THE
PRODIGAL
SPY

ALSO BY JOSEPH KANON

LOS ALAMOS

JOSEPH KANON

THE PRODIGAL SPY

DOUBLEDAY DIRECT LARGE PRINT EDITION

BROADWAY BOOKS ■ NEW YORK

This Large Print Edition, prepared especially for Doubleday Direct, Inc., contains the complete unabridged text of the original Publisher's Edition.

FOR DAVID AND MICHAEL

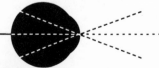

This Large Print Book carries the
Seal of Approval of N.A.V.H.

PART ONE

UN-AMERICAN ACTIVITIES

■

CHAPTER ONE

He was not allowed to attend the hearing. There was his age, for one thing, but he knew it was really the reporters. From his bedroom window he could see them every morning when his father left the house. Mr. Benjamin, his father's lawyer, would come for him—it was somehow unthinkable that he should make the short walk down 2nd Street to the Capitol alone—and the minute they were down the steps Nick would see the clusters of hats swooping toward them like birds. There was even a kind of ritual about it now. No one stood in front of the house. Usually they were across the street, or on the corner, drinking coffee from paper cups, exhaling little puffs of steam in the cold February air. Then the front door would open and they would stamp out their cigarettes, suddenly on duty, and surround his father, falling into step with him and Mr. Benjamin as if they were joining them for a stroll.

In the beginning there had been photographers, their hats pushed back on their heads as they popped flashbulbs, but now there were just the reporters. No one yelled or pushed. The ritual had turned polite. He could see his father in his long herringbone coat drawing the pack with him as he moved down the street, Mr. Benjamin, terrier-like, hurrying to keep up. His father never ignored the reporters. Nick could see him talking—but what did he say?—and nodding his head. Once Nick saw one of them laugh. His father had said the whole thing was a goddam circus, but from up here in the window, watching the hats, it seemed friendly, a gang of boys heading for school. It wasn't, though. At night, alone in the study, smoking in the light of the desk lamp, his father looked worried.

His mother always left separately. She would busy herself with Nora, arranging the day, then stand in front of the hall mirror, touching her hair, smoothing out her wool skirt, while a cigarette burned in the ashtray on the table where they put the mail. When Nick came downstairs she would look surprised, as if she had forgotten he was in the house, then nervously pick up her lipstick to get ready. Her new dress, with its tight cinched waist and fitted top, seemed designed to hold her upright, every piece of her in place.

"Have they gone?" she said, putting on the lipstick.

"Uh-huh. Dad made one of them laugh."

Her hand stopped for a minute, then the red tube continued along her lip. "Did he," she said, blotting her lips, but it wasn't a question. "Well, I'll give them another five minutes."

"They never wait for you, you know," Nick said. It was one of the things that puzzled him. His mother walked to the hearings alone every day, not even a single straggler from the pack of hats waiting behind to catch her. How did they think she got there?

"They will one day," she said, picking up her hat. "Right now all they can think about is your father. And his jokes." She caught the edge in her voice and glanced at him, embarrassed, then went back to the hat.

"There was only one," Nick said.

"I know," she said quietly. "I didn't mean— Check the window again, would you? And shouldn't you be getting ready for school?"

"I am ready," he said, going over to the window. "I don't see why I can't go to the trial."

"Not again, Nicky, please. And it's not a trial. For the hundredth time. It's a hearing. That's all. A congressional hearing."

"What's the difference?"

"Your father's not a criminal, that's the difference. He's not on *trial* for anything."

"Everybody acts like he is."

"What do you mean? Has anyone said anything to you at school?"

Nick shrugged.

"Have they?"

"They said he's on trial for being a Communist."

His mother stopped fixing the hat and lowered her hands. "Well, he's not on trial and he's not a Communist. So much for what they know. Just don't listen, okay? It only makes it worse. They're

5

looking for Communists, so they have to talk to a lot of people in the government, that's all."

Nick came back to the mirror, studying them both, as if the world reflected would be his mother's cheerful dream of before, when all they had to worry about was school gossip.

"They want to hear what he has to say. That's why it's called a hearing. There," she said, pressing the hat like a protective shell. "How do I look?"

Nick smiled. "Beautiful."

"Oh, you always say that," she said lightly, glancing at the mirror again and leaning forward. Nick loved to watch her dress, disappearing to the edge of her careful absorption. It was the harmless vanity of a pretty girl who'd been taught that how you looked mattered, that appearance could somehow determine events. She blotted her lips one last time, then noticed his expression. "Honeybun, what's wrong?"

"Why can't I hear him too? I'm not a little kid anymore."

"No," she said softly, touching the side of his head. "Maybe just to me. But ten isn't very old either, is it? You don't want to grow up too fast."

"Is he going to go to jail?"

She knelt down to face him, holding his shoulders. "No. Look, I know all of this seems confusing. But it's not about you, do you understand? Just—grownups. Your dad's fine. You don't want him to have to worry about you too, do you? It's— it's a bad time, that's all."

A bad time. Nora, for whom Ireland was always

just a memory away, called it troubles. "Before your father's troubles started," she would say, as if everything that was happening to them were beyond their control, like the weather. But no one would tell him what it actually was.

"*You* go," he said stubbornly.

"It's different for me. You're just a child—it has nothing to do with you. It's not *going* to, either. I'm not going to let that happen," she said, holding his shoulders tightly. "Do you understand?"

He didn't, but he nodded, surprised at the force of her hands.

"You'll be late," Nora said, coming into the hall.

His mother looked up, distracted. "Yes, all right. Come on, honeybun, time for school. It'll be all right. You'll see. This won't last much longer, I promise. Then we'll go up to the cabin and forget all about it. Just us. Would you like that?"

Nick nodded. "You mean out of school?"

"Well, in the spring."

"Don't forget you've got Father Tim coming over later," Nora said. "You'll want to be back. Last time he was halfway through the bottle before you were through the door."

"Nora," his mother said, pretending to scold but laughing in spite of herself. "Listen to you. He's not a drinker."

"No, the poor are drinkers. The rich just don't mind if they do."

"He's not rich anymore. He's a priest, for heaven's sake," she said, putting on her coat.

"The rich don't change. Someone else's bottle,

7

that's what they like. Maybe that's why they're rich. Still, it's your bottle, and if you don't mind I'm sure I—"

"Nora, stop babbling. I'll be back. Coast clear?" She nodded her head toward the window. "How about a kiss, then?" She leaned down to let Nick graze her cheek. "Oh, that's better. I'm ready for anything now."

At the door she put on her gloves. "You remember what I said, okay? Don't listen to the other kids if they start saying things. They don't know what they're talking about anyway."

"It wasn't the other kids. About Dad. It was Miss Smith."

"Oh." His mother stopped, flustered, her shoulders sagging. "Oh, honeybun," she said, and then, as if she had finally run out of answers, she turned and went out the door.

After that, he didn't go to school. "At least for a while," his mother said, still pretending that things were normal. Now, after his parents left, the house would grow still, so quiet that he would tiptoe, listening for the sharp whistle of Nora's kettle in the kitchen, then the rustle of newspaper as she pored over his father's troubles with one of her cups of tea. He was supposed to be reading *Kidnapped.* His mother said he was the right age for it, but after the wicked uncle and the broken stairs in the dark it all got confusing—Whigs and Jacobites, and you didn't know whose side you were supposed to be on. It made no more sense than the papers. His father was a New Dealer but not a Communist, and not a Republican either, according to Nora. Then why was he on trial? Some terrible woman had said he was a spy, but you only had to look at her, all made up the way she was, to know she was lying. And a Catholic too, which made things worse. It was the Jews who loved Russia, not people like his father, even though she'd hate to think how long it had been since he'd seen the inside of a church. Still. And the things they said. But when Nick asked her to see the newspapers himself, she'd refuse. His mother wouldn't like it.

So he sat in the deep club chair in the living room, pretending to read but listening instead. While Nora had her tea there was no sound but the ticking of the ormolu clock. Soon, however, he'd hear the scraping of a chair in the kitchen, then the heavy steps in the hall as Nora came to peek in before she began her chores. Nick would turn a page, his head bent to the book he wasn't reading until he felt her slip out of the doorway and head upstairs. After another few minutes, the vacuum would start with a roar and he could go. He would race down the back kitchen stairs, careful not to hit the creaky fourth step, and get the newspaper from behind the bread box, where Nora always hid it. Then, one ear still alert to the vacuum, he would read about the trial. KOTLAR DENIES ALLEGATIONS. COMMITTEE THREATENS CONTEMPT. MUNDT SET TO CALL ACHESON. NEW KOTLAR TESTIMONY. It always gave him an odd sensation to see his name in print. His eye would flash down the column, "Kotlar" leaping out as if it were in boldface, not just another word in a blur of type. But it was *Kidnapped* all over again. Whigs and Jacobites.

The newspapers became part of the spy game. The point at first was to see how many rooms he could visit without Nora's knowing—from the kitchen up to his father's study, then past the bedroom where she was working (this was the best part) to his mother's dressing room, then back down the stairs (carefully now, the vacuum having gone silent) and into the club chair with the open book before she appeared again. Not that she would have cared if he'd left the room—it was just the game. Stuck in the house, cocooned against the cold outside that kept promising snow, he learned its secrets, the noisy parts, the bad floorboards, as if they were bits of Braille. He could even spy on Nora, watching through the crack in the door, crouching halfway down the stairs, until he felt he could roam the house at will, invisible. His father, he knew, could never have done this. You always knew where he was, clunking down the hall to the bathroom at night, all his weight on his heels. His mother said you could feel him a block away. It was Nick who knew how to spy. He could stand absolutely still, like one of those movie submarines with the motors off, on sonar silence, waiting to hear something.

Then one day, by accident, he finally saw his father at the hearing. Nora had taken him downtown to the movies, a *My Friend Irma* picture with Martin and Lewis. She crossed herself when the newsreel began with the Holy Year in Rome, long lines of pilgrims forming at the churches, some from Germany, some even from as far away as America. A crowded open-air mass. A year of new hope for a century half old. Fireworks exploded over St. Peter's. Then, abruptly, the newsreel shifted to Washington, and the announcer's voice turned grim.

"A different kind of fireworks on Capitol Hill, as the House Committee on Un-American Activities and combative congressman Kenneth Welles continued the probe into Communist subversion in our State Department. In the box again, Undersecretary Walter Kotlar, named by Soviet spy Rosemary Cochrane as one of the members of an alleged Washington ring."

He felt Nora move beside him and covered her hand to keep her still as the screen filled with his father walking down a corridor to the hearing room, wearing the familiar hat and herringbone coat. The reporters were more animated now, battering him with questions, as if they had finally thawed out from their morning vigil in the cold. Then he was seated at a polished table, several microphones in front of him, facing a long dais filled with men in suits who kept turning to whisper to aides who sat behind them like shadows, away from the lights.

The man at the center, surprisingly young, was taller than the others, with a thick football player's neck bursting out of a suit that stretched across his wide shoulders like a padded uniform.

"Mr. Kotlar, in 1945 you were a member of the

11

American delegation that attended the Yalta Conference, were you not?"

"Yes."

"In that capacity did you offer views on the political future of the countries of Eastern Europe?"

"No. My views were not solicited."

"But you are Czechoslovakian, are you not?"

"No, sir, I am an American."

"Well, Mr. Kotlar, that's fine. I meant by origin. Would you tell the committee where you were born?"

"I was born in what was then Bohemia and is now part of Czechoslovakia," Nick's father said, but the carefulness of his answer had the odd effect of making him seem evasive. "I came to this country when I was four years old."

"But you speak Czechoslovakian?"

Nick's father allowed the trace of a smile. "Czech? No." But this wasn't true. Nick remembered his grandmother talking in her kitchen, his father nodding his head at the incomprehensible words. "I know a few words," his father continued. "Certainly not enough to use the language in any official capacity. I know a little French, too."

This seemed to annoy the congressman. "This committee isn't interested in your knowledge of French, Mr. Kotlar. Is it not true that as a member of the Yalta delegation, you had access to information the Russians considered very valuable?"

"No. I was there strictly as an adviser on Lend-Lease and postwar aid programs. My information wasn't classified—it was available to everyone."

Welles looked the way Miss Smith did when someone in class was being fresh. "That remains to be seen, Mr. Kotlar," he said. "That remains to be seen." He paused, pretending to consult a paper but really, Nick knew, just allowing his words to hang in the air. "Lend-Lease. We've all heard about your generosity during the war. But after the war, you went right on being generous, didn't you? Isn't it true you wanted to give Marshall Plan aid to Czechoslovakia?"

"The United States government offered the Marshall Plan to all European countries."

"Maybe it would be more accurate to say that certain officials of the United States government offered that aid. Officials like yourself. Or maybe you disagreed. Did you feel that such an offer was in the best interests of the United States?"

"It must have been. They turned us down."

This time there was real laughter, and Congressman Welles, leaning into the microphone, was forced to talk over it, so that when it stopped he seemed to be shouting. "May I remind our visitors that this is a congressional hearing?" There were a few flashbulbs. "Mr. Kotlar, you may consider this a laughing matter. I assure you, the American people do not. Now, this aid you were so eager to hand out. A little money for the old country—even if it was now a vassal state of the Soviet empire."

"I think you have your chronology slightly confused, congressman. At the time of the offer, Czechoslovakia was a democracy, and President

13

Beneš was eager to participate. Subsequently, of course, they declined."

Nick lost his father halfway through—it was Whigs and Jacobites again, too mixed up to sort out—and he could tell the audience wasn't really following either. They could hear only the rhythm of Welles's interrogation, the slow build and rising pitch that seemed to hammer his father into his chair. The momentum of it, not the words, became the accusation. The congressman was so sure—he must know. It didn't really matter what he said, so long as the voice rushed along, gathering speed.

"Round two," the voiceover said, introducing another film clip. "And this time nobody was pulling any punches."

"Mr. Kotlar, I'm sure we've all been grateful for the history lessons. Unfortunately, anyone who changes positions as often as you do is bound to make things a little confusing for the rest of us. So let's see if we can find out what you really think. I'd like to talk again about your background, if I may?" Welles swiveled his head to the other men at the long table, who nodded automatically, absorbed in the drama of where he might be going. "You are, I believe, a graduate of the Harvard Law School?"

For a minute Nick's father didn't respond, as if the question were so unexpected it must be a trick. "That's correct."

"And can you tell us what you did next? Did you join a firm or hang out your own shingle or what?"

"I came to Washington to work for the government."

"That would be, let's see—1934. Is that correct?"

"Yes."

"Of course, jobs were tight then, so I guess government work was pretty popular," Welles said, suddenly folksy and reminiscent. "Kinda the patriotic thing to do in 1934. Yes, sir, they used to say the Harvard Law School ran regular bus service down here right after graduation." This play to the gallery had the expected effect, and Welles, smiling slyly, waited for the laughter to subside. Then he looked back at Nick's father. "But you didn't come right away, did you?"

Nick's father looked at him blankly, saying nothing.

"Mr. Kotlar, is it not a fact that after Harvard Law School you offered your services to the United Mine Workers union during their illegal strike?"

"It was not an illegal strike."

"Just answer the question," Welles shot back. "Did you work for the UMW?"

"Yes."

"And how much were you paid for this work?"

"It was unpaid."

"Unpaid. Free, you mean. Well now, I'm just a country lawyer—I didn't go to the Harvard Law School. They usually work for free up there? Or just the labor agitators?" He rushed on, not waiting for Nick's father to reply. "The party often ask you to do union work, Mr. Kotlar?"

"No," his father said quietly.

"No." Welles paused. "They had other plans for

15

you. Washington plans. Seems a shame, consider-ing. The strike went pretty well from their point of view, wouldn't you say?"

"I wouldn't know. I wasn't working for the Com-munist party."

"No. Just the miners. Out of the goodness of your heart. What made them so special, I wonder. To work free of charge."

Nick's father waited, drawing the room to his side of the table, then let his lips form the hint of a smile. "My father was a coal miner. He asked me to help. I didn't think I could refuse."

There was a slight pause and then the room buzzed. Welles, visibly surprised and annoyed, covered the microphone with his hand and turned to an aide. The other members of the committee began to talk too, as if by looking away Welles had given them all a brief recess. When he turned back to the mike, the room grew still, expectant.

"I'm sure the members of the committee all ap-preciate a son's devotion, Mr. Kotlar," he said, reaching again for sarcasm. But the momentum had gone. Nick wasn't sure what had happened, but his father was sitting up straighter, no longer letting his shoulders hunch in self-protection. "Per-haps they'd also appreciate hearing that you didn't confine yourself to legal services in that strike. It says here that the picket line at the Trousdale Col-liery got pretty violent. You were arrested, were you not?"

"No. There was a scuffle with the company guards, that's all. No arrests."

"Mr. Kotlar, we're not talking about a speeding ticket here. Do you deny there was a violent incident in which you took part?"

"I don't deny there was a fight. I deny I took part in it."

"Oh? What were you doing?"

"I was trying to stay out of the way."

Now there was real laughter, a wave that passed through the room, gathering force until it spilled onto Welles's table, breaking as it hit his angry face.

"Mr. Kotlar," he said loudly, "I think I've had enough. I've had enough impertinence. This committee is charged with the serious business—the very serious business—of investigating Communist activities in this country. I've had enough of your Harvard Law School evasions. And I think the American people have had enough of high-handed boys who use their tax dollars while they sell this country down the river. You go ahead and laugh. But that was no scuffle, and you are no loyal American. When I look at your testimony start to finish, I see nothing less than an attempt to deceive this committee and this great country. Well, we're not going to be deceived. This committee is here to look at un-American activities. In your case, I think the people of this country are going to be grateful we did."

"Congressman," Nick's father said, his voice tight with scorn, "the only un-American activity I've seen is taking place right here in this committee room. I hope the people see that too."

17

Another clip, the announcer's voice more excited now. "But the sparring match drew to a close as Congressman Welles zeroed in on the sensational Cochrane testimony." The clip must have been from another day, because his father was wearing a different suit, the gray double-breasted one Nick's mother said made him look heavier.

"Mr. Kotlar, Rosemary Cochrane testified that on several occasions she received government documents from you in her role as a courier for a Russian undercover operation." The congressman paused. "Do you recall that testimony?"

"Vividly."

"And you denied these charges. In fact, you denied ever having met her, is that correct?"

"To the best of my knowledge, I have never met her."

"To the best of your knowledge?"

"I am trying to be precise. I may have encountered her without my knowing it. Certainly I have no memory of having done so."

"Is that your way of saying no?" Welles said. "Do I have to remind you that you're under oath?"

Nick's father managed a wry smile. "No, you don't have to remind me."

"Mr. Kotlar, have you ever shopped at Garfinkel's department store?"

For a moment Nick's father looked blank. "I'm sorry. What?"

"Have you ever shopped at Garfinkel's department store? The big store down on 14th Street. You're familiar with Garfinkel's?"

"Yes. I suppose so."

"Shirts? Ever buy shirts there?"

"I don't remember."

"You don't remember. Now how could that be?"

"My wife usually does the shopping."

The camera moved to take in Nick's mother, sitting rigidly at the edge of the row behind, her eyes blinking in the unfamiliar light.

Nick felt Nora squirm beside him. "That's it," she whispered urgently. "We're going."

"No, when it's over," Nick said firmly, not moving his head. "I want to see."

Congressman Welles was talking again. "But I suppose once in a while you find time in your busy schedule to shop for yourself?"

"Yes."

"And you never bought shirts from Miss Cochrane?"

"Was she the salesgirl? I don't remember."

"She remembers you, Mr. Kotlar. She remembers receiving envelopes from you during these little shopping trips. Does that refresh your memory?"

"She is mistaken."

"She even remembers your size. Fifteen and a half, thirty-three. Can you at least remember that for the committee? That your size?"

His father smiled. "I prefer a thirty-five," he said. "A longer sleeve."

"A longer sleeve," Welles repeated sarcastically. "Maybe you're still growing. You'd better watch your nose then. They say it gets longer every time you tell a lie."

"I'm watching yours too, congressman."

More laughter, and this time Nick got the joke. He remembered *Pinocchio,* the sick feeling in his stomach when the boy went to Donkey Island and couldn't get back. He felt it now again, that dread, being scared while everyone around him was having a good time. But his father didn't look scared. His smooth, lean face was calm, as if he knew it was all just a movie.

"And so this week's round ends in a draw," the announcer was saying, "as both sides retire to their corners to come back to fight another day."

But it wasn't a boxing match, it was a trial, and Welles was the only fighter who came back in the last clip, surrounded by hand-held microphones on the windy Capitol steps.

"I don't think there can be a doubt in anyone's mind that this country is under attack," he said, his face grave, looking straight at the camera. "These people are using lies and tricks the same way their comrades overseas are using tanks and machine guns to undermine the free world. We saw it in the Hiss case and we're seeing it again here. Walter Kotlar is a Communist and he's going to lose his shirt—no matter what size he says it is."

Then all at once the screen brightened, flooded with Florida sun as the newsreel switched to water-skiing formations in Cypress Gardens. Nick blinked in the light. A man and woman in bathing suits were receiving crowns. After a rooster crowed to end the newsreel, the screen went dark.

Nick watched the curtain close, then open again to start the feature, but he was no longer paying attention to any of it. Nora laughed at some of the movie, but Nick was thinking about the newsreel and missed the point of the jokes and then had to pretend to laugh when everyone else did. He could still see Welles's wide linebacker's face, eyes peering out as if he thought he could make you squirm just by looking hard enough. He was like one of those guys who kept poking you in the chest until you had to fight. But every time Nick's father hit back, he'd get madder. He'd never stop now. The newsreel must be a few days old. Nick wondered what had happened since.

After the movie, on the street, Nora was uneasy. "Don't tell your mother. She wouldn't like it."

"I won't."

"He's a wicked man, the senator."

"He's not a senator."

"Well, whatever he is." She sighed, then brightened. "Still, I'll say this for your father. He gave as good as he got."

Nick looked up at her. "No, he didn't," he said.

Nick could see the Capitol dome from his window if he craned his head to the left, but when he lay in the bed, facing straight ahead, everything disappeared except the tree branches, thin and brittle now in the cold. In the faint light from the street they quivered when the wind shook them, too stiff to bend. Downstairs the dinner party was still going on. Nick could hear the voices rising up through the floorboards, his mother's occasional laugh. Earlier she had been nervous, her red fingernails brushing over ashtrays as she rearranged things on tables, moving the flower vase twice before it seemed right. Then the doorbell, Nick helping with the coats in the hall, the cocktails and the clink of ice cubes, his polite farewells as they finally went in to dinner, his mother's promise to be up later as she touched his cheek goodnight, the air around her warm with smoke and perfume. He had listened on the stairs for a while, straining to make out words in the familiar hum, then come up to bed, lying here watching the branches and waiting. She always looked in while the coffee was being served. But it was his father who came. Nick saw the shadow first against the window, then turned to see him standing in the doorway, taller than he'd been in the newsreel.

"Nicku, you still up?"

"Uh-huh. Where's Mom?"

His father came over and sat on the edge of the bed, moving the covers up under Nick's chin. Nick caught the faint whiff of aftershave. "She and Father Tim are going over old times again. You know what that's like."

Nick smiled. "They're not even old."

"Well, they used to be younger. Anyway, your

mother enjoys it. Father Tim's good for her that way."

"Does he hear her confession?"

"Tim?" His father laughed. "I don't think Tim has time for church business. He's what we call a dinner priest—here's a story and pass the port."

"Nora says you don't like priests. She says you're anti-clerical," Nick said, trying out the word.

"She'd better watch out or I'll get anti-Nora."

"So why does he come here, if you're—"

"Well, he doesn't come for me. He and your mother go back a long way. Since they were your age. To tell you the truth, I think he was sweet on her."

"Dad. He's a priest."

"Lucky for us, huh?" his father said, gently brushing the hair off Nick's forehead. "How about some sleep?"

"When Grandma talks to you sometimes, what language is that?"

"Czech. You know that."

"Like when you say Nicku?"

"Uh-huh. If you put a *u* on the end of a name, it's a way of showing affection. Sort of a Nick-name."

"Dad."

"Why do you ask?"

"You told the man you didn't speak Czech."

"What man?" he said, his hand stopping on Nick's forehead.

"The man at the hearing. I saw you in a newsreel today."

"You did, huh?" But Nick could tell his father

was stalling, not sure what to say. "What did you think?"

"*Do* you speak it?"

Nick's father sat up. "Not in the way he meant. A few words. Half the time I don't know what Grandma's saying. Why? Did you think I wasn't telling the truth?"

Nick shrugged. "No." He paused. "Why did he want to know that, anyway?"

"He wanted to make people think I was foreign. Some people don't like foreigners. They're afraid, I guess. But let's not worry about it, okay? It's just politics. It's his way of running for office, that's all."

"I hope he loses."

His father smiled. "So do I, Nick. Maybe we'll get Father Tim to send up a few prayers, what do you say? If we can get him out the door. Now, how about some sleep?" But he stayed on the bed, looking at Nick. "Does it bother you, all this business?"

"Why did that woman say she knew you if she didn't?"

"I don't know, Nick," his father said, slumping a little so the light caught the shiny waves of his hair. "I don't know. Maybe she thought she did. Maybe she met me someplace and decided she didn't like me for some reason. Maybe she's crazy—you know, the way people make things up? Like when you're afraid of the dark—you think there's someone there even when there isn't. Well, everybody's afraid of the dark now. So they keep seeing things."

24

"Grownups aren't afraid of the dark."

"It's an expression. I mean afraid in general. They're afraid of all kinds of things, so they keep seeing bogeymen everywhere. I know it doesn't make a lot of sense, Nick. Maybe you can't explain a bogeyman—he's just there."

"Communists, you mean."

His father nodded. "That's who it is now. Maybe next week it'll be something else."

Nick said nothing, thinking.

"Not much help, is it?" his father said. "I don't have an explanation, Nick."

"Are they going to stop?"

"They can't—not yet." His voice had begun to drift, away from Nick to some private conversation. "Sometimes I think it was the war. We got into the habit of having enemies. That's a hard habit to break. After a while, you don't know any other way to think. And one day it's over and they turn on all the lights again and expect things to go back to the way they were, but nobody knows how to stop. They're used to it. They have to get new enemies. It's the way things make sense to them."

"For always?" Nick said.

His question brought his father back. "No," he said, "things change. That's why we need people like you," he added, his voice lighter now. He pulled up the covers again. "Who weren't there. Who don't even remember it. It'll be different for you. What's going on now—" His voice lifted, like a verbal wave of the hand. "You'll forget that too. It'll just be history." He paused. "Just a bad dream."

25

"It's not a dream now," Nick said quietly. "I saw it."

His father looked at him, stalling again. "No," he said, "not now." Then he tapped Nick's forehead with his finger. "You're a pragmatist, Nick. That's what you are."

"What's that?"

"Oh, someone who keeps his eye on the ball. Feet on the ground. You know. Not like someone else we know, huh?" he said, pointing to himself.

"Mom says I'm like you. Aren't you a pragmatist?" Nick said, getting it right.

"Sure. Not as good as you, though. You'll have to help me out, okay? Keep me on my toes."

Nick nodded, but he knew, with the same dread he'd felt in the movies, there was nothing he could do to help. His father was just trying to make him feel better—a different kind of lie, like pretending he wasn't worried, pretending it was all going to go away.

"That's the thing about history anyway," his father said. "You have to live through it before you know how it's going to come out. So you keep me on my toes. Of course, to do that you have to grow, and to do *that*—"

"I know. Sleep. But Dad—"

"Ssh. No more. We'll talk tomorrow. It's supposed to snow, you know. I'll bet it's already snowing up at the cabin. Wind blowing it all over the place. Swoosh." His father leaned over and made a wind sound in his ear, tickling him and making him burrow deeper under the covers. It was their

26

old game, from when he was little. "Here it comes, down the chimney." He made another wind sound. "But we don't care, do we? We'll just stay warm and cozy." His father always said that.

"Snug as a bug in a rug," Nick said, as he always did.

"That's right," his father said softly. "Snug as a bug in a rug."

"Dad? If it snows, will you have to go to the hearing?"

His father smiled. "I think Mr. Welles would insist. No snow days for him."

"Don't go," Nick said, his voice suddenly urgent. "He's trying to get you. I *saw* him."

"Ssh. Don't worry, he won't. He's only a bogeyman, and they never get anybody. We make them up, remember?" he said playfully. Then, seeing Nick's solemn face, he nodded. "I know. I'll be careful. This one's really there." He stood up, smoothing the covers. "He made himself up, I guess. Some world, isn't it? All he used to be was a dumb cluck from Oklahoma."

"Walter?" his mother said from the doorway. "Larry's here. Nick, are you still up?"

"We've been going over my defense strategy," Nick's father said. "We're hoping for a snow day."

"Walter," his mother said, shooting him a glance.

"Uncle Larry's here?" Nick said, starting to get up. "Where?"

"Not tonight, kiddo," his father said. "It's late."

Larry wasn't really his uncle. His father had met

27

him in college—over the serving line in the dining hall, according to the family story, when Nick's father was dishing out food to work his way through Penn and Larry, nursing a hangover, tipped a tray onto his father's white jacket without knowing it. His father used to joke that they never changed—he kept working behind the line and Larry kept getting things handed to him on a platter, indifferent to spills. In Washington it had been the dining hall all over again. His father worked long hours in the agencies; Larry moved his tray all the way to the White House, where, his father said, he was one of the fair-haired policy boys. His hair in fact *was* fair, a bright ginger that reminded Nick of Van Johnson, and he had the same open face and easy smile. When he took Nick and his mother to see the White House one day—even upstairs, since the president was away—he moved through the rooms as if they were his, kidding with the secretaries, who waited for his grin, an effortless seduction. It's easy to be charming, his father said, when your family owns half of Philadelphia, but in fact he couldn't resist it either. He was different with Larry—easy and comfortable, the way people were when their jokes are too old for anyone else to remember. But Larry hadn't been to the house for weeks, and it was late to call. Nick wondered what was wrong.

"He's in the study," his mother said. "Go ahead. I'll take care of the others. The Kittredges look as if they're settling in for the night." Nick heard the laugh in her voice, the way she used to be at parties. So maybe it was all right. "Night, Nick," she said, blowing him a kiss. She pulled the door behind her but left it half open, so that Nick could see them starting down the stairs, their heads together.

He didn't wait. When he heard the click of her heels on the landing, he slid out of bed and darted into the hall. He peered over the banister, watching his mother's skirt swish down the next flight of stairs, then tiptoed down to the second floor. He waited until his father's back disappeared into the study before he crept along the wall, angling himself at the open door to see through the crack. Uncle Larry was still wearing his topcoat, as if he didn't mean to stay.

"Long time no see, Larry."

"Sorry. I couldn't get away," Larry said quickly. "We're redoing the speech."

"I didn't mean the dinner. It's been a while," his father said, moving out of Nick's line of vision. "Want a drink?"

"No. I can't stay."

"Don't worry. Nobody saw you. The reporters don't show up until morning."

"For Christ's sake, Walter." Larry looked over toward his father, then dropped his hat on the leather couch. "All right. Maybe a short one," he said, taking off his coat.

Nick heard his father pour the drink at the sideboard. "Good. I thought maybe I'd reached the leper stage. Have I?"

Larry glanced up sharply. "No. But you're not making any friends in there either, Walter. You've got to stop fighting with him."

"I can't help it," his father said, coming back into view and handing Larry a glass. "He's a moron."

"He's a moron who's getting headlines. He's got nothing going for him but a district full of dust farms and a bunch of Indians who don't vote, and you're making him a national figure. How smart is that? Come on, Walter, you know how it works. You're not exactly new in town."

"The town's changed."

"The town never changes," Larry said evenly. "Never. You just got on the wrong side of it."

"That the view from the East Lawn these days?" his father said. "Okay. Withdrawn. Cheers." He took a sip of his drink, then paused. "You don't know what it's like," he said quietly.

"I'm sorry I missed the party," Larry said. "How's Livia?"

"I need your help, Larry," his father said, ignoring the question.

For a minute neither of them said anything.

"I can't get involved with the case, Walter. You know that. We don't go near the Hill these days. Christ, we don't even cross the street. Everybody's too busy ducking under the table."

His father nodded with a small smile. "So I heard. They're starting to get lonely over at State."

"State's like sick bay—everybody's afraid they'll catch something. Anyway, you've already got Benjamin. He's the best lawyer in town for this."

"Devoted as he is to lost causes," his father said, taking a drink.

"You're not going to lose. Just stop fighting with

Welles. He's on a fishing expedition and you keep biting. He hasn't got anything, so he's trying to nail you for contempt.''

"How do you know he hasn't got anything?''

Larry looked at him. "Because he never does,'' he said, tossing back his drink. "Because I know you. The Mine Workers, for Christ's sake. What's next, the fucking Red Cross? He hasn't got a thing, Walter.'' He paused. "If he did we'd have heard about it.'' He turned and started walking, a court-room pace. "One witness who doesn't even *look* stable. You see the way she twists her handker-chief? If this were a real trial, Benjamin would dis-credit her in two minutes. Two minutes.''

"Then I guess I don't have a thing to worry about,'' his father said easily. He leaned against the edge of the desk, looking down at his glass. "Nick wonders why she's saying these things. I'll bet he's not the only one.''

Nick started at the sound of his name, as if they'd caught him and were drawing him into the room.

"Who knows?'' Larry said. "Maybe Welles is screwing her. She wouldn't be the first. Maybe she's doing it for love. She looks the type. The point is, it doesn't matter. All she's got is some cockamamie story about shirts. Shirts. Christ, where do they get this stuff? Anyway, forget her. This is about Welles, not her. Welles doesn't know what to do with her either. Just keep your eye on him.''

His father smiled, still looking down. "That's what Nick said too."

Larry stopped, disconcerted, then walked over to the sideboard to put his glass down. "Well, do it then. All you've got to do is keep your head, Walter. It's her word against yours, and yours still counts for something in this town."

"Let's not kid ourselves, Larry," his father said slowly. "I'm finished in this town. That's why I need your help."

In the quiet Nick could hear the sounds from downstairs, the indistinct voices and clinks of coffee spoons.

"Walter, I—"

"Don't worry, it won't cost you anything. I don't want a lawyer. Just some advice. Advice used to be cheap." He got up and walked over to the window, out of Nick's sight. "You're a behind-the-scenes guy. It's your specialty, isn't it? I need someone like that now."

"To do what?"

"To make a deal with the committee."

"You don't want to do that," Larry said carefully.

"I have to. It's going to get worse."

The room was quiet again.

"What do you mean?" Larry finally said. "Look, Walter, if you're trying to tell me something, don't. I'm not your lawyer. Anything we say—it's not privileged. You know that."

His father came back into view, his face slightly surprised. "You don't have to tell me that, Larry," he said gently. "What's the matter? Do you think I'm a Communist? You too?"

"It doesn't matter. I don't want to know. I mean it. Not any of it. I don't want to know what you joined or who your pals were."

"Larry—"

Larry held up his hand. "No. Listen to me. I don't care if you organized the whole goddam dining hall or had a drink with Uncle Joe at Yalta. Things were different then. Was it innocent? There is no such thing now. They can twist anything. I *can't* know. What if they call me too? They could. I'm an old friend. I don't want to be used against you."

"No," his father said after a minute, nodding to himself. "Not to mention tarred with the same brush."

"That's right," Larry said quickly, embarrassed. "Not to mention. This isn't just happening to you."

His father looked up. "You don't have to tell me that either, Larry. You don't have a wife who wonders why nobody calls her anymore or a kid who can't go to school without hearing his father's a criminal. I know it's happening to all of us. But I'm the one getting beaten up every day. This isn't a trial—I'm already guilty. I'm a Communist whether I am or not. What's the point of going on with it? How do I win?"

"You don't win. You just don't lose it."

"No, they lose. Everybody who comes near me. Just by being around. Even old friends," he said, with a wave of his hand. "It's enough. I don't want to go on being a punching bag just to get Welles elected."

"You don't have a choice, Walter," Larry said slowly. "And if you handle this right, he won't get elected. He thinks he's Nixon, but he's not that good. He's still looking for a pumpkin, and he's not going to find one. All you have to do is let it play itself out."

"Forget the politics for a minute, will you? This isn't about politics."

"Yes it is," Larry said calmly.

"My god, how you love all this," his father said, then turned away.

Larry looked up to answer, then seemed to change his mind and took out a cigarette. "Nobody loves this. Not this. It's getting in the way."

"Of what? Business as usual?" Nick's father said, still sarcastic, handing Larry a lighter.

Larry nodded. "Nothing moves now. We're paralyzed until we get him to run out of steam. Maybe it stops with you, Walter. Who knows?"

"Well, that would be nice. Meanwhile, I'm the one being run out of town." A roar of laughter came up from the first floor, a party sound, and his father smiled involuntarily. "All evidence to the contrary aside."

Larry smiled back and raised his glass appreciatively.

His father, seeming agitated, started pacing across the room. "Look, do you think I like asking for help? I'm drowning. That's what it feels like. Sometimes I think we're all going to go under if it

34

doesn't stop." He paused. "I'm not asking you to lie for me. Or tell the truth, for that matter. I don't want you to testify. I just want you to run a little interference, that's all."

"We don't make deals with the committee, Walter."

"That's right, I forgot. Everyone's ducking under the table."

Larry shrugged. "Anyway, what have you got to trade? Twenty names at State? That's about the going price these days, if you had them. Which you don't."

"Marked down from twenty pieces of silver," his father said.

Larry said nothing.

"I'm going to resign. That's what Welles wants— let's give it to him. He can take credit for hounding another Red out of the State Department. Cleaning out the stables. Without having to go to the bother of proving anything. Since he can't, that should put him ahead. I'll deny it, but it won't matter. Even the people who don't believe it believe it a little. We finish out the hearing in closed session—no more cameras. I don't want my kid seeing me in the movies again, ever. Not a bad cover for the committee either. People will think they really had something. The republic'll be safe and I'll be out of this. End of the drama."

Outside the door, Nick stood still in disbelief. His father always told him never to give up. Why would he walk away from a fight? He wanted to push the door wide open, tell him that he didn't mind the newsreel or what people said, any of it. Instead, there was only the prickling feeling of dread again. Where would they go?

For a minute Larry was quiet. "You're out of your mind," he said finally.

"No, I'm not. It's the way it makes sense."

"Do you think Welles gives a rat's ass whether you're a Communist or not? The only Red he's ever seen had feathers coming out of his head. No cameras. That's what he's doing this *for.* Once they turn the lights off, he's *gone.* And right now, all he's got is you. No one else to call. The girl didn't give them any names. How they tricked her into naming you, I don't know, but it won't work again. You've seen her up there—she never expected any of this to happen. She's not the Bentley type. You're the end of the road as far as Welles is concerned. He's not going to trade you for some musical chairs over at State. You're all he's *got.*"

"Do you know this?"

Larry shrugged. "Nobody keeps a secret in this town. Believe me, his in box is empty. She's not giving him anything. She can't even prove what she said about herself. At this point, he'd be lucky to make the charges stick against *her.*"

"She confessed."

"If you believe her. Maybe she did Judge Crater too. People confess to anything—they like the spotlight. That doesn't make it true. Even Welles is nervous about her. The louder he gets, the less he has to say."

"Then he ought to jump at this."

"He won't. Listen to me, Walter. There is no deal here. Welles is too dumb to make one and you're too smart. You don't have to give him anything—you just have to stop fighting with him. If he can't cite you for contempt, he'll walk away with nothing."

Nick heard his father sigh. "What's the difference, Larry? I'm going to have to resign anyway. I keep waiting for the phone call. No, it'll be a meeting, I suppose. Acheson's office. Just the two of us. Nothing personal. Better under the circumstances—Christ, I've already been through it. Why not get something for it? A little peace of mind at least."

"If you do that now, it's as good as an admission, Walter. We can't have that."

Nick's father raised his eyebrows in surprise. "We?"

"You'd be a political liability."

For a moment they stared at each other, a silent conversation, then Nick's father leaned against the desk again. "I don't care, Larry. I'm going to resign."

"No, it's not going to happen that way," Larry said, his voice low and steady, as if he were explaining something to a child. "He's going to shout and you're going to be polite. Nothing will happen. You'll be the loyal American you always were—maybe a little foolish and idealistic, but nothing worse. One of the good guys. She—let's say she was confused, maybe a nut case, anyway confused."

Larry moved toward the desk, as if he were adjusting the sights of his words, taking aim. "In the spring, two, three months from now, you resign quietly. All that time in the limelight—well, it would make anyone shy. You want the quiet life. The administration regrets. It's a pity reckless accusations are driving talented men out of public life. Or maybe nothing has to be said—no one notices. They've moved on. By the time the elections roll around in the fall, you're not even a memory and Welles is out on the stump with a different fight on his hands. Nobody's soft on communism. Nobody's been embarrassed."

Again, an awful stillness in the room.

"It's been decided, then," Nick's father said softly.

"It's been discussed."

And then Nick saw, without knowing why, that it was over, like a tennis game.

"They don't pay you enough, Larry," his father said finally, now slumped against the desk.

Larry looked at him, and let it pass. "This one's for free, Walter. I'm on your side, believe me."

"I do, Larry. That's the funny part. Well," he said, standing up and straightening, the way he did when he walked over to the net to shake hands, a good sport, "so I get to make a deal after all. What's in this one for me?"

"You've got to think about your future, Walter. What are you going to do after?"

"With my kind of résumé, you mean."

"It never hurts to have friends," Larry said quietly.

Nick's father nodded. "Thanks for explaining everything so clearly."

"Don't, Walter. I'm not the bad guy. I'm trying to help. It's a lousy time."

"I know," his father said, his voice suddenly deflated. "I know." He stood for a minute lost in thought. "Maybe there aren't any bad guys anymore."

"Yes, there are. They're in that committee room." He walked over to the couch and picked up his coat. "Look, I've got to go. You all right?" Nick's father nodded. "Play it smart, Walter, okay?"

His father looked at him, then broke the stare and went over and put a hand on Larry's shoulder. "Come say hello to Livia."

"I can't. I'm late. Give her my love, will you?"

"Late for what?" his father said lightly. "You seeing somebody these days?"

"I'm seeing everybody."

"Nothing changes, does it?"

Larry shrugged. "It doesn't mean anything. You got the only one worth having."

His father dropped his hand. "Luck."

"You're still lucky," Larry said, putting on his coat. He stopped and looked at him. "Just play it smart."

Larry turned toward the door and Nick took a step down the hall, out of sight.

"I'll see myself out," Larry said. "You'd better go

break up the party before the neighbors start complaining."

"Don't be a stranger," Nick heard his father say.

Larry's voice was cheerful again, Van Johnson. "Not me," he said.

He opened the door suddenly, before Nick could race up the stairs, and stood for a second with his hand on the knob, looking at Nick with surprise. Then he winked and pulled the door shut behind him. He put a finger to his lips and motioned with his head for Nick to follow him to the stairs, as if they were hiding together. At the landing he knelt down.

"Hi, sport," he whispered. "You okay?"

Nick nodded.

"You know what happens to guys who listen at keyholes, don't you?" he said, smiling.

"What?" Nick whispered back, playing along.

"You'll end up working for Drew Pearson, that's what."

"A legman," Nick said, his father's expression.

Larry looked surprised again, then grinned. "Yeah, a legman. Hear anything worth hearing?"

Nick shook his head.

"Well, neither do they, mostly," he said, still whispering. "Come on, up you go before they catch us both."

Nick turned to go, then looked back at Larry. "Dad asked you to help him," he said, a question.

Larry stood up. "I can't, Nick. Not the way he wants." Then he smiled and ruffled Nick's hair. "He'll be all right. Don't worry. We'll all help him."

They heard the sound of the door opening and Larry made a face of mock alarm, shooing Nick with his hand up the stairs and turning away to start down the other flight. Nick darted up, out of his father's line of sight, and watched Larry's red hair bob down the stairs. In a minute his father followed. Over the banister Nick could see him stop at the foot of the stairs, waiting until he heard the front door click shut. Then he turned, straightened his shoulders, and went in to join the party.

No one was going to help. All the rest of it, the confusing jumble of elections and deals and witnesses, still came down to that. No one. Not even Uncle Larry, who had just been trying to make him feel better on the stairs. He'd heard them. His father felt like he was drowning. Nick wondered what that was really like, everything closing around you, choking for air, reaching up for any hand at all. No one. It wasn't smart anymore. Not even for his father to help himself.

The draft in the hall seeped through his thin pajamas, making him shiver. He felt like leaping into bed, pulling the covers over his head, and curling his body into a ball, as warm as the cabin fire. Instead he went down the hall to his parents' room. The bedside lamps were on, surrounded by piles of books and Kleenex and alarm clocks. He walked over to his father's dressing area, a mirror and a tall row of built-in drawers that pulled out on smooth, quiet runners, not like Nick's, which always stuck. All the shirts were white, stacked in two neat piles. He took one out. Garfinkel's, all right. But the tag under the laundry mark was 15½–35. Just as he'd said. Nick almost grinned in relief. The next one was the same, and suddenly he caught sight of his pajamas in the mirror and felt ashamed. This wasn't playing the spy game with Nora; it was wrong, like being a burglar. What if his father noticed?

Nick put back the shirts and evened out the edge of the pile. But he'd already started—why not know for sure? Carefully he flipped through the collars of the shirts, looking for the size tags. Some weren't even Garfinkel's. Then, halfway down, he found it. A Garfinkel label, 15½–33. He stared at it, not moving, his finger barely touching the tag. Why had he kept it? Maybe it was a mistake, a present from Nick's mother. But that wouldn't matter. Uncle Larry said nothing was innocent now. They'd find it, just as Nick had. There was a laundry mark, too—he'd worn it. Nick tried to think what that meant. No fingerprints. That woman, any trace of her, had been washed away. And all the shirts looked alike. But what if they had other ways? As long as it was here—

He heard the front door slam, voices downstairs saying goodbye, and without thinking snatched the shirt, closed the drawer quietly, and ran back to his room. He looked around for a hiding place, but then the voices seemed to be coming up the stairs so he shoved it under his pillow and got into bed, breathing fast. Outside the snow had finally begun, blowing almost horizontally across the light from the streetlamp. When his mother peeked in through the door, he shut his eyes, pretending to be asleep. He kept them closed as she crossed the room to tuck him in. For a second he was afraid she would fluff his pillow, but she only kissed his forehead and drifted away again in a faint trail of perfume.

Tomorrow he would find someplace to get rid of it—a trash can, not too near the house—and then his father would be safe again. Then he thought of the laundry mark. He'd have to cut that out. No trace. He turned on his side and put one hand under the pillow, anchoring the shirt. He tried to imagine himself at the cabin again, snug, but the room stayed cold and awake, as if someone had left a window open. His grandmother once told him that people in Europe thought the night air was poison, so they sealed everything tight. But now it came in anyway, blowing through the cracks, making his thoughts dart like flurries, poisoning shelter.

His father was wrong about one thing: Welles did have to delay the hearing. The next day, a Friday, snow covered Washington in a white silence, trapping congressmen in Chevy Chase, swirling around Capitol Hill until the dome looked like an igloo poking through the drifts. In the streets nothing moved but the plows and a few impatient cars, their heavy snow chains clanking like Marley's ghost. By midmorning everyone on Nick's block began digging out, a holiday party of scraping shovels and the grind of cars spinning wheels in deepening ruts. Nick's father helped the other men spread ashes around the tires, then push from behind until the cars lurched into the street, shuddering with exhaust. At the curbs, snow was piled into mounds, perfect for jumping. Even Mrs. Bryant next door came out, tramping up and down the street in her galoshes and mink coat, dispensing cups of chocolate, mistress to the field hands. Afterward Nick and his father knocked the heavy snow off the magnolias with brooms to save the branches, and it fell on their heads, seeping under their collars until they were finally forced inside to dry out. They had soup beside the fire, the way they did at the cabin, and Nick hoped the snow would never stop. The shirt, stuffed now behind a row of books, could wait.

"They'll cancel the dance," his mother said, glancing out the window. "Poor old Miriam. Her first year as chairwoman, too." She giggled. "What do they do with the flowers, do you think? God, she'll be *furious.*"

"It'll be gone by tomorrow night," his father said. "Anyway, a little snow won't stop her. She can fly in on her broom." This to Nick, who laughed.

"Walter."

"It snowed last year too, remember?"

"Yes, and half the people didn't show. Poor Miriam."

Nick leaned back against the club chair hassock, warm from the fire, and watched his parents. It was the sort of easy conversation they used to have, before the troubles. Her new dress. Where the United Charities money went anyway. Whether the president would come this year. When the phone rang it jolted him, as if he'd been half asleep.

His father had barely said "Hello" before his expression changed. He glanced up at Nick's mother, then, seeing Nick, retreated to a series of noncommittal "Yes" and "I see"s. When the call was finished, he went up to the study without saying a word. Nick could hear him dialing, then the low tones of another conversation. His mother, nervous again, followed him, standing outside the study door with her hand against the frame, braced for bad news. Then she went in, closing the door behind her so their voices were no louder than the muffled sounds in the street.

Nick knew they were not going to tell him, whatever it was, and he wondered in a kind of quiet panic whether he'd waited too long to get rid of the shirt. The storm had lulled him into thinking there was time, but now it was starting again. He got up from the floor and headed out into the hall, grabbing his winter jacket from the closet before racing up to his room. The shirt was still there, folded behind the books, and he stuffed it under his sweater, then put on the jacket, buckling the belt to keep the shirt from falling out. His boots were in the back mud room, drying out, so he'd have to go that way, through the kitchen.

"And where might you be going?" Nora said when she saw him.

But he was prepared. "The hill. With the sled. Mom said I could."

"And your boots still wet."

"I don't care. Everybody'll be there," he said, pulling them on in a rush.

"Who's everybody?"

But Nick was already opening the back door. "Everybody."

And then he was free, crossing the back alley courtyard, where all the garages were. The snow was deep here—no one had bothered to shovel in back yet—and it took him a minute or two to reach the garage and find the sled, crammed in a corner with rakes and shovels. Any moment now his mother might appear at the window, calling him back. But she didn't, and after he turned the corner into the alley, he knew it was going to be all right.

The problem was where to dump it. The snow had covered the trash cans along with everything else. He couldn't just bury it in the snow. They'd find it after the melt, like a body. A mailbox would be ideal, but his father had told him it was illegal to put things there. Somebody would report it. Pulling the sled behind him, he walked as far as Massachusetts Avenue, where the plows had been. But it was crowded here, store owners shoveling sidewalks, people carrying paper bags of groceries, so he turned onto A Street, back toward the Capitol.

He had gone two more blocks before he saw it— a storm drain at the curb that hadn't been blocked by snow. He looked around, then knelt down, fishing the shirt out from under his jacket. The label.

46

He took off his gloves and ripped off the black tag, his fingers surprised by the cold, then stuffed the shirt into the space behind the grate, pushing it with his bare hands until it fell with a quiet thud into the drain. He stood up and looked around to see if anyone had noticed, but the street was still empty. He remembered then that he hadn't cut out the laundry mark, but it was too late. And maybe it wouldn't matter. The sun would melt the snow and the drains would run, carrying the shirt along their underground tunnels until they emptied into the Potomac, or wherever they went, miles from the committee room. When he reached the Capitol a few blocks later, making a circle, he felt happier than he'd been in days. Somebody had finally helped.

There were more phone calls in the afternoon and Mr. Benjamin, the lawyer, came to dinner, so Nick ate in the kitchen, catching only bits of the talk in the dining room. No one had to tell him, however. It was there in Nora's afternoon paper. WELLES TO RE-CALL COCHRANE. NEW COCHRANE TESTI-MONY MONDAY. He'd overheard Mr. Benjamin say that it was a typical Welles tactic to tie up the weekend papers in speculation. By the time Monday rolled around, people would think she'd already testified and it would hardly matter what she actually said. But it mattered to Nick. He hoped it would be about the shirt, floating away. When he went to bed that night, his mother told him not to worry about anything and he nodded, as if they'd both forgotten to pretend he didn't know a thing.

The reporters were out in front again the next morning, even though it was Saturday. Nick's father went out to tell them he had nothing to say, but they lingered anyway, drinking coffee and looking up at the house, waiting for clues. No one came. Nick's father was shut in the study on the phone while Nora and his mother fitted her dress for the United Charities that night, because now his mother said they *had* to go, so Nick was invisible again. It was easy to disappear. When his father came out of the study, his face pale and distracted, he looked right past him, not seeing anything. The phone rang, and like a sleepwalker he turned back into the room. Nick had the odd feeling of not having been there at all. His mother told him to go outside—they were building a snow fort across the street—but he wanted to stay close to his father, ready to help. He knew he couldn't leave him now, alone despite the phone calls. Someone had to be there.

He was sitting listlessly in the club chair after lunch when he heard his father in the hall, putting on his boots. Where was he going? He looked out the front window, checking the street, then went back down the hall to the kitchen, obviously heading for the back door. Nick didn't hesitate. He grabbed his jacket in the mud room and pulled on his boots without bothering to close the buckles. When he stepped out into the snowy courtyard, he could see his father already turning the alley corner.

He followed about a block behind, not even worrying if his father turned around, trusting his invisibility. His father walked past the Senate Office Building, then turned down the hill, toward Union Station. He wasn't going out for milk or the afternoon papers. No errand took you to the station. Nick watched the herringbone coat cross D Street, not stopping for the light, then weaving through the moats of clear sidewalks between the banks of snow. Nick picked up his own pace. There were always crowds at the station, and he might lose him.

He darted past the line of taxis and into the great hall, a roar of loudspeaker announcements and newsboys and shoes clicking on marble. Nick moved to the side of the room—a kid alone might be suspicious—and walked quickly past the waiting benches crammed with delayed passengers. His father stopped and looked around, but Nick was lucky, hidden by a swarm of people heading for the track gates. Besides, you never saw what you didn't expect to see. Then his father went over to the row of telephone booths and, taking off his hat, sat down and closed the folding door. Nick waited by the newsstand, trying to make sense of it. Why come to Union Station to make a phone call when that was all he'd been doing at home? But he hadn't bought a ticket, that was the main thing. He wasn't going anywhere. Nick stared blankly at the magazines, warm with relief.

The trip home, up the hill, was longer, and Nick kept his distance, letting the coat stay several blocks ahead. He could probably spin off now, avoiding any risk of being seen, but he wanted to be sure. It was only when his father turned into the alley, back home, that he felt safe again. The sky was darkening for another snowfall, but he couldn't go in yet. Not so soon. Instead he went around the block to the front and pretended to roll snow with the other kids for the big fort. When they started throwing snow, he was the first to get hit, because he hadn't seen it coming. He was looking over the reporters' hats toward the house, protective as a guard dog.

He ate dinner alone again, then went upstairs to watch his parents dress for the ball, his father in a tuxedo with jet cufflinks and shiny shoes, his mother in a tight shoulderless top and a long skirt that swooped out with stiff petticoats. The day was almost over and nothing had happened. Nick kept glancing at his father, wondering if he knew he'd been followed, but he seemed unaware, smoking and fixing his bow tie with some of his old spirit. His mother was wearing her good necklace, the one with the garnet pendant, and she was smiling in the mirror, so that Nick thought maybe their good luck had come back again. It had been like this a hundred times before, the warm busyness before a party, the air rich with powder and after-shave.

The telephone rang.

"Now what?" his mother said, annoyed. "We'll be late."

His father answered the phone and listened for a minute without saying a word. Then he put the receiver back gently, as if he were afraid of waking someone, and looked up at them, pale.

"I have to talk to your mother, Nick," he said simply, and Nick knew that it had come, whatever it was. He glanced at his mother, but her eyes, anxious now, were fixed on his father.

"I'll be there in a minute, honeybun," his mother said absently, and Nick, dismissed, went out and closed the door. At first he could hear nothing, then a quiet undertone of voices, a moan. He had to know. He crept back to his room, then through the door of the connecting bathroom, the way he did to fool Nora, watching her vacuum. But now the spy game was real. The door to his parents' bedroom was open just a crack, and at first he heard only conspiratorial whispers. Then their voices rose, his mother's a kind of wail.

"Why didn't you tell me?"

"I couldn't," his father said. "I couldn't."

"Now?" his mother said, inexplicably.

"I didn't know it would be tonight. I'm sorry."

"No, I don't believe any of it," his mother said, and Nick could hear a cry beginning in her voice. "What about *us*? What about us, Walter?"

"I'm sorry," his father said quietly. Then, more audibly, "Come with me."

"Are you *crazy*?" his mother said. "You must be crazy. Everything—" She broke off, sobbing.

"Livia, please," his father said.

"Don't touch me!" she shouted, and Nick froze. For a moment he heard nothing, but he didn't dare push the door open. Then his father was talking, so quietly that Nick missed the next exchange.

He heard his mother take a quick few steps. "No, you can't," she said. "It's all—Walter, this is crazy. You can't—"

"Livia, I have to," he said calmly. "Come with me."

"Go to hell," she said, almost spitting the words.

"Livia, please," his father said.

Nick heard a new sound, then realized she was hitting his father's chest. "Go," she said. "Go."

"Believe me, I never thought—"

"Never *thought,*" she said, her voice unfamiliar with scorn.

"Never. I love you."

Now his mother was crying.

"I'll call tomorrow. The way I said."

"I don't care," his mother said faintly.

"Don't say that." Nick heard his father move toward the door, then stop. "You are so beautiful," he said softly.

For a moment there was absolute silence. Then, "I hope you die," his mother said.

Nick heard the door close. He rushed into the room and saw his mother sink onto the bed, her head drooping, as if the crying had made her limp. His stomach heaved. Once he had seen a man lying on the sidewalk downtown, people surrounding him and calling for an ambulance, and he'd felt this same fear, of life stopping before he could run away. Then he heard his father below, and he bolted from the room, clumping down the stairs and racing along the hall until, breathless, he caught him at the back door, his coat already on.

"Nick," his father said, turning, dismayed.

"Where are you going?"

"I have to go away, Nick," he said, bending down to face him. "I'm sorry."

"I got rid of the shirt," Nick said.

"You did?" he said, not understanding.

"Fifteen and a half, thirty-three. Like the lady said. I got rid of it. They'll never find it. You don't have to go."

"Nicku," his father said, holding him by the shoulders. Nick watched his father's eyes fill with tears. "My god. I never meant any of this to happen to you. Not you. Do you believe me?"

"You don't have to go."

"I can't explain. Not now. I wouldn't know how." His father got on one knee, his face level with Nick's. "I'll never leave you. Not really." He paused. "Would you do something for me? Make sure your mother's all right?"

Nick nodded, but what he heard was that his father was really going. Nothing would stop him now.

"Don't go," Nick said quietly.

"Could I have a hug? Would you do that?"

Nick put his arms around his father's neck, smelling the smoke and aftershave.

"No, a real one," his father said, clutching him, drawing him tighter and tighter, until Nick felt that he was suspended, without air, holding on for dear life. They stayed that way until Nick felt his father's arms drop. When he finally let go, he looked at Nick and said, "Okay," like the handshake of a deal.

He got up and went to the door.

"You need your rubbers," Nick said, pointing to the shiny formal shoes.

His father gave him a weak half-smile. "It's all right. It doesn't matter." Then he opened the door and started down the stairs, leaving Nick to close it behind him.

Nick watched through the pane of the mud room door. His father didn't go to the garage but headed across the courtyard to the alley. His shoes made holes in the snow, and even after he was out of sight, pausing only once at the corner to look back, Nick stared at the footprints, waiting for them to fill with new snow until finally every trace was gone.

Upstairs his mother was still crying, slumped over on the bed in her pretty dress like a stuffed doll. When she saw Nick, she opened her arms wordlessly and held him.

"Where did he go?" Nick said, but his mother didn't answer, just sat rocking him back and forth, the way she did when he was hurt. Finally she wiped her eyes, reached back to undo the clasp of the garnet necklace, and let it fall slowly into her hand. She sat looking at it for a moment, then closed her hand over the bright red stone and got up to put it away with the rest of her things.

CHAPTER TWO

The phone rang early the next morning, but Nick knew it wasn't his father because his mother said, "No, I'm sorry, he's not here," and immediately hung up. When, a little later, it rang again, she didn't answer but let it go on and on, shaking the quiet house until Nick thought the entire street must have heard. Then it stopped and she picked up the receiver, put it under her pillow, and went down to make coffee.

Nick found her in the kitchen, holding a steaming mug and smoking, staring at nothing. He took out some cereal and poured milk.

"What if he calls?" he said.

"He won't."

Afterward she built a fire and they sat in their bathrobes looking at it, curled up on the couch, pretending to be snowbound. Her face was drawn and tired, and after a while the rhythm of the clock and the crackling of the fire made her drowsy, and he saw her eyes droop, released finally into sleep. When he covered her with an afghan, she smiled without waking up. Nick lay with her on the couch and drifted too, worn out by the night.

The key in the lock startled them. Nora didn't

come on Sundays, and for one wild moment Nick thought it might be his father. But it was Nora, on a draft of cold air, a glimpse of the reporters outside behind her.

"Your phone's out of order," she said, stamping her snowy boots on the hall carpet.

"I took it off the hook," Nick's mother said, half asleep, sitting up.

"Where's Mr. Kotlar?"

"He's out," Nick's mother said simply.

"Well, he's picked a fine time."

"I just wanted some peace, that's all," his mother said, still on the earlier thought. "Don't they ever give up?"

"Mother of God, haven't you heard?" Nora said, surprised.

"What?"

"She's killed herself, that's what. That Rosemary Cochrane. Jumped." She held out the newspaper. Nick's mother didn't move. "Here, see for yourself," Nora said, putting the paper down and taking off her coat. "It's a wicked end. Even for her. Well, the burden on *that* conscience. Still, I won't speak ill of the dead."

"No," his mother said absently, reading the paper, her face white.

"I thought I'd better come. There'll be no peace today, for sure. The vultures. You'd better put the phone back or they'll be breaking down the door. Where's Mr. Kotlar gone, out so early?"

But Nick's mother didn't answer. "Oh god," she

said, dropping the paper, and walked out of the room.

"Well," Nora said, "now what?" She looked at Nick, still lying under his end of the afghan. Then, puzzled, she followed his mother down the hall.

Nick stared at the photograph framed by blurred type. She was lying face up on the roof of a car, peaceful, her legs crossed at the ankles as if she were taking a nap. Her shoes were gone and one nylon was visibly twisted, but her dress, high on her thighs, seemed otherwise in place. Only the strand of pearls, flung backward by the fall, looked wrong, tight at the neck, dangling upside down in the dark hair spread out beneath her head. She didn't look hurt. There was no blood, no torn clothing, no grotesque bulging eyes. Instead the violence lay around her in the twisted metal of the car roof, crumpled on impact, enfolding her now like a hammock. When you looked at it you could imagine the crash, the loud crunch of bones as the body hit, bending the metal until it finally stopped falling and came to rest. The new shape of the roof, its warped shine caught in the photographer's flash, was the most disturbing thing about the picture. In some crazy way, it looked as if she had killed the car.

Nick's first thought was that his father could come back now. The hearing would be over. But that must be a sin, even thinking it. She was dead. He couldn't stop looking at the picture, the closed eyes, the flung pearls. Was she dead before she hit the car, her neck twisted by the fall? She was dressed to go out. Had she looked at herself in the mirror before she opened the window? Then the rush of cold air. But why would anyone do that, the one unforgivable sin? What if she changed her mind after it was too late, not even the split second to repent? Damned forever. And then, his body suddenly warm with panic, another thought: Was it somehow his father's fault? Was she ashamed of lying? Or was it some kind of new attack? They'd blame him for this too. Nick felt a line of sweat at the top of his forehead. The hearing, their troubles, wouldn't end—they would get worse. A dead body didn't go away. It would start all over again—new questions, new suspicions. Her jump from the world would only drag them down deeper.

Now it was important to know. His eyes scanned the surrounding blocks of type, trying to reconstruct what had happened. A room on the sixteenth floor of the Mayflower Hotel. She had checked in that afternoon under a different name. Why go to a hotel? Her apartment was a few blocks away, off Dupont Circle. But a three-story house—too low. So she had planned it. And the newspaper speculated that in the Mayflower she'd found more than just height. All of Washington was in the ballroom below, for the United Charities ball. If she wanted a dramatic final appearance, she'd picked the right stage. Nick imagined her at the window, the cabs and hired black Packards pulling up under the awning, watching all the people who'd tormented her. Welles had been there, everybody. Nick stopped for a moment. His father was supposed to have been there too. Was that it? A final strike against him, in front of everybody? Larry had said she liked the spotlight. There would even be photographers on the street, to record the evening and its unexpected climax. She was dressed to go out.

The other details were sketchy, lost in long paragraphs of people's responses. Welles, still in black tie in his photo, was shocked and saddened and reserved further comment pending an investigation. She had jumped at 9:35, according to the doorman who'd heard the crash. The ball had been in full swing. She had fallen wide of the sidewalk, hitting the roof of a waiting car and injuring the driver, who had needed treatment. According to the front desk there had been no visitors and according to the District police no signs of struggle in her room—this was a new idea to Nick—but she had ordered liquor from room service and it was assumed she had been drinking. She had made no calls. There was no note. She was survived by a sister, living in New York.

And that was all. Nick read through the reports again, then went back to the picture of her body, staring so hard that he saw the grains of ink. What had she been like? For an instant he hated her. Why had she done this to them? Drawn them into this personal mystery that spread, touching everything, like a spill. It wasn't just politics anymore. Now someone was dead. And his father wasn't here. Nick could hear the phone again. What would happen when they found out he was gone? Larry said they could twist anything. Nick looked at the woman, peaceful and inert. They'd blame his father somehow. She'd only sold him a shirt and look what they'd made of that. Nick felt a pricking along his scalp. She hadn't lied about the shirt. His father had. But only Nick knew that. Had his father seen her at the hotel? There would have been time—he had left the house before the ball started. But no one knew that either. No one would ever know, if he came back.

Nick thought over everything that had happened the night before, remembering the words, the desperate hug, sifting for clues, but none of it seemed to have anything to do with the woman at the Mayflower. Nothing to connect his father with her. Unless she had been the call at Union Station. Nick looked up from the paper. No one, not even his mother, could know about that. Then his father would be safe. No connections at all. It was only his being away that could make things worse now, make people wonder why he was hiding. He had to come back.

Nick grabbed the newspaper and ran upstairs to dress. Through the bathroom door he could hear running water and knew his mother was soaking in the tub, hiding in a cloud of steam. They were all hiding. But they couldn't, now. He threw on some clothes and went down to his father's study, closing the door behind him. When he picked up the phone he heard Nora's voice, polite and normal. "No, he's out. Would you like to leave a message or try back later?" He waited for the click, then

pressed the receiver button again to get the operator to place a call to the cabin. There were a few
more clicks, then the burring of the line ringing a
hundred miles away. It was a new line, finally put in
last year, and it rang loudly enough to be heard
outside. Nick imagined his father shoveling a path
in the snow, picking up his head at the sound, then
stamping his boots on the porch as he came in to
answer. It's all right, Nick would tell him. But the
rings just continued until finally the operator came
back and asked if he wanted her to keep trying. He
hung up and turned on the radio. Perhaps his father hadn't got there yet or the snow had blocked
the road.

The radio was full of the suicide. Welles was
asked if the loss of his witness would call a halt to
the hearings. No. Not even this sad tragedy would
stop the American people from getting at the truth.
Mr. Benjamin was saddened but not surprised. The
poor woman's instability had been obvious from
the beginning. It had been irresponsible of Welles
to use her as a political tool, and now with such
tragic consequences. The bellhop who'd delivered
the liquor wouldn't say that she seemed particularly depressed. Pleasant, in fact, a real lady. She'd
given him a dollar tip. But you never knew, did
you? Meanwhile, Walter Kotlar was still unavailable
for comment. Nick listened to it all and he realized
that nobody knew. It would still be all right if he
could reach his father in time. He tried the number
again.

It was Nora's idea to take a tray up to his mother, as if she were an invalid.

"She got no sleep, I could tell just by the look of her. And where've you been all morning?"

"Reading."

"So it was a ghost, was it, with the radio on?"

"I can do both."

"Your father's picked a fine time. Not that I blame him. That phone would drive anyone out of the house."

But her eyes were shiny with excitement and Nick could tell she was enjoying it all, playing nurse and secretary, busy and important. So his mother hadn't told her.

After lunch he sneaked back into the study and tried the cabin again. He was listening to the rings, willing his father to come to the phone, when his mother walked in, surprising him.

"Nick," she said vaguely. "I thought I heard someone. What are you doing?" She was dressed, her skin pink from the bath, but her eyes were dull and tired. She moved across the room slowly, still underwater.

"I'm calling the cabin."

She looked at him, her face softening. "He's not there, honey."

Nick hung up the phone and waited, but his mother didn't say anything. It scared him to see her withdrawn, drifting somewhere else. They needed to be awake now.

"Where is he?" he said, as if the question itself, finally asked, would break the spell.

"He went away," she said. "You know that."

"But where?"

"Not to the cabin," she said to herself, her voice unexpectedly wry.

"Where?"

"Did he say anything to you? When you saw him?"

Nick shook his head.

"No, he wouldn't. He'd leave that for me to explain." She took a cigarette out of the box on the desk and lit it. Nick waited. "I'm not sure I can, Nick," she said. "Not yet. I'm not sure I understand it myself." Then she looked up. "But it's nothing to do with you. You know that, don't you?"

"I know. He wanted to stop the hearing, that's all. But now—"

"Is that what he told you?"

Nick shook his head. "I just know." He stared at her, waiting again.

She leaned her hand on the desk, unable to take the weight of his eyes. "Not now, Nick, okay? I need some time."

"So you can think what to say?"

She looked at him, a half-smile. "That's right. So I can think what to say."

There was a knock, then Nora flung the door open, her eyes wide with drama. "There you are. We've got the police now." His mother met her eyes, then glanced to the phone, expecting it to jump. "No. *Here,*" Nora said, cocking her head toward the stairs.

Nick saw his mother's face cloud over, then retreat again. She closed her eyes for a second, waiting for this to go away too, then opened them and looked at her wristwatch, as if she were late for an appointment. "Oh," she said and left the room in a daze. He and Nora glanced at each other, a question mark, then, unable to answer it, they followed her down the stairs.

Nick had expected uniforms, but the two policemen were in suits, holding their hats in their hands.

"We understand your husband's not here," one of them was saying.

"Yes, I'm sorry. Can I help?"

"Could you tell me when you're expecting him?"

"I'm not sure, really. He didn't say."

"Any idea where we might be able to reach him?"

"Have you tried his office?" his mother said lightly, not meeting Nick's look.

"We did that, Mrs. Kotlar."

"Oh. Well, that's odd. Is something wrong?"

"No. We just wanted to talk to him. You've heard about Miss Cochrane?"

His mother nodded, then raised her chin. "My husband didn't know Miss Cochrane," she said plainly.

The policemen looked at each other, embarrassed. "Well, we have to talk to everybody. You know. In cases like this. Get some idea what may have been on her mind."

"That's one thing we've never known."

In the awkward pause that followed, Nick looked at his mother, surprised at her tone.

"Yes, well, we don't want to bother you. Just have your husband give us a call when he gets in, would you?" The policeman handed her a card.

His mother took it. "Do you want to talk to his lawyer, Mr. Benjamin?"

"No, just have your husband give us a call."

She jumped when the phone rang, involuntarily glancing at her watch again. "That's all right, Nora," she said quickly. "I'll get it. Excuse me," she said to the policemen, picking up the phone on the second ring. "Hello. Yes?" Nick couldn't see her face, but her body leaned into the phone as if she were trying to make physical contact, and Nick knew it was his father. A prearranged contact. Now he understood her distraction. A chance to talk, ruined now by the need to pretend, her voice unnaturally brisk. "Yes, that's right. Yes." She was listening. "No, I'm afraid I can't." Would his father know the police were there? Nick wanted to push them out of the room, grab the phone, and tell his father to come back. "I'm sorry, but he's not here just now. He's out." Her voice was odd again, so far from intimacy that Nick knew it must be a message, her own kind of warning. "Yes. Yes, I know." Now a faint crack, or did only Nick hear it? "He's fine," she said, almost softly, and Nick's heart skipped. His father was asking about him. A pause as the caller talked. "You'll have to try later," she said, formal again, her voice rising slightly at the end. "Oh. I see." Then, finally, her real voice. "Me too."

She kept her back to them for a minute when she

65

hung up, composing herself, Nick thought, and when she turned he saw that it was only partly successful. She looked the way she had after the bath, slightly drugged and confused. She tried a small smile.

"It seems everyone wants to talk to my husband," she said apologetically.

"We don't want to bother you," the policeman said again, getting ready to go. "What time did you say your husband left?"

"What time?" she echoed weakly. Nick looked up in alarm. She was trying to think what to say again and the call had drained her.

"About eight o'clock," Nick said suddenly. "He made me cereal first."

The policeman turned to him, not catching Nora's surprised expression.

"Eight o'clock? Is that right, Mrs. Kotlar?"

"Nick—"

"Mom was still asleep. He didn't want to wake her." Nick thought of the shirt, floating down the drains. Now he had lied to the police too.

"Did he say where he was going?"

Nick shrugged. "A meeting, I guess. He took his briefcase." That was stupid. They'd find it upstairs. "The little one," he added, digging deeper.

"I see. Eight o'clock. He get a taxi out front?"

Nick saw the trap. They'd already asked the reporters.

"A taxi?" he said, pretending to be puzzled. "No, he went out the back. He always does that

66

when he doesn't want to talk. To the guys out front. You know."

The policeman smiled. "No, but I can imagine. Must be like living in a fishbowl here sometimes." This as a kind of apology to Nick's mother. "Well, we don't want to bother you," he said again, as if he really meant it. "Oh, Mrs. Kotlar, one last thing? You didn't go to the United Charities ball last night?"

"No."

"You and your husband were in all evening, then?"

He saw his mother waver again.

"We played Scrabble," Nick said.

"Oh yeah?" the policeman said, friendly.

"I won," Nick said, wondering if it was another trap. Who would believe that? "My dad lets me win."

And then they were gone, in a small confusion of thank-yous and promises to call, swallowed up by the reporters' hats outside.

"That was Dad," Nick said flatly when he heard the door close. His mother looked at him nervously, afraid to answer. "Is he all right?" She nodded.

"Would someone like to tell me what's going on around here?" Nora said. "Making cereal," she added, scoffing.

But his mother's eyes were filling with tears. "Do you think they knew?" his mother said to him. "I tried—"

"No, just me," Nick said.

"What?" Nora said again.

"She's worried about Dad," Nick said, answering for his mother. "He said he'd be back for lunch."

Nick's mother looked up, helpless to correct him.

"Lunch," Nora said, working at a puzzle.

The phone rang again and Nick's mother slumped, covering her eyes with one hand. Nick nodded to Nora, who raised her eyebrows and answered it. He led his mother to the couch, sat down beside her, and put one arm around her shoulder.

"When is he going to come back?" he said, almost in a whisper, so Nora wouldn't hear. His mother shook her head. "But he has to," Nick said.

"He's not coming back, Nick," his mother said wearily. "I wasn't sure until now."

Nick looked at her in confusion. "The police will come again. He has to be back before that. They'll look for him."

His mother put her hand to the side of his face, shaking her head. "It's just you and me now. You don't have to lie for him, Nick. It's not right."

But she still didn't understand; her mind was somewhere away from the immediate danger. "He was here last night," he said, looking into her eyes. "You have to say that."

"What are we doing to you?" his mother said in a half-whisper, still holding the side of his face.

"Call Uncle Larry," Nick said.

"Larry?"

"He'll know what to say. Before they come back."

His mother shook her head. "It doesn't matter," she said, dropping her hand.

"It does. They'll blame him. Where is he?"

"I don't know, Nick."

"I'm good at secrets. I'll never tell. Never."

"So many secrets," his mother said vaguely. "You don't understand. I don't *know.*"

"But he's safe?"

She nodded.

"Mr. Welles won't get him?"

She looked at him, and then, as if she were starting to laugh, her voice cracked and she sobbed out loud, so that Nora looked over from the phone table. "No," she said, her voice still in the in-between place. "Not now. Nobody will."

"Why not?" Nick whispered, his voice throaty and urgent. "Why not?"

Then she did laugh, the other side of the crying. "He's gone," she said wispily, moving her hand in the air. "He's fled the coop."

Before Nick could take this in, Nora loomed in front of them, her face white and dismayed.

"I'll take her upstairs," Nick said quickly. "She's upset." It was his father's voice.

Nora stared at him, more startled by his self-possession than by his mother's behavior. When he took his mother's elbow to lead her out of the room, Nora moved aside, stepping back out of their path.

He led her down the hall, but at the stair railing

she stopped, slipping out of his hand. "I'll be all right," she said softly, her voice coming back. "I'll just lie down for a while."

But Nick stopped her, placing his hand over hers on the rail. "Why won't they get him?"

His mother turned her head, looking for Nora, then lowered it. "He's not here," she said finally. "He's left the country."

She took in his wide eyes, then looked nervous again, so that Nick knew she hadn't meant to tell. He felt lightheaded, the same frightened giddiness as that time when their car had skidded on the ice coming down the hill from the cabin, spinning them sideways. Steer into the slide, his father had said aloud, giving himself instructions, gripping the wheel hard until finally they connected with the road again and he heard the solid crunching of snow. There wasn't time to think, just to steer.

"Mom?" he said, looking into her frightened eyes. "Don't tell anyone else."

By the next day his father was no longer unavailable for comment: he was missing. There were more men outside, and Nick saw that one was now watching the back too. Nora moved into the guest room, bringing her things over in a small valise, settling in for a siege. The radio said his father had been distraught at the news of the Cochrane suicide, but how did they know? Mr. Benjamin came, and Uncle Larry, and the police again, two men from the FBI. The phone rang.

Each day that week, as the spill spread, the headlines grew larger, so that the mystery itself became the news, begging for an answer. Welles appealed to his father to come out of hiding, implying that he had become guilty simply by being absent. Still, there was a new hesitancy in his voice, as if, having pushed one victim to a desperate act, he did not want to be blamed for another. Walter Kotlar had eluded him after all. There was an article about the rot in the State Department, the pumpkin field again, the China lobby, the unaccountable disappearance, proof of some larger conspiracy. But the story refused to stay political. The mystery seemed too complete for that—it frightened people. Nobody ran away from a hearing. It seemed to belong instead to the tabloid world of personal scandal and WANTED posters and cars speeding away in the night, a more familiar fall from grace. Was he still alive, sitting in some hotel room with his own open window? One day the papers ran some old family pictures. Nick and his mother, she squatting next to him proudly on the pavement as he showed off his new suit to the camera. His father as a young man, smiling. The house on 2nd Street. The car, still parked in the garage. All the pictures of a crime story, without any crime.

All week, as the newspapers grew louder and louder until finally, like a fire out of oxygen, they choked and went out, what struck Nick was the quiet in the house. With all the phones and visitors and black headlines that seemed to carry their own sounds, hours went by when there was nothing to hear but the clock. People spoke in low voices, when they spoke at all, and even Nora walked softly, not wanting to disturb the patient.

His mother was the patient. She spent long stretches sitting on the couch, smoking, not saying a word. Her silence, her intense concentration on nothing at all, frightened him. At night, alone, she drank until finally, her eyes drooping, she would curl up on the couch, avoiding her bedroom, and Nick would wait until he heard her steady breathing before he tiptoed over and covered her with the afghan. In the morning, she never wondered where it had come from. She seemed to forget everything, even what had really happened. She told the police—a relief—that his father had left Sunday morning, just as Nick had said. Yes, they'd played Scrabble. No, he hadn't seemed upset. When Uncle Larry suggested she get away for a few days until things died down, she said to him in genuine surprise, "I can't, Larry. I have to be here, if he calls." The secret, at least, was safe. She had begun living in Nick's story.

"Are you all right for money?" Larry said.

"I don't know. Walter took care of all that."

"You have to know, Livia. Shall I go through his things? Would you mind?"

She shrugged. "It's all in the desk. At least I suppose it is. The FBI went through it yesterday. I don't think they took anything away."

72

"You shouldn't let them do that, Livia," Larry said, a lawyer. "Not without a warrant."

"What's the difference, Larry? We don't have anything to hide," his mother said, and meant it.

The FBI came often now. In an unexpected see-saw of attention, as the newspapers grew bored with the story, the FBI became more interested. They went through his father's papers, opened the wall safe, asked the same questions, and then went away, as much in the dark as before. His father had signed a power of attorney for her on Saturday, which seemed suspicious, but his mother didn't know anything about it. And what, anyway, did they suspect? In the quiet study, everything was in order.

Nick grew quiet too. He wanted to go over things with his mother, plan what to do, but she didn't want to talk, so he sat listening to the sounds of the house. He thought of everything that had happened, every detail, studying the Cochrane photograph to jolt him into some idea for action, but nothing came back but the creak of floorboards, a windowpane shaking back at the wind, until it seemed that the house was giving up too, disintegrating with them. He read the Hardy Boys books he had got for Christmas, with their speedboats and roadsters and mysteries that were always solved. They rescued their father in one, wily and resourceful. One day, after the snow melted, he walked down A Street to check on the drain, but the shirt was gone, and he barely paused at the corner before turning back.

It was his decision to go back to school, stifled finally by the airless house. When he opened the door that Monday, the reporters swarmed around, expecting his mother, then backed away to let him pass, like the water of the Red Sea. "Hi, Nick," one of the regulars said, and he gave a shy wave, but they let him alone. At school, the kids backed away too, nodding with sidelong glances, deferential to his notoriety. His teacher pretended he'd been out sick and apologetically piled him with back homework. She never called on him in class. He sat quietly, taking notes, then went home and worked all evening while his mother sat smoking, still drifting. He finished all the make-up work in three days, turning in assignments that were neater and more complete than before, because now it was important to be good, to be blameless.

In the weeks that followed, nothing changed at home, but outside the reporters dwindled and at school people began to forget that anything had happened. When Welles suspended the hearings, the papers barely noticed. As Uncle Larry had predicted, things moved on. And it was Larry who brought his mother back.

"You can't just sit in the house. I'm taking you to New York for the weekend."

"To do what?"

"Go to a show, go out to dinner. Get dressed up and show your pretty face all over town," he said, winking at Nick, Van Johnson again, cheerful and take-charge.

"I can't."

"Yes, you can. Livia, you can't sit here. You've got to get on with things."

"By going to New York with you?"

Larry looked at her and smiled. "For a start. We'll take the train. I'll pick you up here at five. *Five,* no later. And no buts," he said, waving his forefinger.

Surprisingly, she went. Nora stayed the weekend and she and Nick went to the movies, treating themselves to tea at the Willard. In the long lobby of red carpets and potted palms, no one noticed them. On Sunday, when they went to meet his mother at Union Station, he glanced at the telephone booth, then averted his eyes, as if he were being watched. But his mother seemed better, the quiet around her beginning to thaw, like the melting snow.

It was only at night that it came back, the dread. It was the not knowing. Everyone acted as if his father were dead, but Nick knew he wasn't. He was somewhere. Nick lay under the covers watching the tree branch and tried to play the cabin game. Over the years, they'd thought of a lot of places where the wind was blowing—the cabin in the mountains, a tent in the desert, that big hotel at the Grand Canyon where they'd gone one summer— but Nick couldn't picture any of them. Instead there was the committee room, Welles glowering and accusing. A body falling in the cold. The strange walk to the telephone booth. And then, always, the back courtyard filling with snow.

I hope you die, his mother had said. But she hadn't meant that. Nick just wanted to know, and then he could rest. It seemed to him that their lives on 2nd Street had ended without any explanation. There had to be a reason. The hearings were starting again. They were looking for more Communists. So things went on. Was that all it had been? Politics, a piece of history? The trouble with history, his father had said, is that you have to live through it. But he hadn't meant this, half-living in a mystery. One day it will all seem like a dream. But it wouldn't, just the same mystery. That was the dread: he would never know.

His mother ended it that spring by selling the house. They would start over in New York, where nobody cared, and Nick would go to Rhode Island, where Father Tim had arranged for a place at his old school. Tim was taking them there himself, in the big DeSoto he drove like a carriage, hands on either side of the wheel as if he were holding reins.

Nick went with him for gas while his mother finished packing—an excuse, Nick suspected, for one of Father Tim's chats. But Tim was bubbly, as far away from homilies as a man on a picnic. They drove around the Mall, a last tour.

"You'll like the Priory," he said. "Of course, people always say that about their schools. I suppose they're really remembering themselves when they were young." Nick looked over at him, unable to imagine the ruddy face over the white collar as anything but grown up. "But this time of year," he continued, taking one hand away to gesture to the tree blossoms, "well, you won't find a finer sight. And then you've got Newport down the road. All the boats. I used to love that. Hundreds of sails, all across the bay." He stopped, aware of Nick's silence. "You'll like it," he repeated. "You'll see."

"My father wouldn't like it," Nick said. "He didn't want me to go to a Catholic school."

Father Tim didn't say anything to that. Nick watched him shift uncomfortably in his seat, avoiding the subject, his father's name like a cloud over the bright day.

"Well, give it a chance," Father Tim said. "You'll see. But a fair chance, mind. You don't want to be a burden to your mother. Not now. She's had worries enough to last a lifetime. Rose isn't as strong as she looks. It's been a difficult time for her, you know."

What about me? Nick wanted to say, but he was quiet. Then, "Why do you call her Rose?"

Father Tim smiled. "Well, she was Rose when I first knew her. She hated 'Livia' in those days. Like a Roman wife, she said. You know, Calpurnia. Names like that." He smiled again, glad to reminisce. "She was just Rose Quinn then. The prettiest girl at Sacred Heart."

"Maybe you should have married her," Nick said, curious to see if his father's joke had been right.

"Well, I married the church," Father Tim said, but he'd misunderstood Nick and looked at him, troubled. "He's still your father, Nick. No matter what."

This was so far from what Nick had been thinking that he didn't know what to say. Instead, he changed the subject. "Is it a sin to wish somebody would die? To say it, I mean."

"Yes," Father Tim said, "a great sin." Then, misunderstanding again, "You don't wish that, do you? No matter what he's done."

"No," Nick said. "*I* don't." But he was disconcerted. Tim had opened a different door. What did Tim think his father had done?

They stopped for a red light and Nick looked across at the Smithsonian, surrounded by flowering trees.

"Of course you don't," Father Tim said. "Anyway, that's all past now. You'll both have a fresh start."

But not together, Nick thought. He remembered the night his father went away, his mother clinging to Nick. He'd imagined going on like that, just the two of them. Now it seemed she'd be better on her own, putting Nick behind her with everything else. Maybe it was because he looked like his father, a visual reminder of what they were all supposed to forget.

"It's not easy making a new life," Father Tim said, as if they'd already disposed of the old. "But she'll have you to help her now."

This struck Nick as unfair, coming from the man who'd arranged to send him away, but he said nothing.

"You'll settle in before you know it," Father Tim went on. "And it's just a train ride from New York. You'll make new friends. It'll be a fresh start for you too."

"They'll know," Nick said. "At school."

Father Tim paused, framing an answer. "It's not Washington, Nick. They're a little out of the world up there. That's one of the nice things about the old Priory. They don't hear much."

"I don't care anyway," Nick said, looking out the window at the Mall. They were climbing the hill now, up toward the Capitol.

"You mustn't mind what people say, Nick," Father Tim said gently. "We're not responsible for what our parents do. There'd be no end to it then. God only asks us to answer for ourselves."

Nick said nothing, staring up at the Capitol, where everything had started. The flashbulbs and microphones. Maybe the committee was meeting now, banging gavels on the broad table, driving someone else away.

"If you commit suicide, do you go to hell?"

Father Tim glanced at him, visibly disturbed, then nodded. "Yes."

"Always?"

"Yes, always. You know that, Nick. It's a sin against God."

"What if you helped? What if you made someone do it? Then what?"

"You mean that poor woman," Father Tim said quietly. "We don't know why she did that, Nick.

You mustn't judge. It may not have anything to do with your father."

"No, not him. I was thinking about Mr. Welles."

Father Tim looked at him in surprise. "Mr. Welles?"

"They said in the papers he was pressuring her. What if—"

"I don't think that's true, Nick. And even if it were, we mustn't judge. He's only doing what he thinks is right."

"No. I *saw* him. He's—" Nick searched for a word, but it eluded him. "Bad," he finally said, knowing it was feeble and childish.

But his inadequacy seemed to relieve Father Tim. "Not necessarily," he said smoothly. "I know it's hard for you to understand. I don't condone his methods either. But Communists are godless people, Nick. Sometimes a man does the right thing the wrong way. That doesn't make him bad."

Nick looked at him, stunned. Tim thought his father was godless—that's what he'd done. We mustn't judge. But Tim had judged and now he was going to save Nick, shipping him off to the priests and a world where people didn't hear much. Save him from his father.

"Now this won't do, you know," Father Tim said, catching his look. "Taking the world on your shoulders like this. They're still pretty young shoulders, Nick. The right and wrong of things—that's what we spend our whole lives trying to figure out. When we grow up." He smiled. "Of course, some people never do, or I'd be out of business, wouldn't I?"

Nick saw that he was expected to smile back and managed a nod. There was nothing more to say, and now he was frightened again. Even Father Tim was with the others.

"What you've got to do now," Father Tim said with a kind of forced cheer, "is get on with your own life. Never mind about your father and his politics and all the rest of it. That's all over. You've got to look after your mother now. Right?"

Nick nodded again, pretending to agree.

"You have to let go," Father Tim said quietly, his final point.

"He's still my father," Nick said stubbornly.

Father Tim sighed. "Yes, he is, Nick. And you're right to honor him. Just as I do mine. That's what we're asked to do."

"Your father's dead."

"But your father's gone, Nick," he said as if Nick hadn't interrupted. "Maybe forever." His voice was hesitant, struggling for the right tone. "He wanted it that way, I don't know why. You can't hold on to something that isn't there. No good comes of that. It just makes it harder. He's gone. I'm not telling you to forget him. But you have to go on. He's like my father now. It's an awful thing. And you so young. But it would be better if—" He floundered, slowing the car at the light, then turned to face Nick, his eyes earnest and reassuring. "You have to think of him as dead."

He reached over and placed his hand on Nick's, a gesture of comfort. Nick stared down at it, feeling the rest of his body slip away, skidding on ice.

Nobody was going to help. Ever. Tim was waiting for him to agree. His father was godless and he was gone, better for everybody. It's what they all wanted, all the others. If he nodded, Father Tim would pat his hand, the end of the lesson, and leave him alone. You've got to stop fighting with him, Uncle Larry had said in the study, and his father had.

"I'll never do that," Nick said quietly, sliding his hand out from under, free.

Father Tim glanced at him, disappointed, and took his hand back. He sighed again as he made the turn into 2nd Street. "You will, though, you know," he said wearily, sure of the future. "Things pass. Even this. Nothing is forever. Except God."

And suddenly Nick knew what he would do. He would remember everything, every detail. He looked at the street, the pink-and-white blossoms, the bright marble of the Supreme Court Building catching the sun, and tried to fix them in his mind. The curly iron railing in front of Mrs. Bryant's house. Lampposts. The forsythia bush. Then he saw the moving van, the big packing boxes scattered all over the sidewalk in front of his house like the mess their lives had become. The prettiest girl at Sacred Heart was standing on the stoop, her vacant eyes animated now, giving directions to the movers. Crates for the china. The end tables sitting on the patch of city yard, spindly legs wrapped in protective brown paper. Two men in undershirts sweating as they heaved a couch into the van.

Suitcases by the door, ready. They were really going.

In that instant, as his mother saw the car and
waved to them, picking her way through the boxes
to the curb with a fixed smile, he thought, finally,
that his heart would break. He wondered if it could
literally happen, if sadness could fill the chambers
like blood until finally they had to burst from it. He
wouldn't cry. He would never let them see that.
And now his mother was there, pretending to be
happy, and Nora, all blubbery hugs, was handing
them a thermos for the ride, and Father Tim was
saying they'd better be starting. In a minute they'd
be gone.

Nick said he had to go to the bathroom and
raced into the house, leaving them standing at the
car. He walked through the empty rooms, trying to
fix them in his memory too, but it felt like someone
else's house. Maybe Father Tim was right. Things
passed, whether you wanted them to or not. He
went up to his father's study and stood at the door.
His mother hadn't taken the desk and it still sat
there, just the desk and the blank walls. The window was closed, and in the stale air he thought he
could still smell tobacco. His chest hurt again. Why
did it have to happen? He stared at the desk. He
wouldn't cry and he wouldn't do what Father Tim
had said. He wouldn't forget anything. His father
was somewhere. But not in the empty room. There
was nothing left but a trace of smoke.

He heard his mother calling and went down the

stairs to the car. Nora cried, but he got into the back seat, determined not to crack. He wouldn't even look back. But when the car turned the corner, he couldn't help himself and swiveled in his seat toward the back window. It was then he realized, trying to remember details, that something was missing. There were no reporters. It was over. There were just the boxes being loaded into a van.

Three years later, in the summer of 1953, after the death of Stalin and the murder of Beria, Walter Kotlar at last gave a press conference in Moscow. In the chess game of the Cold War, the move was meant to dismay the West, and it did, another blow after the disappearance of Burgess and Maclean. Like them, Kotlar denounced Western aggression as a threat to world peace. But his remarks were limited, and he made no reference to the circumstance of his defection. His presence was the story.

Nick had waited so long for his answer that when it came, a grainy newsclip, he felt a numb surprise that it didn't explain anything after all. It solved a puzzle, but not the one he wanted to solve. His father looked well. There was the expected storm in the papers, the events of 1950 retold as news, and for a day Nick and his mother wondered if their lives would be exploded again. But no one called.

The country had moved on. And by that time Nick had a new father and a new name, and their troubles, everything that happened to them, had become just a part of history.

PART TWO

THE RED
MENACE

■

CHAPTER THREE

"Vanessa Redgrave's supposed to show."

"Super. Where?" The two boys, obviously students, looked over the iron railings toward the tall houses lining one side of the square.

"I don't know, but she's supposed to show. Check out the cameras."

"Far out. We'll be on TV."

Eavesdropping, Nick smiled and looked toward the embassy steps, where the camera crews were setting up. The turnout was bigger than he'd expected. The day was raw and cold, damp morning mist still hanging from the trees, but the line snaked all around Grosvenor Square, ringing the enclosed park and spilling out down Brook Street. They couldn't all be American. The streets were still open to traffic, and the police, polite and wary, walked along the edge of the curb, asking the crowd to stay on the pavement.

The rally, like London itself, was gentle and friendly. In front of the embassy there were microphones for the demonstration speeches and Americans Against Vietnam signs, but no one broke out of line or heckled the secretaries going into the building. A few faces stared out of the upper-story windows, more curious than besieged, but no one called out to them. The confrontations and shouting belonged somewhere else. They were here to listen to speeches and then, one by one, to read the names of the dead.

Nick looked around for his LSE group, but they'd become separated earlier and were now swallowed up in the queue. One of the organizers, megaphone dangling from his neck, was moving down the line, handing out index cards.

"When you get to the mike, just read off the name and place and say 'dead' and then drop the card in the coffin. Got it? Don't yell—the mike'll pick it up. And keep it moving, okay? No stunts."

Nick took the card. *Pvt. Richard Sczeczynski. Nu Phoc, 1968.* That would have been during Tet, when the body bags flooded the airport, a hundred years ago.

The organizers looked like teenagers, but then everyone in the crowd looked young to him. Earlier he had noticed a middle-aged group in drab overcoats—academics, presumably, or English radicals old enough to have tramped to Aldermaston—but everyone else seemed to have stepped out of a dorm party, smooth-faced and eager, wrapped in capes and leather and old army greatcoats. A few had peace signs painted on their foreheads. Underneath the bushy mustaches and lumberjack beards their cheeks were pink. It was a thrift shop army—cast-off shawls and buckskin fringe and tight jeans with shiny studs planted along the seams. None of them had been there.

"Excuse me," a girl behind him said, holding out her card. "Do you have any idea how to pronounce this?"

An American voice. He looked at her—long blond hair held away from her face by an Indian headband, shoulders draped with a patterned gaucho cape—and took the card.

"Hue," he said automatically, wondering why she'd asked. She was pretty but slightly drawn, dressed to look younger than she was. Had she been standing there all this time?

"No, the name. I mean, he's dead—awful if I couldn't pronounce it. I mean—"

Nick looked again at the card. "Procházka," he read.

"Chaw?" she said, drawing out the flat *a.* "Like that? Russian?"

"No, it's a Czech name."

"Really? Do you know that?"

Nick shrugged. "It's a common name. Smith. Jones. Like that."

"Common if you're Czech," she said. "Are you?"

Nick shook his head. "Grandmother."

"You take it, then. I'll never say it right. Swap, okay? Do you mind?"

Nick smiled. "Be my guest," he said, handing her his card. He watched her face as she read it, did a double-take, and then gave a wry smile.

"Okay, you win. I can't even start this one. Is this like Jones too?"

"No. Che-chin-ski," he pronounced. "Polish."

"You can tell? Just like that?"

"Well, the 'ski' is Polish. The rest, I don't know. I'm just guessing."

She looked at him and smiled. "I'm impressed." She reached over and took back her card, grazing his fingers. "Forget the swap, though. I think I was better off the first time. Imagine, two in a row. Maybe we're the Slavic section. How do you say yours? In Czech. *Z*'s and *y*'s and all that?"

"Warren."

"Oh." She smiled. "Sorry."

"No," he said, studying her face, her quick brown eyes meeting his without embarrassment. "They're funny names."

"But not to them. I know. Mine's Chisholm, by the way. With an *l.*"

"Imagine what the Poles would do with that."

She smiled. "Yes, imagine."

He looked at her again. Wide mouth and pale skin, a trace of freckles over the bridge of her nose.

"Where are you from?" she said, the usual American-abroad question.

"New York."

"No, I mean where here. Are you with a group?"

"LSE," Nick said.

"You're a student?"

He laughed at her surprise. "Too old?"

"Well, the tie—" He followed her eyes to the senior-tutor wool jacket and plain tie he'd forgotten he had on. "Are you a teacher?"

"No, I'm finishing a dissertation," he said, the

92

all-purpose explanation for his time away, the drift. "Late start. What about you?"

"Oh, I'm—just here." She looked away for a second, avoiding him, and adjusted the heavy bag hanging from her shoulder, a shapeless but good soft leather that seemed at odds with the hippie cape. When she turned back, he was still staring at her. "What?" she said.

"Nothing," he said, catching himself. "I was— never mind."

"What?" she said, a laugh now in her throat.

"Well, I was going to say, Do you come here often? And I realized how dumb it sounded. What I meant was, have you been to one of these before?" But what he really meant was, why are you here? He wondered if she was like the girls in *Hair,* floating in a haze of smoke between protest marches and concerts, interchangeable parts of the same scene. But she was looking at him again with the same frank scrutiny, anything but mindless.

"Of course," she said simply. "I don't understand people who don't."

"Even over here?" Nick said, his own doubt.

She shrugged. "It all counts. Somehow. Why do you?"

"Same reason, I guess," he said, letting it drop.

The line moved a little now, people drawing nearer to the steps where the speakers had appeared, and he began to move with it.

"So do you always wear a tie?" she said, trying to keep his attention.

He smiled. Was she flirting with him? "I have to meet somebody after," he said. "That's all. Tie people."

She looked up at him and squinted her eyes. "Tie people?"

"Parents."

"Parents?" she said, disconcerted.

"Am I too old for that too?"

She looked at him oddly, as if his answer had thrown her, a piece for the wrong puzzle. "They live here?" she said unexpectedly.

He shook his head. "Flying visit. One meal. One tie. Not too much to ask." He glanced at his watch, reminded of the time. Larry and his mother were expecting him in just under an hour. "What's the matter?"

"Nothing. I—"

She seemed flustered again, but now there was a movement in the crowd, and before she could finish, people began to surge politely around them, looking down the street.

"It's her!" someone shouted. "She came."

Nick glanced toward the corner, where a black taxi idled as a tall woman leaned in to pay the fare. Two women with her greeted the organizers and collected their index cards, then steered her away from the photographers who had begun to move in their direction. "Miss Redgrave, over here!" She was dressed in a plain pea coat with a long muffler wrapped around her neck as camouflage, but in her high boots she towered over the other marchers, drawing attention like camera light. Now the rally had point.

She ignored the commotion at the steps and quietly joined the line not far from Nick, thanking the students who moved aside to make a place. They nodded shyly, pretending to be indifferent, but it was a face they had seen twenty feet high and soon they were staring openly, sprinkled with the same fairy dust that drew the press.

"Can you give us a statement?" one of the reporters shouted, Cockney and insistent.

"No, sorry," she said, turning away and staring straight ahead, removing herself.

"And will you be speaking today?" he asked quickly.

One of the women with her waved an arm to take in the crowd. "We're all speaking today," she said. "Just by being here." The students around her nodded, flattered.

Nick wondered who she was. An actress he didn't recognize? Or a hanger-on, the willing mouthpiece?

"What about charges that demos like these are actually undermining the progress of the Paris peace talks?"

"What progress?"

"Right," he said, smiling, finally jotting something down. "Film stars in politics?"

"Come on, Davey, not again," the woman said, surprising Nick with the intimacy. Had they been around this dance floor before? Maybe she *was* famous, part of the new culture that seemed to have sprung up overnight, while he wasn't looking, a music without history. "Everyone's in politics," she said, almost offhandedly. "Whether they want to be or not."

"Even the dead, eh? These soldiers here," he said, nodding toward the index cards. "Think they'd be pleased? Being part of this?"

There was a question, Nick thought. He wasn't even sure how he felt, still alive.

"We honor them as victims, not soldiers," the woman said, then stopped, aware that the reporter was writing. "That's all now, please."

And, surprisingly, it was. The reporter, still scribbling, nodded and started to back away, apparently satisfied with an interview that hadn't really happened. Nick remembered the reporters in Vietnam taking the handouts from the press office, knowing they were lies, printing them anyway.

"Davey's all right," the woman now said busily to Redgrave, who seemed not to hear, her Valkyrie head still above the crowd.

The line continued to press from behind, drawn to limelight, and Nick felt himself pushed against the girl at his side.

"Hey, Nick!"

He turned to the yell and saw the crowd rearrange itself as Henry, from the LSE group, pushed through. He came up to them, clearly excited by the day. "Hi," he said to the girl. "I see you found him."

Nick looked at her, puzzled, and saw her face color with embarrassment.

"I thought he'd be over here," Henry said to her, still unaware of her discomfort. "Description fit?"

"Perfectly," she said quietly.

"How'd you get lost anyway?" he said to Nick. "Old Wiseman came. He was asking for you."

But Nick was still staring at the girl. She met his eyes as frankly as before, then shrugged, found out.

"Hey, is that Vanessa Redgrave?" Henry said, looking around. "Where's Annie? Annie *loves* her." He finally made eye contact with his girlfriend and jabbed his finger in the air toward the tall woman.

"I just wanted to meet you, that's all," the girl said, still looking at Nick but smiling now. "Is that so terrible?"

Nick didn't know how to respond. Was she trying to pick him up? Is that the way it worked now? He looked at her, trying to imagine what it would be like. A few light exchanges, the walk back to her flat, the awkwardness until they finally touched— just like that, as easy as the music. In spite of himself, he grinned.

"No. So what do you think?" he said finally, spreading his hands to present himself, making a joke of it.

"I'm not sure yet," she said, matching his tone. "I like the tie, though. Look, maybe I'd better explain—" But she was drowned by the megaphones starting the demonstration and settled for another helpless shrug of the shoulders and a smile that didn't explain anything.

The crowd grew quiet around them, alert and

solemn, as the speaker welcomed them and asked them to begin the roll call of the dead. They stepped forward one at a time to read the names, the first few barely audible, unsure of the microphones. In the distance they could hear a buzz of traffic, but the square itself had become a hushed theater, and as one name followed another they took on the rhythm of a muffled drum roll.

"Corporal Ronald Stanton. Ben Hoa, 1967. Dead."

"Private Anthony Moro. Hue, 1968. Dead."

On and on, all the body bags. The line shuffled forward, holding index cards.

Nick listened for names he might have known, ashamed suddenly of flirting. He could feel her next to him, but she was looking straight ahead, serious, and it occurred to him that he had got it wrong somehow. Not a pickup. Why ask Henry anyway? None of it made sense, except his wanting it to be true, flattered by the attention, as eager as a teenager splashing on aftershave before a dance.

"Lieutenant Charles Macomb. Mekong Delta, 1968. Dead."

Not even a town, just a stretch of swamp. At the demonstration in New York they had wanted Nick to wear his uniform. "It's important, for moral authority," the organizer had said, a nice kid from Columbia still spotted with acne. But he had refused. Did it make him any better to have been there? It seemed to Nick that he had spent half his life in uniform, being good—Boy Scouts, with the proud sash of merit badges; ROTC, always pressed; the tropical-weight khaki—and it had all come down to a drum roll of names. There was no moral authority in a uniform, not even this new one of beads and headbands. He wondered how many of them had come to a funeral, to read the names, and were thinking instead about getting laid.

"Corporal Leonard Bauer. Lon Suc, 1968. Dead."

Nick looked up, startled. He had been to Lon Suc, before he'd been transferred back from the field, a semicircle of huts and scratching chickens steaming in a hot clearing. But who was Bauer? There'd been a little boy, killed when the bomb he'd been hiding—for whom?—went off, taking a few soldiers with him. Maybe Bauer. Afterward they had shot the parents, who never said a word, grateful perhaps not to have to live through the grieving. The huts were torched. Maybe Bauer had been one of these, shooting flames and yelling, hit later by a sniper. Maybe they were honoring a monster. And maybe he hadn't been there at all, just a jungle casualty, and someone in the office had looked at a map and picked a place of death for his tag. Now he was another piece of evidence, a name for the Fulbright scholars and draft evaders and movie stars to drop in a box as the line moved on. Who could sort it out? Larry was on his way to Paris to negotiate, which made him the enemy to Miss Redgrave's friend. And maybe he was.

"You go first," the girl said, and he saw that they were coming up to the microphones, a few steps above the young faces and careful policemen. He must have been drifting again, because she was looking at him curiously, as if she were trying to read his thoughts. Odd, the dark eyes in the blond face, unless there were hints of green that only showed in the light. He tilted his head a little to see and suddenly wished they could go for a walk in the park, away from the confusion and mixed motives of a rally that wouldn't matter anyway. A blanket on Hampstead Heath, an afternoon of absolute nothing. Talking idly. The image was so real that he wanted to laugh, surprised to be thinking in song lyrics. Instead he nodded, back in the raw, damp morning, and felt guilty. He was here for the names. He read his card and stepped away from the microphone.

"Private Leonard Procházka. Hue, 1968. Dead." She read the name perfectly, so that he wondered whether she had needed his help at all. Or had that been playing up too?

The steady line of readers coming down the steps pushed him farther back into the formless crowd, and for a minute he thought he'd lost her. Then he saw her craning her head near the curb, obviously looking for him, and made his way over.

"Spoken like a native," he said easily.

"Thanks."

"Pani Procházkova would be pleased," he said, testing her, but her face was blank. "His mother," he explained.

"Oh." She looked around at the crowd. "Now what happens?"

"Speeches."

"Do you want to get some coffee?"

"I can't. Really. I'm meeting somebody." He fingered his tie. "Remember?"

"One tie. One meal." She nodded. "Look, it's not what you think," she said, suddenly hesitant.

"It's not?"

She met his look, debating, then gave it up. "Screw it," she said. "As if you'd believe me now anyway. Look, I didn't do this right. I just wanted to see—" She stopped. "One of my bright ideas. Not exactly the best place, though, was it?" she said, extending her hand toward the steps, where the names were still being read. "You probably think—well, I know what you think."

"Take it easy," he said, smiling. "Want to start this over?"

She smiled. "I thought you had to go."

"I do. Can I call you?"

"I don't want you to think—oh, what's the difference? You probably wouldn't call otherwise. Anyway, we can't talk here."

He watched her, intrigued, feeling that he was eavesdropping on a conversation she was having with herself. "So can I call you?"

She looked at him again, the same appraising once-over. "Flaxman nine, double-oh two nine," she said carefully. "Better write it down."

"I'll say it three times. Then it's mine for life."

But this seemed to throw her.

"Like the game," he said. "You know, for new vocabulary words."

"Does that really work?" she said, genuinely curious.

"Usually. Flaxman nine, double-oh two nine," he repeated. "Chisholm, with an *l.*"

She smiled at him. "Molly. Two *l*'s," she said, extending her hand to shake his, just introduced.

"And I'm Nick." He held her hand for a moment. "I'll call," he said, wondering if he would.

He watched her cape as she worked her way through the crowd. When she turned to look back, he felt caught and she laughed at his expression, then wiggled her fingers in a wave and was gone.

"What was that about?" he said to Henry, still staring after her.

"I don't know. She asked if you were around."

"Really? By name?" Nick said, puzzled again.

Henry grinned. "Maybe you were recommended. They talk, you know."

He looked for the cape, but it had disappeared, taking the answer with it. A girl at a rally. He grinned back. "Yeah, right," he said, the locker-room answer Henry expected. If he really wanted to know, all he had to do was call.

"I told you. Demonstrations are the best," Henry said.

Nick listened to a few of the speeches. Wiseman, the historian, who had served Churchill in the great days, spoke of the folly of imperial adventures. Then an expatriate writer spoke on the criminality of the bombing, the tear in the social fabric at home. Nobody talked about the Lon Suc boy's parents, bowing their heads to the inevitable. But

102

what was there to say to that? Nobody here had pulled the trigger. They weren't the problem. They were the good guys, even Henry, who only pretended to be frivolous, and Annie, in her white makeup and Twiggy eye shadow, listening hard. It was easy to dismiss them and their tie-dyed politics, but what about the others, who used the dead soldiers to justify sending more? Because otherwise what had been the point? Private Bauer had to be redeemed. Nick had the same sense of futile dislocation he'd felt at the other rallies. They were here to talk to themselves, but the war had taken on a momentum of its own, killing everything. Who cared why it was crazy if it couldn't be stopped? As if he was doing anything about it either, dropping a name in a box.

Nick slipped away to the edge of the crowd, not even bothering to say goodbye. There was nothing worth hearing, and he was already late. He headed toward the Brook Street end of the square, then turned right, down past the bright flags on the Connaught to Mount Street, past the antique shops and the smart butcher where dressed fowl hung in the window like pieces of rare furniture. The crowd had been yelling back responses to one of the speakers, but even that had disappeared by the time he got to Berkeley Square, drowned out by the traffic zipping around the auto showrooms and the old plane trees that had survived the blitz.

It was a different London here, window boxes and polished brass, gleaming with privilege. With each block he felt he was leaving his own life for the smooth deep pile of his mother's world, where every step was cushioned and even the light was soft, filtered through trees in the park. In New York her windows looked out over the reservoir, and here, he suspected, she would be high over Green Park, exchanging one eyrie for another without bothering to come down to earth.

When he reached the Ritz he hesitated, reluctant to go in, and instead walked over to the park to have a cigarette. They'd still be groggy from a jet-lag nap, grateful for the delay. But Larry never napped. It was Nick who wanted the few minutes, to clear his head.

Aside from a few dog-walkers, he had the park to himself. He sat looking at the canvas lawn chairs scattered on the grass, hoping for sun, then glanced toward the hotel windows. Of course they'd be up. What did they talk about? After all these years, their life was still a mystery to him. He knew he should be grateful. Larry had rescued his mother from the bad time when she sleepwalked through the days and had made her happy. But she'd become someone else. There were moments still when she met Nick's eyes and he felt they were back in their old life, but then the phone would ring or the flowers would arrive and she would turn away, literally facing forward as if, like Lot's wife, the past would kill, turn her into a pillar of salt. Instead she seemed to spin in a circle of dinners and fittings and weekends and museum commit-tees until, exhausted, she was too tired to think of anything else.

It was useless to pretend she didn't enjoy it. Larry adored her and she answered him with an affectionate attention that Nick knew was more than simple gratitude, some emotional payback for security. They were a couple. Larry had given them a new life and his mother reveled in it, drawing on the blank check of Larry's wealth. But she had paid something too. Her laugh was different. Or was it only age, a settling in? Nick knew that, finally, it wasn't his concern, that he had no right to be uneasy. Nothing stays the same. But when she sat at her dressing table now, in her perfect clothes, her hair brushed into place, he felt that only part of her came back through the mirror and that in all that soft luxury it had become something shiny and hard, lacquered with money.

He stubbed out the cigarette and started back to the hotel. In a way, Nick thought, he'd been luckier. Larry had offered the protection and anonymity of his name without asking anything in return. His mother had been anxious about them in the beginning, but Larry had approached him as a kind of thorny government assignment, and with his usual tact and steady whittling away had won this negotiation too. He'd brought him back from the Priory. He did not ask to be called Dad and, except for those Sundays lugging gear to hockey practice at Lasker, hadn't tried to be one. They got along. It came, probably, as a surprise to them both. They were careful and then they were attached, in a family neither of them had expected, and when Nick had left home they found they missed each other, the reluctant father and his accidental son. Larry always introduced him that way—"my son"—and it had been years since Nick had felt guilty hearing it. Out of deference to his mother, they never spoke of his real father, because they were conspirators in this, keeping his mother happy, while she stared out of high windows and never looked back.

The Ritz, however, had only managed a second-story room facing Piccadilly, and as he padded down the corridor, past the pink walls and faux Louis XVI chairs, he smiled to himself, imagining their arrival scene—his mother frostily put out, Larry accommodating.

Larry opened the door, still in stocking feet and suspenders, and drew him in with the familiar broad smile and a hand on his shoulder.

"Nick, come in, come in. Good to see you. Just let me finish this," he said, pointing to the telephone lying on the desk. The years had thickened him and the Van Johnson hair was gray, but the face was still boyish, as eager as a soldier's on leave. "The duchess is still in her parlor," he said, nodding toward the closed bathroom. For a second Nick wondered if it was an unkind joke, for in his worst moments he had begun to think of her like the Duchess of Windsor, idle and groomed. But Larry was incapable of that kind of crack. It was just the winking camaraderie of men waiting for their women to dress. "I'll only be a sec," he said, returning to the phone.

Nick looked past the flowers and the messy coffee tray toward the bedroom piled with suitcases, and went over to the window. The room was quieter than he'd expected, the traffic on Piccadilly barely audible through the double glazing. The bed was still made, so no one had napped. Coffee, a wake-up shower, the phone calls—their morning was laid out before him like a map, already on schedule.

"What time is it there? Seven? Try him at home," Larry was saying. "Well, then *get* him up. I'm seeing David later and he'll want to be briefed. Yes, I know, but it's a courtesy. Let's not make this into a crisis, Jimmy. They're not *going* to walk away from the table. It's probably just another goddam Buddhist holiday. They've got a million of them. But find out."

Nick listened to the wheels of power while the midday traffic floated by outside.

"Fine," Larry said, signaling to Nick that he was finishing. "And use the telex line, will you? I'll be in and out. Right, later." He hung up. "Nick," he said fondly, shifting gears.

"How's the Insider?" Nick said, a joke between them. A *Newsweek* cover story had labeled him Mr. Insider, the old Democrat who served both parties and seemed beyond either, the surprise Nixon appointee to the negotiating team, brought back by the wrong party from his banishment to the wilderness during the Johnson years. That had been the one transition he hadn't survived, trickier than Truman to Eisenhower, because Kennedy had liked him and that, for Johnson, had been that. Now he was in because he'd been out, his hands so clean in Asia that he'd become a statesman, not a fixer.

"Outside looking in, from the sound of it," he said, smiling. "Seems I'm going to face an empty table in Paris tomorrow."

"They're objecting to you?" Nick said, surprised.

"They'll get over it. They have to."

"What's wrong with you?"

"This time? Old Cold Warrior, something like that. Hard-line—that's the actual phrase. Funny, back then I wasn't supposed to be hard-line enough. Still, who was? Except Stalin."

Nick smiled at the play of his mind. "Is it serious?"

But Larry was clearly enjoying himself. "No. Ho's probably still away for the weekend, but nobody wants to say. The minute he gets back we'll be bowing and drinking tea and off we go."

"Good luck," Nick said, looking at him seriously.

Larry looked up, not sure how to respond, but before he could say anything, Nick's mother opened the bathroom door.

"Nick," she said, smiling. "I didn't hear you." She was already dressed, a Chanel suit with a short skirt, and had clearly been putting on fresh makeup, so Nick expected an air-kiss, but she rushed across the room to hug him with the old warmth, her cheek tight against him.

"You'll smear," he said, laughing.

"Oh, darling, I don't care," she said, holding him. "Here. Let me look at you." She pulled back, holding his upper arms, gazing at him fondly, and Nick wondered again if she saw his father. "I think you've grown. Is that possible? We're supposed to *stop*. But Nick, the hair." She touched the back of his neck.

"Too long?"

"Too scraggly. Just a trim? I'm sure they have a barber downstairs. It wouldn't take ten minutes—"

"Mother."

"Oh, I know, I know. But honestly, Nick, you can't go to the Bruces' like that. You really can't."

"We're going to the Bruces'?"

She sighed. "Oh, I know, darling, I'm sorry. We came to see you and now Evangeline's carrying on about dinner. She's been on the phone half the morning. I told her we'd said drinks but apparently she's got half of London coming to some reception. So now it has to be dinner after, and—Anyway, it can't be helped. You know what she's like. You don't mind, really, do you? Sasha will be there, I suppose. Weren't you at school together?"

"No, she's younger."

"Oh. Well—"

"It's my fault, Nick," Larry said. "I can't say no to David. He's still the ambassador. Anyway, we can talk at lunch."

Nick smiled to himself. One meal. One tie. "Fine," he said. "Don't worry about it. This all right?" He touched the lapel of his jacket. "For tonight?"

"Don't tease," his mother said lightly, enjoying herself. "A proper suit. I know you have one.

109

Funny, isn't it? Men used to come to London just to *buy* suits, and now look at everybody.''

"You'll feel better at the Bruces'. I'll bet the rot hasn't spread there yet."

"Ho-ho," his mother said, waving her hand. "But you do see about the hair. She'll ask. I suppose they still have barbers here." This to Larry, a dig at the hotel left over from an earlier conversation. "I knew we should have stayed at the Connaught," she said, as if somehow the barbershop had already let them down.

"You wouldn't want to be there today anyway," Nick said, skating over it. "It's a little noisy." His mother raised her eyebrows. "There's a demonstration right around the corner."

"At the embassy, you mean," she said, fixing the geography in her head. Then, looking at him, "You were there?"

Nick nodded.

"Oh, Nick, you didn't. It's not fair to Larry, it really isn't. Think how it *looks.*"

"I wasn't thinking about that," he said, glancing at Larry.

"Darling, you have to. It's just what the papers—"

"Nobody was looking at me," he said. "Vanessa Redgrave was there."

"What's it got to do with her?" his mother said sharply.

Nick shrugged. "What's it got to do with anybody?"

His mother sighed. "I'm not talking about poli-

110

tics. I'm talking about this family. Larry's in a sensitive position right now—"

"I'm going to be a lot more sensitive if I don't get something to eat," Larry said. "Anybody else hungry? I'll just go get my tie." He ducked into the bedroom.

Nick's mother followed him with her eyes, saying nothing, then went over to the coffee table and lit a cigarette. "It's just—I don't want anything to go wrong. He's so happy being back. It might even do some good. This *war*," she said, exasperated, as if she'd been given another inferior room. Then she paused, hearing herself, and lowered her voice. "You know what they're like at the White House—they don't trust anybody, and they *hate* the protests. They think it's about them."

"It is about them."

"You know what I mean. They take it all personally."

"They should."

She glanced up at him, stubbing out the cigarette. "Oh, I can't talk to you. Do you think you're the only one against the war? Everybody's against the war."

"Not everybody."

"Well, Larry's trying to *do* something about it." She softened. "Look, I'm not trying to tell you what to do. As if I ever could. But—well, Larry's who he is. He's public. And that makes you public too. They'll use you to embarrass him."

"Mother, nobody even knows who I am. There

were thousands of people there today. Thousands.''

"But only one of them has a father going to the peace talks.''

He stopped, amused in spite of himself at the end run. "Well, I can't argue with you there.''

She blushed, taking the salute, then said, "Oh, let's not argue at all. I can't bear it. Nobody talks about anything else anymore. I haven't come all this way to argue about Vietnam.'' She stopped, catching herself in the glint in Nick's eyes, almost laughing. "Oh. Actually, I *have,* haven't I? Well, Larry has. No wonder he doesn't want me to stay—I suppose I cramp his style or something. Anyway, I just came to see you.''

"Between fittings.'' He grinned.

She smiled back and came over to him. "Nick, I am on your side, you know. How do you think I felt when you went there? If anything had happened—''

"It didn't. I was transferred out of the field, remember?'' he said, a trial balloon, because he had always suspected Larry had arranged it. But if so, he could see from her expression that Larry had kept it a secret from her too.

"What difference did that make? You don't stop worrying just because—Anyway, never mind. You're here.''

"And now it might happen to somebody else. Lots of them.''

She took his point but ignored it, following her own thought. "I've never been so scared in my life.

I never understood it. Everybody else got a deferment. Why didn't you? If you feel the way you do?"

"I didn't know I felt it then."

"No," she said, shaking her head. "Something else. Proving yourself, I suppose. Men. And we're the ones who end up worrying."

Nick looked away, seeing himself for a minute as he had been, the blind desperation to be thought loyal, beyond reproach. Like everyone else. His friends, who were safe, without a past, could afford to be different. So he'd gone, not fighting for his country, just asking for its good opinion. Not that that was any excuse. He turned back. "You know why."

Her eyes widened, as if they had felt the crack that opened up in her, and for a moment he thought the crack would widen, that at least she could admit this. But the lacquer worked; she came back together, sealed up. He saw that he had frightened her and he retreated, literally taking a step back.

She looked at him for a moment but didn't answer, and then began her own retreat, walking back over to the coffee table.

"Would you do something for me? Could we just not talk about any of this at lunch? I don't think I'm up to it. I really don't."

Nick spread his hands. "No politics. No religion."

"Oh god, that reminds me. Did I tell you? Father Tim had a heart attack. You might send him a note."

113

"Serious?"

"Well, *he* thought it was indigestion," Larry said, coming out of the bedroom, smoothing his tie.

Nick laughed.

"You're both terrible," his mother said indulgently. "I don't know why you're so mean about him," she said to Nick. "He's very fond of you."

"He means well," Nick said, tongue-in-cheek.

"Well, he does. Anyway, at his age anything's serious. It would be sweet if you did write."

"I thought you were the same age," Nick said.

"Not quite," his mother said. But her eyes were happy again, enjoying herself.

"What gets me," Larry said, "is how anybody dares to confess anything to him. Man's the biggest gossip I've ever met."

"That's because you're not a Catholic. You don't confess to a man—a priest is someone else then. Tim takes that sort of thing very seriously, you know, whatever you might think."

"Come on," Larry said. "I'm starving. You two solve all the problems of the world while I was in there?"

"We left a few for you," Nick said.

"You go ahead," his mother said. "I just want to fix my face."

"Should we start without you?" Larry said, implying the usual long wait.

"Don't be fresh. Five minutes. Not everybody slept all the way over. I need a little armor."

"Don't do any damage."

114

"Go on. Off," his mother said, shooing them out the door.

They passed up the elevator for the thick-carpeted stairs, Nick quickening his step to keep up.

"So how are things, Nick?" Larry said, putting a hand on his shoulder as they walked. "Do you like it here?"

"It beats law school."

Larry stopped. "You can always go back and finish, you know," he said seriously.

"Larry—"

Larry held up his hand. "Withdrawn," he said, smiling, and started down the hall again. "But what are you actually doing? Except having a good time. You are, I hope. When I was your age—You seeing anybody?"

Nick shook his head. "You know, a girl tried to pick me up this morning. At least I think she did."

Larry grinned. "If you don't know, then it's time to get out of the library."

"I guess," Nick said, returning the grin. "It suits me, though. For now," he added, wondering if it did, if the long afternoons in the stacks were anything more than an academic time-out.

"Well, it's your life. Sounds a little quiet to me. What do you do all day?" Larry said, his voice filled with telephones and secretaries and agendas.

Nick smiled to himself. "At the moment I'm doing some research for Aaron Wiseman."

"So he said." Then, catching Nick's look, he

smiled. "I ran into him when he was in the States last month."

"Checking up?"

"Just a little. Old habits." He brushed it aside. "What exactly are you writing?"

"He's writing. I look things up. He says history's like a criminal investigation. The documents are the clues."

"And you're the detective?"

Nick heard it, the tiny edge under the geniality. Instinctively he glanced over, but Larry was nodding to the bellman at the bottom of the stairs, ignoring him.

"So the students do the spade work," Larry said easily. "The old fox. No wonder he keeps churning them out." They turned into the long corridor of the lobby. "What's this one? Something about HUAC, I gather."

"He didn't tell you more?" Nick said, amused at Larry's cat-and-mouse. "One old fox to another?"

"You tell me."

"Jacobinism," Nick said flatly. "How the patterns never change. HUAC, the other committees. He's got me on SISS, the Senate committee."

"Mr. McCarthy," Larry said after a pause, as if he'd been trying to place the reference. "You know, he never really cared one way or the other," he said, his voice oddly reminiscent.

"He did a lot of damage for not caring."

"He didn't, though. I think he was surprised anybody took it seriously." They had passed the Palm Court, with its swirl of angels and gilded moldings,

116

when Larry stopped and turned to him. "Do you think this is a good idea, Nick?" he said, still trying to be casual, but Nick was alert now.

"You don't."

"I'm not sure what it means to you, that's all," Larry said softly. In his voice Nick heard the old protection, transferring him back from the field again.

"It's a research assignment, Larry, that's all. There are four of us. Nothing personal," he said. He smiled at Larry. "It's okay."

Larry looked at him, but apparently decided not to press the point. "Well, you know your own mind. I just don't want you picking at scabs." He hesitated. "Don't mention this to your mother." Nick nodded, wondering for a second if that had been his real point all along.

"You know, when you live through it—" Larry said suddenly, talking to himself. "Wiseman never knew them. Drunks. Opportunists. Little men who wanted to be somebody—that's all it ever was." He paused. "They're not worth your time, Nick. Anyway, they're gone."

"Not all of them," Nick said, looking straight at him. "Your new boss is still there."

Larry held his eyes for a minute, then turned toward the dining room. "Let's go in."

The maitre d' recognized Larry and took them across the pink room to a table near the tall windows facing Green Park. The day was still gray and dreary, but overhead, clouds floated across the painted ceiling sky. Gold ran along the walls and hung in long swags between the bright chandeliers, giving the room the summer luster of a giant jewel box. As they opened their napkins, waiters swarmed around them, removing cover plates, dishing out butter, taking drink orders, so that finally, when they were gone, Nick smiled at the sudden peace.

"Imagine what it's like at dinner," he said, apologizing by moving on.

But Larry refused to be distracted. "I didn't elect him."

"It's none of my business."

"Yes, it is. I don't want you protesting me too. You think—well, what do you think?"

"I don't see how you can do it," Nick said simply. "Nixon. Of all people."

"Yes. Of all people," Larry said slowly, looking down at the table. "Leader of the Free World. One of history's little jokes." He paused as the waiter filled their wineglasses, then looked up at Nick and said quietly, "He isn't Welles, you know."

"Was he any better?"

"Times change, Nick," he said gently.

"You think he's changed?"

"Dick? No. He doesn't have an idea in his head. Never did." He took a sip of wine. "He had instincts, though. I guess that was all he needed."

"And now his instincts are telling him to end the war."

"No, the polls tell him that. He just doesn't know how."

"So you're going to help him."

"I'm going to help him." Larry nodded. "My gray hair. My years of experience," he said sarcastically. "You can read about it in the papers. I'm going to give him—" He searched. "Credibility. Self-preservation's a powerful instinct. You can work with somebody who's got that. They'll do anything, if you find them an out."

"No matter what they said yesterday."

"They don't remember yesterday. They're not stuck in the past."

Nick took the point and looked away. "What if you're kidding yourself?"

"Well, what if? I don't think we can wait another four years to find out. This thing—riots, for Christ's sake. It's like watching somebody having convulsions. Sometimes it feels like another country to me." His voice was almost wistful, and Nick saw suddenly that he was older, propped up by the straight shoulders of his tailored suit. "You wonder where the other one went." Larry looked up. "Nothing's been happening in Paris, you know. Nothing. They argue about where to sit."

"And you're going to change that."

Larry said nothing, then leaned forward, a gesture at once earnest and conspiratorial. "We have to save face, Nick. We can't get out of this otherwise. Does it really matter if it's Nixon's face that's being saved?"

Nick looked away. "Why tell me, Larry? What difference does it make?"

Larry kept his eyes fixed on him. "When you lie down with dogs, you pick up a few fleas. Maybe I want you to know why I'm doing it before they start to bite. You're my son, Nick," he said, the words drawing Nick back. "I don't want to be one of your bad guys."

Nick looked at him, touched and disoriented, as if someone had tried to embrace him in this public, overdressed room. "I'd never think that," he said.

Larry leaned back in his seat, drawing away. "I know what he is. I'm not buying a car from him. I just want him to make the peace. You don't have to be honorable to do that. Not even a little. Not to make a deal."

"You just need a good lawyer."

Larry nodded, with a faint smile. "You just need a good lawyer."

"Who knows his way around. God, how you love all this, Larry," he said, then stopped, suddenly hearing another voice, back at the study door.

But Larry had heard only his. "That's how it gets done, Nick. Nothing ever got decided in the streets." He paused, letting the ball hit its court, then shifted in his chair. "Anyway, I didn't bring you down here to argue about Nixon. I wanted to talk to you before your mother comes down. She hates this sort of thing—she thinks we're all immortal. Of course, she may be," he said, smiling.

"What do you mean, immortal? Is something wrong?"

"No, no, nothing like that. I'm in the pink. Twenty pounds too pink, according to my doctor, but what does he know?" He caught Nick's look. "I'm *fine*, Nick. It's not that." He motioned to the waiter to refill his wineglass. "But I'm not getting any younger either, so we have to think about these things."

"What things?"

"Money." He reached in his pocket and pulled out his wallet. Then, seeing Nick's face, he laughed. "No, I'm not trying to give you a fiver. Here." He handed Nick a card. "There are some papers you need to sign. Needles is sending them to that address—it's the firm they use over here. They may already be here, for all I know. Anyway, give a call and they'll set up a time, okay? It's not very complicated, but they can walk you through them. Of course, you can still draw on the trust, but this will be yours outright."

"Larry, what is all this? I don't need any money."

"It'll all be yours one day, Nick. Unless your mother runs through it first. Which she's capable of doing," he said, a verbal wink. "Anyway, it's taxes. Needles says if I don't start signing some of it over now, the government will get it later. I've given Uncle Sam the best years of my life. I don't have to give him all my money too. So why wait?"

Nick looked at the card, too surprised to respond. Larry's heir. He ran his finger along the edge. It was just a card, a harmless token of this easy generosity, yet he felt that merely putting it in his pocket would mark a turning, make what had been provisional something permanent, a formal acceptance.

"You don't have to give me anything, Larry," he said quietly. "I never expected—"

"Who else?"

"What about your family?"

"Who? My sister? I wouldn't give Phyllis the time of day. Besides, she's got her own money." He leaned forward again. "Nick, you're my family. Legally you're my son. I'm not likely to have another one." He covered Nick's hand with his own. "Anyway, I'm happy with the one I've got."

Nick looked up from the card. "I don't know what to say."

"Well, 'thank you' is always appropriate."

Nick nodded slowly. "Thank you," he said, then pocketed the card, feeling a lightheaded letting-go. He took in the jewel-case room and grinned. "Does this mean I'm rich?"

"Comfortable. You don't have to vote Republican yet."

Nick smiled. "No strings?"

"No strings. Of course, you have to take care of it if you want to keep it. There's always that string. But talk to Needles when you get back. He never loses a dime."

"Am I coming home?"

"When you do," Larry said, maneuvering. "You don't want to stay away too long."

"What's wrong with London?" Nick said lightly. "I'm having a great time. Girls try to pick me up in the street. People take me to lunch and give me money. I'd be crazy to leave."

"Just don't let Wiseman talk you into another year. You're not getting any younger either."

"And now I have—responsibilities," Nick said,

toying with it. "All those money strings reeling me back in. Was that the idea?" He smiled. "You're an operator, Larry, I have to hand it to you."

"You haven't got it yet," Larry said, playing along. "It has the opposite effect on most people. Maybe you'll go wild instead."

"No. You know me. I was an Eagle Scout, remember? Look," he said, leaning forward. "I know what you're worrying about. I haven't gone AWOL. This is"—he waved his hand—"I don't know. R and R, I guess. I'll finish the degree. Then after, I'll go home and put on a suit and everything'll work out just the way you want it to. You don't have to buy my way back."

Larry looked at him and smiled. "Then there's nothing more I could ask," he said, and for an instant Nick thought he would actually reach over and shake hands.

"You'll think of something," Nick said, teasing.

"Well, don't tell the ambassador where you were this morning. Ah, here's your mother." He glanced toward the entrance. Two maitre d's were leading her across the room, a liner guided by tugboats, and Nick watched, amused, as heads bobbed up in the wake.

"They'll take you at two-thirty," she said, touching the back of Nick's neck as she took her seat. "Downstairs. Evangeline's thrilled you're coming."

"I'll bet."

"Well, she is. You know how she loves a party. Sad, really, their having to leave. She'll miss all this," she said, waving her hand, as if the room were an extension of the ambassador's residence. "Have you ordered? They've got five *hundred* coming for drinks, if you can believe it. Sort of a last hurrah, I suppose. I wonder who they'll send."

"They're talking about Annenberg," Larry said.

"Who?" Nick's mother said, reaching for the menu.

"*TV Guide,*" Larry said, smiling. "Campaign contributor. Generous."

"It's too bad," his mother said. "They love David here. Which Annenberg? Philadelphia?"

Larry nodded. "Remember Moses? Nailed before your time," he said to Nick, "for income tax evasion. Eight million penalty—in 1940 dollars. Makes you wonder what he really did. Now the son's on his way to the Court of St. James's." He shook his head. "It's a wonderful country. Nobody remembers anything."

And for a moment, in the pink Watteau room, it seemed nobody did. Water over the dam, the merciful absolution of time. Larry, grinning and casual, was on his way to Paris, and Nick's mother, studying the menu, hadn't heard a thing.

"Maybe he'll be better than you think," Nick said.

"I'll tell you one thing," his mother said. "The parties will never be the same. Never."

CHAPTER FOUR

The cars were backed up to the gate at Winfield House, so Nick paid off the taxi and walked the length of the driveway. Behind the hundred lighted windows Regent's Park stretched for miles, as dark as the night sky, so that the party seemed at first like a country-house ball, with Marine guards instead of livery men and Daimlers and Bentleys rolling up like coaches. Nick had come late to avoid the crush, but there was still a line on the steps, another for the coats, then a final clot at the entrance to the big room where the Bruces were receiving the guests. Nick worked his way around the edge, sure that the Bruces wouldn't recognize him anyway, and grabbed a glass from a passing tray. The room was pretty, but so crowded that the walls and furniture receded into a flat backdrop, blocked out by all the people onstage. There was a room beyond, and presumably another beyond that, bright and noisy, and waiters moved between them, their plates of canapes emptying and reappearing with the magic of the loaves and the fishes. Nick passed one of the makeshift bars covered with flutes of champagne and kept moving. There was nothing as anonymous as a big party, so long as you pretended you were on your way to something and didn't stand against the wall.

The crowd was hard to read, a hodgepodge of English and American voices, and Nick guessed that it was a general payback party—embassy workers, F.O. civil servants, transatlantic businessmen. They talked shop and the weather, polite and innocuous. Somebody's new posting. A skiing holiday. No one mentioned the demonstration. In the next room he spied Davey, the journalist who'd tried to interview Redgrave, but he had moved on too; his hair was slicked back now, part of the pinstriped crowd. Nick wondered if he was working, finding an item for tomorrow's chat columns, or just enjoying a perk. He was staring over his wineglass, his eyes fixed, and Nick followed the gaze to see what had caught his attention.

She was standing at the edge of a small group, her back to Davey, wrapped in a sleeveless red dress whose skirt, hugging her, ended somewhere on her upper thighs. When the man behind her moved, the full length of her legs sprang into view, a jolt of flesh in the crowded room, and Nick's eyes followed them down to her high heels. He glanced back at Davey, who had tilted his head for a better view, and grinned in spite of himself. Only a crowd this polite or self-absorbed would miss the only thing worth noticing. Davey, all bad manners and frank appraisal, had her to himself. Nick watched, fascinated, to see if he would make his move. But the wonderful legs seemed wasted on him too—he took another drink, then looked away, back on the job.

Nick walked over to her. It was an outrageous dress for a reception, about six inches short of propriety, a Chelsea skirt. She was probably one of the English secretaries at the embassy, who had dressed for a real party and ended up here instead. Her hair was piled on top of her head, swept up tightly in her one concession to formality, but a few strands dangled to the side like loose promises. When she turned toward him, he stopped. He saw the freckles across the bridge of her nose, then the eyes, as surprised as his.

"Flaxman nine, double-oh two nine," he said, smiling.

"What are you doing here?" she said, too surprised to stop the question.

He laughed. "What are you doing here?"

"Oh, I was brought," she said, waving her hand and the small silver purse that hung from her wrist. "But really, what *are* you doing here?"

"I was brought too. Don't worry, I'm not following you," he said, stepping closer.

"You look different," she said, nodding at his suit.

"So do you. I like your dress."

She blushed. "I didn't know. I've never been to an open house before. I thought—" She stopped. "It's not just the suit, it's the hair. You cut your hair."

He shrugged. "Part of the dress code. It'll grow back. Who brought you?"

"What? Oh, nobody. I mean—god, that sounds terrible. A friend of mine at the *Observer.* He thought I'd like to see the other half."

"Well, here they are. You're a journalist?"

"Just freelance. I had some stuff in *Rolling Stone* last year, though. A few other places."

"Is that what you were doing this morning?"

"No, that was me."

"You know, I've been wondering all day—what happened there? Did we just meet or what?"

She smiled. "They said at your flat that you were there. I was going anyway, so—"

"But—"

"Look, it's no big mystery. Somebody told me to look you up and I thought I'd check it out first, that's all."

"And?"

"I'm still checking."

He held her eyes for a moment. "Come to any decision yet?"

"About what?"

"About whether we're going to go out."

"Is that what goes on at these parties?"

"If you wear a dress like that."

She looked away. "Look, let me ex—"

"Nick, there you are," Larry said, coming up to them. "Having a good time?"

"Hi, Larry. Larry, Molly Chisholm," he said, "an old friend. My father, Larry Warren."

She looked rattled, either at the introduction or at Larry's appreciative look, but managed to shake hands.

"I told you you'd find someone you knew," Larry said to Nick, still looking at her. "It's a Bruce specialty. I don't suppose you've seen your mother anywhere?"

Nick shook his head.

"Then she's probably looking for me. I'll see you later. Nice to meet you," he said to Molly, nodding. "You're joining us later, I hope?"

"That's just what we were talking about," Nick said.

"Good, good. I look forward," Larry said, moving off.

"You will, won't you?" Nick said, but she was watching Larry slipping into another group, his hand already on someone's shoulder.

"You remembered my name," she said, turning back to him.

"Seems only fair. You already knew mine. How did you, by the way?"

"I told you, a friend—" She stopped, putting something together. "You're *that* Warren? I didn't know."

Nick smiled. "That Warren. He's my father. Come and have dinner anyway. You can see what it's like in the enemy camp."

"I had no idea," she said, suddenly nervous. "God, this is all mixed up. I never expected—"

"They're friends of the Bruces'. That's why we're here. You all right?"

"It just threw me for a loop, that's all. You throw me for a loop." She glanced around her, as if looking for an escape hatch.

"Is that good?"

She looked back and then laughed. "I guess so. I'm not making any sense, am I? Oh, this *place,*" she said, then looked up at him with a grin. "Hey."

"What?"

"Want to do a joint?"

"Here?" he said.

"The Beatles did one at Buckingham Palace."

"Are you serious?" he said, intrigued by the daring, as if she'd proposed having sex.

"Come on, we can go out there," she said, gesturing toward the French windows.

"You'll freeze."

"Come on."

He followed her out onto the shallow terrace, avoiding the look of a waiter who clearly thought they were ducking out to make love. At one end of the terrace two men smoking cigars near a giant potted plant looked up, then turned away discreetly. She fished an already rolled joint from her silver bag and handed him the box of matches. When he struck a match, her face glowed in the tiny flare.

"Light a cigarette just in case," she said, drawing in deeply. "No one will know the difference."

The sweet, pungent smoke, a smell of Vietnam, hung in the damp air.

"You like taking chances," he said.

"It's not much of a chance. I don't think anybody in there even knows what it is." She took another drag. "That's nice. Clears the head."

"Sometimes," he said, exchanging the cigarette for the joint and drawing on it.

"Who are these people anyway? This man I was talking to—agricultural development in the Third World. What does *that* mean?"

"It means he's a spook."

"Really?"

"Guaranteed," he said, smiling again. "The room's full of them."

"Can you always tell?"

"Agricultural development, for sure. Otherwise you have to look for signs. Journalist is usually pretty good."

"Oh, really," she said, playing. "You think I'm one?"

"Are you?"

She took the joint back. "We're not supposed to tell. What made you suspect?"

"You keep popping up in unlikely places," he said, spreading his hand toward the house.

"You know, I really didn't expect to see you here. I don't believe it now. I never thought—it's funny, isn't it?"

"What? You being here or my being here?"

"You. Maybe you're the spook." She glanced up at him quickly. "No."

"You sure?"

"I'd recognize you, wouldn't I? Here," she said, handing him the joint, "finish it. I'm on duty." She laughed to herself. "I interviewed a Hell's Angel once. I asked him how they picked an Angel and he said, 'We don't pick 'em, we recognize 'em.' So I guess I'd know."

Nick smiled, feeling a buzz. "Where was this?"

"California. A while ago."

"The summer of love," Nick said idly.

"Well, it was for the guys."

Nick flicked the roach out into the night and lit a cigarette, leaning against the building. The tall shrubs had taken on some definition in the misty air. In a few months it would be light all evening, England wide awake in the late northern light.

"What brought you over here?" he said.

"I don't know. Last year, after the assassinations, I just thought, enough, you know? I mean, all you could do was watch the news. So I thought, well, Europe. I had a friend in Paris, and of course just as I get there they start tearing up the streets, so it was all the same anyway. *Les événements,*" she said wryly, her accent deliberately broad. "So I just kept going."

She turned so that her face came into the light from the windows. Nick watched her, unaware that he was staring until she raised her eyebrows. Then she reached over and took his cigarette. "Let me have one of these," she said, putting it in her mouth with a casual intimacy. "What?"

"You're a quicksilver girl," Nick said, still watching her.

"Steve Miller Band," she said, placing the phrase. "I actually met a guy in that band." She handed back the cigarette, touching his fingers. "Like a chameleon, you mean."

"No, like quicksilver. Whenever I look, you go somewhere else."

She met his gaze and then, as if to demonstrate his point, looked away and leaned back against a potted plant. "Well, I'm here now. Where is here, anyway? I thought this would be at the embassy. Like this morning."

"It's the residence. Used to belong to Barbara Hutton."

"Who?"

Nick smiled. Maybe Larry was right—nobody remembered anything. "Woolworth heiress. She was married to Cary Grant. This used to be her house."

She looked up and down the terrace, then back through the windows at the party, a realtor's gaze. "Do you think he used to come out here to smoke too?"

"I don't think they were here together. Later. Maybe she bought it to get over him."

"Instead of a good cry," she said, looking at the house again. "What's it like to be that rich?" Then she glanced back at him. "Are you rich? I mean, Warren—"

"No. It's his money, not mine." He nodded at the house. "Nobody's this rich anymore."

"Who owns it now?"

"You do. Taxpayers."

"So that's where it goes." She giggled. "Makes me feel better about crashing."

"Come to dinner. You paid for that too."

"I can't."

"Yes, you can."

133

She looked at him, not saying anything, reading his face.

"Who's the friend?" Nick said.

"It's not that. I just can't." She paused. "Maybe I can join you later," she said, a polite dodge. "Where is it?"

"Here."

"Here?"

"Hmm. As soon as the taxpayers clear out."

She laughed. "You're crazy. I can't do that. What would they think?"

"The Bruces? They're used to it. All she has to do is rearrange the plates. It's her idea of a good time."

"Just like that."

Nick nodded. "If I ask her. I thought you wanted to see the other half."

"Not that close up. Look, it's nice of you—"

"Stay," Nick said, putting his hand on her arm. "I'd like you to."

She looked down at the hand, then smiled. "Don't you think it's a little soon for a family dinner?"

"I may not keep running into you. Maybe I won't get another chance."

"You could call."

"And then what?"

She grinned. "I guess you'd ask me to dinner."

He spread his hands, palms up, resting a case.

"God, what am I going to tell Brian?"

"Tell him you have an interview with the ambassador."

"Why am I doing this?" she said, laughing to herself. Then she looked up at him. "You're not what I expected," she said.

"What did you expect?"

But she let it go, making a joke of it. "I don't know. Somebody in agricultural development, I guess. I better find Brian." She held herself by the arms. "It's cold. No wonder Barbara what's-her-name sold it. You're sure?" she said, looking up again.

Nick nodded. "Go find Brian." She took a step toward the French window. "Hey," he said, stopping her, because in the new light from the window her pale skin did suddenly begin to gleam, shifting like mercury. "Don't disappear, okay?"

"Promise," she said, and because the day had been lucky, he took her at her word.

The intimate dinner sat twenty-four and she disappeared after all, behind the floral centerpiece, so that like Davey, he had to tilt his head to see her. At this angle her hair bounced on top of the stems, another flower, and he watched her turn back and forth between her dinner partners, two gray-haired diplomats who preened for her attention like rival suitors. When she caught his look, her eyes laughed in a private joke. The dope had worn down to a familiar lull of well-being, but his senses still seemed sharp, catching the light off the crystal and the glow, refracted, in the soft red wine. With Larry near one end and his mother near the other, he was marooned in the middle, surrounded by people talking to each other, free to watch her. It was easier without words, he thought. This is what animals did—looks and body movements and smiles, tapping a sexual Morse code across the table.

"It's not polite to stare, you know." A woman's voice, next to him.

"Sorry. Was I?" he said, turning to her, embarrassed.

But she was smiling. "I wish someone looked at me that way. She's very pretty. Are you together?"

"Sort of," he said, taking her in. She was still an attractive woman, but her face was loose and round, padded, Nick guessed, by years of too many extra glasses of wine. She seemed slightly drunk, shiny and amused, but not fuzzy.

"Sort of." She laughed. "Well, you will be, if you keep that up. Youth," she said, suggesting she'd enjoyed hers. "I tell you what. You just look and pretend to talk to me. I don't mind a bit. I'm Doris Kemper, by the way. Jack Kemper's wife." She spoke the name, unknown to Nick, as if it guaranteed instant recognition.

"Nick Warren."

"Ah. Larry's son?"

Nick nodded.

"Well, that explains it. Your father always had an eye for the girls."

"Really? Did you know him?"

"Not *that* way, if that's what you mean. But I must say, I always wondered a little," she said, oddly flirtatious. "He was quite the man about town. Do they use that expression anymore? Of course, this was all about a million years ago. Thank you," she said to the waiter refilling her glass. "You can't imagine how different Washington was then. People had *fun*."

Nick watched her take another drink, trying to imagine her slim and eager for a night out. It occurred to him that if he just smiled encouragingly he wouldn't have to talk at all.

"Well, they did," she said, misinterpreting his look. "Of course, children don't believe their parents were ever young. I know mine can't. Then I heard he got married. We were overseas and I thought, well, that's that. They'll be hanging crepe all over town. If it lasts. But here you are, so I guess it did."

"Where overseas?" Nick said, making conversation.

"Oh, everywhere. Athens. Rabat. Everywhere you had to boil the water." She laughed to herself. "We were in Delhi for four years—that was the longest stretch."

"Did you like it?"

"Well, Jack did. I had the children to raise. You know the tropics—one little scratch, and before you know it, it's infected. You had to watch all the time. And the snakes." She waved her hand, dismissing India, and when he followed it he found himself looking across the table again. Molly was listening to one of her suitors, fork poised in the air, her bare arms pale in the candlelight. He wondered if they would sleep together tonight. She'd stayed for dinner.

"You do have an eye," Doris Kemper said. "I suppose he passed it *on.*" She picked up her glass. "Now tell me about yourself. What are you doing in London? Are you a lawyer too?"

"No, I'm finishing a degree at LSE."

"That sounds interesting," she said, clearly not believing it. "What in?"

"At the moment I'm doing research on the McCarthy period. You know, the witch-hunts."

"People study that? Now I do feel old."

"My professor's writing a book about it."

"But it's such an exaggeration. Witch-hunts. I suppose to young people—but really, you know, the whole thing has been blown all out of proportion. I remember the loyalty oaths. We all had to do that. The army hearings. But to hear people talk, you'd think that's all that was going on. Not any of the good things. Most people didn't even notice."

"HUAC held over two hundred hearings then," Nick said calmly, a statistician. "Three thousand witnesses. And that was just HUAC. Not McCarthy."

"Really?" she said, too surprised to be offended. But she was already moving away, the lesson of a hundred dinner parties. "Of course, we were overseas most of the time."

She leaned back to let the waiter remove her plate and looked at Nick as if the new angle had suddenly brought him into focus. "Now I remember," she said. "Larry's wife. *She* had a child.

138

That's right. There was a boy—" She stopped. "Oh." Nick could see in her slack face the rest of it coming back to her. "I'm so sorry. I didn't—" She floundered, in such obvious distress that Nick, almost as a reflex, helped her.

"That's all right," he said quietly.

But it wasn't. It happened so rarely now that he was unprepared for it, that moment when someone knew. He felt the sinking in his stomach, always the same, found out by the giant pointing finger. He wished he weren't still high, unguarded, because now it would all come back. He knew the sequence, the pictures that would flash through his mind and always end with the woman lying twisted on the roof of the car. Instead he turned to the bright table, willing himself to be distracted by the opulent silver and the spray of flowers, an imperial banquet. Doris Kemper, who misinterpreted the gesture and thought he was angry, put her hand on his arm.

"I didn't mean—" she said, and because she was silly but still kind, Nick smiled back, letting her off the hook.

"I know," he said. How quickly it could happen, he thought, when you weren't expecting it. But that was his problem, not hers. She never meant a thing. She'd had a life of amahs and swimming pool parties and only remembered the snakes, dreaming of Maryland. And now, of course, she'd be curious. He could already see the irresistible questions forming in her eyes.

They were both rescued by the tinkling of a knife

against a glass as the ambassador rose to propose a toast. Not a speech, he said genially, just a word of welcome, because it was always good to see old friends and particularly good when those friends were about to render a service to their country. They were all aware of the importance of Larry's mission, and they were all grateful, he was sure, that the mission had been placed in such competent hands. If there was progress to be made, he would make it, and he carried with him, at the very least, the hopes and good wishes of everyone at this table and countless other tables back home. There was a little more, and a few "Hear, hears," and they raised their glasses. Nick raised his too, feeling more than ever the anomaly of his position, the son of a traitor invited to sit at the high table. But Larry, smiling modestly at the group, seemed entirely at ease, and his mother, on the ambassador's right, looked radiant. No one, in fact, saw anything but a happy family, not even Doris Kemper, who thought he had an eye.

The table was breaking up now, heading into the sitting room for coffee, and when he looked over at Molly towering over her diplomats, who turned out to be short, his mood changed. The hell with them all, tangled up in their money and pious hopes for Paris. Their world, not his. He was going to spend an evening with a girl who'd actually met someone in the Steve Miller Band. But when she returned his look she seemed nervous, flustered by the toast, as if the evening had been a high and they were coming down, back where they started, and he wondered if they would sleep together after all.

"Good luck with your project," Doris Kemper said, shaking hands.

"I'll try to look for the good things," he said pleasantly.

"You do that." She smiled, almost winking. "It's still the greatest country in the world."

The informality of the coffee hour made it easier to slip out early, and after paying his respects to the Bruces, he collected Molly and headed for the door. A hug and faint protest from his mother, but no one else seemed to mind, absorbed on their side of the generation gap.

"She's a nice girl," Larry said when Molly went to get her coat. "I thought you said you weren't seeing anybody."

"I'm not seeing her yet," Nick said. "First date."

"Quite a restaurant," Larry said, nodding at the room. Men smoked near the fireplace, ignoring the women, who perched on the edges of the deep couches, busy with each other. A waiter was passing brandy. It looked to be a long night.

"Quite an invitation," Nick said. "Thanks. Good luck tomorrow."

Larry nodded and shook his hand. "Don't forget to call the lawyer."

"I won't. By the way, who's Jack Kemper?"

Larry grinned. "What did he tell you?"

"He didn't tell me anything."

"Well, he wouldn't. He's CIA."

In the hall, Molly was being helped into her

gaucho cape, a remnant of her morning self. The servant, stiff and correct, held it as if it were mink, and as she slid into it, the two halves of her life seemed put together without matching.

"Shall I call you a taxi, sir?"

"No, thank you. We'll find one."

The man raised a dubious eyebrow, but nodded and opened the door. "Mind how you go," he said, indicating the dark driveway, dense now with night mist.

But it was the obscurity Nick wanted. He took her arm on the steps and they walked out of the range of the house lights, over the canal toward Prince Albert Road.

"You okay?" he said.

"I've never felt so out of place in my life."

"No, you were the hit of the party."

"I kept thinking, what if they knew?"

"Knew what?"

"Oh, I don't know. That I didn't belong there, I guess." She paused. "What was it like, growing up like that?"

"I didn't grow up like that. It was just—normal, you know. The usual stuff. School. Sports. They went to parties, I did homework."

"An all-American boy."

"Mm. Eagle Scout."

"You're kidding."

"On my honor," he said, holding up three fingers in the oath position.

She stopped, looking at him. "You're not what I expected."

"You said that before. Anyway, I'm not a Scout any more."

"No."

"There's something I've wanted to do all evening." Before she could say anything, he put his hands on her shoulders and kissed her, pressing her lips gently until she opened her mouth and he tasted the faint trace of wine. But then she pulled back and put her hand between them.

"Don't you want to?" he said, surprised.

She nodded. "That's the problem. Then later you'd think—"

He grinned. "I'm not old-fashioned. I'd respect you in the morning. Promise. Scout's honor."

She bit her lower lip. "No, you don't understand. Look, I need to talk to you. Let's go somewhere."

"No, here. What's wrong?"

She looked to the side, avoiding him, then took a breath and turned back. "Okay. I was going to explain, but I couldn't in there. And then—" She stopped. "Let me have a cigarette, will you?"

He fished one out of his pocket, still looking at her. He was amazed to see her hand trembling slightly as she took it. "What's this all about?" he said, lighting it for her.

She inhaled as if drawing strength from it.

"I told you someone asked me to look you up. You never asked who."

"Who?"

"I was supposed to give you a message. I never meant to—"

"Who?" he said, impatient now.

143

She looked up at him as if she were afraid of his reaction. "Your father."

"Larry?" he said, so that he wouldn't have to think anything else.

"No, your father. Walter Kotlar. I met him. He asked me to—" She paused, taking another drag on the cigarette. "He wants to see you."

CHAPTER FIVE

It was her idea to go to Jules Bar. A pub would have been noisy, her flat impossible, and when they got into the taxi he seemed incapable of suggesting anything, so she said the first thing that popped into her head. He was quiet all the way to Jermyn Street, not sure where to start or whether to start at all, one thought canceling out the other until he felt empty, staring at the meter. She didn't try to talk either, and for one crazy moment it seemed to him that they'd already entered the clandestine world, afraid to be overheard in taxis.

He wants to see you. Why? How? When the taxi stopped, she got out and paid and he just stood looking at the blue neon martini glass, now a little wary of her because, like a lover, she knew the most intimate thing about him.

"Who are you?" he said when they sat down. The bar was supposed to be like a New York cocktail lounge, dark and cool, little tables with flickering votive candles.

"Who I said. I just met him, that's all."

"Two vodkas," he said to the waiter, then turned back to her. "That seems appropriate, doesn't it?"

"Do you want to hear this or not?"

"I don't know. Yes. Of course I want to hear it. Christ." He lit a cigarette. "What were you doing in Moscow?"

"He's not in Moscow. He's in Prague."

"All right. What were you doing in Prague?"

"That doesn't matter."

"We have to start somewhere. Tell me. Or are you with the CIA too?"

She looked at him blankly, having had a different dinner partner. "Well, if you must know, I went to see a guy I knew in Paris. He's from there. There were lots of Czechs in Paris last year. You know, before the invasion."

"But he went back."

She nodded. "I thought we were—well, wrong again. Imagine my surprise. He didn't even want to see me—I suppose he thought it would get him in trouble. So like an idiot I show up at his door, and *voilà,* the new live-in girl takes one look and—anyway, what's the difference? Satisfied?" She looked up at him and smiled. "I'm not a spy. I just went to Prague to make a fool of myself."

"My father was a spy," Nick said simply.

"I know who he was."

The waiter brought the drinks in Jules's widemouthed martini glasses and he gulped his, managing half before it burned.

"So how did you meet him? After the girlfriend threw you out."

"Well, that's the funny thing. Jiří let me stay there—I think it was her idea, actually. To torture him or something. But I really didn't have anywhere

146

else and I'd already exchanged my money, so I just hung out and saw Prague. They took me places. To tell you the truth, I think Jiří liked the idea of people thinking he was with both of us. You know, that he had some *ménage à trois* going."

"Did he?"

"No." She glared at him, then let it go. "Anyway, they took me to a party one night and that's where I met him. Your father."

"At a party," Nick said. "When was this?"

"Last month."

"You took your time."

She shrugged. "I went back to Paris. I wasn't sure what to do. But I kept thinking about it. So."

"So here we are." He paused, looking down at his glass. "How did you find me?"

"Oh, he knew where you were. He knows all about you. I guess he keeps tabs."

For a second, his life seemed to tilt on its axis. He kept tabs. He never left.

"How is he?" he said finally.

"He's fine," she said, which told him nothing he wanted to know. "I mean, I guess he is. I only met him once. Well, twice."

He looked up at her. "Go ahead."

"I met him at the party. I knew who he was. And I thought, well, maybe there's a story. Maybe he'd talk to me—you know, give me an interview. He's never given one."

"No, never," Nick said.

"So I thought there'd be a piece in it."

"For *Rolling Stone,*" Nick said sarcastically.

147

"For somebody."

"They weren't even born," Nick continued. "Do you honestly think anyone cares?"

"Are you kidding? Walter Kotlar? After all these years? Everybody'd want that piece." She paused. "It would be a huge break for me. Anyway, I thought it was worth a try. So I asked him and he agreed to meet me."

"You must have made some impression. He's never talked to anyone before."

"He didn't then, either. Except about you. We met on the Charles Bridge and then we went for a walk. That's when he asked me to get in touch with you."

"On a bridge. Just like in the movies. In your trenchcoats."

"Well, it's like that there. You have to talk outside."

"And maybe somebody was putting you on. How do you know it was him? How do I know?"

"He said if you asked that to tell you he always remembered how you helped with the shirt. Whatever that means. He said you'd know."

He felt his stomach move again, another tilt. The snowy street. The drain.

She looked at him. "It was him, wasn't it?"

Nick nodded and then signaled to the waiter for another round. "Now what? I'm supposed to call him up and chat about old times?"

"No, he wants to see you."

"What makes you think I want to see him?"

"Don't you?"

"No."

"Oh," she said, at a loss.

"What did you expect? I'd be so thrilled he wants to see me after twenty years that I'd catch the next plane?"

"I don't know what I expected. I thought you'd be—I don't know, curious."

"Curious. Is that how you'd feel if you saw a ghost?"

She looked at him for a minute, studying his face. "No. I guess I'd feel scared."

"I don't feel scared," he said, taking a sip of his drink. "Let me tell you about my father. He walked out on us. Just left. *Defected.* That's the word everybody prefers. Gives it a sort of ideological cast. But what he really did was run. And we had to clean up the mess. My mother. Larry. Christ, not to mention the country. Sometimes I think that's the worst thing he did. That stupid fucking committee—he made them legitimate. They got something right finally. They just stepped right into it, and after that there was no stopping them. There *were* Communists in the State Department. Well, one. And they couldn't get him. So then how many others? And on and on. That's another little gift he left us."

"You can't blame him for that," she said quietly.

"But he did it," he said, placing his hand on hers for emphasis. "That's the point. They were right. Before him they had nothing. And then—" He caught himself, pulled back his hand, and took another drink. "We had to pretend he was dead. And after a while he *was* dead. I don't want to bring him back. You saw a ghost, that's all."

He stopped, waiting for her reply, but she said nothing.

"You know what I did the day he gave his press conference? That was the first time he came back from the dead. I played baseball. There was a game that afternoon and I saw him on television and I thought, Oh god, it's starting all over again, everybody will know, they'll throw me out of the game or look embarrassed or something. They'll know. But they didn't. I went to the park and nobody said a thing—the kids, the coaches, nobody. We just played ball, as if nothing had happened. Because it hadn't. That's when I realized it was over. I wasn't his son anymore. I was somebody else." He looked at her. "I'm still somebody else."

"If you say so."

"What's that mean?"

"It means I don't believe you."

He felt the lurch again, found out, back at the table with Doris Kemper.

"Have it your way. You delivered your message. Why did you, anyway? I mean, why bother? What's in it for you?"

"I told you. He promised to talk to me."

"And you believed him? He's been known not to tell the truth, you know. In fact, he's famous for it."

"He's not like that."

"Really. What is he like?"

"He's—" She searched for a word. "Sad."

Nick looked at her, not quite sure how to take

this. "Am I supposed to feel sorry for him? Forget it."

"Old-sad," she said thoughtfully. "He's old. Don't be angry. He just wants to see you."

"So why not pick up the phone? They have phones there, don't they? Why you? I don't get it."

"He wants me to bring you."

Nick stared at her, dumbfounded. "Come again?"

"He said you'd need a cover. I guess that's me. You'd be with me. He told me you had a different name. I didn't realize it was *that* Warren."

"Wait a minute. Let me get this straight. He walks up to you at a party and says go get my son and I'll give you an interview. But don't tell anybody, because I'm being watched. And you agree to do it? This doesn't strike you as a little crazy? If you're that hard up for a story, why not interview Barbara Hutton? Nobody remembers her either."

"I'm just telling you what he said."

"But why go through this? He's not a prisoner, you know. He's allowed visitors."

"I know. I kept wondering about that too. What I think is, he doesn't want them to know who you are. I don't know why. He wants them to think you're somebody else."

"Your fiancé."

"Look, I thought it was crazy too. All the cloak-and-dagger stuff. Why do you think it took me so long? But I kept thinking about it. First of all, it's like that there. They're all a little spooky. Jiří thought everybody's phone was tapped. So

151

maybe it's crazy, but they ought to know. They live there. They're always arranging to meet in parks, things like that. So I thought, well, maybe he thinks that way. He's used to it. But the more I thought about it, the more I thought there was something else. Not just being careful. Like he had it all worked out. The problem was, I couldn't figure out what. Then it occurred to me that maybe I wasn't supposed to know, but you would. That you'd know what he meant." She had been leaning forward, her voice eager, but now she sat back, opening her hands. "So I thought I'd better tell you. Just in case."

Nick shook his head, staring at the glass. "What exactly did he say to you?"

"Exactly? He wants to see you. Don't tell anybody. He said you'd understand."

"No, about the shirt."

"Oh." She frowned, concentrating. " 'Tell him I always remembered how he helped with the shirt. He'll know.' Like that, anyway. I don't know exactly. At the time, I didn't think—is it some kind of code?"

The word made Nick smile. "No. And this isn't Nancy Drew either. No codes. No invisible ink. There was a shirt, so yes, I know it's him. That's it."

"But what do you *think* it means?"

Nick looked at the table for a minute so she would think he was trying to sort out his thoughts, not push them away. It was starting again. Secrets. Listening at doors. But it didn't have to start. All he had to do was push it away.

"I think it means you met an old man at a party. Maybe he's sorry about what happened. So am I. But that doesn't mean I want to see him. It's a little late for apologies."

"You're wrong. There's something else—it's not that simple."

"Look, I'm sorry you came all this way—"

"I was coming anyway," she said, annoyed. "Don't worry." Then she leaned forward again, making a last effort. "What if I'm right? How could you not want to know?"

He looked at her, then signaled for the bill. "It takes practice. After a while, it works. Everything goes away and the last thing you want to do is bring it back. What do you think would happen if we went? A few awkward days with someone I don't even know anymore? All taped by you for some magazine?"

"That's not fair. I never said I wanted to do that. You don't have to take it out on me."

"Take what out?"

"Whatever it is that's making you like this."

"Right. Sorry." He pulled out some money to put on the plate with the bill.

"So you won't," she said, gathering her purse.

"You go. Tell him you saw me and I said he owes you the interview. Ask him why he defected. Ask him why that woman jumped out the window. I'd buy a copy of that story myself."

She looked up. "Why she—?"

"Forget it. Come on, we'd better go." He shook

his head. "It's been a strange day." He looked at her. "I thought—well, never mind what I thought."

"I didn't do this right."

"No, you were perfect. How else? It's like telling someone he's got cancer—it's hard to warm up to it. Anyway, I got the message."

"But you're not going to see him."

"Look, it isn't just me. You've met my family. How do you think they'd feel about this little weekend reunion? I can't do that to them. It's impossible."

"Don't tell them. They don't have to know. Nobody has to know."

"Just me and every photographer in Moscow."

"You're not listening. That's the last thing he wants. Nobody would know it's you. Anyway, he's in Prague. It's different."

"What makes you think he's still there? Maybe he's gone back."

"No, he lives there now. His wife is Czech."

He had been about to stand up to leave but now he stopped, amazed. "His wife?" It had the full shock of the unexpected. He had imagined his father as he was that night, back in the snow, literally stopped in time. Now suddenly he too had become someone else. Nick sat back in his chair, as if he'd been winded. "Christ. His wife."

"Didn't you know?"

"I don't know anything about him," he said, and for the first time he saw that it was true. What had his life been all these years? It hadn't stopped at the press conference. There'd been jobs and apartments and wives, a whole unknown life.

But Molly took his surprise for disapproval. "Your mother remarried," she said gently. "After the divorce."

"They weren't divorced," he said offhandedly. "It was annulled."

"Annulled? But how—"

"You mean because of me? Oh, that wouldn't stop the Church. It just—never happened. They're pros at that. My mother had connections," he said, thinking of Father Tim and his puppet strings. "Not that there was any problem. A Communist? They don't think there's anything worse than that. Let's go," he said, standing up.

"I never met her," she said, trying to hold him. "The wife. I saw her at the party, but I didn't meet her."

"I don't want to know," he said, holding up his hand. "Really." He stopped. "Are there children?"

"Not that I know of." She put the cape over her wonderful dress. "Just you."

"Not me," he said, and led her out of the bar.

It was late, but there was a taxi outside, unexpected luck.

"Will you drop me?" she said, an invitation.

"No. I'll walk."

She looked at him. "Well, at least I got to meet the ambassador." She hesitated at the taxi's door, listening to the motor turn over like a rickety machine. "For what it's worth, I think you're crazy.

He's worth ten of them, those people at dinner. I don't care what he did."

Nick smiled slightly. "I know. They've probably done worse. They just didn't do it to me."

"Neither did he."

"I don't want to see him, Molly. I can't."

"You don't want to see me now either, do you?"

He leaned against the open door, waiting for her to get in. "I wish I did. No one ever wanted to meet me before."

"No?" She smiled, then shrugged. "Well, don't let it throw you. I just turned up at the wrong door again, that's all." She got into the cab, then almost immediately pulled down the window. "I hate to ask, but do you have a fiver? I'm flat. I'll pay you back."

He took out the note and handed it to her. "That's okay. I'm feeling rich today," he said, thinking of Larry.

"Thanks. You know where to find me if you change your mind." She tilted her head slightly. "By the way, did anyone ever tell you? You look like him."

He stared at her through the window. "Who?"

She rolled her eyes, giving up, and sat back in the seat as the taxi pulled away.

He walked all the way back to his flat, cutting through Soho and its halfhearted dingy lights, then the quiet squares north of Oxford Street.

In the months after his father left, when he knew he would hear, he would listen for the phone, check the mail even after they had moved, always ready. It was only a question of when the message would come. If there were people in the room, he was prepared to cover, the way his mother had in front of the police. Code. But the message didn't come, and after a while he forgot what he'd been waiting for. No, he always knew. Come with me. Join me. And now that it had come, delivered by this unlikely girl, he felt ambushed, standing at the phone too startled to reply. Why now? This way? A summons like an old long-distance connection, scratchy and unclear, barely audible over the thin wires. What did his father want?

He could fly there in a few hours—Vienna was farther—not the end of the world. He wouldn't have to cross the barbed wires and guard dogs in the movies of his youth. Just show a passport, with its harmless new name, and join the line of German tourists waiting for the bus. In and out. See where Kafka lived. Wenceslas Square, which wasn't a square but a long street. He knew because he'd seen the Soviet tanks on television last year, lined up against the students.

What would they say to each other? Where did you go that night? How was it arranged? Why didn't—? But what was the point? Everything he wanted to know, that drew him, was further away than Prague, back irretrievably on 2nd Street. That was where they still lived, in some dream of the past. It was what he couldn't tell Molly, because he hadn't known it then himself. He was afraid of ghosts. They were too fragile. If you disturbed them, they vanished. If he saw a nice old man living with a Czech wife somewhere west of Vienna, his father would be gone for good.

The house was quiet; even vigilant Mrs. Caudhill in the ground-floor flat had gone to bed. It was an ugly Victorian redbrick, one of four whose bay windows stuck out like prows in a row of modest Regency terrace houses, and he'd been lucky to find it. A room at the top back, "overlooking the garden," which turned out to be a birdbath and a clump of rhododendrons that never bloomed. When he opened his door and switched on the desk lamp, still tiptoeing from the climb up the dim stairs, he could see everything in a glance: a bookcase of boards and bricks with a record player in the middle, a daybed and a cast-off easy chair, a desk with typewriter and stacks of index cards, an electric fire in front of the bricked-up fireplace. He flicked the fire on, rubbing his hands. It was always cold in England, and they put the water pipes outside the houses, where they could freeze.

He sat down, still in his suit, then got up to make some tea on the gas ring. It was only when he went over to look out the window that he realized he was pacing, jittery and caged. He wouldn't sleep. Anxiety had sopped up the alcohol, leaving his mind too sharp to rest. He thought of rolling a joint, but that would run the risk of an unwelcome thought floating in, and he didn't want to think. Everyone smoked in Vietnam because it was surreal and then you couldn't tell the difference. Now he needed to do something, crossword puzzles or solitaire, to keep his attention on the immediate.

The kettle whistle startled him and he hurried to make the tea. Why now? He sat back down in front of the electric fire, counted the orange bars, and sipped from the mug. He could will himself to be calm. Read something. As long as he didn't think. Then he glanced out the window and saw the top branches of the leafless tree and 2nd Street came flooding back, racing through his body until he actually felt memory, a tingle in his fingers on the cup. Everything he'd pushed away at Jules. Scene after scene. Had she thought he was indifferent? That it wasn't still there, just waiting? Welles and his stupid gavel, rattling ashtrays for the cameras. The swarm of hats outside the window, drinking coffee. His mother all dressed up for the charities benefit. The pearls flung backward on the dented car roof.

He stopped. That was the other thing. She'd left her apartment, checked into the Mayflower, and jumped. That was all. A girl at Garfinkel's. But before that, what? Discussion groups about capitalism? Saving the world from fascism? What had made her come forward, unraveling her lethal thread? What did the committee know, anyway? His father's judges. One of them, it turned out, had been a member of the Klan, convinced the Communists were organizing Negroes. It was there in the index cards. He glanced over at the desk. Indifferent? Then why the stacks of cards for Wiseman, the trail back? Larry had known instinctively that the research was a pose. He was studying the mechanics of history to find out something else. Had his father gone there that night, a last stop at the hotel? And now the one person who could tell him had sent a message and he sat with a mug of tea, too afraid to ask.

The room was warm enough for him to change now, and he went over to the closet to put his jacket away. He could read something until he fell asleep. Trollope, maybe, who'd probably seen houses like this going up and thought they were handsome. But his hand fell on an omnibus Stevenson, and there was memory again, *Kidnapped* in the club chair. He took it out anyway, a gesture of refusing to be intimidated, and threw it on the bed. He'd never read *Dr. Jekyll and Mr. Hyde,* just seen the movie, and that seemed safe enough. Then he realized, with a sighing irony, that he wasn't going to escape it. Who was that, after all, but his father, one person, then another? Except that Dr. Jekyll couldn't help himself, once he'd taken the medicine.

He folded his pants and put them on a hanger and started unbuttoning his shirt, staring down at the pile of laundry on the closet floor. He'd have to go to the Chinese tomorrow. When it hit him, he held on to the open front of his shirt, literally dizzy.

The shirt. His father hadn't been able to help himself then; Nick had helped him. It was something only they knew, that Nick had tried to help. In his child's mind, he had even been willing to break the law, anything. He was asking for help. That was the code.

Nick stood for a minute, arguing with himself, but he knew beyond reason that he was right. There had never been any point in making the message cryptic—why not just "Come see me"? "He'll know." And he did know. I need your help again. Don't tell anybody. Between us, like before. It couldn't mean anything else. His father might have used a hundred references from Nick's childhood, but he used the shirt, their secret. Molly could have thought it was an old family joke, nothing more. Was that what his life was like now, so cautious he didn't even trust his own messenger? But he trusted Nick. Nobody else had ever tried to help him. And now there was another shirt.

Nick walked over to the desk, pulled by strings that stretched so far back he was afraid mere movement would make them snap. What if he were wrong, standing there in his socks and underwear in the middle of the night, reading things into an innocuous hello? Or maybe just telling himself a story that would make him do what he wanted to do anyway. What if?

He picked up the phone and started to dial, surprised at the clunking sound in the quiet room. Flaxman nine. A Fulham number. Maybe he was still stoned. But he had never felt more alert in his life.

"Hullo?" The phone was picked up on the first ring, as if she didn't want anyone else to hear.

"It's Nick."

"Do you know what time it is?"

Why hadn't he waited until morning? But it had already been a month. "I know. I'm sorry. It couldn't wait."

"What?"

"I've changed my mind. You still willing to make the trip?"

"Maybe we'd better talk about this in the morning."

"Are you?"

She paused. "What made you change your mind?"

"It doesn't matter. You were right. I have to go. Can you leave right away? Tomorrow?"

"Are you crazy? We have to get visas. It takes a few days. You can't just walk—"

"Okay, where do we go for the visas?"

"Czech consulate," she said, suddenly practical. "It's in Notting Hill Gate."

"Will you meet me there? First thing in the morning?"

"Try noon. They don't open till late. And you just have to wait in line anyway. But go early if you want."

"No. We have to go together. You're my fiancée, remember?"

She laughed. "Do I get a ring?"

"I hadn't thought of that."

"I was kidding, for god's sake. Are you all right?"

"Okay, noon. Where in Notting Hill?"

"Meet me at the tube stop. It's about a block. Nick?"

"What?"

"Are you sure? I mean, you seemed so—I have his phone number, you know. I can just give it to you, if you want."

"No. The way he says. You'll be the contact."

There was a silence. "I thought you didn't want to see him."

"Now I do."

CHAPTER SIX

In the morning he saw Larry's lawyer, who droned on for half an hour about financial responsibility before he finally let Nick sign the papers.

"When can I draw on this?"

"This week, if you like. I'll arrange a wire transfer. Are you planning to buy something?"

"A car."

The lawyer smiled. "That's usually the first thing, isn't it? I've seen it time and again. A young man will have his car."

At Cook's, overflowing with brochures, they were happy to arrange anything, the whole world for a price. Bratislava was only fifty kilometers from Vienna, a tram ride in the old days. There was a Danube cruise, highly recommended, though of course it was early in the season. Prague was a bargain, since tourists were still a bit skittish about the Russians, but Budapest might surprise him. They had several groups going to Budapest.

By the time Nick got to Notting Hill Gate, he had a plan and the beginnings of an itinerary. He found Molly waiting on the street, looking at a Czech phrasebook, and she had changed herself again—plaid skirt, knee socks, sweater, and hair pulled back into a pony tail, a conventional American girl. Passport officials would know the type in a second.

"I thought I'd better start boning up," she said, holding out the book.

"Perfect," Nick said, implying that it was a prop.

"No, we'll need it. Unless you speak German. They hate it, but they speak it."

"Come on, let's go. We need to hit the Hungarian consulate later."

"We're going to Hungary?"

"Vienna and Budapest. The old empire. I thought it would be better if Prague was a side trip. You know, as long as we're in Vienna, so close, you couldn't resist showing it to me. In case anyone checks."

"When did you think all this up?"

"Last night. It has to be casual—a quick look-see and we're on our way, before anyone notices. With an itinerary to prove it."

"Why should we have to prove it?"

"I don't know. Why did my father send you?"

"Are you trying to scare me? He just wants to see you."

"Secretly." He looked at her. "Do you want to back out?"

"You're overreacting."

"Maybe. I've never done this before." He looked up at the modern building with the plaque of the Czech lion rampant bolted into the brick, as official as a jail. "It's still a police state. We have to be careful."

She shrugged. "Tell you what, then. You do all the talking. I'll just think about my engagement trip. Budapest, for god's sake."

Nick smiled. "It's nice. Lots of thermal baths. They told me so at Cook's."

"You went to Cook's?"

"I want it all on paper. Tickets. Reservations."

"Like an alibi."

"Yes," he said, looking at her. "Like an alibi."

But in fact the process was no more sinister than getting a driver's license. There were guards and applications to fill out and pamphlets about currency restrictions. On the walls, a portrait of a jowly man Nick assumed to be Husák. A few old people in line arguing in a language as remote as Chinese. Then forms were stamped and routed to out boxes, an iron curtain of paper. The visas would be good for three weeks, and they were required to exchange dollars for the whole period.

"But we'll only be there a few days," Nick said.

"Those are the currency regulations," the woman said tonelessly. "You will perhaps find many things to buy." An explanation from Oz, utterly without irony.

"When will they be ready?"

"Come back in three days. It's possible."

"We're anxious to start."

"Yes," the woman said, shuffling papers. "All the world wants to go to Prague."

Nick wondered if this was an office joke, but her face was impassive, already looking at the next person in line.

166

They paid the extra five pounds for the car and took the early hovercraft, skimming across the Channel to Ostend. They made good time through the flat, sprouting landscape, but by afternoon the mountains slowed them, and it was late when they finally reached Bern, as neat and atmospheric as a stage set. They found a pension on one of the arcaded streets not far from the bear pit, and after some soup and Alsatian wine in the empty dining room, went up to bed. Molly had said little during the drive but now began to unwind, turning playful from the wine.

"So how do we do this?" she said, pointing to the bed. "I've never been to bed with a man before. To sleep, I mean."

"Pick a side."

"Like brother and sister." She threw a flannel nightgown on the bed and went into the bathroom to brush her teeth. When she came back, toothbrush still in her mouth, Nick had already stripped to his shorts.

"Briefs. I knew it. We used to take bets—you know, in school. Briefs or boxers. I knew you'd be briefs." She watched as he turned back the covers. "Do you sleep in them?"

"Tonight I do."

"Don't worry. I'm too tired to look."

"Is that really what girls talk about?" he said, getting into bed.

"Of course. What do boys talk about?"

"Other things."

"I'll bet."

She went into the bathroom to rinse, then came back and put on the nightgown, slipping the clothes off underneath. Nick sat in the bed, blanket pulled up to his chest, watching her.

"How do you do that?"

"Hooks. Trick of the trade," she said, pulling in her arms and struggling with her shirt. "Ta-da." The shirt fell to the floor, then, after a few minutes of wriggling, the bra. She held it up for him, dancing a little. "See?"

"If you want to put on a show, take my advice and don't wear flannel."

"Serves you right," she said, sinking into the chair, propping her feet on the bed.

"Aren't you coming to bed?"

"In a minute."

"Well," he said, snapping off his light but still sitting up, looking at her.

"This would be my mother's idea of a perfect honeymoon."

He watched her for a minute, then said, "Let's not complicate things."

She moved to the bed. "No."

"Turn off the light and go to sleep."

"Just like that."

"Try it," he said, rolling away from her on his side.

She got into bed quickly, pulling the covers up. "Want to hear something funny? I feel—I don't know. Embarrassed. It's like we're married or something. Do you snore?''

"No," he said, still on his side.

"How do you know?"

"Will you go to sleep, please? We want to make Vienna tomorrow."

"It's farther than you think."

"Then we'll have to start early. Go to sleep."

She turned out the light and was quiet for a minute. Then she said, "Another day or two won't make any difference, you know. I mean, he's waited this long."

Nick turned over, but there was no light to catch her face, so that his words seemed spoken to the darkness. "So have I."

He turned away from her again, convinced they would spend hours pretending to sleep, but after a while he drifted off, no longer aware of her. It was the army's one gift: you learned to sleep anywhere. When the rain started he was back at the cabin, listening to the steady drip on the roof, safe in his room. It got louder and he thought about the gutters, his father cleaning out the clumps of leaves so the water would run down the drainpipe at the corner, making a puddle near the porch.

A rattling noise woke him, and, disoriented, he was startled by the figure at the open window until he realized it was her. She was looking out, smoking, her head in profile against the dim light.

"What's the matter?"

She jumped, as if he had tapped her on the

shoulder. "Nothing," she said quietly. "I couldn't sleep, that's all."

"Would it be better if we had separate rooms?"

"It's not that. Go back to sleep," she said, her voice gentle again.

"You all right?"

"Just nerves. Middle-of-the-night stuff. That ever happen to you?"

He nodded in the dark. "What is it?"

"There's no 'it.' It's just that feeling you get when you know you're going to make a mess of things. I do that a lot—make a mess of things." The rain blew in and she stepped back, brushing the front of her nightgown. "And now I'm wet. My mother always said I didn't have enough sense to come in out of the rain."

"Do you want to go back?"

"Not now." She stopped, talking into the dark as if she could see him. "That's the thing about making a mess—you can't help it, even when you see it coming."

"What are you worried about?"

"You, I guess. I mean, I got you into this. And now you're so—I don't know, *up* for it." She paused. "You never know how things will turn out."

He sighed. "Then let me worry about it. I want to go, Molly. You just—came along for the ride, okay? Come on, get into bed. It's late."

She stood still for a minute, then started lifting the nightgown over her head. "I have to take this off. It's wet." He heard the rustle of cloth, then saw

170

the pale white of her skin, indistinct in the dark. She slipped naked into bed, curling up on her side in a protective ball. "Nick?" she said. "Don't expect too much, okay?"

"I know."

"I mean, things never go the way you expect."

"I know," he said, but lightly this time, edging further away. "Look at us."

The next day was bright and clear and she began to enjoy herself, as if the rain had washed away the nighttime jitters with the clouds. They drove past steep meadows dotted with cows and wide farmhouses with window boxes, a calendar landscape without a smudge. The road swung through the mountains in perfectly engineered switchbacks and tunnels, encouraging speed, and they seemed to fly through the high, thin air, not even pausing at the rest stops, where tourists photographed each other against patches of glacier and the miles of valley just over the rail. It all looked, in fact, the way Nick had imagined it, Heidi meadows and bright wildflowers, but more painted than lived in, and by midmorning, feeling guilty because it was beautiful, he began to be bored. He knew he was meant to admire it—think of America, raging in its streets—but after a while all he wanted to do was turn the radio on, to disturb the peace.

"What kind of people stay neutral?" Molly said, somehow reading his mind. She was in jeans, down in the seat with her feet up, content to let him drive. "When you're traveling, you never meet anyone who says he's Swiss. Germans, yes, everywhere you go, but never Swiss. Imagine liking a place so much you never go anywhere." She pulled out a cigarette, lighting it away from the draft at the window. "It must be nice, not taking sides."

"Everybody takes sides."

She looked at him for a second, then waved her hand toward the landscape. "They didn't. They just let everybody go to hell. And they're doing okay."

"Up here in cloud-cuckoo-land. You wouldn't last a day."

"No? Maybe not. Anyway, it's probably just the air. Not enough oxygen to decide anything one way or the other."

"How much more of this?" he said, nodding toward the road.

"Miles. Austria's pretty much the same. This part, anyway. You can hardly tell the difference." She took a long pull on the cigarette, blowing the smoke out in a steady stream, suddenly moody. "Of course, they weren't neutral there. They were Nazis."

"So much for your theory," he said. "About the air."

"Maybe they got talked into it," she said quietly, still looking ahead.

"That's not the way I heard it."

She glanced at him, surprised, as if he'd interrupted another thought, then shrugged. "Who knows? Maybe the air's heavier over there."

Oddly enough, it was. As they crossed the border the sky grew dark with clouds, so that the morning seemed more than ever like some bright Alpine mirage floating above the gray. The middle of Europe was overcast, too far from the sea for the winds to lift its gloomy cover. Even the buildings began to take on a leaden weight, dreary with concrete and slate. They had lunch on a terrace built for sun with a small cluster of middle-aged ladies wearing overcoats and hats.

"What's it mean, anyway, briefs or boxers?" Nick said, to break her mood.

She smiled. "Well, boxers are a little country club, maybe." She paused. "Can I ask you something? Why did you change your mind?"

He looked at her face, open and curious. "I didn't change it," he hedged. "You just took me by surprise. Of course I want to see him. Wouldn't you?"

"I don't know. If I felt the way you did—"

"How do I feel? I don't know from one day to the next. I won't know until I see him, I guess."

"Okay," she said, backing off.

He leaned over, putting his hand on hers. "Look, I think I owe him this much, that's all."

Her eyes widened. "Owe him?"

"Remember before when I said people always take sides? What if it's the wrong one? That ever happen to you?" He felt her hand start under his, trapped, and he realized he'd been pressing down, so he released it. "It happened to me. I went to Vietnam. People change. Maybe he needs to tell somebody, get it out."

She moved her hand away, drawing it down into

her lap. "He's been there a long time, Nick," she said softly.

"Don't expect too much—I know. So maybe he hasn't changed. Maybe he just wants to tell me his war stories."

"Are you nervous?"

He glanced up, feeling her eyes on him, then covered the moment by pulling out some notes to put on the bill. "Well. This isn't getting us there."

She watched him put the money on the plate. "Would you do something for me?" she said. "Let's pretend we're not going there. Until we do. Let's just be tourists."

"All the world wants to go to Prague," he said.

She smiled. "But not today. Prague can wait a little."

They stayed the night in Salzburg and the next day left the main highway for the old road through the valley, storybook Europe with monasteries perched on bluffs over the river. The farther east they drove, the more remote the landscape felt. Nick saw the chemically sprayed vineyards and mechanized farms, but what he imagined were ox carts and peasant houses with superstitious chains of garlic at the window. Churches swirled in Baroque curves and flared out on top in bulbs. The German signs, funny and indecipherable at the same time, made the roads themselves seem un-real, as if they were traveling away from their own time.

They decided to stop at Dürnstein, where the ruined castle, almost theatrically gloomy now at dusk, was likely to guarantee a few tourist hotels, and were amazed to find the town full. They went from one inn to another in a light drizzle, achy from the long day's drive, until finally the desk clerk at the Golden Hind sent them to Frau Berenblum's, a block away. She had been slicing bread when they rang the bell and, alarmingly, answered the door with the knife still in her hand, but she had rooms.

"Zwei zimmer," she said to Molly.

Nick, who understood this much, said, "Tell her we only need one."

"Zwei zimmer," she repeated, glowering at him and pointing at Molly's ringless finger.

"Two rooms," Molly said. "She's worried about my virtue. If she only knew. Cheer up, though, we get to share a bath, and you never know where that's going to lead. Want to get the bags? She already thinks you're a pig, so try to be polite."

Frau Berenblum nodded through this, evidently because she thought Molly was asserting herself. Then, knife still in hand, she guided Molly up the stairs, leaving Nick to play porter.

The rooms were spotless and plain, down quilts rising high on the beds like powder puffs, but the bathroom was wonderful, with an old Edwardian box tub with rows of colored bath salts along its shelf, and after dinner Molly claimed it, soaking for what seemed hours. When she finally appeared at his door, her head wrapped in a towel turban, Nick was half asleep, nodding over the map. Then it was his turn to sit in the tub, listening to the sounds below—the slap of dough on the wooden table as

175

Frau Berenblum kneaded tomorrow's bread, the faint background of radio music. He wondered if she were listening too, cocking her ear for the telltale creak of springs. It was absurd. They weren't tourists. They were wasting time.

He could smell the dope as he passed Molly's door, and paused, not believing it. He tapped lightly, more aware than ever of the lights downstairs, and opened the door, still hoping it was his imagination.

She was sitting on the bed painting her toenails, small wads of cotton wedged between her toes, and she looked toward the door in surprise. The flannel had been replaced by silk, held at the back by two thin straps and cut low in front, and as she leaned over to apply the polish her breasts seemed on the verge of tipping out of the fabric. She had hiked the skirt up to mid-thigh to keep it out of the way, so that her entire leg was exposed in an arch of flesh.

He stopped for a moment, taking her in. It was the first time, in all the flirting and awkward sleeping arrangements, that he had really wanted her, wondered what it would be like to run his hand along her inner thigh, where she would be warm, quick to the touch. Then he saw the ashtray on the bed, the bulky home-rolled joint, a thin stream of sweet smoke still rising from the tip.

"Are you crazy?" he whispered.

She angled her head toward the open window. "It's okay."

"She'll smell it. *I* smelled it."

176

She grinned. "You think she's with the DEA?"

"It's not funny. Christ. You *brought* it? Over the border?"

She nodded, a little surprised at his anger. "Tampax. They never look. Never. It's okay." She swung around on the bed, dropping her leg so that she faced him in the low-cut nightgown, her skin white. He looked at her, an involuntary glance, then moved over to the ashtray.

"It's not okay," he said, putting out the joint. "Where's the rest of it?"

"Why?"

"Because I want to get rid of it, that's why. When were you planning to dump it? Just before we hit the iron curtain?"

"Iron curtain," she said. "It's just a border."

"I don't believe this," he said, his voice rising. "If you want to spend some time in a Communist jail, save it for your next trip. Did you ever think what might happen if you got caught? To both of us?"

"All right, stop yelling at me." She went over to the cosmetic bag, took out a tampon, and tossed it on the bed. "There."

"Is that all of it?"

"Would you like to search me?" she said, spreading her arms.

"Christ, that's all we need, to get nailed for drugs. Then what?"

She walked over to the bedtable and lit a cigarette, annoyed now. "I don't know. You've got connections. Maybe your father would get us off."

"That's not funny."

"All right," she said. "I'm *sorry.* What do you want? I thought it wouldn't matter. It's not legal in the States either, you know."

"We're not in the States. We're in fucking Austria, with Ilsa Koch downstairs and a trip to Husák's workers' paradise just down the road. They put people in jail for reading *Playboy,* for Christ's sake."

"No, they don't."

"You know what I mean. You want to test them? 'Welcome to Czechoslovakia—you're busted.' Christ, Molly, what were you thinking?"

"All *right.* You made your point. Go flush it down the toilet." She walked over to the open window. "Boy Scout."

As she stood by the window, he could see the length of her, the filmy material of her nightgown outlining the lean body, and he bounced between being aroused and irritated, his senses made alert by contradiction, as if the air around him were scratchy. It always seemed to work this way with her, feeling taunted and protective at the same time, then becoming impatient with himself for being distracted. He saw, looking at her, that it wasn't going to go away, the static, and that most of it was coming from somewhere outside them, the larger interference of the trip and what he would find. Meanwhile, they rubbed against each other, not sure why they were nervous in the first place.

"Sorry," he said, quietly now. "I just don't want anything to go wrong."

He picked up the tampon and walked toward the door.

"Nick?" She came over to him, a peace gesture, and held out her palm. "I'll do it. What if Frau Berenblum's out there?" She smiled. "How would you explain this?"

He handed it to her. "I was looking at the map before. If we backtrack to Freistadt, we can head straight up to Dolní Dvořísté tomorrow."

"Tomorrow?" she said quickly. "You can't."

"Why not?" he said, puzzled at her reaction.

"We're supposed to be in Vienna. I thought we had to keep to a schedule. You know. Anyway, don't we have reservations?"

"We'll cancel. Change of plan." He turned away from her. "I want to get this over with. We can see Vienna later."

"But—" She paused. "Are you angry? About the dope? Is that what it is?"

He shook his head. "Forget it. I just want to get there, Molly. Don't you? What's so important about Vienna?"

She looked down, at a loss. "Nothing, I guess. It was the plan, that's all. A little more time."

"We can be in Prague tomorrow. We're so close. A drive away. I used to think it was impossible—to go there—and it's just a drive away."

"Only from this direction," she said.

■

179

They had their last salad in Freistadt and drove to the border through gently sloping, wooded country, still and empty during the long rural lunch time. He had expected the road to the border to be grim, but the land was placid and rich, neat farms and stretches of old forest promising mushrooms. Then the road curved and the woods fell away and they were looking across a long cleared tract to the checkpoint. Beyond it another empty stretch rose uphill to the Czech crossing. In these open fields it would be impossible to hide.

Without thinking, Nick slowed down, already intimidated. He looked at the guardhouse, the tall watchtower, fences of barbed wire, all the props. But real to them. If you ran out across the field, you would be shot. The Austrian farms ran right up to the border like some jaunty declaration of freedom, but on the Czech side the land was empty. Just the fence. There would be searchlights at night. The guards, playing by the rules, wouldn't hesitate for a minute. So you kept away, behind the other side of the forest. Maybe nobody ever came this close, to see the elaborate watchtower. If you don't see the bars, you can pretend you're not in a cage.

The Austrian border police were bored and perfunctory, stamping their passports and waving them through. Nick wondered how useful they'd be to any escapees. He put the car in gear and moved slowly up the broad hill, aware that they had now left Austria and whatever protection it offered. It was crazy—he had not expected to be frightened, but the years of pictures and warnings flooded through him. They had crossed, just a plain field, into enemy territory.

The Czech guard waved them over to the side of the road. A machine gun hung from his shoulder.

"Dobre odpoledne," he said, which Nick understood as good afternoon, and then a line of incomprehensible Czech. When they didn't respond, he pointed the gun toward the guardhouse.

"He wants us to go in," Molly said.

"What's wrong?"

"Nothing. It's like this. Relax."

She got out of the car, smiling, but the guard ignored her, looking at the back of the car, peeking in through the window.

Inside they managed the essentials with Molly's smattering of German, but the uniformed officials seemed to be moving underwater, drugged by their heavy lunch. Finally they were led into a plain room—nothing but Husák on the wall—that reminded Nick of interrogation rooms in movies. But there were no questions, just nods and papers being taken to another room, visas being examined, then passed on to someone else, even the offer of tea from the gas ring in the corner. Then they were left alone.

Nick stared out the window at the two guards going over the car. They had placed their guns on the ground and seemed to be examining everything, one of them lying underneath, the other bent over to catch what seemed to be a running commentary. Earlier they had asked for the keys, and now they opened doors and explored the trunk.

Inexplicably, they didn't touch the suitcases, just poked their heads in for a look, then continued to walk around the car. For a second Nick thought they might actually kick the tires, like customers in a showroom.

"There's something wrong. I can feel it," Nick said, jittery.

"Maybe," Molly said. "I don't know. I flew in before. It's different at the airport."

One of the officials came in, handed them their passports, and spoke to Molly in rapid German. Nick watched the exchange, a verbal badminton, waiting to be told.

"It's the currency form," Molly said, her voice amused. "It says we changed sterling, but we've got American passports, so it's a confusion."

"What does he want?"

"He wants you to change money again. Got any dollars? Amazing what a dollar buys here. I hope his wife comes in for a piece."

"But—"

"Do it, would be my advice."

Nick shrugged and pulled out a traveler's check. "This any good?"

"As gold."

The exchange, with its forms, took a little longer. They were allowed to wait outside now, and Nick stood by the car, looking up at the watchtower and the soldier staring down at him, gun ready. How could his father want to live here? Russia would be even worse. In the patchy sunshine, Nick began to sweat. The barbed wire was higher than he'd expected—you'd have to cut it to get through. He took a cigarette pack from his pocket.

"American?" a guard said, walking up to him. For a wild moment Nick thought it might be contraband, but the guard's eyes were friendly and Nick realized he was just trying to cadge one. When he offered the pack, the guard smiled and took two.

"*Děkuji vám.*"

"*Prosím,*" Nick replied, trying it.

They stood side by side, smoking, staring down the road to Austria. Nick wondered if guards ever made a run for it. But they seemed sleepy and content, as if the guns and fences were invisible parts of the landscape, like power lines.

Nick felt the guard straighten before he saw the smudge in the distance. It grew into a bus, and the guard alerted the soldier in the watchtower, shouting up in Czech. The soldier answered, then another came out of the guardhouse. Something was going on. The guard next to Nick noisily drew in the last of the American smoke, stubbed it out with his boot, and stood straighter. The second guard joined him, and Nick had the feeling that the others inside were watching too.

The bus drew up at the Austrian crossing and pulled to the side of the road. The Czech guards were talking back and forth. People began filing out of the bus, and even at this distance Nick could see the tennis shoes and bright colors that meant a tour group. He imagined them crowding the interrogation room, exchanging money, flooding the counters with passports. The guards were imagining it too, their conversation a mix of groans and anticipation. The tourists stood to one side of the striped crossing gate, taking out cameras and aiming them directly up the hill at the iron curtain. Nick and the guards stood there, zoo animals. Then, pictures taken, the tourists got back on the bus. In a few minutes it turned around and, like a mirage, was gone.

Nick saw the disappointment on the guards' faces and wanted to laugh out loud. Nothing was wrong. An American passport, an English car—they had been the only event of the day. The tourist buses, memories of the busy months last year when the border was porous, passed them by now. It wasn't about him and Molly. Here, in this Cold War diorama, dressed up with the old symbols, the players had nothing to do.

At last they were allowed to pass. Beyond the Czech frontier, Nick could tell the difference immediately. The road, a major one, developed ragged shoulders, asphalt crumbling away at the sides. There were no houses, no billboards, few road signs of any kind, and even the landscape itself began to look rundown, dingy and ill kept around the edges. In only a few miles they were in another world. The road became the main street of villages, the way roads did before they were highways, passing mud puddles and ducks and women in babushkas, the timeless Eastern Europe of the folk tales. There were few cars. The villages depressed Nick—peeling plaster and old electric wires and a rim of dust extending up from the bottoms of the buildings, as if the whole town had been in a bathtub that drained, leaving a ring. People looked up as the car passed. The propaganda was true—nobody smiled.

"Do you want me to drive?"

"What?"

"I said, do you want me to drive? You seem a little preoccupied."

"I'm fine," he said, brushing it off. "How do we contact him?" He was staring straight ahead, edging away from an oncoming truck.

"We call him up," she said, smiling. "It's a city. Phones. Garbage. Everything."

But he didn't want to play. "I thought you said all the phones were tapped." He drove quietly for a minute. "What if he's not here? I mean, it's been a month. What if he left?"

"Where would he go? You can't just walk down to Cook's and buy a ticket."

"Back to Moscow. He could go back to Moscow."

"Will you stop?" she said, rolling down the window. "Look, the sun's coming out. Spring."

There were in fact blossoms now, not just buds, and the countryside was coming to life, as if the border had been a poison leaching into the soil. Here and there Nick saw an old manor house, a steepled church, left over from engravings of old Bohemia, but he found it impossible to imagine himself back in time. The grim present was always around them—the housing blocks of damp concrete, the dusty streets, the pervading sense that he was somewhere foreign, on the other side. He knew this was silly—an American wouldn't be in any danger—but he felt vulnerable and aware at the same time, as if he were walking down a dark street at night. Things were different here, as arbitrary and whimsical as a policeman's goodwill. He felt like a child. Maybe the Czechs did too, made wary and fretful by unpredictable authority. Even in the spring sunshine it seemed to him a country of shadows.

They were in Prague before they realized they had entered it. In America, the skylines offered a sense of arrival, but here there were simply more houses, then street signs, red with white lettering, and tram rails, everything getting denser as they moved toward the center. They came down a long hill, running along the wall of a park, and found themselves circling a World War II Soviet tank at the bottom before the road shot off toward the river. It was here, finally, that the city opened up to a vista, Kafka's castle high on the hill to their left, yellow buildings with tile roofs, the graceful bridges, the sky spiked everywhere by steeples.

They drove toward the cobbled streets of the Malá Strana, and Nick could see that beneath the dust and the scaffolding the city was beautiful. There was no color—no ads, no splashy shopfronts, not even the usual variety of cars in the street—so the buildings themselves became more vivid. Their Baroque facades of light mustard and green and terra cotta dressed the town. The architecture seemed to have been put down in layers,

186

one period after another, until the unremarkable hills along the river had become an astonishing city, one of those places where Europe rises to its high-water mark, rich and complicated. Mozart had introduced operas here. In the afternoon light, the city was a painting, full of brushstrokes and perspectives and lovely forms. It was also falling apart. Up close, some of the wonderful houses were buckling, the lemon plaster torn with cracks. The scaffolding he saw seemed like a finger-in-the-dike attempt to shore up the years of neglect. The buildings, unmaintained, were slowly dying. How the Russians must hate it, Nick thought. The whole city was a beautiful reproach. The gifts of centuries were wasting away in a system that could not even produce salad.

They crossed the Vltava, past the imperial National Theater and the nineteenth-century streets of the New Town to the hotel on Wenceslas Square. To Nick's surprise, there was a doorman and an old man to help with the luggage, a service class he thought did not exist. The room was heavy and ornate, deep red that wouldn't show the dirt, wardrobes instead of closets. The old porter lingered, pretending to adjust the drapes, clearly expecting a tip. Their windows faced the street, and Nick could hear the tram bells outside.

"Did I give him enough?" Nick said after the man left. "He looked disappointed."

"He was hoping for dollars. Technically, they're not supposed to get anything, so don't worry about it." Molly started walking around the room, looking at it. "Well, here we are. God, I'm dead. Aren't you? All that driving."

Nick shook his head. "Now what? It's still early. Should we call my—"

She put a finger to his lips, then raised it and pointed around the room.

"You're kidding," he said.

"I don't think so. The Alcron was popular with journalists. They all stayed here last year. So we have to assume—"

Nick stared at her, not sure whether to laugh or be frightened.

"The phone too?"

"That for sure. How about a little air?" she said, moving toward the window. Traffic sounds floated in with the spring air. When he came over, she leaned close to him. "I'll call," she said to his ear. "Just be careful. No names. You'll get used to it." He felt her breath, warm and smooth, on the side of his face, and it startled him, as if she had just whispered an erotic secret. He pulled back. "What?" she said.

He shook his head, to make the feel of her go away. "Nothing."

She went to her purse and took out a small address book, then started toward the phone. The tapping on the door surprised them both, as if someone had been watching them. But it was only a difficulty about the car, a few minutes of Pan Warren's time, if he would come down to the desk. Nick followed the old man, feeling, crazily, that he was being taken away.

The difficulty turned out to be an extra fee for the garage—he could not park in the street. Nick was so relieved that he forgot to be annoyed. "I'm sorry for all these bothers," the desk clerk said, and Nick found the English charming. He paid and looked around the lobby, imagining it buzzing with reporters just a few months ago. Now it was nearly deserted, an elderly couple having tea and a man hidden behind a newspaper, so obvious that Nick thought he couldn't actually be a policeman. Outside some students were gathering in the street, walking in a half-march toward the university. He didn't care about any of it.

She was saying goodbye on the phone when he opened the door, and he stood there for a moment, waiting and apprehensive.

"Dinner?" he said finally.

She shook her head. "Some other time. They're busy tonight."

Nick looked at her in disbelief, the tone of her voice, social and pleasant, making the moment unreal.

"Busy?" he said dumbly.

"Mm. A concert," she said evenly, looking straight at him. "At the Wallenstein. We might think about that, actually. It's pretty. What about it? Are you too tired?"

"What's the Wallenstein?" They were going to see him.

"A palace in the Malá Strana. They give concerts in the courtyard. It's nice. What do you say?"

"Can we get in this late?"

She pointed to the phone. "Try the concierge."
She raised her voice, taunting the microphone.
"You have dollars. You can get anything you want
with dollars."

CHAPTER SEVEN

The students were lighting candles in the middle of Wenceslas when they left the hotel. The crowd was small, a fraction of the old rallies, but the police were out in force, patrolling the long street and pretending to ignore the students. No one wanted any trouble. From the candles Nick assumed it was a memorial service, but the signs they held up, in Czech, might have meant anything.

"I wonder what it says," he said idly, looking at the quiet group. Behind them the street rose up to meet the giant columns of the National Museum, still scarred from the previous year's shelling.

" 'Be with us. We are with you,' " she said.

"You can read Czech?"

"No. It was the slogan. You used to see it everywhere. It's their way of telling the police they're all on the same side."

Nick wondered what they expected the police to do—drop their guns and walk off the job? But it was all, from the incomprehensible signs to the sad, divided loyalties, someone else's problem.

They walked down toward Národní Street, past the *párky* stalls, then threaded their way through the narrow streets of the Old Town to the river. This was the tourist route, full of marvels and medieval towers, but Nick found himself hurrying, oblivious. The Charles Bridge, with its ornate statues, was full of couples looking down at the water, arms around each other, the girls all with bleached-blond hair that seemed to hang straight from poor chemicals. On the other side, the Malá Strana, there were thick arcades and cobblestones, lit by dull street-lamps and the glow of passing trams.

The Wallenstein was not far from the river, and when they got there a crowd had already gathered on Letenská Street, waiting to get in. Most of them wore coats against the spring chill, and Nick saw that they had dressed up, men in ties, women in cloth hats. No one was young. The street door led through the honey-colored stone wall directly into the formal gardens. At one end of the central court-yard, musicians sat in front of the high arches of a portico, tuning instruments. Folding chairs had been set up on the pebbled ground, and people claimed them, first come, first served, then stood looking around for their friends, waving and chat-ting, just as they must have done when the palace was first built. Behind the walls, away from the tanks and the lines for carrots, Prague still had its evenings.

Nick found chairs toward the back, so he could look out over the crowd, and stood watching the people file in. What would he look like? Was it pos-sible he wouldn't recognize him? He would be how old now? In his sixties, like most of the audience. Gray? White?

"Don't crane. It's too obvious," Molly said. "Maybe we'd better sit down."

"No one else is."

It was true. People stood talking, their voices rising over the violins and cellos being stretched into tune. Did they all know each other? A few people near them stared frankly at their Western clothes. Why so public a place? Why meet in front of an audience? The lights were being lowered now, people finally taking their places.

"What are we supposed to do, save seats?" Nick said.

"He just said he was coming to the concert. Don't worry. He'll find us."

A couple sat down next to them and the man nodded at Nick, but it was just a concertgoer's greeting, polite and vacant. The music started, a series of Mozart divertimenti, as formal and airy as the gardens. Only the portico was lighted now, and Nick looked around the dim courtyard at profiles and shapes of heads, waiting for someone to turn in the dark. How would his father find them? It was Nick who would have changed, no longer a boy. It occurred to him—a new thought—that his father would know him only because he was sitting with Molly.

At the intermission, while people smoked and drank beer, he stood near the bright stage, impossible to miss, but no one came up, and only a few people looked toward him at all, glancing at his shoes. Molly said nothing, but he could tell from the way she bit her lower lip that she was worried, that it should already have happened. Czech, fluent and guttural, surrounded them, making him feel isolated, not even free to eavesdrop.

When they sat down again, he knew his father wasn't coming. Something had happened, or maybe he had balked, unable to go through with it after all. Nick stared at the Baroque walls, not hearing the music, and realized that he felt a kind of relief. It was better in so many ways to keep things as they were. His body began to sag a little, coming down to earth. The past wasn't meant to come back. Except there it was again, the walking away. In the pretty courtyard, listening now to Brahms, he was at the back door again, being left.

"I'll be right back," he whispered to Molly, and when she looked alarmed he smiled and said, "Bathroom," and slid out of his seat, crouching as he slipped farther back into the dark garden, trying not to crunch pebbles.

A long arcade led back to an ornamental pool, and he stopped for a cigarette near one of the pillars, away from the crowd. Phones were tapped. Maybe he had had to change plans at the last minute, to keep the secret. Who knew what his life was like now? Maybe he would be idling on Letenská Street when they came out, a chance meeting. And maybe not.

Nick went into the bathroom. Damn him, anyway. He wasn't going to do it twice. Molly said he lived here; she'd spoken to him. What did it matter if Nick called? Who cared who listened? He was still taking precautions, and in America nobody even remembered his name. Old politics, all forgotten, as dated as a hemline. But his son was here. How could he not want to see him?

Nick came out into the soft light of the arcade and stopped. The man near the other end was walking carefully, as if he had forgotten his cane in his rush to get to the bathroom. No, not that old. The waves were gone, thinned to a dusting of hair across his scalp, and his body had thinned too, so that the suit hung loosely, the sleeves too wide for his wrists. He kept coming. Nick couldn't move. There hadn't been years to watch the change, just this one minute. An awful mirror. He was looking at himself old. This is what he would be like, bony, almost bald, shoulders slightly drooped. And the face. It was coming into the light now, as inevitable as a ghost. Paler than before, the skin still tight over the cheekbones, then a little slack, a gravity pull. His own face. But the eyes. The shine of liquid full to brimming over, catching all the light, so full Nick thought he might drown in them.

"Nicku."

The voice seemed to touch the back of his neck like a shiver, drawing him nearer. Voices didn't change. The same sound, wrapping around him, his earliest memory.

"Nicku. My god."

And now the eyes did spill over, a wetness at the corners, as he raised his hands, putting them on Nick's arms. Nick thought of the day they had left Washington, when his heart had literally hurt in his chest, a kind of practice death. He felt it now. Take a breath. He had wondered what it would feel like, this moment, and now he saw that it was like falling. His stomach was light; the ground had slid away. But his father had taken him in his arms. He could feel his cheek, the head leaning into his shoulder, the arms circling his back, holding on to him for dear life.

They sat by the ornamental pool in the dark, his father clutching Nick's hand, holding down a balloon that threatened to get away. Without the light of the arcade there was only his voice, so that Nick slipped back into it, not distracted by having to see him.

"So tall," his father said, his voice shaky, "so tall." And then, patting his leg, he said simply, "You came."

"I got your message."

"So you knew. I wanted you to be sure it was me. I thought maybe that's why you didn't answer before. You couldn't be sure."

"Answer?" Nick said, lightheaded again.

"My letters." His father paused. "I see. You never got them."

"You wrote to me?"

"Of course. In the beginning. I should have known they would stop them," he said, his voice suddenly older. "But I thought—never mind. You're here. Look at you." Touching him again.

Nick wondered if he could see in the dark; maybe just the shape of him was enough.

"Who stopped them?" Nick said. "Mother—"

"No, no. My friends." An edge of sarcasm. "How is your mother?"

The question itself seemed absurd, as if everything that had happened to them could be reduced to a polite inquiry.

"She's fine," Nick said, at a loss. "She's married."

"Yes. To Larry. You took his name."

Nick glanced up at him, trying to read his face in the faint light. "She thought it would be easier, I guess. You were—famous."

"Famous," he said, almost pouncing on the word. Then he edged away, conversational again. "But you didn't have to be. Yes. I suppose I should be grateful to him. He's been a good father to you?"

"Yes."

He nodded, then looked away, to his own thought. "Is she happy?" he said, but when Nick didn't answer, he brought himself back and sighed. "Well, what a question. How do we talk? There's so much—" He put his hand on Nick's knee. "You came. You don't know what it means. I thought, what if he never wants to see me again?"

"No," Nick said.

"But I had to try. It was a chance."

"Why now?"

"And not before?" He stood up, looking toward the music. "I'm not sure. I suppose I thought you were better off. Maybe I was afraid you wouldn't answer, like with the letters. But then, when I heard you were working with Wiseman—oh yes," he said, answering Nick's expression. "I keep up. I have your graduation picture."

"What?"

His father smiled. "So much information from America. They still work overtime at it, my friends. Like addicts. I thought, why not a little for me? Don't they owe me that much? Of course, the newspapers I could see for myself at the institute. But the rest—" He paused. "I didn't want to miss everything in your life."

"Wait a minute." A sudden anger. "You had people spy on me?"

His father shook his head. "No, no, nothing like that. Just what anyone would know. The public record." He stopped. "Well, once. In the beginning. I was so desperate—I couldn't bear it. So I asked someone at the institute. You know, it's so easy. To arrange that. He brought me pictures. Hockey in Central Park. You were still a boy. Then I saw how crazy it was. How could I do that to you? It was my fault, all of it. I had to let go. So I made them stop." He turned to him. "It was just that once."

Nick stared up at him, not knowing what to say. In all the years, he had not once imagined what his father had felt. Now he saw, as in the science experiment, that if you just took a few steps to the side, the angle of the world was different.

"What else?" he said, curious.

His father shrugged. "It wasn't much, Nick. A picture. A few clippings. I couldn't watch you grow. Remember the height marks?"

Nick nodded. The notches on the side of the cabin door, measuring him every six months.

"It was like that. Just the marks. So I'd know how you were doing."

His father was quiet for a minute, and Nick could hear the music rising in the background, almost at an end.

"So college and then the army and—" His father stopped, took a breath. "All the time, I thought, he doesn't even know me anymore. Leave it—it's over and done with. But then you went to London to work with Wiseman. Un-American activities. And I thought, it's not over for him either. It's time."

"For what?" Nick said, standing up. "Why now?"

His father looked around, disconcerted, as if the question had come too soon, then turned to face him.

"Because I'm dying, Nick," he said, his voice almost a whisper.

Nick stared at him, seeing now that what he had taken for age was really illness.

"No, don't look like that," his father said quickly, concerned. "It's all right. I don't say it to upset you. It's just—a fact." He paused. "So it has to be now." He looked away from Nick's gaze. "Please don't. I know I'm a stranger to you. I didn't ask you to come to—"

"Why did you, then?" Nick asked, unexpectedly bitter, his voice unsteady. "To say goodbye?"

"No. I wanted to see you, it's true. Selfish. But there's something else." He reached up, putting his hands on Nick's shoulders. "I want to put an end to that time. For both of us. I need you to help me."

"But—"

"Don't you see? You're the only one I can trust."

Nick looked at him, amazed. In the distance, the applause began. "To do what?"

His father looked up at the sound of the clapping, the lights beginning to come on, and patted Nick's hand. "Not here. We'll talk. It's a long story. We can't start it here." Then he held him by the arms again. "Tomorrow."

But the lights seemed to bring with them a kind of urgency. There would never be time to catch his breath, sort out the noises that were a jumble in his mind. He watched me grow. He's dying. Something's worrying him. Was any of it real? He felt somehow that his father might rise up and float away, like the applause.

"Nick!" He heard her voice from the other end of the arcade, tentative, obviously looking for him, and he grabbed his father's shoulder.

"One thing," he said. "I have to know."

His father looked at him, surprised at the strength of his grasp. "What?"

"Tell me the truth. The *truth*. Just to me. That night, when you left—did you go to the May-flower?"

His father stared, assessing, then looked down, almost with a smile. "So you think that too. I thought I was the only one." He looked back up. "No, I didn't go there. Somebody else killed her."

There it was, as simple as that. Nick felt empty with it gone, the relief of an aching limb finally removed.

"But you do think she was killed?"

"Oh, yes."

"Nick." Molly again, closer now.

"Who—"

"It's all the same crime, you see," his father said, leaning toward him, conspiratorial. "What happened to her. What happened to me. That's why I need your help. I want to know. While I still have time."

Before Nick could respond, Molly was with them. His father glanced at him, a flicker of the eye to signal an end to the conversation. But why shouldn't she know? Secrecy became a reflex. Nick looked at her, waiting to see if she'd overheard, but the words, so loud to him, evidently hadn't carried.

"There you are," she said. Then, to his father, "Hello again."

His father took her hand. "Thank you. For bringing him. I owe you a great debt."

"I'm glad someone does," she said cheerfully, refusing to be solemn. "You've had a visit?"

"A sighting," his father said. He looked around at the people milling toward the garden door. "Tomorrow we'll visit."

"You're going?" Nick said.

"It's better."

"But we've just—I'll come back with you."

"No, no. Tomorrow. The country." He smiled at Nick's surprise. "The weekend is sacred here. To stay home would be noticed. We leave our flat every Saturday at eight. Like clockwork. So we must keep the clock running."

"You're going away?" Nick said, incredulous.

"And you. Leave the hotel early, with your camera. There's a lot to see in Prague. I can pick you up by the tram stop—"

"We have a car."

His father smiled. "Rich Americans. I forgot. Even better. Two cars. You know the tank at the bottom of Holečkova?" This to Molly, who nodded. "Eight-ten. It's quite safe. They never follow us there."

His voice, growing faint, ended in a small cough. Then the coughing came again, stronger, until he was forced to give in to it, partially doubling over to catch his breath. He took a handkerchief out of his pocket to cover his mouth.

Nick leaned forward, peering at him. "What's wrong?"

His father waved his hand dismissively, still catching his breath. Then he managed a smile. "Nothing. Overcome with emotion."

He tossed it out casually, and in that second Nick heard his father again, young, unable to resist an ironic turn. But he looked drawn, shaken by the cough.

"It passes," he said, and fumbled in his pocket for a small tin box, the kind used for pastille candies. When he opened it, the pills seemed enormous. "Soviet medicine," he said wryly. "Not for the weak."

"There's some water in the men's room," Nick said, turning to get it. To his surprise, his father leaned on his arm and began walking with him.

"Just a moment," his father said to Molly, attempting to be jaunty, but his voice was raspy now, and Nick wondered if it really was just a coughing spell.

In the men's room, people were lined up at the urinals. Nick's father went over to the washbasin, taking his time with the pill. He chased it down with water and stood quietly for a minute calming himself. A few men left.

"Better?" Nick said.

His father nodded. "What we talked about before? It's better, I think, not to say anything."

"To Molly, you mean. Why?" A man at the urinal glanced in their direction, surprised at the English, but Nick ignored him.

His father was nodding again, stifling the beginning of another cough. "Not yet. Not even her. Not until I'm sure. I'll explain."

"You all right?" Nick put his hand gently on his father's back, afraid that a stronger pat would set him off again.

"You think it's crazy, don't you? Whispering in corners," he said, his voice now in fact a whisper. "You're not used to it."

203

Nick looked around the room. The overhead vents might be hiding mikes, but why? Who would bother to bug the men's room at the Wallenstein Palace? It occurred to him for the first time that his father, this man he didn't know, might really be paranoid, common sense and skepticism worn down by the years to a membrane too thin to stop suspicion seeping through.

"Is it always like this?" Nick said.

"No. Sometimes they really are listening."

Nick smiled, relieved. It was the kind of offhand joke his father would have made on 2nd Street, having a drink with his mother before they went out. A throwaway, not a story, and she'd be smiling, just happy to be with him. His father smiled now too, pleased with himself. But when he spoke, his voice was serious. "I don't do it for myself," he said, looking straight at Nick. Then another cough, his face crinkling up a little in pain, and he turned around to the basin so that Nick had to look at him in the mirror.

"What's wrong with you?" Nick said, alarmed, frustrated at not knowing how to react.

In the mirror his father lowered his head, eyes dropping out of sight, and waved his hand again. "It's all right. You go. Please. I'll be fine. Tomorrow. By the tank."

But Nick wouldn't let go. He took the back of his father's shoulders, turning him. "It's not all right. You're sick."

The man at the urinal had zipped and now came over, saying something in Czech. His father answered quickly, the sound of Czech surprising Nick.

"He thinks you're molesting me," his father said, his head still down, trying again for a wry joke. "You'd better go."

"Tell me what's wrong." Nick still held him by the shoulders, but when his father lifted his face Nick let go, stung by the look of dismay.

"It doesn't matter. Just a side effect. Please," his father said quietly. "I don't want you to see me like this."

Nick looked down in confusion and saw the stain. His father had wet himself. When he looked back up, his father's eyes were moist with embarrassment. "It's all right," Nick said, words to a child.

But his father shook his head. "No. Now you'll always think of me this way." He looked up, his eyes a kind of odd plea, past all the jokes. "I can't make it up to you. I'm not expecting—" He stopped, his voice almost feverish. "But not this. Not some stranger with wet pants."

Now it was Nick who reached out to him, bringing him close in the dingy men's room, holding him, whispering into his ear so that no one could hear. "You're not a stranger," he said.

"He's all right. He wants us to leave separately," he said to Molly outside.

"He doesn't look all right."

"I know. He's been sick."

"You look a little shaky yourself," she said, studying him.

He led her toward the last of the crowd funneling through the garden door.

"I can't stand it," she said. "What did he say? What did you talk about?"

He looked at her, unprepared. Why not tell her?

"He's not just sick. He thinks he's dying. That's why he wanted to see me," Nick said, surprised at how easily it came out. It had begun already, the convenient half-truths, covering tracks.

"Oh," she said, deflated. Then, an afterthought, "I'm sorry. How do you feel?"

"Ask me later. Right now, I'm not sure."

The street was a small eddy of Tatras and Škodas, loud motors and clunky headlights shining on the cobblestones. In the square a large crowd bundled in coats waited for late trams. Instinctively, Nick headed away, toward the bridge, where couples were still loitering by the statues.

"What else did he say?" Molly said. "I mean, why doesn't he want anyone to know you're here? What difference would it make?"

"Maybe he doesn't want anybody to know he's sick. You summon the family, it's a kind of tip-off. I don't know."

She shook her head. "There's something else." But when he stopped and looked down at the water, she let it go, sensing his reluctance.

"This is the way cities used to look," he said. "Just enough light to see where you're going." A delayed thought from the walk over, when he had taken in the streets without ads and lighted shops, just corner lights like sconces and recesses that were really dark.

"Nick? What was it like, seeing him? Do you mind my asking?"

He turned to her. "It was easy. It was him." He looked back at the mist gathering along the surface of the river. Soon everything would be covered, insubstantial. He glanced over his shoulder as if he could catch a last glimpse of his father on the streets twisting up to Hradčany, a proof he'd really been there. "All this time. For years—*years*—I thought he was, I don't know, on the other side of the moon or something. But he's been here. In an apartment. All you have to do is drive in, spend a few dollars. All this time."

She put her hand on his arm. "He hasn't always been here."

"Moscow, then," he said, a little annoyed. "What's the difference? The point is, he's been *somewhere*. I could have seen him. They stamp a passport. That's it. What did I think it was? Some fucking Checkpoint Charlie? I could have seen him, not waited until he was sick. So why didn't I?"

She was quiet for a moment. "Nick, you're not the one who left."

Nick nodded. "I know." He reached into his pocket for a cigarette and handed her one. "He wrote to me."

"Wrote to you?" Her face was caught in the glare of the match.

"In the beginning. He says. Anyway, I never got them." He lit his own and exhaled a long stream, looking back at the water. "It's like I missed a train. And I don't know why."

She took his arm, leading him away from the railing. "Come on. You're tired," she said, her voice familiar, as if they were already a couple. "Maybe this wasn't as easy as you thought."

Karlova fed into the Old Town Square, where the clock was ringing to nearly deserted streets. There were no cars; the town had reverted to its medieval life. He could hear the click of her heels. Like him, the city was brooding and quiet, slipping back into its own past.

They were on one of the side streets that led toward the lights of Wenceslas when they heard the whistle, an urgent shriek of authority, and the clomp of boots, the sounds of a dozen war movies. Two figures were racing toward them, chased by a group of uniforms. Shouts, indistinguishable words, a Gestapo bark, and then the whistle again, flying toward them like a pointed finger. Nick froze. The sound of fear, always directed at you, so that even when it was merely overheard, you felt caught too. Here, in the foreign street, it had the anxious confusion of a bad dream—it was coming to get you. Shoes cracked against the pavement.

Before the men were halfway down the street, he felt a yank, Molly pulling him into the dark shadow of a doorway. She put her arms around his neck, drawing him to her, and the figures at his back became lost, just a background sound rushing

208

past while they pretended to be lovers. No one stopped. He heard the boots, more shouts, all of his senses alive now with the adrenaline release of the whistle. Her breath was on the side of his face and suddenly he smelled her—skin, not perfume—and felt her against him, a touch as loud and surprising as the whistle. He kissed her almost by reflex, not thinking about it, and the kiss was surprising too, immediate and natural, like the smell of her, so that when he pulled back to look at her he seemed puzzled, not sure how it had happened.

"I thought you'd never ask," she said, her voice low in her throat, as if they were still hiding from the police.

He leaned into her again, and this time the kiss was sexual. Her mouth opened to him and he could feel his body react, another reflex, unwilled. He moved his hands behind her, low, and she let him pull the curve of her closer, until she was pressed against him, warm beneath her clothes. She drew a breath, a swimmer's gulp, before his mouth was on her again, pressing now, the kiss itself a kind of entry. She gave in to it, her mouth rubbing against his, then pushed away, putting her hands on his shoulders.

"No, don't," she said, a whisper, still catching her breath.

"I thought—"

"So did I." She shook her head, then looked up at him. "It's different."

He said nothing, the silence an open question.

"You have other things on your mind."

"Not now, I don't."

She smiled a little, then put her hand on the side of his face. "Yes, you do. No complications, remember?"

"It doesn't have to be complicated," he said, moving closer, but she held him away.

"It will be, though. I'm not as easy as you think, either."

He stared at her, then dropped his hands.

"Come on," she said, moving into the street. "The police must be breaking up the demonstration. We don't want to get caught in that."

"Sorry," he said, embarrassed to hear the sulk in his voice.

She turned. "No, don't. It's not that. It's just not right. Not now."

"Is that a rain check?"

"I guess." She looked up, biting her lip. "But things never work that way, do they?"

They walked without touching, keeping a space between them, but when they reached the long sweep of Wenceslas, alive with lights and patrolling soldiers, she took his hand again, slipping them back into their roles. The students with candles were bunched near the mounted statue, surrounded by police, who appeared to be moving them off one by one. The chase in the alley must have started this way, a sullen resistance that broke ranks, an unexpected scuffle. Now things moved with a ritual formality. No trouble. Several of the students were holding up an enlarged photograph on a poster.

"Jan Palach," she said, nodding at the picture. "It must be a memorial service." He looked at her quizzically, reluctant to speak English now that there were people around. She was moving them away from the top of the street, skirting the crowd to skip across unnoticed. "He set himself on fire in January, to protest the invasion."

Nick stopped, appalled. "Like the Buddhist monks," he said, seeing the image before him, the shaved head and saffron robes in flames, the black gasoline smoke. But that was in another world, tropical and alien, not fairy-tale Europe where people listened to Mozart in gardens. "Christ," he said, his voice a mixture of awe and scorn. "And it didn't change a thing."

There were shouts in the square as they reached the hotel and they ducked in quickly, finally safe in the cocoon of art nouveau woodwork and faded chairs. The usual newspaper readers had thinned out so that the few still there glanced up at once, on the alert. Molly took his arm, the clinging fiancée, and there it was again, the jarring feel of her.

"Pan Warren," the desk clerk said, handing him the key. "You had a pleasant evening? It was not too cold for the concert?"

Nick took the key, feeling somehow watched. But of course he had arranged for the tickets. It was nothing more than the oily smoothness of a concierge with too few clients. "No. The music was wonderful."

"Yes, it's good, the Wallenstein. I'm sorry for the disturbance," he said, his eyes indicating the protest outside. "It is too bad. Perhaps a drink in the bar? Our Pilsner beer is excellent. It should not be too much longer." He glanced at his watch, as if the demonstration too had a closing time. "A half-hour at most. There will be no problem with the sleeping." He was smiling. A weary familiarity with protests, or some more practical arrangement with the police? Business went on. Jan Palach had become an excuse for a nightcap.

"I don't think so," Nick said. "It's late. Oh, I'll need my car in the morning."

"Your car?"

His question took Nick by surprise. He hadn't expected to explain himself. But why couldn't it be just a bland inquiry?

"We wanted to see Karlovy Vary," Molly said quickly, leaning into him. "Is it too far?"

"Karlovy Vary. Yes, very beautiful. Far, but you can do it." He looked at them hesitantly, then brought out a tourist map and marked it with his pen. "For the *benzin*," he explained. "You can fill there. It's sometimes difficult in the countryside. I'm sorry," he said, spreading his hands, an apology for the country itself, short of fuel.

Molly was leaning over the map. Her body was still close to his, and when she leaned back she brushed against him and he felt it again, the heat on her skin. If he reached down, he could run his hand along the curve of her hip. Instead he saw them in bed, her figure turned over onto itself, away from him.

"Well, maybe one drink," he said, nodding to the

desk clerk and drawing her away to the bar. "What was that all about?" he said as they walked.

"His brother probably owns the gas station."

"No, Karlovy Vary," he said carefully, trying to get it right. "Whatever the hell that is."

"Karlsbad. It's a spa. I couldn't think of anything else, right on the spot."

"You're good at this."

She glanced at him. "All women are," she said lightly. "You learn to think fast. It's just part of the game."

"Like saying no when you mean yes?"

"Like saying no when you mean no. Do you really want a drink?"

"No, but if we go to bed now we'll start something."

She stopped and touched his shoulder, smiling. "Try the plum brandy, then—you'll pass right out."

The bar was deserted except for a short gray-haired man at the end, chain-smoking and nursing a beer. Nick had become used to the furtive glances of Prague, but this one stared openly, frankly taking Molly in, a barroom appraisal. They ordered Pilsners.

"I never know where I am with you," Nick said, automatically lowering his voice so the words became a murmur in the room.

"That's what you said you liked."

"I did?"

"Well, you implied it. At the Bruces'."

"The Bruces'? When was that, anyway? A year ago?"

She smiled. "At least."

"And you had that dress." He took a sip of beer, then put it back slowly on the coaster. "We didn't go to bed that night either. You had a message to deliver."

"Yes."

"But now we're here. End of message." He reached over and ran his finger along hers, barely touching, but she moved it away.

"Let's not start this, okay? It was just a kiss."

"No, it wasn't."

"Oh, how would you know?" she said suddenly. "Has it occurred to you, you've had kind of an emotional day? You're all—I don't know. Excited. I want it to be me. Not like this. When it's just us."

He looked at her, surprised. Her mood seemed to come out of nowhere, a shift in the wind. "Okay," he said quietly. He brought his hand back, but she stopped it, covering it with her own.

"Look," she said, "when I started this, I didn't know it was going to be you. Who you are, I mean."

"Who I am," he echoed, not following her.

But now she backed away, almost tossing her head to clear the air. "I want this to be over. God, I hate being here." Then, hearing herself, she turned to her beer. "Everybody watching. Everybody *not* watching. You can't breathe. Politics," she said, almost spitting the *P.*

Nick said nothing, waiting for the calm to return, a cartoon husband, lying low. "How about him?"

he said finally, trying to change the subject. "He doesn't look very political."

"Is he watching us?" she said, not looking up.

"Well, he's watching you," Nick said.

She turned and the man held her gaze, studying her face as if he were trying to place her.

"You're right," she said, moving back to Nick. "That's not politics. He doesn't even pretend not to look. Men. I suppose it must work sometimes or they wouldn't keep doing it."

"Well, you try."

She smiled, the squall gone. "Good luck," she said, taking in the empty bar. She stood. "I'm going up. No, it's all right." She put her hand on his shoulder. "Finish your beer. I'd rather pass out with a good long soak." She stopped, hesitating. "Look, don't mind me. I'm just nervous, I guess. About tomorrow."

"Why?"

But she ignored the question and leaned over. "Don't talk to strangers," she said playfully, glancing again at the gray-haired man. "You never know."

He turned on his stool, watching her leave.

"Fight, huh?"

At first Nick thought it was a foreign phrase, a bar order, but the voice was unmistakably New York, and he turned back to see the gray-haired man smiling at him. Nick shrugged, a universal nonanswer.

"Better give in," the man said. "No matter what it is. That's the way it works." He got off his stool, moving unsteadily, and it occurred to Nick that the man was drunk, hazily eager for contact. Nick took another sip of beer, anxious now to finish. "You're American," the man said flatly, taking the next stool. Nick raised his eyebrows, a question. "The shoes," the man said, nodding toward Nick's feet. He extended his hand. "Marty Bielak. Where you from?"

"New York," Nick said, and then, because some kind of response seemed called for, "You?"

"I'm from here."

"You live here? I didn't know there were any Americans here."

"A few. Of course, we're not Americans any-more." He paused. "Except we are. They think we are." He was drifting into his beer. "I came over in fifty-three. Long time ago."

"You came here?"

He smiled a little at Nick's confusion. "I'm a Communist."

Nick looked at him more carefully. His eyes were shiny, but the words had been flat, without belliger-ence.

"You're too young. You wouldn't know about that. They were arresting everybody then. I didn't want to go to jail, so I came here." He said some-thing in Czech to the bartender, who brought him another beer.

"What did you do?"

"Do," he said, a kind of snort. "I voted for Wal-lace. You didn't have to *do* anything. Just have a card, you know? The summer they killed the Rosenbergs I thought, that's it." He stared at Nick. "You don't know what I'm talking about, do you? Anyway, it was all a long time ago."

"You like it here?"

The man shrugged. "Same as anywhere. What was it like living there? You couldn't take a piss without somebody reporting it. That's what it was like there. You think I'm kidding? My wife got fired. She'd go to work, they'd have guys following her. It got to the point—" He stopped, taking another sip. "The hell with it. You're too young. My daughter, she couldn't wait to see it. Last year, when you could travel, she goes to the Bronx, to the old building, and it's crawling with schwartzes and she says no wonder you came. She thought we lived in a slum. But it wasn't like that then. That's not *why.*"

"So you never went back?"

"What's to go back for? Last year—well, she went. I didn't have money for all of us. Maybe someday. Anyway, it's all different, isn't it? I mean, they don't even have the Giants anymore. What's New York without the Giants?"

"What do you do here?" Nick said, intrigued now.

"Radio. I monitor the VOA broadcasts. Well, I did. But now I'm American again. You know, after last year. Even the old Reds. But that'll change. We're going through an adjustment now. You have to expect that."

A believer's rationale, still. Nick thought of the index cards in Wiseman's study, all the facts of the

217

witch-hunt, which had somehow overlooked Marty Bielak in a misplaced file. This is where some of them had ended up, perched on a barstool, stranded, like debris swept up on the beach by a storm.

"Can I ask you something?" Nick said impulsively. "Why did you? In the first place?"

"What, become a Red?" He looked back at his beer. "You think we have horns? Let me tell you, we didn't. Who else was there? You think anybody cared about the working man? Anti-Semites playing golf. That's what it was then. Anti-Semites playing golf." He stared at the glass, then caught himself. "It's the beer talking," he said, trying an apologetic smile that stopped midway. "You ask me, you know what I'd have to say? Who else was there? That's it." He picked up the glass. "Anyway, here I am talking—it's good, you know, the English—and you've got a pretty girl to go to. What are you doing here, anyway?"

"Just seeing the sights," Nick said easily.

The man nodded. "Not so many come now. Unless they have family. You have family here?"

"No." He shook his head. "My grandmother was Polish, though," he said, improvising. Molly was right. You could learn to do it fast, part of the other game.

"And that's close enough," Bielak said, laughing to himself. "You'd have to be American. They're the only ones who think it's the same thing." He paused, then looked up at Nick. "Let me ask you, could you use a guide? I know this town inside out.

I could use a little cash." His voice, the brash sound of the Polo Grounds, had dropped an octave, suddenly older. Nick caught the embarrassed pleading in his eyes, still shiny with beer. "Dollars, if you have them. My sister, she still sends, but these days—I have the time."

Nick looked at him. Not an index card. "I don't think so. We're only here a little while. Thanks, though."

"Just see the castle and on your way. Okay. Don't miss the Jewish cemetery—it's the best thing. Sounds crazy, but it is. Well, think about it." He reached for a pen, wrote a number on the coaster, and handed it to Nick. "If you change your mind, I can show you the stuff the tourists don't see." Nick heard his voice begin to slur. "A special tour. You want to see all the old Reds? That might be interesting," he said, his voice suddenly sarcastic.

Nick stood up, putting the coaster in his pocket. " 'Night," he said, almost a mumble. He threw some crowns on the bar, not bothering to count them. "Good luck."

"Luck." Marty Bielak winked. "We don't need luck here. We have socialism."

When he got to the room, Molly was still up, reading by one of the two dim bedside lamps. The flannel nightgown was back and her face glistened with cold cream, an almost comic body armor. The heavy drapes, drawn tight by the maid, still sealed the room, and he crossed to open them, hungry for air.

"What happened to you?" she said. "I was about to give up." She closed the book and snapped off her light, leaving only the small glow by his side of the bed.

"You were wrong about that guy," Nick said, opening the windows. "He's an American. He lives here. It was your English." He began unbuttoning his shirt, looking down at the streetlamps.

"Lives here? You didn't tell him anything, did you?"

"No. Why?"

"Oh, Nick," she said in mock exasperation. "Who do you think hangs around the Alcron bar talking to foreigners?"

He stopped, his hand still on the button. "You think?" he said quietly.

"Who else could afford it?" When he didn't answer, she turned over. "Goodnight."

He continued staring out the window, not wanting to turn around. What if she was right? What was that like? He saw Marty Bielak writing up reports on tourist conversations, taking another step for the working man. Do you have family here? Did that make it easier? Maybe cadging dollars for a tour was worse, a seduction without even the self-respect of betrayal.

The protesters had gone, just as the desk clerk had predicted, leaving behind their candles. Now the police were clearing them away, tipping over the lights until the space under the good king was empty again, a patch of dark. He'd set himself on fire. How many ways are there to take away your life? A lost family, as irretrievable as childhood. A careless exile, eavesdropping in bars. At least Jan Palach had only done it to himself. But you always take somebody with you. There must have been parents, left with a martyrdom and an empty house. And sometimes somebody did it for you, flinging you out the window before you had a chance to hold on.

Molly moved in bed, and the sound carried to him, a disturbance in the air. It pricked at him, not letting him drift, and as he raised his hand to draw on the cigarette he suddenly saw her at the window in Bern, a reverse image. Maybe she had felt it then, the same disturbance, something right here, not some feint with ghosts. Now it was his turn. He thought about her in Dürnstein, then down in the bar, and he saw that they kept colliding and moving on, like electrons. What if he made the same mistake as the others? Losing everything for an idea. He stood still. In the courtyard with his father, he had felt that his life had come back to him, but it was only a piece of the past that had come back. It was the side street that had been alive with an adrenaline touch. Maybe there was no idea. Maybe it was as simple as a rustling of bedclothes that wouldn't leave you alone, a disturbance. No more than that. So that if you didn't hear, it came and then, like the luck Marty Bielak didn't need, slipped away for good.

CHAPTER EIGHT

The day began with sun, but by the time he'd finished coffee the clouds of middle Europe had rolled in, a lead weight pressing down on the city, turning everything gray. They crossed the Vltava over a different bridge, downriver from the Malá Strana.

"Is this the right way?" Nick said. "I don't remember this."

"Just keep going to the end. Soviet Tank Square."

"They call it that?"

"Mm. *Namesti sovetskych tankistu,*" she said, the accurate pronunciation its own joke. "Of course in those days they were liberating, not invading."

"How do you know all this?"

"All what? It's just tourist stuff. I had a lot of time to get to know the city."

"Are you going to see him, your friend?" Maybe the split hadn't been as casual as she had said.

"Jiří?" She was looking out the window. "No, not this trip. One reunion's enough, don't you think?"

There was no one near the tank and they drove

around the traffic circle once, then parked near the corner and pulled out a map, pretending to plot the trip. The place names, brimming with consonants and accent marks, might have been Chinese.

"Let's hope he doesn't drive too fast," Nick said. "I could never follow this."

But his father had thought of everything. When the Škoda pulled alongside, he got out to switch cars. In the daylight he looked less drawn, more like himself, and Nick felt a jolt again, as if a photograph had come alive.

The woman in the passenger seat was handsome but full-faced, and when she stepped out to change sides he saw that her body was thick, rounded by time and gravity. To his surprise, she was shy and nervous, brushing a stray hair back into place with the automatic gesture of a girl wanting to look her best, and Nick realized that she was apprehensive about meeting him. She smiled hesitantly, glancing into his eyes.

"Anička, this is my son," his father said. "Nick, my wife, Anna." So easy. The whole tangled mess reduced to a simple introduction. She held out her hand.

"How do you do," she said, a formality from a phrasebook, but her eyes were warm, scanning his face now, tracing her husband's features. "You are very like," she said pleasantly.

"Miss Chisholm, would you go with Anna? Then no one gets lost."

"Molly," she said to Anna, shaking her hand too. Anna placed her hand on Nick's father's sleeve, familiar and affectionate, and said something in Czech. Then she got in the car and started around the tank, noisily shifting gears.

"What did she say?" Nick asked.

"Not to be too long. I thought I'd show you the sights. We don't want to travel in convoy." He walked toward the passenger door.

"Why not? Do people follow you?"

"No." He smiled. "Force of habit, that's all."

Nick started the car. "Where to?"

"Just drive around. Head for the castle."

"Can I see where you live?"

"It's just up here. Up Holečkova. We'll come round the other way. We don't want to surprise anyone."

Nick drove along the river, then climbed the steep hill to Hradčany. His father said nothing, glancing in the rearview mirror.

"I suppose she's my stepmother," Nick said, and then, when his father didn't answer, "How did you meet?"

"At the institute. In Moscow. She was an archivist."

"When was this?"

"Well, when? Fifteen, sixteen years ago."

Nick counted backward. No, not right away. A decent interval.

"Do you love her?" he said, surprised at his own prurience. But how else could he ask it?

His father looked at him, then back at the street. "I married her. We've had a good life. I owe her this." He motioned his hand to take in the city. "I

224

never would have got out of Moscow otherwise. She's a Czech national." He paused. "I loved your mother. It's different."

Nick looked straight ahead at a church with several towers, green copper domes. "How long have you been here?"

"Just a year. She retired, you see, so they let us settle here. Kind of a gold watch. Ordinarily you have to stay put. But I guess they knew I wasn't in any shape to worry about, so why not?"

"What's wrong with you?" Nick said quietly. "Is it cancer?"

"No, my heart. I've had one operation, but it doesn't seem to have done any good. That reminds me." He took out a plastic vial and opened it. A different pill from the one last night. "Thins the blood," he explained. "Of course, if you cut yourself you have a hell of a time, because it won't clot. Fix one thing and something else goes." He swallowed the pill without water. "Anyway," he said, steering away from the subject, "we came to Prague. My gold watch too, I guess."

"It's beautiful."

"Hitler thought so too. He made it an open city. That's why it's still beautiful—no bombs. Imagine, having Hitler to thank for this."

"What's Moscow like?"

"It's like Brooklyn. Everyone there thinks it's special and you can't imagine why."

Nick smiled. The same rhythm.

"At first I couldn't get used to the quiet," his father said. "It's very quiet for a big city. You never hear an ambulance or a fire truck. I don't know why. Not much traffic. And then in the winter the snow muffles everything. Sometimes I used to open the window and just listen to the quiet. It was like being deaf. You think you want quiet, and then when you get it—" He paused. "But after a while you get used to it. Like everything else." He took out a cigarette and rolled down the window. "The funny thing about that was in the bad old days, they used to send the cars at night, so no one would know. But it was so quiet everyone did know. You'd hear a car in the street—you couldn't miss it—and you'd know it was an arrest. The whole block. Maybe they planned it that way. You didn't go back to sleep after that. You'd just lie there, waiting to hear the next car. But that was before, when Stalin was alive. Turn here by the church. We'll swing around the Strahov."

Nick said nothing, imagining the nights, now just an anecdote. People talked about the knock on the door, but it had been something else, a car motor idling in a quiet street. No screaming, no people being dragged out, just the faint sound of a car door being shut, a deaf man's terror.

"Were you ever arrested?"

"No. Of course, I was debriefed. That took months. I still don't know where. But after there was a flat. In the Arbat. Two rooms—a palace, then. And a job. They gave me a medal."

Nick heard the tone, a hint of pride, and was disconcerted. Was he supposed to congratulate him?

"What kind of job?" he said, not sure again how to ask. "Did you—work for them?"

"As an agent, you mean?" his father said, almost amused. "No. Who would I spy on? The diplomats, the journalists—they were already taken care of. There wasn't anybody else. Just the defectors. We kept to ourselves—maybe we were *kept* to ourselves, I don't know. For a while I worked with Maclean on *International Affairs.* The magazine," he said to Nick's unspoken query. "Like your *Foreign Affairs.* I think with the same level of accuracy. A nice man. A believer, you know. Still. But the others—" He let the phrase drift off. "Not exactly people you want to spend the weekend with. Besides, I was trying to learn Russian, not speak English. I was never very good at languages. I still can't speak Czech, not really."

"I thought you could."

"You did? Oh, the committee. No, I never could. I picked up a few words from your grandparents. But they tried not to speak around me. They wanted me to be—" He paused, framing the words. "An all-American boy." Nick said nothing, letting the thought sit there. "I was, too. I had a paper route. I still fold a paper like that, like I'm going to throw it on a porch. Sixty subscribers—a lot for then. The things you remember."

Nick heard the fade in his voice and resisted its pull. "Too bad about the language. It would have come in handy," he said lightly, indicating the street.

"Well, Anička takes care of all that. That's a little

like being deaf too, when you can't speak the language. People talk to you and you just look. You even get to like it, not hearing things. When I first got to Moscow, I would spend days not hearing anything. It was quiet. Like the streets."

The sound, Nick thought, after a door had closed.

They had made the circle and were coming back down Holečkova. "Slow down a little if you want to see it. Where I live. Third building there on the left. The white one. Not too slow," his father added, automatically putting his elbow on the window to cover the side of his face.

It was a multistory apartment building with simple art moderne lines in a section of the street that must have been developed before the war, when straight edges and glass were still a style. The white was tired now, but had escaped the cracks and watermarks of the newer buildings across the river, put up on the cheap. It was set back from the street, reached by a flight of concrete steps set into the hill. There was nothing remarkable about it at all, except that his father lived there.

"We were lucky to get it," his father said. "The views are wonderful. Not the Old Town, but then the plumbing's better. Two bathrooms."

Nick glanced quickly at him, feeling again a peculiar sense of dislocation. He was in Prague with a ghost, discussing real estate. He noticed the hand at the side of the face.

"Does someone really watch the house?"

"Or do I just imagine it?" his father said wryly.

"No, the Czechs take a look from time to time. The STB. You see, to them I'm a Russian. They want to know what I'm doing here."

Nick took this in, toying with it. A Russian. They passed the Soviet tank again and headed across the river.

"What did they give you a medal for?"

"Services to the state. All of us got one. Mostly for going there. Once they've brought you in, they don't know what to do with you, so they give you a medal. It's cheap and it gives you something to hold on to. So you don't wonder why you're not doing anything anymore. They don't trust foreigners—they can't help it, it's in the bone. After the magazine, I got the job at the institute, so at least they thought I wasn't going to do any damage. Some of the others—English lessons, make-work."

"What did you do?"

"Policy analyst. American policy. Of course, by the time they trusted me to do that, I'd been away from Washington so long I didn't know any more about American policy than the next man. They have a habit of defeating their own purpose. But maybe that's what they wanted all along. Anyway, they never listened to anything I had to say."

Nick realized that the answer, easy and smooth, was what he wanted to hear, and for the first time he wondered if his father could be lying. Had he really done so little? For an instant he felt as if he were back at the hearing. So plausible and persuasive, and all the while—. Nick stopped. Was he

229

Welles now? The inquisitor to outflank? Who cared whether they listened to him or not? And it might after all—which was worse?—be the truth, a glib answer to mask a marginal life.

"Seems a shame—for them, I mean," Nick said.

"Not taking advantage of my wisdom? Who knows? I was wrong about Cuba. I never thought we'd go that far."

Nick paused. "We who?"

"We Americans," his father said softly, clearly thrown by the question.

There was nothing to say to that and Nick drove quietly, skirting the top of Wenceslas to follow the streets behind the university. The mood in the car was uneasy now, as if, improbably, they had nothing more to say.

"Tell me about your mother," his father said finally. "Tell me about Livia."

"She's—fine. Busy. Lots of parties. You know."

"Yes, she loved parties." A beat. "Does she ever talk about me?"

"No."

The word, blunt and final, hung between them, and the instant Nick heard it he wished he had lied. Another door closing, louder this time. The silence, as leaden as the sky, was its own response, and there was nothing to break it but the sound of the car. At a corner, Nick stopped and reached into a back pocket for his wallet. He pulled out a photograph and handed it to his father, then put the car back in gear and drove on, allowing him to look in private.

"She's cut her hair," his father said quietly. "She used to wear it longer."

Nick kept driving, not wanting to intrude. From the corner of his eye he saw his father holding the picture, absorbed.

"I may have this?" he said finally, a foreign intonation. Nick nodded. "She's the same." He put the picture in the breast pocket of his jacket. "Don't tell Anna," he said, and Nick felt drawn against his will into some odd complicity. Why was even the simplest gesture tangled?

"Would she mind?"

"It's better this way," his father said, not answering.

"Sometimes the way she looks at me," Nick said, "I think I remind her of you." A small offering, to soften the no.

But his father wanted to move on. "No. Just the eyes." He was looking at Nick now. "So tall."

"We're the same height."

His father smiled. "Well, you used to be smaller. And now. You still bite your nails." Involuntarily Nick moved his hands on the wheel, turning in his fingers. "Always something going on inside."

You were going on inside, Nick wanted to shout. Instead, he said, "Do you have children? You and Anna."

"No, there's only you. We're not so young." He paused. "She's nervous, you know, about you."

"Why?"

His father shrugged. "She thinks you'll change

things." He took out another cigarette. "But what is there to change?"

"Are you supposed to smoke those things? With your heart?"

"No, of course not. I'm not supposed to do anything. No excitement. If you listened to them, you'd be so careful you'd go without knowing the difference."

"Is it bad for you? My being here?" A new thought.

"Very bad," he said, teasing gently. "It's the best thing in the world."

The houses—smaller now, with patches of garden—were thinning out, and they could see the country ahead.

"Is this right?" Nick said.

"Yes, keep going. I want to show you something."

"Are you going to tell me what?"

"It's not a mystery," he said, making it one. "Everything in its time."

Nick glanced at him. There was an agenda, everything planned. And what was at the end? The Wallenstein, the switch of cars, the country. Step by step. Even their conversation now seemed to him a kind of testing, his father leading him further into his life, where nothing was open. Secrecy became a habit. He saw now that his father wanted to be sure of him somehow, and he felt unexpectedly wounded. Wasn't it enough that he had come?

In the woods there were still blossoms on the

trees, not the lush flowering of Virginia but a thin sprinkling of white, a Bohemian lace.

"Remember the dogwood," his father said, seeing them too. "On 2nd Street? I wonder, is it still there?"

"Magnolia. I don't know. The neighborhood's changed."

"But not the trees," his father said, not hearing the shift in Nick's tone.

"I've never been back. We sold it. Right after."

"Ah. What became of Nora? Do you see her?"

"Just Christmas cards. She's still there somewhere. Arlington, I think."

"I always wondered, was she working for the FBI?" his father said easily. "Old Edgar had a real fondness for housekeepers."

The words, like a trigger, exploded something in Nick. This was crazy, yet another descent through the rabbit hole. Even Nora. Who *cares*? It's not important. He felt things fall away until there was nothing but the gulf of all the years between them. Why were they talking about this? The realtor view from Holečkova. Two bathrooms. Moscow in the snow. Surreal, all of it. They gave me a medal. *Talk* to me.

"I loved that house," his father said dreamily.

It snapped again. Everything in its time. Now. He felt his breath shortening and gripped the wheel, bringing the car to a stop on the side of the road, his foot on the brake. He heard the motor, his own breathing, sensed his father turning in alarm.

"Why did you do it?" he said, his voice wavering, staring straight ahead, pulling the words out of himself, not enough breath for a wail. "Why did you leave me?"

Then there was no sound at all, a suspension even of air.

"I didn't leave you," his father said finally, in a whisper. "I left myself." A distress real enough to touch. Nick knew it was true and knew that if he reached out for it they would lose the moment, put everything aside in some evasive forgetting.

"No," he said, still looking at the wheel. "Me. You left *me.* Why did you?"

His father said nothing. Nick kept his eyes ahead, afraid to look. What could there be on his face but loss?

"I want to explain—" his father said weakly, then stopped.

"Why did you ask me here? What do you want from me?"

At this his father stirred, flustered. "If we could wait," he said hoarsely. "The right time. So I can explain."

"Now," Nick said angrily, finally turning to him. "Tell me now. What do you want?"

His father met his eyes, the nervous fluttering gone, giving in. "I want to go home."

Nick started driving, too stunned to do anything else. "Please, let me explain in my own way," his father had said, and then, when he didn't, Nick didn't know how to press. The outburst had unnerved them both—they were afraid of each other now—so that driving seemed a form of apology. Don't worry, I won't do that again. It was safer to concentrate on the road.

"You know that's impossible," Nick said. But it had been impossible for him to come, and he had driven right in. A two-lane road, through the wire.

His father said nothing, determined to follow his own timetable, and Nick went back to the road, the ragged asphalt and lacy trees. Had he actually worked out the logistics? Nick's imagination couldn't take it in. Passports and border crossings and newsmen at the end, like the men in hats. No. Not that. It was a kind of metaphor, a way of talking, one of his father's riddles.

"Turn up here."

Nick saw the sign. "Terezín?"

"In German, Theresienstadt."

"The model camp. Where they took the Red Cross."

His father nodded. "That's right. The model camp. In the museum, by the Jewish cemetery in Prague, they have the children's drawings. They are—well, you'll see them."

They parked outside an old fortress, the walls of a castle town.

"Why are we doing this?" Nick said. "I don't want a history lesson. I want to talk to you."

"This is what we're talking about. I want to start at the beginning. So you'll understand."

There were no other cars, and when a guard ap-

235

peared, grumbling in Czech, Nick thought it must be closed, but his father flashed some card in his wallet and the guard, straightening himself, nodded a salute and passed them through.

The air was utterly still, not even moved by birds, and it carried the crunch of their shoes on the dirt. All the buildings were not just empty but abandoned, like a western ghost town whose mine had played out. There had been no attempt to turn it into a museum park, no flower beds or lawns, as if the ground itself had resisted any signs of new life. Just the graveyard stillness. The buildings, some of them old, pieces of architecture, had been left to rot, exhausted by their own terrible history. It was not the kind of concentration camp Nick had seen in a thousand photographs—the railway tracks to the smokestacks, the long barracks, wrought iron twisted into messages—but there was no mistaking the stillness. They had left their dread behind, and it still hung in the air, as real as blood.

"People have the idea that it wasn't so bad here," his father said, taking them farther into the compound. "You know—the orchestra, the children's drawings. Like summer camp. But sixty thousand died here. The rest they sent to Auschwitz, the other camps. Everybody died. You see the bunks." He gestured toward an open door, where Nick could see bunk beds stacked to the ceiling. "Nine in a bunk. Sometimes more. You can imagine. Typhus. Dysentery. Well, you can't imagine. Nobody can. People think that because there were no ovens—but over sixty thousand. Here, not

236

shipped out. They didn't need gas chambers. They just shot them, one by one. Or the gallows. Not very efficient but maybe more satisfying. They could watch."

Nick followed him down the dusty street, saying nothing. This happened in my lifetime, he thought.

"At the end there, through that gate, is where they shot them."

"I don't want to see this," Nick said, claustrophobic.

"There's just one thing." He stopped at a house near the end. Next to it was an empty swimming pool, with bunches of old leaves stuck in rain puddles on the cracked concrete. "This was the commandant's house."

"He had a swimming pool?"

"For his daughters. Little girls. The prisoners would march by here on their way to the firing range." He pointed again to the open area through the gate. "They shot them over there."

So close. The sharp crack of gunfire. Not once. All day.

"They would hear," Nick said, picturing it.

"Yes. While they were swimming. The first time I saw this—what kind of people were these? Little girls swimming, and all the time—"

"Maybe there was a fence," Nick said dully. "So they couldn't see."

"No. No fence."

Then the prisoners would see them too, Nick thought. Splashing. The last thing they would see.

"Why are you showing me this?" he said, turning away from the pool.

"I want you to understand what they were. Nothing will make sense without that."

Nick looked at him, sensing where he was heading. "You don't have to explain yourself to me."

"No? I think I do. The politics of another generation—they're never real, are they? What was the point? Thirty years from now, they'll ask you. What was so important? But it *was* important."

Nick thought of Jan Palach. Important enough to light a match.

"In Prague," his father said, "you see all the statues. Hussites. Catholics. What was that? Nobody remembers. But at the time, if you *lived* then."

Nick looked down, moving his shoe across the dirt like a visible thought. "You didn't know about this. Not then."

"The swimming pool, no. But we knew what they were. All you had to do was listen."

"And?"

"And no one was stopping them. No one. America First. It'll all just go away. Or maybe it's a good thing. People thought that then, you know. We had our own Nazis. My god, Jim Crow. People with sheets over their heads. That doesn't seem real anymore either, does it? Father Coughlin on the radio, that prick."

Nick glanced up, oddly reassured by the familiarity of his father's scorn. Still an anti-cleric. But his father was racing now.

238

"And you could see what the Nazis were doing. Austria—just like that. They weren't going to stop. Then Czechoslovakia. The Sudeten, but we knew it meant the whole thing. Why not just hand it over? The English," he said, waving his hand. "And nobody in Washington lifted a finger. Couldn't. It would have been bad politics. Nobody was trying to stop them."

"Except the Communists," Nick said quietly, following his logic. "That's when you became a Communist."

"Yes. After Munich. That was the last straw. Strange, in a way. I didn't have any special feeling for the Czechs. Your grandparents had family here—in the Sudeten, in fact—but I never felt Czech. I don't feel Czech now. I think it was the helplessness, the feeling that you had to do *something*." He stopped, then managed a shrug. "Another generation's politics. How do you explain it? Maybe I was ready, and then Munich came along." He glanced up at Nick. "I wasn't the only one, you know. A lot of people joined in the thirties. There were good reasons then. Well, we thought there were."

Nick looked at him. "They didn't become spies," he said. He turned back toward the entrance gate. "Let's go."

His father followed him. Outside the walls, near the car, he touched Nick's elbow. "Let's walk for a bit."

Involuntarily, Nick drew his elbow in. "Not in

there," he said, but he began to walk. "What made you ready?"

"I was impatient." Nick caught the tiny barb and slowed to his father's pace. "The times," his father said vaguely. "You can't imagine what things were like then. You remember where Grandma lived?"

They had visited a few times when Nick was a child. Collieries and slag heaps and cookie-cutter company houses. The big coal stove in the basement kitchen, where his grandmother seemed to live, held by the warmth. A photograph of Roosevelt on the wall. The Last Supper, draped with a frond from Palm Sunday. Upstairs, the parlor with doilies where the priest visited once a year and no one sat.

"People literally went hungry in those days. I had friends, children, who worked in the breakers. Half the miners were on relief. You picked up coal by the tracks, the pieces that fell off the cars. In a burlap bag. You had to drag it home if it got too heavy. But I was lucky—I got out. I was going to change all that."

"She never believed you did it," Nick said. "Grandma. She wouldn't look at the papers. She said it was a mistake."

His father stopped and took a breath, as if he'd been punched.

"In the early days we did change things," he continued, refusing to be distracted. "Washington was exciting. The New Deal." He pronounced it for effect, like a foreign phrase. "We were just out of law school—what did we know? We thought we

240

could change anything. Nothing could stop us. But they did. I think we just knocked the wind out of them, and then, when they caught their breath, there they were again. The Welleses, the Rankins—they were always there, you know. We didn't invent them after the war. Defenders of the faith. Whatever it was. Themselves, mostly."

He turned, looking at Nick. "You know, when I first went to Penn, I remember I had a suitcase. Your grandmother bought it for me, and I saw right away it was all wrong. I hid it in the closet. Embarrassed, you know? And then I thought, what the hell? I'll catch up. This was my *chance.* I had the scholarship and the job, and sometimes I didn't even sleep, there was so much I wanted to do. But what I couldn't understand—it was the first time I'd met people who thought they *deserved* their luck. They didn't know they were lucky. They didn't think at all about the ones who weren't there. How can people be like that? Not see they're lucky? Not have some—" He searched. "Compassion."

"They're afraid someone will take it away," Nick said simply.

"Yes." His father nodded. "But what makes them think they should have it in the first place? That's what's interesting. What do they believe in? What did Welles believe in? I still don't know. Of course," he said, a faint smile on his face, "they're not very bright, are they? Maybe that's all of it. Kenneth B. Welles. I remember when he first came to town. Not even a lightbulb on upstairs. He never did have anything except his *amour propre.*"

241

"And the right suitcase."

His father glanced at him appreciatively. "Yes, he had that. His father—natural gas, of all things. That certainly ran in the family," he said, a throw-away. "Anyway, things just—stalled. Maybe we ran out of steam. Maybe Welles and the rest of them learned how to block. Bills just sat in commit-tee. After a while all we were doing was fighting them. Not politics, schoolyard stuff. And mean-while things kept going to hell—there wasn't *time.*" He stopped. "Impatient, you see. So I was ready."

"What did you do? Walk into some office and sign up? Like that?" Nick said, sounding more sar-castic than he intended.

"No, they come to you," his father said, ignoring the tone. "They fish. First the bait, then they play the line—it turns out that's what they did best. In those days, that's all they were doing, but I didn't see that. No change. Just recruiting."

"Who recruited you?"

His father stopped and looked toward the for-tress walls. "Names. Well, what difference does it make now? He's dead. Richard Schulman, a teacher at Penn. He was never exposed. You're the only one who knows this," he said, his voice sud-denly conspiratorial.

Nick looked at him. "It was thirty years ago," he said. "No one—"

"Cares," his father finished. He shook his head. "Old battles. Still, it's not easy, you know, even now, giving names. Anyway, he kept in touch. He came to Washington now and then. We had dinner.

I think he saw I was—what? Discouraged. Ready for something else. It was a long process. A seduction."

"Literally?"

His father smiled. "Like the Brits? No, he had four wives. I think he changed them if they got suspicious. None of them knew, not even them. I think that's what he liked, the secrecy. Of course, in my case it made sense, being a secret member. If you were in government, you couldn't be public. That's how it started. We were secret for my protection, so I could keep the job. At least I didn't have to go to the meetings," he said lightly. "Self-criticism, that was the thing then, you know—all that breast-beating. I heard the stories later. I don't think I would have made it through that, so it's just as well."

He glanced at Nick, expecting him to be amused, but Nick was still looking at the ground, waiting. "So. I was in place. Secret and in place. What else could the next step have been? It started with the trade agreement. We were being stupid about that—still trying to collect old war debts. Anyone could see the Soviets didn't have that kind of money to spare. They couldn't rearm against Germany without hard currency. But the talks just dragged on and on."

"So you decided to give them a push."

"Yes, a push. A little one, to move things along. It was important for them to know how to speed up the negotiations. We're not talking about tank designs, just position papers, memos. Half the people involved had access to them. They weren't sensitive."

"Then what good were they?"

"Well, you have to understand the Soviets. They have a mania for information. It comes, I think, from feeling so isolated. During the war, they took planeloads of documents out. On the lend-lease planes—bags of them. Memos. Newspapers. Useless, most of it. Paper. But they always wanted more."

"I don't want to know what you gave them," Nick said, flustered. "What matters is, you did."

"No. It's important for you to know. For what I'm going to tell you."

Nick waited.

"It was never anything military. Office paper. Like emptying a wastebasket. Things we should have told them in the first place. Why not? We could tell England, but not them. They had to rely on—people like me. Just to know. But what could I tell them? Diplomatic reports. What Ambassador so-and-so thought, assuming he thought anything. What was the harm? I never gave them anything that would hurt us. I never *had* anything like that. Just my in box."

"Your in box," Nick said, facing him. "Is that why you sent for me? To tell me how innocent it all was? Just a little private lend-lease, out of the goodness of your heart? My god. Don't you think it's a little late for this?"

"No," his father said, shaking his head. "I didn't mean that. I knew what I was doing. I thought they had a right to know. It was never—innocent. The point is, I never gave them anything important."

"So?"

"So why bring me out? Do you think I was Philby? I wasn't. What made me so important to them?" It was a new idea to Nick, unexpected, but his father's voice was even, the patient tone of a teacher leading him through a theorem proof. "All that trouble for me. Why?"

"You got caught."

"No. I was accused. I was never caught." Nick looked at him, picking up the odd, twisted pride in his voice. "What did they have? A salesgirl who said she knew me. Her word. My word. We could have beat it," he said, a lawyer again, still preparing the case.

"The papers said she had more."

His father waved his hand, an easy dismissal. "What more could she have? She was the messenger. That was Welles grabbing a headline. He did that, you know. On Fridays. By Monday people would forget he hadn't actually told them anything. He was just trying to turn up the pilot light, make that poor girl think he had something. Shake her up a little and see if any more came out. It's been known to work. Anyway, this time it went with her. But he didn't have anything."

"Maybe she'd already talked to him."

"No, we'd have heard. Why would he keep it to himself? It cost him, that hearing. Smoke and no fire. People get fed up. He started looking like a bully. She didn't tell him anything about me. She

245

couldn't have—there was nothing to tell. She sold the shirt, I left the papers. That's all there was to it. Simple. Nothing to connect either of us. Of course, one way or the other, after the hearing I'd be out of business. That kind of spotlight doesn't go away. As far as they were concerned, I was finished. But Welles was stuck—he didn't have enough to put me away. So why not just retire me? Why bring me out?"

Nick stopped, rattled. "I thought it was your idea."

"No." His father slowly shook his head. "I had no choice, Nick. You believe that, don't you?" He took Nick's elbow, a physical plea. "To leave everything— No. I thought we could sit it out." He took his hand away, dropping it with his voice. "We could have."

"What are you trying to say? That it was all a mistake? Somebody jumped the gun?" This was worse somehow, their whole lives turned around in a careless haste.

"I did think that at first," his father said, starting to walk again. "I tried to tell them. But there were orders. You didn't argue with that. Ever."

"In the phone booth," Nick said quietly. "In Union Station."

His father turned, amazed. "How did you know that?"

"I followed you."

"You followed me," he repeated. When he looked at Nick, he softened, as if he could see a child's face again. "Why?"

246

"I knew something bad was happening. I thought, in case—" He stopped, surprised to find himself embarrassed.

"In case," his father said, still looking at him. "So I made you a spy too." Then he smiled. "A better one, it seems. I had no idea."

"You weren't looking."

"We're supposed to, you know," he said wryly.

Nick shrugged. "People don't see kids. You had things on your mind." He saw him again, in the herringbone coat, walking slowly up the hill, looking down at the snow, preoccupied. "Is that when you decided? After the phone call?" As if the chronology mattered.

"I didn't decide, Nick. I did what I was told."

"But if Welles didn't have anything?"

"We didn't know that then, only later. I suppose I believed him too. That there was something. I didn't want to go to prison." He stopped, turning. "So I went."

"Without us," Nick said, picking at it.

"Yes. Without you. It was usual to have the families follow. Like Donald's."

"But we didn't."

"No. Did I think your mother would come? I don't know. At first I hoped, but I never heard. And then—well, by that time I knew Moscow better. It was the terror all over again, until Stalin died. No one was safe. War heroes." He snapped his fingers, making them vanish as casually as the black cars in the night. "Even Molotov. He denounced his wife. The fool thought it would save his job. She

247

spent seventeen years in the camps. Soviet justice." He turned to Nick. "It was no place for you. I didn't want you there, can you understand that? It would have killed your mother, that life. Later, when things got better—" He spread his hands. "You were already someone else."

They had made a circle through some trees and were heading back to the fortress, to the stillness. The guard had left his post and in their absence was inspecting the car, running his hand along the smooth finish as if it were an exotic animal.

"It's clearing," his father said, looking up. "We'll have sun."

"Then let's finish."

"Yes." He stopped, touching Nick's elbow again. "A moment."

The words sounded translated. Nick looked at him quickly, wondering whether the walk had tired him. Or was he trying to keep a distance from the guard? But his face, lost in thought, showed something else: an old man trying to find his place in a prepared speech.

"So why bring me out?" he said finally, picking up the thread. "The propaganda? That was part of it. Just being there. They like to show us off. Like the Africans they bring to the university. Living proof. Marx is everywhere—even in the jungle. No color bar in the International. Of course, the people think they're savages—they just stare at them in the metro—so who's fooling whom?" He paused, catching himself. "But they never used me that way."

"They gave you a medal."

"Yes. One press appearance, then no more. A lot of trouble to take, don't you think, for a minute on the stage?"

"They had to help you. Isn't that part of the deal?"

"For a Russian, yes, they would do that. But the rest of us—it would depend on what we knew. And what did I know? So why take the chance, if I was being watched, for instance?" he said, glancing slyly at Nick. "Someone had to get me out. Why put anyone at risk? Why not just leave me to the wolves?"

"Okay, why?"

His father looked at him, his eyes burning, finally there. "To protect someone else."

For a moment Nick was silent, trying to take it in. "Do you know that?" he said quietly.

His father nodded. "I've had a lot of time to think about it. At first you flatter yourself—you want to believe you are important. But I wasn't. It was never about me, Nick, what happened. It was always about someone else."

Nick stared at him, so carefully led to the point that now he felt pinned by its sinking inevitability, the event of his life reduced to an accident. Not about them at all.

"Who?" he said.

His father began to walk again, his voice slipping back to its instructor tone. "Well, who did I know? The logical person was Schulman. It fit. He recruited me. He must have been valuable to them.

249

He would insist on being protected. Richard Schulman. I didn't know it was possible to hate someone that much. During the bad times I had that to hang on to. He'd get caught—it would happen to him, too. It didn't, though." He took a breath. "Which was just as well. It wasn't him, you see. It was someone else."

"Who?" Nick repeated.

"That's what I want to find out."

For an instant Nick wondered if his father was all right, his anger finally curdled over the years into an old man's obsession. "Find out? How?"

"The woman is the key. I was sent away and she—died. So someone would be safe. Schulman? No. It should have been him, but he died too." He glanced at Nick. "Quite naturally—later. There was no question about that. I saw the coroner's report."

Nick looked at him, appalled. How long had his father been working out his old puzzle, playing detective while his life passed by? Then he saw himself in London, arranging index cards like clues.

"So," his father said, a blackboard pointer in his voice, "a new question. Who else did *she* know? Who recruited her?"

They were almost at the car now, and Nick turned to him, away from the guard. "Does it matter anymore?" he said gently. "So many years. Maybe he's dead too."

His father shook his head. "No, you don't understand. It does matter. He's still there."

The guard, no longer shy, called over to them in rapid Czech, and Nick stepped aside when his father answered, jarred by the sudden volley of foreign words. Even the familiar voice seemed different, guttural and slurred. He looked at him, half expecting to see his face changed too, broad and Slavic.

"He wants to know what it can do on the highway, how fast," his father said.

"I don't know," Nick said, his mind elsewhere. "What do you mean, he's still there?"

"Later," his father said quietly, then spoke in Czech again, affable now, sharing a foreign joke. Nick watched the guard widen his eyes, then shrug. "I told him ninety easy before it starts to rattle. He says his Tatra would fall apart." The guard gave the car an admiring pat. "I think you've made a convert to the West."

"Stop it," Nick said, annoyed at his tone.

"Just smile and get in the car," his father said, almost under his breath, and then spoke Czech to the guard again. Nick watched them chat for a minute, idle car talk outside the old camp walls, and felt again how surreal ordinary life was here. The past wasn't forgotten, just ignored. Down the road, little girls had played in a pool.

"Never leave a bad impression," his father said, getting in the car. "People remember."

Nick put the car in gear and pulled away. "How do you know he's still there?"

His father lit a cigarette. "Because I've been following him. Every agent has a pattern."

"Following how?"

"Well, at first by accident," he said, blowing

251

smoke, easing into it. "We always acted alone in Washington. Burgess staying at Philby's house—that kind of thing would have been impossible for us. We never knew each other. I had my contact, my control, at the Russian embassy, and that was it. No one else."

"Then how do you know—"

"The code names. They liked to group us—it's a convenience. Fish. Birds. Mythology. Whatever came to someone's mind. I've often wondered who did that, who assigned the names. They're supposed to be completely at random, but you know how it is, someone can't help being clever. San Francisco was Babylon, Washington Carthage. Capitals of fallen empires. Some clerk's idea of a joke."

"What was yours?"

"Coal. I thought it was because of the union work, but it turned out we were all minerals. It had no significance at all. Schulman was Gold. Panning for gold? Maybe he was just first. Of course, I never had the cross-files, only the code names. But it became a kind of game to figure it out, to see whether I might have known any of them. I was pretty sure Iron was Carlson over in Commerce—the reports had his tone, just as dull as talking to him, and sure enough, when he died the reports stopped, so it must have been. Copper was someone at the *Post,* but I'm still not sure who. The others were mostly illegals, Soviets who were there without diplomatic immunity, so I wouldn't have known them even if I had had the cross-files. Not that it mattered. It was just a game, to help pass the time."

Nick stared ahead, amazed. A boys' game for grownups, code names and passwords.

"Of course, this was all later," his father continued. "After Josef, my embassy control, came home. At first I didn't see anything. They had me reading newspapers. I was a sort of *Reader's Digest* for Moscow Central. Then I got the traffic from the San Francisco residency."

"They had an office in San Francisco? What for?"

"Originally to monitor the UN conference in '45," his father said easily. "Afterward, well, some of the old GRU contacts were still there. It was useful to keep tabs on the Soviet merchant marine. Sailors had a bad habit of jumping ship once they were in Babylon. Defectors. That kept the office busy."

"What happened to them, the sailors?"

"Does it matter?" his father said quietly.

"Yes."

"They were found and shipped back home."

Not a game. Hunted down, thrown into ships, sent back to prison camps.

"With your help," Nick said.

His father was quiet, then sighed. "Yes, with my help. What do you want me to say, Nick? That I didn't know?"

"No," Nick said, absorbing it. "Go on."

"So Josef came back—this would be after they finally got rid of Beria, lots of changes then—and we got together. He liked a drink. I'm a political

253

analyst, I said. Isn't it time I had something to ana-lyze? I'm wasting my time here. No one is going to waste time now, he says. We're going to clean house. You'll see. Very important. As if it were up to him. It's the drink talking, I thought. But no, reports did start coming. They threw out half the section, Beria's goons, and Josef had everything his way for a while. He liked me, I don't know why. I never liked him much, but we don't pick our commissars, do we? I finally had some real work to do.

"Then, one day, a funny thing. Josef used to assign the reports, but he was out, so his secretary brought them straight over from cryptology. She was the type who knew everything—she came with the place. No one could ever get rid of her, not even Josef. I think maybe she had a protector. Anyway, she handed me a report and said, 'So Silver's back. Now we'll really have something,' as if I knew all about it. 'Good,' I said. 'It's about time.' Conspirators, you see. And she was right—we did have something. Committee minutes. House ap-propriations. Much better than the other stuff I was seeing. So where did this come from? I wondered. Not Carlson. Not an illegal—the access was too good. The next day I said to Josef, 'Who's Silver?' Not that he would tell me—that wasn't allowed. But I thought he might say something, a hint. For the old network. It only took a second, that look of surprise. He shouldn't have hesitated—we live for seconds like that."

Nick thought of the guard, of his father's seam-less affability, not even a second's pause.

254

" 'There is no Silver,' he said. 'What are you talking about?' But I knew. It was that second. I showed him the report. 'Oh, this,' he said. 'That idiot in cryptology—he keeps getting the names wrong. There is no Silver.' So I went along with it—what else could I do? I waited for the next one. Of course it never came. So one day I took a report back to the secretary and said, casually, you know, 'This one's no Silver. When's he going to deliver again?' and the old cow smiled that little superior smile of hers. 'Oh, Josef Ivanovich reads those himself.' So there it was. But what? Why not let me see them? I was reading everything else. We used to cross-check the reports, to verify information when we could. Evidently these didn't need verification. Josef never said a word. I would get him drunk, talk about the old days, but never a word. The others, yes. How Carlson used to bungle the meetings. Lots of stories.

"Then one night he said something interesting. We were talking about the Cochrane woman. 'That was wrong,' he said, which surprised me. I thought he was talking about her being killed. Josef wasn't the squeamish type. His hands were never— Then he said, 'You can't run things that way. The postman shouldn't know anyone.' 'She knew me,' I said, thinking I'd catch him, but he just shrugged it off. 'From the newspapers.' He wagged his finger at me, I remember. 'I always said, stay out of the newspapers.' Scolding me, a joke. So we laughed. But all I could think was, she knew somebody else."

"Silver," Nick said.

"Yes. It had to be. No one else was that important. Maybe Schulman—he was a talent spotter, he would have known names, but he had a different contact. Not in Washington. She never knew him. It had to be Silver. No one in the old network was worth protecting. Not that way—killing somebody. Josef wouldn't talk about him. They were *still* protecting him, even from me."

"What made him so important?"

"His information. They were right—it didn't need verification. No guesswork, no mistakes."

Nick glanced over. "You got this from one report?"

"No, I saw others. I told you, I followed him. Nothing lasts forever in the service. Including Josef. He was a good man, too, as far as that went. His problem was, he was from the old days, all the way back to the Comintern, when people believed in things. He didn't grasp what it had all become. Just smoke and mirrors. And perks, if you knew how to work them. Which he didn't."

"What happened to him?"

"I don't know. We never asked."

"You never asked?"

"Does that seem strange to you? You see how long I've been here. You have to live through the terror to understand. '52. You'd hear the cars. The next morning no one would say a thing, even the neighbors. It happened in my building once. Like a plague—no one wanted to touch the sick. You went to work. You went about your business. After

256

Stalin died it was different, but who knew for how long? It was always better not to ask. So we didn't. People just—went away." He paused and lit another cigarette, coughing slightly. "Once a whole hockey team, the VVS, national heroes. That was Vasily's pet project—Stalin's son, a drunk. Vasya ordered them to fly to Kazan in a storm, on a Politburo plane, no less. It went down. But there were no disasters in the Soviet Union, not even natural ones. So no publicity. They just disappeared, the whole team. No one said a word." He drew on the cigarette. "Vasya," he said scornfully. "His father was always cleaning up one mess or another. He tortured people, I heard. For the practice. But what could they expect, given the father? They had to wait until Stalin died before they could send him away. Then he disappeared too."

His voice had begun to drift, an old man's ramble, away from Nick, and Nick saw now that he would never know his father's other life. Even the palace gossip was as chilling and remote as whispers from outer space.

"We were talking about your boss," he said.

"Yes. Josef. Another victim. But in this case also an opportunity. Now we had Alexei, somebody's nephew, a kid. He didn't even know where the files were. Josef's secretary ran things, when he let her. He was suspicious of everybody—well, he was right to be suspicious—but he trusted me. An American defector. I'd be the one person who'd never have his job. So I helped him. Among other things, I told him that the Silver reports were supposed to come to me, no one else. Of course, it was his department now, and if he felt it would be better to change the procedures— He didn't. He brought me the first one himself, like a puppy. So I followed Silver.''

"Who was he?''

His father shook his head.

"You never figured it out?''

"Neither did Hoover. But I knew where. Hoover showed me where.''

"Hoover?''

"Strange, isn't it, to end up on the same side. We were both looking for him. And he helped me.'' A small smile, a twist of history. "You see, I thought it had to be somebody I knew. The mind plays these funny tricks when you don't know where to look. You turn things over and over—you suspect everybody. Everybody. Your best friend. Why not? He took my wife. Or your housekeeper.'' He nodded. "Even Nora. Imagine. The best one was Welles himself. Just the kind of elaborate bluff the comrades would like.''

He stopped and shook his head. "So much time wasted. Then Hoover showed me. I got some of Silver's early reports, the ones Josef had kept to himself, and that's when everything began to fall into place. After I left Hoover went on another witch-hunt, this time internal. Right through the Bureau. Now that was interesting. He had never done this before, at least that we knew. So how did we know now? I studied those reports over and over. You see, we'd never been able to crack the

Bureau. And now here it was, details, how he was turning the place inside out, what he was thinking. Not low-level information—someone close to him. And everything else began to make sense. The access everywhere, not just one department. The personal information—who else had files like that? Why he had to be protected—Dzerzhinsky would have done anything to keep someone close to Hoover. A prize. And that hunt, for Hoover to go after his own—I know what that's like. It's always the worst fear in the service, a renegade agent, someone who *knows.* Now it made sense why it was so hard for me to track him. The others, they'd reveal themselves one way or the other. You can't imagine the mistakes. They don't follow their own rules. Sometimes, by accident, even their own names, or their colleagues'. But Silver was different. He was a professional, careful. Nothing to indicate where he was. But when Hoover knew, then I knew too. He was there. Our man in the Bureau. If it hadn't been for Hoover, I never would have known where to look."

"But you said there's always a pattern."

"To the reports, yes. A certain style. But never *how* he knew. The others, they made regular reports, even when they had nothing to report. But with Silver, months would go by. No unnecessary risks. Then, when he had something, there'd be several in a row, all complete. Then nothing again. You had to wait. When he stopped, I didn't know it for months. I kept waiting. But he was gone."

"What do you mean, he stopped?"

"No reports. No documents. It got to be a year. That's a long time. I thought he was dead, or Hoover had finally got him and covered it up. What else? The others were all gone, one way or another. He had a long run, longer than most. People get caught, or die. Schulman. Carlson. Now Silver. It was the logical thing. You don't retire, you know."

"You did," Nick said.

"I wasn't in the field," his father said smoothly. "Just an office worker. With a pension. In the field it's different. You keep going until something happens. But he was never caught. We would have heard that. He had to be dead."

"But he wasn't."

"No. I didn't know for years. Of course, I wasn't in a position to know. They reorganized the department again. I had other things to do. But I could still hear the gossip, and I never heard anything."

"Then how do you know he's still there?"

"The secretary again. What was her name? You'd think I'd remember. Pani Know-it-all. She finally retired, just before Christmas. They gave her a party." He caught Nick's surprise. "They have parties, you know, just like everyone else. A big one this time. Toasts all night. Sturgeon. For a secretary. Maybe they wanted to make sure she wouldn't come back. Anyway, they invited all the old crowd, those of us who were left."

"This was here?"

"No, in Moscow. I was there at the time."

"Why?"

260

"It's not important, Nick," he said, impatient at the interruption. "Anička had to go. I'm not in prison. I'm allowed to travel."

"That's right. I forgot. You have a medal."

"Yes," he said quietly. "A medal. All the privileges. They gave the secretary one too. Not Lenin," he added quickly, as if it mattered, "just a service medal. She wore it all night. Pinned here." He put his hand on his chest. "She was glad to see me. Sentimental. You know how those things are. The good old days. My god, the good old days— Beria. We saw the best of it, she said. Nonsense like that. Tears even, with the drink. So what can you do? You play along. 'It won't be the same without you,' I said. I wonder if she thought I meant it. I suppose so. What else did she have then? A room somewhere out in Sokol? Her medal? 'You were the last.' And she nods, the cow. Yes, yes, we were the last. She takes my arm, all tears—I thought she was going to kiss me. 'Now there's only Silver,' she says. 'He never stops.' I remember she had my arm and it jerked—I couldn't help it. 'I thought he was dead,' I said. 'Him?' She just shook her head, Miss Know-it-all again. 'Not him. He's too clever for them. Not like the ones they have now. Amateurs. Not like the old days.' As if it had been different then," he said to Nick. "What did she think we were? 'I can't believe it,' I said. 'All this time.' She patted my arm, like a child. 'Yes, just like before,' she said. 'Just like before. They don't retire him.' And I knew then she'd been forced out—she wanted to die at her desk, I suppose. In the saddle.

Nina, that was it. Her name." He smiled to himself, as if remembering it had been the point of the story.

"And was he?" Nick said. "Still there?"

"Oh, yes. I checked. I still have some friends inside—I saw one of the reports. She was right. It was the same. Same style, same name. So I knew he was operating again. He's still there, Nick. The one who sent me here. And now I know how to get him. Not Hoover. Me."

Nick waited, but his father seemed to have finished.

"Why are you telling me this?"

"So you would know it's not just for me. In case—" He hesitated. "I didn't know if you would do it for me."

Nick felt the soft words like a slap. In case.

"Do what?"

"I told you. I need your help. To come out."

"You can't be serious."

"Yes. It's possible."

"What am I supposed to do? Hide you in a trunk and drive across the border?"

"No," his father said steadily. "I would never put you at risk, never. You believe that, don't you? I want you to take a message, that's all."

"That's all," Nick repeated dully.

"Something for your country," his father said. "Call it that. You were a soldier. You were willing to—now, just take a message. I can expose Silver. It's important. Do it for that, not for me."

Nick was quiet, following his father's logic. "Sort

of a patriotic act," he said finally, his voice unexpectedly sarcastic. "One for our side."

"Yes, one for your side."

"And whose side are you on now?"

He meant to provoke, unable to stop himself, but his father just shrugged. "Sides. We both lost this war. What was it all about—does anybody know? Like the statues. Hussites. Catholics. No one remembers. What war?"

"You're living behind barbed wire."

His father shook his head. "It's over. Look at us here. All those ideas. Pan-Slavism. Only twenty years ago. Now look. There are half a million troops in Czechoslovakia. We're at war with ourselves. No idea survives that. And America. Communists in the State Department. Now Communists in Asia. They don't know it's already over. We're fighting our children now. That's how it's ending for both of us."

Nick said nothing, surprised at the outburst. What had he been like young, before everything turned to disappointment?

"Then let it go. Make peace."

"I can't," his father said, quiet again. "I can't let it go. For me it's personal." His voice picked up, ironic. "But for you. A spoil of war for your side. I owe that much."

Nick lowered his voice, sensible. "You can't go back, you know. It's impossible."

"No," his father interrupted, "it's possible. I have it all worked out. I can make it worth it to them."

"Is it worth it to you? To go to prison? They're all still there. Welles, all of them—Nixon's the president, for god's sake. There *was* a Communist in the State Department—you. Do you want to go through all that again?"

"I won't go to prison," he said calmly. "I'm an old man. Aside from anything else, there's the statute of limitations. That ran out a long time ago. Anyway, I was never charged with anything. Who's going to charge me now? The witch-hunts are over. Nobody wants that again."

"Yes, they do. You were a spy. You said so. In public."

"And now they'll have a bigger one, brand-new. It can work, Nick. I'm not asking them to roast a fatted calf. Just make a quiet deal. They will."

"It won't be quiet," Nick said, seeing the flashbulbs.

"Maybe they'll like that. Who knows? Nobody's ever asked to come home."

Nick felt the sinking sensation again. The almost jaunty self-importance. The old game. One for our side. Brass bands and bunting. But that was now a country of the imagination, as distant as an old grudge. Maybe it happened like that. Maybe after all the years of dingy streets and bad clothes, America began to be a dream. He didn't know he'd been forgotten.

"They'll never let you go. Here."

He turned to Nick. "That's the risk. But I can do it."

"I'll come see you," Nick said, a last try. "It's

easy for me. You don't have to risk anything. We can start over."

His father was quiet. "I don't want to die here, Nick. Not here." He placed his hand on Nick's arm, a reassurance, not a plea. All worked out. "We'll talk more," he said, patting him. "Take that next turning, by the plum tree."

The tree, heavy with blossoms, had scattered white markers over the one-lane road. Nick thought of Hansel's pebbles, leading deeper into the forest. A mile later, they forked onto a narrower dirt road dotted with mud puddles.

"It's almost time for lunch," his father said, glancing at his watch. "I didn't realize."

"What kind of message?" Nick asked, still absorbed.

"Not now," his father said quickly, as if they could be overheard. "And nothing in front of Anička."

"She doesn't know?" Nick said.

"No. It could be dangerous for her."

"Why does she think I'm here?"

"I wanted to see you, before it's too late. It's natural."

"Yes," Nick said flatly. A cover story.

"She'll be worried," his father said. "She worries when I'm late."

CHAPTER NINE

They were in the garden, hammering in stakes for tomato vines. Anna wore rubber boots and worker's overalls, which had the effect of making her look even broader, her hips ballooning out like Churchill's in his siren suit. Nick thought of his mother at the embassy party, slim and glossy. Molly, holding the stakes, had rolled up her jeans and taken off her shoes, playing peasant in the mud. They had clearly been at it for some time, their faces damp with perspiration in the humid air.

Molly waved at the car and grinned, and he felt her smile like a wakening hand at his shoulder, something real again. Her hair, piled on her head, fell down in wisps around her face, but the back of her neck was clear, as white and vulnerable as a child's. She seemed too fresh for the tired countryside, with her freckles and American teeth.

Anna wiped her hands and started over to them, her face tentative and somehow relieved. "We started. Before the rain comes. You had a good trip?" she said to Walter, glancing at Nick.

"Yes, perfect," his father said easily, not answering her real question. "Here, let me help you with that."

266

"No, no. You sit. I'll start lunch."

"She treats me like an invalid."

"You are an invalid."

"And you always expect rain," he said, smiling.

She looked up at the cloudy sky, unimpressed by the patches of light breaking through, then leaned against him to take off her boots, holding on to his upper arm for support. "There are left a few," she said to Nick, handing him a hammer. "You don't mind? Your father should rest."

"Sure," Nick said automatically, staring down at her feet, surprisingly small and pale.

"Is there beer?" his father said.

"For you?"

"Anička," he drawled, a mock pout.

She giggled good-naturedly and turned to the house. It was small, ordinary stucco with wooden shutters and sills, but placed at the top of a rise so that the lawn in front looked out over the trees to a field beyond. The landscape was unremarkable, not the dramatic rolling hills of Virginia, but the trees enclosed them in privacy. A rusty gas tank at the side. A stack of firewood, like the one at the cabin where they used to hide the spare key. A tiny tool shed in the back. A spigot with a green plastic garden hose attached, curled in a pail. Beyond the muddy driveway, woods to keep out the world. They came every weekend.

"Having fun?" he said to Molly as he reached the garden.

"You can't imagine. Gidget goes to Prague," she said. "Careful of the beans."

He sidestepped a row of tiny green seedlings.

"You had a good trip?" Anna's question, with the same edge.

Nick hammered in the stake. "We went to Theresienstadt."

"The concentration camp?"

"My father seems to think it's a tourist attraction."

"The Germans go," Molly said simply. "Pretty amazing, when you think of it." She moved to the next stake. "How was it? With your father, I mean."

"Fine," he said. Then, "I don't know. One minute he's the same, then the next—I can't get a fix. You know when you're adjusting binoculars? It's fuzzy, then it's clear, then it's all fuzzy again. Like that."

"Why? What did he say?" she asked, curious.

Nick moved away from it. "It's not what he says. It's—maybe he's just getting old. I never thought of him as old. I don't know why. Of course he'd be old. What's she like?"

"Not old. She doesn't miss much. Her English is better than you think. She's nervous about you."

"Why?" Nick said quickly.

"Well, why not? Here she is, cozy in her garden, and you drop in. The long-lost son. She wants you to like her—it's natural."

Natural, his father's word. "Yes," he said again.

"So smile a little," she said, pretending to be airy. "You look like you've just seen a concentration camp." She stepped back from the last tomato stake. "There, that's done. Just in time. Looks like soup's on."

She nodded toward the cottage door, where Anna was waving to them. She had changed the overalls for a skirt and blouse, and Nick noticed that her hair was brushed back, all tidied up.

"I hate soup," Nick said absently.

"You'd better like hers," Molly said.

She sprayed her feet with the hose and stamped them dry on the ground, taking down her hair and finger-combing it while she slipped into her loafers. Involuntarily, Nick smiled. Both Kotlar women seemed determined to make a good impression.

And, in fact, lunch was pleasant. The round dining table, set near the window corner of the room, was draped with a crocheted tablecloth anchored with a porcelain jug of fresh wildflowers. Across the table Anna had spread plates of pickles and hard-boiled eggs and salami arranged in pretty concentric circles. Nick glanced at the larder shelf, just like the one in their old cabin, but filled here with glass jars of cucumbers and tomatoes and beets, a garden preserved all year in vinegar and dill. He looked for the rainy-day snacks of his youth—peanut butter and saltines and cans of tuna—but this was a serious pantry, with real food to last a season. Anna ladled some form of borscht, beet red, from a decorated tureen and poured tall glasses of beer.

"Did you do all this yourself?" Nick said to her, indicating the shelves.

She nodded. "In the winter it's difficult for vegetables. We are fortunate to have the garden."

"Difficult. Nonexistent," his father said. "Carrots—that's it. Of course, the Americans have lettuce. Once a week the car goes to Germany. The lettuce run. Sometimes they share with their friends—the British, the Czech staff. Everyone in Prague knows someone who can get a German cabbage from the Americans. But Anička doesn't like to do that. She thinks it's disloyal," he said playfully.

"Not disloyal. Illegal. Ruzyně for a salad? No."

"Ruzyně," Nick said. "The airport?"

"A prison," his father explained. "Nearby. Same name." Then, smiling at Anna, "Where they put you for groceries."

"In the summer it's different," Anna said, ignoring the tease. "We have cherries down below. Plums. For jam."

"Jam," Nick said to his father. "Remember the time Mom tried with the blackberries?" It had slipped out before he could catch it and now it hung there, an embarrassment, but Anna smiled.

"Your mother was a gardener too?" A figure of the past.

"No. She said it would ruin her nails." A half-truth, making her seem frivolous. Why had he said it? To make one feel comfortable at the expense of the other? But Molly was right—Anna didn't miss much, and sensing his discomfort, she examined her hands and sighed.

"It's a price, yes. She was right, I think."

"But look how we eat," his father said, pointing to the array of pickles. "Anna can make anything grow. A magician."

"Oh, a magician. With peasant hands. That's the price. For the planting thumb."

"Green," Molly said. "Green thumb."

"Yes?" Anna giggled. "Green thumb. English—why do you make it so difficult?"

"You should try Czech," Molly said.

Anna found this funny, or chose to, and laughed, and Nick suddenly saw her as she must have been, bright and attractive, before weight and time had drawn her face closed. When had they met? Did they have jokes together? Nick thought of his parents, laughing downstairs after the guests had gone. He had been looking at Anna as a kind of nurse, dispensing pills and telling his father to rest. Now he sensed a different intimacy. Not a nurse, a wife. Who broke her nails pulling weeds.

So, improbably, they talked about gardens, about temperamental peas and what to do when the squash came in, as if the morning with his father had never happened at all. Anna passed plates. Molly asked the names of things in Czech. Small talk, a conspiracy of cheerfulness. He found himself slipping into the easy familiarity of a family lunch, where nothing important was said because everything was already known. He sat back, listening to his father's voice telling stories about the neighbors, feeling oddly at home. It was the last thing he'd expected here. Maybe things really were the same everywhere, fresh produce aside.

The room had been dim when they'd first come in, but now he could see it clearly, and his eyes moved lazily from the pantry shelf to the sitting area, the usual heap of books next to the couch. The side table with the Order of Lenin in its velvet box. The shelves on either side of the fireplace— no, not a fireplace, a wood stove, but framed by the same kind of shelves. He glanced toward the record player in the corner, then back to the couch, facing the easy chairs, each glance like a snap- shot. He stopped. It felt the same because it was the same. The desk under the window with its por- table typewriter, the table behind the couch for lamps and messy piles of books, even the radio on the windowsill—all the same. For a moment the slipcovers and crocheted doilies, Anna's touches, disappeared. Arranged exactly the same, all of it. His father had recreated the cabin.

Nick stared at the room, half hoping to see the fishing poles near the door, and sank back into the old photograph. Did his father know? Or was it a longing so unconscious that even furniture fell into place, just part of the natural order of things? He'd never left. And what about Anna? Did she fall into place too, curled up on the sofa with a book in his mother's spot? Maybe she liked it. Maybe she didn't know she was living in someone else's house.

"Did you have a place in Russia?" Nick said, clearly a question out of the blue, because they all looked at him, surprised he hadn't been following their conversation.

"In the country?" Anna said. "Yes, a dacha. Small, like this. We had to bring everything with us. You can see the condition. So old. But new furniture—who can get it? Of course, your father didn't mind. Men," she said to Molly. "They like everything the same."

"Hmm," Molly said. "Like dogs."

Anna laughed again, covering her mouth with her hand, a girl.

Afterward, Nick helped with the dishes while Molly and his father sat out in the sun in fading canvas chairs like the ones in Green Park. His father had taken another beer from the tiny fridge, hiding it from Anna and winking at him.

They worked at an old pedestal sink, Anna slipping wet plates into the drying rack, Nick wiping and stacking. She seemed preoccupied, uneasy now that they were alone, as if the others had taken the high spirits of the lunch table with them.

"How did you meet?" Nick asked to break the silence.

"Meet?" she said, surprised. "At work." She brushed it away like a fly. She took a second, then turned to him, her hands still in the water. "He's very ill. Did you know?"

"Yes. He told me."

"It's not good for him, to be excited."

"He doesn't look very excited." Nick nodded toward the lawn chairs, trying to be light.

"He is," she said flatly. "To see you—" She hesitated. "When he told me, I was afraid. That you would quarrel. So many years. But it's all right, isn't it?'' She looked at him, more than a question.

"Yes. It's all right." He smiled. "No quarrels."

"You think I'm foolish to worry like the mother hen. But I know him. All this month he's waiting. 'What if he doesn't come?' "

"But I did."

"Yes." She turned back to the sink. "Your mother—she didn't object?"

He glanced at her. "I didn't tell her," he said cautiously, not offering any more.

"Ah," Anna said. "You thought it would upset her? Still?"

"I don't know. She never talks about it."

She nodded to herself. "Like Valter," she said, translating his father's name, making him foreign, hers. "Never of her. Only you." Then, unexpectedly, "She's a woman of fashion."

It was another trick of language, the archaic phrase wrapping his mother in gowns and powdered wigs, a figure in a Fragonard swing. Nick smiled.

"I suppose. She thinks so, anyway." There it was again, the easy disloyalty.

"Yes. I saw photographs. Beautiful. I was maybe a little jealous," she said shyly.

"Jealous?"

Anna laughed. "When we get old, we become invisible to our children. But we still see. He was in love with her, I think."

"That was a long time ago," Nick said, embar-

274

rassed. Did she want to be reassured, this thick-waisted woman with her hands in the sink?

"Sometimes it's easier to love a memory. In life, things change. What would Zdeněk be like now, I wonder sometimes."

"Who?"

"Excuse me. My first husband. It was a long time ago." She smiled, echoing Nick's words. "He was killed."

"In the war?"

"No, when the Germans first came. They arrested him. They arrested all the Communists."

Another life, closed to him. More than his father's wife. Why had he thought she had no history?

"So to me he's always young, like then. Now what would he be? An old man at the Café Slavia, arguing politics. Well, who knows? We change." She turned and dried her hands on the towel, her eyes soft and concerned. "Even your father. Sometimes, you know, when a memory comes to life, it's not what we expect."

"You don't have to worry," Nick said. "I don't expect him to be the same."

She shook her head. "No. Him. What does he expect? All these years, he sees you as you were—not a man, not different. And then—" She reached over and touched his arm. "You'll be careful. You won't—excite him."

Nick looked down at her hand. "You didn't want me to come," he said simply.

She sighed. "The wicked stepmother? No. It's

good for you to see each other. But perhaps Valter's right, I am always looking for the rain. Why now? What does he want?" Nick moved his arm away, afraid of the question, but she had her own answer. "I think he's getting ready to die. So, this meeting. But I'm not ready for that. We have a life here. Not rich. Not—fashion," she said, almost spitting the word. "Quiet. But you don't know what it means to have this. What it was like before."

She stopped, turned back to the draining board, picked up a kettle, and held it under the faucet. For a minute the only sound was running water.

"I'm not trying to upset anything," Nick said lamely.

"No," she said quickly. "Excuse me. Such foolishness. How happy he is—you can see it in his eyes. So maybe it's good." There was a popping sound as she lit the gas ring.

"Two days. That's all," Nick said, as if they were bargaining for time.

She nodded. "Go talk to him. I'll bring the tea." She glanced out the window, a caretaker again. "It's too much beer—he'll fall asleep."

But he was animated, talking with Molly in a patch of sunlight. In the low-slung canvas chairs they looked like a Bloomsbury photograph, droopy sun hats and cigarettes, waiting for tea.

"Nick. KP finished?" he said. "You'll make someone a good husband. What do you think, Molly?"

She looked up at Nick. "Hmm. A catch."

"I was telling Molly about when they took down

Stalin's statue here, in Petřín Park. Crowds kept coming—cheering, you know?—so they had to do it at night. But you could hear the dynamite way over on Holečkova. All those years, and he still wouldn't go quietly.''

"Chair?'' Molly offered, but Nick sat down next to them on the grass.

"What's down there?'' He pointed to the clump of trees below. "Where the mist is.''

"Water. What we used to call a crick,'' his father said, smiling at the word. "There's always mist here, all over this part of Europe. It's the cloud cover, I think. No wind, unless the *föhn* comes up from Vienna. Then everybody gets headaches. Maybe it explains the politics.''

Molly giggled. "And Freud.''

His father shot her an appreciative glance. "Yes, and Freud. Maybe it was the weather all along.'' He lit a cigarette. "So, Nick, what will you do now?'' A father's question, innocent. "After LSE.''

Molly turned to him, frankly curious.

"Larry wants me to go back to law school.''

"Well, he would. And you?''

Nick shrugged. "We'll see.''

"All the time in the world,'' his father said. "Well, why not? Of course, someday you'll have to earn a living.''

The tone, so unexpectedly paternal, annoyed Nick. Maybe Anna was right—he'd always be as he had been, a child.

"Larry settled some money on me,'' he said bluntly.

His father was quiet for a second. "Did he? That was generous."

"I told you he was a catch," Molly said.

But this time his father ignored her. "What do you want to do, work with Wiseman?" He leaned back, smoking. "Of course, it's the great subject. To know what happened. You know, when I was your age I thought history was—what? Sweeping forces," he said, his voice ironic. "We were all swept along. Playthings."

"A dialectic."

"Yes, like that. The clash of forces. Something almost abstract."

"And then?"

"Then, I suppose, biography. I saw the effect of one man. What if there hadn't been a Stalin? Would things have been the same? No, utterly different. What if he'd never existed?"

"Who?" Anna said, coming out to them with a tray.

"Stalin."

She hesitated, then handed his father a mug and two pills. "Here," she said, as if nothing had been said.

"The great man theory," Nick said.

"Great man," Anna said. She passed out the mugs. "Such talk," she said to his father, the words a kind of clicking of the tongue. Then she put the empty beer bottle on the tray, looked at them worriedly, and turned back to the house.

"She's offended?" Nick said.

"No," his father said. "She thinks the trees have

278

ears, like all good Czechs. Someone's always listening." He sipped the tea. "At Stalin's funeral, several thousand people died. Trampled. In the crowd, to say goodbye. To the man who tried to murder them."

"There's no one like that now," Molly said quietly.

"Now? No. Petty crooks. Bureaucrats. So much for the theory. I was wrong. They were aberrations, the Stalins. Great forces, great men—such melodrama. And all along, what was it? A crime story."

Nick looked up at him.

"Of course, it's interesting," his father said, gazing back to Nick. "To solve the crime."

"That's what Wiseman says."

"Yes, well, he should know." He smiled slightly. "Maybe it's a hazard of the profession. He worked for the British, you know. SIS." He caught Nick's look. "No, not now, during the war. Everybody did. He must have seen plenty of crimes. All in a good cause, of course. They're always in a good cause. Even Stalin's, who knows? People thought that. Sometimes even the victims thought that—it gave them a reason why it was happening to them." He shrugged. "History."

The air was still, not even a rustle of leaves. A crime story. But what if you were in it?

When Molly stirred in her chair, it felt like an interruption. "Well," she said, pushing herself up, "I'll let you two figure out who done it. I'm just a farm girl." She looked toward the garden, where

Anna was digging, then up at the clouds. "I'd say about an hour, if we're lucky."

They watched her move across the grass, waving to Anna.

"She's a nice girl, your Molly."

"My Molly?"

"She likes you," his father said simply, a matchmaker's tease that caught Nick off guard.

In spite of himself, he flushed. "Don't complicate things."

"A girl like that is never a complication. Your mother had it, that spirit."

"She doesn't have it now." He looked down. Anna had been right. They were quarreling.

But his father sidestepped it, saying nothing. He put his hand on Nick's shoulder, stroking it lightly, the way he used to when they sat together on the dock, waiting for fish.

"Do you still go to the cabin?" he asked idly.

"No. It was sold."

His father nodded. "So. Every trace." Then the hand stopped, just a weight now. "Will she see me, do you think?"

Why hadn't he thought of this before? "Yes," he said. They'd all see him. His mother, staring out of windows. Larry, who'd patched up their lives. All the carefully constructed years. Where would they meet, in the apartment? Nick tried to picture it, the tentative first words, but nothing came. And he realized, shocked at himself, that he didn't want it to happen. He didn't want him to come back, splintering things again. The old dream. And now that it might be real, like the weight of his father's hand, he wanted to shake it off, walk away. But the hand was there, pulling him.

His father leaned back and sighed. "I'd like that," he said dreamily. "What will I say?" A conversation with himself. "Where do you start? I don't know how to start with you. What do you like for breakfast? What do you read? It seems silly, doesn't it, not to know these things."

Nick didn't say anything. His father, too, seemed to retreat from the day, closing his eyes against the weak sunlight. Nick could hear Anna and Molly talking in the garden, a faint insect buzzing.

"Anna doesn't know," Nick said. "What we talked about this morning."

"No. I told you, no one. It's too dangerous for her."

"Why dangerous?"

"If they thought she helped—" He let the thought hang.

"What about Molly?"

"Molly? There's no danger to her. What does she know? That I wanted to see you, that's all," he said drowsily. "It's good she likes you. It looks better."

"You took a chance with her."

"No. I checked."

"What?"

"There are not so many Americans in Prague. We know who they are—the embassy staff, the journalists. We watch to see if they recruit Czechs, so there's a list. I checked. She's not working for them. A love affair." He smiled, his eyes still closed. "At that age, there's always a love affair. She was safe. You were the chance—if you would come. But you did. I knew. It doesn't matter, you see, all the rest of it—what you like for breakfast. I knew you would come."

Nick looked over to the garden at Molly's face, fresh and guileless. A security check, just in case. In his father's world, suspicion hung over everyone, like the permanent cloud cover.

"Who keeps a list?"

"Nick." Indulgent, to a child. "We have our people too. That's the way it works."

But how exactly? Nick thought. Maids in the embassy? Repairmen going through desks? Somebody nursing a drink at a bar, all ears?

"Like Marty Bielak?"

His father frowned. "Who?"

"An American. He lives here. He was at the bar in the Alcron."

"Bielak," his father said, evidently remembering. "You talked to him?"

"No, he talked to me. Don't worry—I didn't say anything. Just a tourist. Is he one of yours?"

"Well, a Winchell," his father said dismissively. "A legman. He collects items—do they still call them that, items? He worked for the radio. Then his wife left, last year, when people could go out. So now he's a legman. To rehabilitate himself, I suppose. I met him once. He's a believer. For him, still the workers' paradise."

"Then why does he need to rehabilitate himself?" Nick said, slipping into the language.

"They won't trust him now. Unless she comes back, of course. Anyway, better avoid him—you don't want to become an item."

"But is it useful, what he does?"

"It gives them something to read. What else is there, *Rudé Právo*?"

Nick said nothing, and in the stillness that followed he could hear his father's faint breathing. He looked over at the closed eyes, the lined face smoothing out with sleep. He had drifted off with a cigarette still in his hand, and Nick leaned over and gently slipped it from his fingers, taking a puff himself, familiar, like sharing a toothbrush. A lazy afternoon. But nothing was peaceful here, not even the torpid landscape, tense with rain.

He looked toward the garden, where Anna was planting. Why bother? Soon it would be overgrown, abandoned. But she didn't know. If they thought she had helped—he felt the cigarette hot on his finger as the thought swept through him, stiffening him with dread. She didn't know because she wasn't going. His father was going to leave her, walk away from this life the way he'd walked away from theirs. Leaving everything behind. Only this time it would be Nick on the other end in the phone booth. That's what he was being asked to do.

He let the cigarette fall, staring ahead, not trusting himself to look at his sleeping father. The same crime all over again. He saw his mother weeping on the sofa. But Anna wouldn't be rescued by a rich man. She'd need to be rehabilitated—to denounce him, make them trust her. He watched her work, bending and straightening, unaware, and he could feel the heat in his face. We have a life here. But it would go too, the dim cottage and the jars of food, whatever peace they'd managed to scrape together. How could he do it? But how could he have done it the first time?

Nick got up and moved away from the chairs. The lawn sloped west, into the sun, and for an instant he wondered if he could keep going, all the way through the barbed wire, until he was home. In Prague they kept reminding you they were west of Vienna, Molly had told him, as if their history had violated a logic of geography. It was forty, fifty miles to the border, not far. He could simply walk through. But his father needed someone to help. A small favor. A message. And then it would never stop, one step after another until everyone was swept up in the turmoil again. Not history, just his father's endless mistake.

As he reached the trees he could hear the sky begin to rumble, a sound effect. He followed the path down to the water, pushing past bushes until the house was hidden behind him, out of sight. He stopped. What if the message were never delivered? A small betrayal, for everyone's sake. He started down again, with something like relief. It was that easy. Stop it finally. His father would never know. But he'd wait, expecting a call, some signal. That's how it would end, waiting, wondering why nobody came. The way Nick had waited. Could he do that to him? I don't want to die here, Nick.

The water was a crick, just as he had said, channeled by a low bank. Nick picked up a few small stones and began throwing them into the stream, listening for the familiar plops. He'd have to tell him, not let him waste what life was left here. Don't excite him, Anna had said, but which was worse? You can't expect me to do this. But his father had expected it, sure of him. So he'd sent for him, finally. That had been the point all along. Not to see him; to get an accomplice. He threw another stone, staring at the ripples.

"Just a boy at heart," Molly said, behind him. He turned, surprised, her voice bringing him back. "You never see little girls throwing rocks, but boys can do it for hours. Now why is that?"

He smiled. "I don't know. We used to pretend they were grenades. Here, try it."

She took a stone from his hand and pitched it, then shrugged. "Nothing. It must be one of those throwback things. You know, from the caves. When you were out there hunting and we were home stitching hides." She paused. "Anything wrong?"

He shook his head. "My father fell asleep. Pretty exciting, isn't it, life behind the iron curtain?"

"I don't know. My father used to spend the weekend watching golf on TV. Compared to that, it's a hoot."

He threw another stone. "How's the garden?"

285

"She's starting dinner. It takes hours, apparently, whatever it is. I suppose I should help. Boil nettles or something. God knows what little treat she's cooking up this time." She stopped. "Now why am I being like this? She's nice. It's just—I don't know, a little strange. Different, anyway. I feel like I'm meeting the in-laws and I haven't even been asked out yet."

He smiled at her. "Will you go out with me?"

"Oh." She glanced up at him. "Soon," she said, light again. Then she turned to the water, and in the silence that followed he felt her mood shift, like a faint stirring in the heavy air. "Want to tell me what's going on? The two of you were thick as thieves."

"He wants me to do something for him. I don't think I can."

"Then don't," she said quickly, trying to be casual. "What is it? Smuggle something out? It's usually that. Letters and things. They call it the tourist post."

"No. He—"

But she swung around suddenly, holding up her hand. "No, don't tell me. Really. I don't want to know. It's better. Just don't do it." The urgency in her voice caught him by surprise. "Don't do anything."

He nodded, still surprised, waiting for her to go on, but she turned away.

"God, I wish we could go," she said.

"Go?" His own idea, thrown back at him, a lifeline. Drive through the fence.

"Before anything happens."

"Like what?"

"I don't know."

"Nothing's going to happen."

"We could, you know," she said. "Just leave. Tomorrow. We could do that stupid Danube boat if you want. Anything." She turned. "We could start over."

The words made him look at her, an unexpected twirl of the binoculars. He saw her freckles, suddenly clear. Not complicated.

She raised her head and held his eyes for a moment. "Couldn't we?"

He touched her arm, an almost involuntary movement, and nodded.

"Would you like that?" she said, her eyes still on him.

There was a streak of dirt on her forehead, left over from the garden.

He nodded again. "But not on the Danube."

"No." She leaned closer. "Where?" she said, her voice low.

They stood for an instant, not moving, and then it was too late. The rain came all at once; no first drops, just the sudden burst of a punctured water balloon shocking them into place. They looked at each other, startled at being wet, then Molly, catching the water on her face, started to laugh. Nick took her hand and pulled her under a large tree. They stamped their feet, shaking themselves.

"Christ," Nick said. He picked at his shirt, sticking coldly to his back. Molly shook her hair, then leaned against the tree, her breasts showing through her blouse.

She smiled. "Not here, I guess."

They were both gulping air, as if they'd been running, and he stared at her for a second, watching the rise and fall of her chest, then moved nearer to the tree.

"Isn't that what they do in the army?" she said. "Cold showers?"

He leaned down, rubbing his hand along her face, slick with rain.

"It's what they advise," he said, his mouth almost touching hers.

But the rain had broken the mood. She pulled back. "Well, what's got into you?" she said, but pleased, still holding him. "We don't have to start over before dinner."

"The ground's dry." He bent forward again.

She reached up, putting her hand to his face. "We're a little old for this. Rolling around in the mud." She moved aside, shaking her blouse.

"Is that what you used to do?" he said, watching her.

"What? In my hippie days?" she said airily. "No. I like it better in a room."

"What's so special about a room?"

"You will, too."

"Promise?"

She grinned. "I guarantee it." Then she looked up at him, serious. "There's plenty of time. Now that you've asked me out."

"Okay, I'll get us a room," he said.

She rubbed her hair between her hands. "Mm, with hidden microphones." Her eyes widened, a glint of mischief. "I hadn't thought of that. What's *that* like? Do they listen? You know."

"If we make noise."

She stepped over to the edge of the dry area, facing the rain. "Should we make a run for it? They'll be worried."

Beyond the first few feet, the woods had become a blur. A few drops were coming through the leaves overhead now, but the leaky tent held, shutting everything else out.

"Not yet. Stay a little."

She glanced at him. "A little time out?" she said softly. She walked over to him. "Got a cigarette?"

He took out the pack, half dry, and lit one, then handed it to her. "Isn't this what we're supposed to do after?"

She looked away. "Everything's backward, isn't it? Maybe we're ahead of ourselves." She shook her head, a weak smile. "Now, too. We're ahead of ourselves."

"Molly—"

"It's all right. He's why you're here. I—I just came along for the ride."

"That's all?" he said.

She looked up at him, her eyes caught. "I thought so." She took a drag on the cigarette. "Anyway, it's too late now. Let's just get through it. Two days. But no tourist post, okay? No letters. They look for that. You don't want to end up in a Czech jail."

"It's not that."

"Oh. I thought—" She stopped short, waiting now.

He looked at her. They had started together, a bar in London. "He wants to go home."

"What?" As if she hadn't heard, had missed a joke. "What are you talking about?"

"He wants me to arrange it—to get him out."

"Are you crazy?"

"Maybe he is. But that's what he wants."

"He can't be serious. You think they're going to let him out? It's not the kind of trip you make twice."

"He thinks he can."

She took a breath. "Nick, listen to me. Don't get involved with this. I mean it. You don't know—it's different here."

"I don't have to do anything here. Just deliver a message."

She looked up at him. "To whom?" Then she looked away, as if she had overstepped. "Tell him to deliver his own message. Go to the embassy or something."

"He can't. You know that."

"Why not? Maybe they have forms for defectors. I wouldn't be surprised." She stopped. "I'm sorry. It's just too crazy. Why would he *want* to?"

"He's sick, Molly. He wants to go home."

"To jail?"

"He won't. Not now."

"Home free," she said, with a hint of sarcasm.

"What makes him think anybody wants him back?"

He looked away. "Maybe nobody does."

She said nothing for a minute, watching him. "You do. It's what you've always wanted, isn't it?" She shook her head. "I don't believe this."

"He's my father. I can't just leave him here. He doesn't belong here."

"Nobody belongs here. The Czechs are stuck, that's all. So is he." She walked back toward the rain, folding her arms over her chest. "How is it supposed to work, anyway? Swap him for one of theirs?"

"I don't know yet. I don't think he wants me to know. He seems to have it all planned."

"He's crazy. You don't go back. You just don't. It's a one-way thing."

"And what if he could? And I didn't help?" he said, almost to himself.

"So you're going to."

"I don't know."

"I do. I can tell. Look, I don't want any part of this."

"It doesn't involve you."

"That's right," she said sharply. "I just came along for the ride." She looked up at the leaves, dripping now with rain, closing in on them. "Well, you're full of little surprises today. No wonder you're all excited. Nick to the rescue. God. He still thinks he can get away with it."

"He didn't get away with anything. It's a long

time, twenty years, to live like this. For something you didn't do."

She glared at him, a sudden inexplicable anger. "Is that what he said?"

"He's not a traitor—not the way you think."

"Really? How many ways are there?"

He looked at her, surprised at her tone. "What's wrong?"

"Him. Everything. I can't believe he's doing this."

"He's sick."

"I know he's sick," she said quickly. "Why do you think I came? I thought that's what he wanted—to tell you about her. You know, a little confession. So good for the soul. I'd finally get to hear it from him." She looked at him. "All right, from you. Why not? I wanted to know how it happened."

"How what happened?"

"Ask him. Before you start all this."

"I'm asking you."

"He can't go back, Nick. He killed her. He thinks they don't know, but they do. They've always known."

"He didn't kill her."

She nodded. "He did, though. He was there, in the hotel room. It's in the police report. You can see it for yourself. He was *there.* He's lying to you, Nick." She turned to him. "Still want to get him out?" Then she stepped out into the rain and started up the hill without looking back.

The storm went on all afternoon, trapping them indoors, and Nick retreated into a kind of hangover wariness, afraid that the smallest gesture might give him away while he waited for his head to clear. Around him they busied themselves with the usual motion of a rainy day. A fuss was made about their wet clothes, exchanged for dry upstairs, Anna's old slacks and sweater hanging loosely on Molly, a child playing dress-up, his father's fitting him comfortably, uncannily like his own. He watched his father make a fire in the wood stove, poking at the kindling, and then they were in their usual cabin places, his father in his rocker, sitting opposite, Molly curled up in the corner of the couch with a mug of tea. Nick looked at the coffee table, half expecting to see the Sunday paper folded open to the puzzle, a pencil lying across the filled-in blocks. What did they used to do? Play Hearts. Read. Now they talked, not free to withdraw, moving words like pieces in a board game to fill the time.

Molly avoided him, chatting lazily with Anna, afraid to meet his eyes. What police report? But the presence of the others, the makeshift family, made it impossible to talk about anything he wanted to know. They picked at conversation, strained, like old army friends who think they want to see each other but have only the past in common. What they should see in Prague. What it was like last August when the tanks rolled in, everyone's trace memory.

The almost comic surprise of the Soviet soldiers, expecting to be welcomed, dodging stones. Finally Anna got up to start dinner, leaving an empty moment of silence.

"Where did you go that night?" Nick said suddenly. "The night you left?"

His father looked at him, surprised by the shift. "That night?" He sat back, as if he needed to refresh his memory. "To Canada. There was a ship. I went to Detroit. It's easy to cross there. We had to go all the way to Philadelphia to catch the plane, in case I was recognized at National. So unnecessary. That long drive—it took hours, I remember, because of the snow. The roads were still slippery. There had been a lot of snow."

"Yes," Nick said, remembering footprints.

"Hours. We almost missed the plane. I remember I was dying for a cigarette. I'd forgotten my lighter, and the driver didn't have any matches. Can you imagine, a Russian who didn't smoke? Finally I made him stop at a gas station outside Baltimore. He went in—he wouldn't let me. I'd be recognized. By someone pumping gas in Baltimore." He shook his head. "It never changes."

Nick could feel Molly stir beside him on the couch, sitting erect, watching his father.

"I mean in Washington. Where did you go in Washington?"

"In Washington," his father said, puzzled. "New York Avenue, I suppose. We took the Baltimore Pike. He picked me up out back and we took the

294

pike, so it must have been New York. Does it matter?"

"You didn't stop anywhere?"

"No," he said easily, "of course not. We were in a hurry. He knew the roads would be bad. We could have had an accident, the way he drove. How different everything would have been. But he didn't—we made it. Does it matter to you?" he said again. "All these details?"

"Yes."

But his father eluded him, lost now in other details, telling stories beside the fire.

"I remember the ship. My bunk, anyway. I couldn't go on deck. The crew wasn't supposed to know I was there. They locked me in. Nothing to read. No air. A cell. I never knew what they were carrying. Grain? Pig iron, maybe. Who knows?"

Nick leaned back, listening.

"Then I got seasick, so they let me out, for the air. It was freezing. You had to hang on to something or the wind would knock you over. But at least it was outside. The crew pretended I wasn't there—it was dangerous to ask questions in those days. I don't know who they thought I was. I ate by myself. The captain had a little English, but nobody else. I don't think I said ten words the whole trip." He paused. "I had a lot of time to think."

"About what?"

"You. Your mother. What would happen. I still thought I could work things out, that you'd join me. I suppose I thought it would be like Yalta, not so bad. Pleasant. When it got calmer, not so rough, I began to enjoy it a little. Something new. The way you feel on any trip. I'd never been on the ocean before. At night the sky—" He broke off. "Anyway, none of that happened. It was just the first cell. But I didn't know that then."

"They put you in a cell?"

He smiled faintly. "House arrest. First for the debriefing, then for my protection. It was worse than the ship in a way, that town. I could walk around, like on a deck, but the air wasn't as good. And of course now I wasn't going anywhere. I was already there."

"Why did they wait so long before they let you appear?"

"The news conference? It was like the ship. They didn't know what to do with me. Nobody knew what Stalin wanted. He never trusted foreign operatives, never. To him they were something from the old Trotsky days—internationalists. Real Communists were Russian. He was a peasant. People thought he was some kind of statesman because they saw his pictures at the conferences, but he had a local mind. A little like Welles, in fact," he said, smiling slightly, amused at the comparison. "Never trust a foreigner. And I think he liked the game. Let the Americans wonder—was I there, was I dead? Why give anything away if it might come in handy later? He could afford to wait. I wasn't going anywhere. If he hadn't died—" His father paused. "But that changed everything. Now they wanted to show us off. Me. The English. They wanted you to think spies were everywhere. And of course it worked. How many of us were there? Three? Four? Not so many. And Welles had everybody looking under beds. But the only one he ever found got away. At least I had that satisfaction."

"He found two," Molly said.

Nick's father looked at her, as if noticing her for the first time. "Yes, two," he said quietly, and nodded.

"And she got away too," Molly said. "Just in time."

Nick felt it, the edgy disturbance in the air, but his father seemed not to notice.

"I saw the paper on the ship. The captain got it before we left Canada, to give me something to read. I don't think he had any idea who she was, why I kept looking at it."

"So you had that satisfaction too."

This time his father caught it, unmistakable, a piece being moved into place. He looked at her for a second, unsure why he was being attacked, and his voice, when he answered, was patient, calming a willful child. "No. I never wanted that. Never. Is that what you think?"

"None of it would have happened," she said evenly, "if she hadn't started it." Another piece.

"She didn't start it. Welles did. Do you think I blamed her?"

"Didn't you?"

"No." He paused. "At first, yes, of course. But I never wanted her dead."

"Somebody did," Molly said.

297

In the silence, Nick saw his father hold her eyes, debating.

"Yes," he said finally. "Somebody did."

The answer rattled her. Not an admission. An invitation to join sides, in the open.

"But not you," she pressed.

"Why would I?" his father said calmly. "By that time it didn't matter what she said. I was gone. Why would I want such a thing? A terrible death like that."

"But so convenient."

"Not for me," he said, checking her.

"For everyone," Molly said. "No more names. It must have been a relief. For everyone, I guess, except Welles. She was his only witness. Not so convenient for him."

He stared at her, waiting, then moved. "Unless she was going to change her testimony."

His voice, so reasonable, stopped her. She looked at him, surprised, as if he had turned the board around. "Why would she do that?"

"It's possible. It would have been the easiest thing to do. It's what I would have advised, if I'd been handling it," his father said, a lawyer walking her through it. "She thought she'd recognized me, but now she wasn't sure. It might have been somebody else. She couldn't swear under oath. She wouldn't want to do that, make a mistake. She'd been so nervous when they first talked to her—" He broke off, looking at Molly, who had sat back, letting him lead. "She was young, you know, younger than you are now. They were already worried about her. Communists weren't supposed to be young and pretty, not real ones. She was just an impressionable girl—they took advantage of people like that. She didn't know what she was doing, and when the committee first talked to her, she panicked. But now—Anyway, she could have done it. Of course, he'd still have her, but what was that worth? You didn't get elected by locking up salesgirls, not when you promised a conspiracy. If he could lock her up. He knew about her, but how much? Enough to convict? I'm not sure. She might have walked away. And that would have ruined everything, made him look—unreliable. No conspiracy. So maybe it *was* convenient for him. With her gone, the smear would stand—I'd always be guilty, at least in the press, which is what mattered. The court of public opinion, always his favorite. You don't have to prove anything there. You can build a career on it. But then I got away, so he ended up with nothing." He glanced pointedly at Molly. "That was the only satisfaction."

Molly said nothing, turning it over, and Nick saw that his father had shifted things again, that the story, just the possibility of it, was a kind of reproach.

"Of course, we'll never know what she intended to do," his father said.

Molly looked at him steadily, still examining the brief. "But why do that—to save you?"

"No. Herself."

"Then why go to Welles in the first place? She was his witness."

He looked at her curiously. "But she didn't go to him. He went to her. She wasn't an informer, you know. Did you think that?" he said, then shook his head. "She wasn't the type. It was Welles. He hounded her until he got a name."

"Yours."

"Yes, mine. One. If she'd been a friendly witness, she'd have told him everything she knew. Why volunteer if you weren't going to talk? Look at Bentley, or—who was the other one? Coplon. They couldn't stop. She never wanted any of it—you could see it in her face. She was afraid of him. She made a bargain, and then she saw it wasn't a bargain. He'd never let her alone. With that press? She was all he had. He had to keep squeezing. Once he knew about her—"

"How did he, if she didn't tell him?" Nick asked.

His father nodded as if they'd finally arrived. "Well, that's the great question. How did they know about anything? Hearing after hearing. Where did it all come from?"

"If you throw enough mud, some of it sticks," Molly said.

"But how do you know where to throw? Where did Welles get his information?" He turned to Nick. "What does Wiseman say?"

"FBI files, usually."

"Yes, usually. Hoover. Our own Dzerzhinsky. Helpful to a fault. As long as someone else took the credit. Which of course they were eager to do. Welles, the great inquisitor. Or McCarthy, when he was sober. Where would either of them have been without those files? There was plenty of mud there to go around."

"And Hoover supplied it," Molly said skeptically.

"I said usually. There were other sources. Subscriber lists, donations. Sometimes they got lucky—the mud would stick. But the Bureau was the best. It was all there. It's not easy to set up a police state. Which is what they were trying to do. It takes time. Files. Secretaries. Field agents. Legmen," he said, glancing at Nick. "A whole organization. I know a little about this—it's the one thing the comrades are good at. The committees didn't have those resources. Who were they? Lawyers, football players." Another glance at Nick. "Politicians, not detectives. You have to remember the scope of all this. The hearings were only a part of it. Most of the time HUAC was operating as a personnel agency, giving information to employers. A vetting service to make sure you had the right people. God knows how many they ran checks on."

"About sixty thousand," Nick said. "Roughly."

"Roughly," his father repeated, taking it in. He looked at Nick. "I see. Wiseman. Think what it means, the work involved. And that was just HUAC, not the Senate committees, the state committees. All of them looking for information so they could run their own circus. People didn't ask where it came from. Maybe they thought Welles dug it up all by himself. But where else? Only the FBI had that much. Those were Hoover's committees. McCarthy's especially, but Welles's too. Hoover fed them, and then, when it suited him, he cut them off. The trouble was, they didn't know what to do with the stuff. McCarthy, for god's sake. Welles, always shooting from the hip and never hitting anything. Disappointing, the horses Edgar picked." He paused. "But it came from him."

"How?" Molly said, fascinated now.

"The usual ways. Hoover had to be careful. The leaks were illegal, for one thing, a small point. But there was his reputation—not a small point. He couldn't be seen to be leaking information. Sometimes the field offices would help the local police. Then they could pass it off as *their* detective work. Sometimes a journalist would be tipped, one of the friendly ones. With the committees it was usually more direct—that was helping the government, after all. But in this case I think it might have come directly from him—he was close to Welles and this was sensitive, the sort of thing he liked to handle himself. He might not have wanted anyone else to know, even in the Bureau."

"But does it matter? The fact is, they *did* know about her."

"But how? Did you ever wonder why it started with her? That's always been the strangest part of the whole business. She was the last person in the chain who'd be under suspicion. She wasn't in the government. No access. No history. You didn't have to pass a security check to work at Garfinkel's. Why investigate her? She should have been at the *end* of the trail, the small fry you round up with the others. But there weren't any others. They never connected her to anybody except me. So what led them to her? How did they know to go after her?"

Molly said nothing, so Nick's father answered for her.

"Somebody told them. That's how it all started, all of it. That's what I thought about on the ship," he said, looking at her. Then he sighed, finished. "I still think about it."

Dinner was roast pork and dumplings, whose lightness Anna demonstrated by slicing them with a string stretched taut between her forefingers, Czech style, but which then sunk back heavily in the thick gravy. Molly picked at her food, quiet and withdrawn, no longer interested in playing cat and mouse with his father. Instead she talked to Anna, complimenting her on the elaborate table setting, old china swirling with painted flowers spread across a stiff white tablecloth embroidered with gold thread.

"It's all I kept from the house in Bubeneč. My mother had three closets just for the linens. And dishes—she prided herself on her china. All the women did. Of course, they had maids. So different then. You know, I never cared about these things when I was a girl. It was just the way we lived. Now it seems so beautiful—it reminds me, I suppose. Of that life. We had a large house, a villa. A music room, even. A greenhouse in the back—

we always had flowers. But that was before the war."

"Is the house still there?"

"Oh yes. But my father was killed, so we had to leave. The Germans took it. My mother lost every-thing—all those closets. But she kept these."

They were still talking about the world before Munich, all parties and piano lessons, when they heard the car in the driveway. The rain had gone, leaving only the sound of water dripping off leaves, and in the quiet the engine seemed a roar, sput-tering, then stopping, unmistakably there to stay. Anna raised her eyes, her fork stalled in midair, and Nick saw that she was looking at him in alarm. He would have to be explained. The day, so placid and ordinary, had become a guilty secret. Even here, safe in the country, she was always expecting a knock on the door.

His father, seeing Nick's face, smiled. "Don't worry, Beria's dead." He got up and went over to the window, peering through the curtain. "Fran-tišek," he said. Then, to Nick, "A friend. It's all right."

"What does he want?" Anna said, still uneasy.

"A drink. What else?" his father said lightly, opening the door.

But František had already had one. He was a bear of a man, tall and bearded, and when he en-tered the cottage, stooping to get through the door, his eyes had the wild, shiny look of drink. He stopped for a minute, weaving slightly, disoriented by the unexpected strangers and the formal table, then spoke to Nick's father in rapid Czech. Without language, Nick watched them as a silent movie, forced to follow the story through gestures. He didn't mean to break up the party. No, no, it was all right, come sit. Was something wrong? More Czech. Anna's hand flew to her mouth in dismay, like Lillian Gish. No, his father said, then more Czech, placing his hand on František's shoulder. At this, the tall man leaned into him, a sentimental embrace. Anna got up, then went over and led him to her chair, as if he were too upset to find it by himself. He looked at Nick and Molly and Nick saw his father introduce them. "Friends from America," he said in English, at once a courtesy and a signal to Nick. The man nodded, too preoccupied to be curious, and the Czech began again, a volley of questions, Anna shaking her head. His father slumped into his chair, placing his hand on František's. Anna brought out a bottle, some kind of brandy, and put it before him with a glass. Then, noticing Nick and Molly, she said, "I'm sorry. His brother has died."

"No telephone," the man said to them in accented English, waving his hand to take in the cottage, apparently apologizing for having come.

Nick's father poured him a glass, then some for himself.

"A suicide," he explained to Nick, but the man understood the word and covered his forehead with his hand, and Nick saw his eyes moisten. When he spoke, in Czech, his voice was deliberate, almost without inflection, so that again only the gestures meant anything.

Molly got up and began to clear, motioning to Anna to sit down, and Nick, excluded from the low murmur of Czech, retreated into the solemn politeness of funerals, his eyes fixed on the emptying, the painted china removed piece by piece until there was nothing between them but white cloth and the amber bottle. The drink made František moody, and finally silent, until he sat staring at the table too.

"I'll make some coffee," Anna said.

František answered, but Nick's father said to him, "In English," nodding toward Nick.

"English, yes. Excuse me. You don't speak Czech?"

Nick shook his head.

"It's better, Czech, for bad news. Very expressive. The Eskimos have the words for ice. But we—" He poured two more glasses. "What do you say, Valter? We have the words for bad news, yes?" A look of disgust. He took a drink.

His father turned to Nick. "His brother was a writer."

"A writer. Under Dubček, a writer. Then, poof, a tram driver, for Husák."

"He was fired from the Writers' Union," his father explained, "so he had to work on the trams. That's the kind of job they give you. An embarrassment, so people see."

"They make you eat their shit," František said. "To fill your mouth. No more words." He glanced at

306

his glass. "Then you're quiet. So there is his brotherhood of Slavs. You remember that? He believed in that. We're Slavs. They're Slavs. Who else is there, the Germans? Now look at him."

"A writers' movement," his father said to Nick, a text gloss.

"You like Prague?" František said suddenly. The opening, hopeless question.

"It's beautiful," Nick said, the expected answer.

"Yes, beautiful. For tourists. The Germans used to come. Not so many now."

But what was he supposed to answer? That it was sad and dingy? That the crabbed, suspicious life inside the lovely architecture depressed him? A judgment no guest was allowed to make.

"America." František took another drink and looked up at Nick. "You were in Vietnam?"

"Yes," Nick said, embarrassed, expecting the usual arguments, the usual averted eyes, silent accusations. Aren't you ashamed? Yes.

"Good," František said, slamming down the glass. "Kill the bastards. All the Communists."

Nick said nothing, too surprised to answer. Was that really how they saw the war here, a world away from America, turned now on itself? Maybe their suffering had brought them, finally, a simple myopia. There were no other politics but theirs.

"Franku, please," Anna said anxiously, putting down a coffee cup. "Here, drink."

But he had already turned from Nick, back in his grief. "They took Miloš's book," he said to Nick's father. "The notes, everything. Do you know what they said? It must have affected his mind. Now he's a suicide too. Just like Masaryk. The pigs. That's what they said to me."

"There must be a copy," his father said.

"How? Something like that."

"On film," his father said simply. "It's easy to hide on film."

Nick looked at him, curious, but his father misinterpreted his interest.

"He was writing a book on Jan Masaryk," he explained. "His death. It's still a controversy here, how he died."

"Yes, Masaryk," František said. "You know about Masaryk in America?"

"Yes," Nick said, to be polite, but in fact who did anymore? A forgotten name. Twenty years ago, a famous leap from the Czernin Palace that was the end of the republic. A national hero's funeral. Pictures in *Life.* In the West, a murder no one could prove and everyone forgot. But here, evidently, still an open wound, a reminder of the world before, like Anna's china.

"He couldn't hide the book," František said. "Everyone knew what he was doing. Last year, when they opened the case, even the police wanted to help him. Everyone wanted the truth about Masaryk. Last year. Now they won't even let you go to Lány. No flowers."

"His grave," his father said to Nick. "The family grave. Not far from Lidice. We're a country of symbols here. It's a way to talk to each other. Last year people started taking flowers there. A shrine. Now

308

that would be an embarrassment to the government, too Czech, so they put an end to it."

"People remember," František said vaguely, his words a little slurred.

"What did he mean, when they opened the case? Who's they?"

"The government—the old government, Dubček. One of the first things he did was order an investigation into Masaryk's death. It's time to know the truth, he said. Of course, the Russians weren't pleased. They knew what it meant. Another symbol, you see."

"It's twenty years ago."

His father looked at him. "Yes. But a crime like that—to know the truth can be a political act."

Nick looked back, reading the code. "Here," he said.

"Like Masaryk," František said again, lost now in drink.

"Is that how he did it?" Molly stood behind him, a dishtowel in her hand. "Like Masaryk? Out the window?"

"No, pills," his father said, then to František, "He felt no pain. You just go to sleep. It's the best way."

František nodded. "The best way."

"Such talk," Anna said.

Nick looked at his father. Had he ever thought about it? Those years now were a story, a walk around the boat deck, but what had they really been like? Bad enough to wonder? A glass of water before bedtime. You just go to sleep.

"Masaryk said the window was the housemaid's way out," his father said. "A servant's death."

"Hah. That's good, the housemaid's," František said. "Those fools. Did they think we would believe it? That he'd go like that?" He took another drink. "He thought he could work with them. Like Milos."

"Our clothes must be dry," Molly said, excusing herself.

The two men kept staring at their glasses. Nick listened to the sound of Molly on the stairs, Anna rattling the dishes in the sink. "Ach," František said finally, out of words, tired of it all. He poured again from the bottle, clearly determined to pass out. Now Nick could hear the clock. Neither of them seemed to notice when he got up and left the room.

Upstairs, a low room under the pitched roof, Molly was brushing her hair, already changed. Finally alone.

"We should go," she said casually, nodding toward his clothes. "He's here for the night."

"Look at me. What's going on?"

"Nothing." A sharp tug of the brush. "Everything's lovely. A perfect weekend."

"Stop it," he said angrily, then lowered his voice. "Why are you hounding him? What police report?"

She glanced at him, then picked up her bag. "Not now. Let's just go," she said softly. "I'll help Anna finish up."

Nick sat on the bed for a minute, frustrated, looking around the room. A heavy crocheted bedspread, like a giant doily. A few books. He picked up the picture frame on the night table. His father and Anna, younger, smiling shyly. He still had all his hair. They were dressed for snow, bundled up, standing in an empty city square. Moscow? He wondered what the occasion was, who had taken the picture, then put it back. Their life—still a blank to him.

When he went back down, František was laid out on the couch, not yet really sleeping but no longer there. His father was covering him with a blanket. "You're leaving?" he said, seeing the changed clothes. "So soon."

"We have to get back."

"No, no, he'll sleep now. One more drink."

He moved unsteadily, a little tipsy. Nick glanced toward the kitchen, where the women were working, then shrugged and joined him at the table.

"No more," Anna said from the sink.

His father winked and poured out a glass. When had the drinking started?

"Na zdravi," he said, raising the glass slightly, and Nick drank, trying not to cough as the rough liquid hit his throat.

His father said nothing, just looked at him, his eyes gentle, a little clouded. Then he reached over and patted Nick's hand, his touch as hot as the drink. "I knew you would come," he said, his voice low.

Nick nodded. A few hours ago he'd wanted to walk away, right through the woods, but he saw in the face, so like his own, that he could never do it.

Upstairs, a stranger in a picture, and now, suddenly, a touch he'd known all his life.

"You see what it's like here."

His color had begun to drain, a sickly pale. What would he become, another František, sleeping it off on the couch?

"What I see is that you've had too much," Anna said, coming over with some water and his pills. She put a hand to his forehead, shiny now with sweat. "How do you feel?"

His father placed the pills in his mouth, the movement deliberate and slow. "Perhaps a little tired," he said quietly.

"It's late," Nick said, standing, eager now to get away. "You should get some rest. I'll help you upstairs." Anna moved toward him. "No, I'll take him."

"I'm all right." His father waved his hand, a mild protest, but allowed himself to be lifted up and led by the elbow across the room.

Nick followed him up the stairs, then turned down the bed as his father began to undress. His body was bony, frail, and Nick looked away.

"You see what it's like," his father said again. "I can't stay here."

Nick faced him. "It may not be possible. You know that, don't you?"

But his father grabbed his arm, clutching him. "No. It is. You think I don't know what they want? I know. Something valuable. I can pay."

Nick looked at him, dismayed. There was no

talking to him. "Okay. But now let's get some sleep," he said, like a nurse.

"We'll meet tomorrow—I'll come back early. The Národní Gallery." He began to cough. "Go around noon," he gasped, trying to hold down another cough, so that it came out a desperate wheeze.

He took off his shorts and moved to the bed naked, his thin legs and ropy behind as white and vulnerable as a child's. Nick turned away, hanging things in the wardrobe to avoid the sight of his body, and when he finally looked back his father was under the covers, his eyes closed, his hands folded over his chest. In that instant, Nick saw him as he would be, lying in a coffin, and his own breath went out of him, an unexpected panic. He stood holding the hanger, utterly alone in the room, as if he'd been abandoned. It was only when he saw the blanket stir, a faint rise, that he could move to the bed and lean over to arrange the covers.

His father opened his eyes and smiled. "Nicku," he whispered. He reached up to smooth Nick's hair back from his forehead, the old gesture. "Now you tuck me in."

Nick nodded, feeling his father's hand slip back.

"Are you all right now?" he said.

His father smiled, closing his eyes. "As snug as a bug in a rug."

CHAPTER TEN

The drive back was long, slowed by patches of low-lying fog and wet mist that condensed on the windshield, forcing him to lean forward to make out the road. Occasionally tiny lights appeared in the darkness, like fireflies coming out of the woods, then joined the halting stream of cars inching toward Prague. He hadn't expected traffic. In town, the streets had been almost empty, conduits for trams, but here in the country he saw that the cars had only been in hiding, parked in secret pockets of free weekend air.

Molly was restless, fiddling with the heater, then turning the radio knob to scratchy bursts of Czech that faded in and out until, fed up, she snapped it off and stared out the window. He could feel her next to him, bottled up, wanting to talk but not knowing how to start. He fixed his eyes on the road, where there were only red taillights, not old men with stories, a frail arm reaching up to him from the bed. Now she was rummaging through her bag, pulling things out as she dug deeper, crinkling paper, then finally extracting a thin, misshapen cigarette.

"Don't say a word," she said, lighting it. "Just don't."

She drew on it deeply, and the smell of dope filled the car.

"I thought you left that in Austria."

"I lied." She rolled down the window, letting the smell escape into the air, shivering a little at the sudden chill. "Don't worry. I just kept one. For a rainy day."

He glanced in the rearview mirror, half expecting to see police lights, but there was only the dark. He rolled down his window a little, creating a draft.

"What report?" he said finally.

She sighed. "The D.C. police report, from the night she died. I asked to see it."

Nick looked at her. "Just a reporter doing her job," he said, still angry. "Is that the story you're writing? You want to make him a killer too? Great."

"He did kill her," she said quickly, then looked away, her voice apologetic now. "I'm not writing anything. I just said that."

"Then why—"

She took another drag, stalling, then exhaled slowly. "Okay. She was my aunt. Rosemary Cochrane. My mother's sister. That's how I knew who he was. You're not the only one who—" She stopped, looking over at him. "I know. I should have told you. I was going to. And then, things changed, and I thought, let it go. What's the good? She's dead. Why upset everything? Let him take it with him. And all the time here he is, packing his bags."

Nick said nothing, too stunned to reply.

"I'm not writing anything," she said again. "It was personal, that's all." For a minute there was no sound but the swish of the tires. Then she reached over and handed him the joint, a peace offering.

"Want a hit?" she said, and suddenly he did, a piece of the world they'd left at the border. He extended his right hand, eyes still on the road, and felt her place the joint in the *V* of his fingers. He drew on it, aware of the quick glare at the tip, then held the smoke in his lungs. They passed it back and forth, still not saying anything, until he felt it grow hot in his fingers.

"Keep it," he said. "I'm driving." He saw her place the end between the tips of her fingers and finish it with sharp intakes of breath.

"There. Clean," she said, flicking it out the window.

"Feel better?"

"No. But I will," she said. "Give it a few minutes."

But he could feel it already, moving through him with his blood, relaxing and buoyant at the same time. He eased into it, letting his mind drift with the mist on the road.

"God," Molly said, leaning back in her seat, "that dinner."

He said nothing, listening to another conversation inside his head.

"It's interesting, the way he does it," she said slowly.

"Does what?"

"Tells the story. It's all there, isn't it? All the way to Canada. Everything but the first stop."

Nick let a minute pass, watching the road.

"Were you close?"

"No, I never knew her. I mean, I must have known her, but I don't remember. We never talked about it. You know, the one unforgivable sin."

"But what was she like?"

"Well, let's see. Also born in Bronxville. She wanted to be a singer."

"Really? An opera singer?"

"A band singer. You know, nightclubs and things. She had this picture—one of those professional pictures they put in delis? 'Best wishes to Mel.' Like that. She's got this big smile and a flower in her hair. All *set,* you know? I never heard that she actually sang anywhere, though. She probably just did it to freak out my grandparents. Nightclubs. I *mean.*"

"Pretty radical."

"It was, in a way. She was always doing that. Of course, it wasn't hard with them. My grandfather got on a train in the morning and walked through the door at six-twenty every day of his life. They wanted her to go to Manhattanville—where else?—and when she went to NYU there was this big fight, and the next thing you know she's waiting tables for money and—do you really want to hear this?"

Nick nodded.

"Of course, I got most of this from my grandmother, so consider the source. She *still* blamed

317

NYU, right to the end. All those 'undesirable influences'—that was the phrase. Anyway, there was Aunt Rosemary, waiting tables and being influenced. Funny, isn't it? In a way my grandmother was right. I mean, that must have been when she—became political."

"Became a Communist, you mean," Nick said, saying it.

"If she was. An actual Communist, in the party. They never said that." She stopped. "Talk about splitting hairs."

"Then what happened?"

"Then she dropped out of school and went to Washington. She was a secretary for a while, I think. During the war. And then—well, the rest you know."

"Except we don't."

"No," she said thoughtfully. "I used to think about it, the way kids do. We had this box in the attic, you know, with the Mel picture in it, and I'd go through it, making up stories about her. Then I put the picture up in my room and my mother had a fit. I suppose she thought I'd turn out the same way."

"What, a Communist?"

"No, man-crazy. She always thought that was the start of all the trouble."

"What made her think that?"

"Oh, there's always a man." She waved her hand. "She had to tell herself something. The more she didn't talk about what happened, the more it was there. You know when she told me? When they sent the suitcase back. The one she had in the hotel. I guess the police took it as evidence and then, months later, out of the blue, they delivered it and my mother had to explain it to me. She just sat there crying, and I guess that must have upset me, her crying, because that's when she told me."

"What was in it?"

"Nothing. You know, just overnight stuff—cosmetics, a nightgown. Nothing. It was the fact of it. And because they'd torn it all up. The lining was sliced—I guess they were looking for secret messages or something—and they never even apologized. She just sat on the couch with this beat-up bag and that was her sister, what was left of her, and—"

A nightgown, Nick thought. Planning to spend the night. A bag packed to meet someone.

"Anyway, that was Rosemary," Molly said. "Public Enemy. Part of the Communist conspiracy. Remember that, in school? I thought they were talking about *her.* And I used to think, I know one but you don't have to worry about her. She turned herself in."

"Except she didn't."

"According to him."

"But why would she?" Nick said, brooding. "The others who talked, they were all tied up in the politics of it. You know, you lose one faith and you replace it with the opposite. And then the opposite has to destroy the first. They really *did* believe a conspiracy was threatening the country, because they used to believe in it themselves. So in some crazy way it was their duty to expose it, now that they were on the other side. But that doesn't sound like her at all. Not from your description. How many nightclub singers have a problem with apostasy?"

She looked at him, the helpless beginning of a smile. "You know, I've never heard that word used before. In speech. Only in print. Is that how it's pronounced?"

"You don't want to talk about this."

She shrugged. "I don't know what to say. Maybe she had political convictions, I don't know. What are they, anyway? What would you do to stop the war? Besides rallies and things. Suppose there was a way. What would you do? Name names? Maybe it wouldn't seem like much if you really thought they were the enemy. Maybe you're right—maybe she didn't care about any of that. I don't know. Maybe she just wanted a little attention. Anyway, she got it." She paused. "While he was on his way to Canada."

"You still think he's lying."

She said nothing, as if she had to think about it, then sat up and reached for a cigarette. "Yes." He watched her light it, her movements stretched in time by the dope. "Now I know it."

"How?"

"Remember that drive in the snow? All the little details. How he was dying for a smoke but he left his lighter behind?"

"So?"

"So they found it in the hotel room. *That's* where he left it—it's in the report. He still doesn't know. I was watching. He probably still thinks he left it at home." She turned to him. "He was there, Nick."

"How do they know it was his?"

"They didn't use these," she said, indicating the disposable plastic lighter in her hand. "They had real lighters. With initials. W.K."

"And O.K.," he said softly.

She looked at him, puzzled.

"My mother. It was from her. She was always giving him stuff like that." He stared at the road. "That still doesn't mean he was there."

"Have it your way. How else would it get there?"

"Somebody could have planted it."

"Do you really think that's likely?" she said quietly.

"No." He remembered it in his father's hand, shiny, always with him, like the wave in his hair.

"He was there," she said, an end to it.

"That still doesn't mean he killed her. I don't believe it."

"You mean you don't want to."

"Do you?"

"Want to? No. But that doesn't change things." She paused, biting her lip in thought. "I'll give you this, though. I sat there and I thought, could he really do that? It doesn't feel right."

"How is it supposed to feel?"

"I don't know. Threatening. But he's not."

"No."

"Whatever that's worth. Maybe that's how they get away with it. They stop believing it themselves. So there's nothing to pick up on."

"Killer vibes."

"I know, it sounds stupid. But there should be *something.* A little radar blip, you know? A little ping."

"A little ping."

She looked at him, then tossed her cigarette out the window and slumped down in her seat, burrowing in. "You're right. It's stupid. I mean, he was there. We know that. It's just—"

"What?"

She shook her head. "Her lover. I can't see them together."

Nick was quiet, following his own thought, a blip across the screen.

"They weren't together," he said finally, sure. "He was devoted to my mother."

"Yeah. So was mine. Every time he came back. Anyway, I don't mean him. I mean her. He wasn't her type. Not—I don't know—flashy enough."

Nick thought of him changing upstairs, the pale, slack skin. "No, he's not flashy."

"Still. People change."

"No, they don't."

By the time they got to town they were alone again; the other cars had melted away into the dark edges of the city as mysteriously as they had come. The streets were deserted, wet cobblestones cut by the bumpy tram rails, whose metal caught their headlights and gleamed back at them through the mist. Dim pools of yellow light from the streetlamps. It was, finally, the Prague of his imagination, Kafka's maze of alleys and looming towers, spires poking suddenly through the fog. They drove along the river, Hradčany somewhere off to the right, then turned into streets where nothing was visible beyond the reach of the car's lights and, still lulled by the dope, Nick felt that he had begun driving through his own mind, one confusing turn after another, going in circles. How could anyone live here? When they reached Wenceslas, the empty, lighted tram that appeared clanging in front of them seemed to come out of a dream.

The *párky* stalls were closed but the Alcron was still awake, the doorman leaping from the bright door as if he'd been waiting for them. The lobby was empty. Nick saw the bellhop and desk clerk glance up. The drug was wearing off, leaving only a pleasant tiredness and now the familiar sensation that everyone was watching them. For an instant he stopped, then smiled to himself. They *were* being watched; it was what people did here. Did they notice he was walking slowly? Then the bellhop yawned, and he saw that his cover would be exhaustion. It was only eleven, but everyone seemed ready for bed.

"A long day, Pan Warren," the clerk said, handing him the key. "Not so nice for Karlovy Vary, the weather."

Was he checking up or only being polite?

"You took the waters?"

323

Nick looked at him blankly, but Molly said, "Why do the glasses have those pipestems?"

"Pipestems? Ah, like a *pipe,* yes. To drink in. For the minerals, you see. To get past the teeth. Otherwise they would stain."

"Ah," Molly said. "Well, goodnight."

The desk clerk smiled and bowed at them, satisfied.

"That was good," Nick said as they crossed to the elevator.

"It's the only thing I remembered about the place, those funny little glasses. Thank god. Now he can put it in his report. Our day at Karlsbad."

Nick stopped. "But it wouldn't be true. I mean, just because something's in a report. There it is in black and white, but we were never there."

Molly looked at him for an instant, then lowered her eyes. "But the lighter was."

"How can we be sure?"

"Ask him."

Their room was stifling, the heavy drapes drawn tight, and while Molly ran her bath, he opened the windows, then lay on the bed in his underwear, feeling the cool night air move over him. His body was tired but alert, and when he closed his eyes he could hear the sounds around him with a sharp clarity: water splashing in the tub; the bells of the late trams below, carried in by the mist, disconnected, like the sounds of ships at night. He went over the day, putting it in order, as if the chronology would tell him something. In the report. What if all of it was true? None of it? Why would he lie? Or was it the usual mix, the half-truths of things left out or just forgotten? But which? Then he was in the cottage bedroom, his arm gripped, caught. Snug as a bug.

There was a shaft of light from the bathroom when she opened the door, and he squinted at her, wrapped in her thin robe, toweling her hair. Her movements were languid, almost swaying.

"Are you asleep?"

"Thinking."

"About what?" she said idly, moving toward the window. When he didn't answer, she said, "Okay. A penny? A Czech crown?"

"About what it's like for you. When you see him. I mean, if you really think he—" He trailed off, not able to say it.

"What's it like for you?"

"I don't see what you see." He paused. "I can't leave him like this. Whatever he's done. I thought I could, but I can't. But that's me. You don't have to go on with this. Not anymore."

She stopped, still holding the towel to her hair. "You want me to leave?"

"Don't you? You must hate him. All of it. I didn't know. Why keep it a secret? No wonder you didn't want to—"

She looked at him. "Is that what you think?"

"You can see what it's going to be like. You'll just get more involved. With someone you think—"

She stared at him for a second. "You're a real jerk sometimes, you know?" she said softly. He looked up at her. "I'm not involved with him. I'm involved with you."

A beat. "Are you?"

He watched her drop the towel, then heard the faint rustling silk of her robe as she came toward the bed. She ran her hand along his bare leg, stopping at the knee. "Don't think so much, okay?" she said, moving it up to his thigh, stroking. "Why don't we finish what we started. Before you started thinking." She looked toward the stirring in his briefs and smiled.

"What are you doing?" he said, unable to move, paralyzed by the hand making slow circles on his thigh.

"I'm seducing you, before you throw me out." She leaned close to him and shook her head slowly. "No more secrets okay?"

He closed his eyes as her fingers moved across his pouch, lightly grazing his balls, to the inside of his other thigh. Then both hands were stroking him, moving up along his waist. She took the elastic band of the shorts and with elaborate slowness started pulling them down. "Want to help?" He raised himself slightly from the bed, a reflex, and felt the shorts slipping out from under him, his erection springing free. "Look at you," she said, then ran her fingertips under his scrotum. He could feel the delicate scraping, then his penis swelling harder as her fingers moved up along the shaft, wrapped around the base in a slow pumping motion. "Still want me to go?" she said, gripping it

326

gently, so that the tip seemed to get even harder, full to bursting.

"Not with that in your hand."

She moved up onto the bed, straddling him, then leaned over, and her robe opened, filling the air with the smell of soap and bath oil. He reached up to touch her breasts, warm and smooth, and then her open mouth covered his and he could feel her hair around him, still damp from the bath, as if they were back in the rain. She drew a breath, kissing him lightly, and he moved his hands behind her, rubbing the silk, then pulling it up in folds until he could feel bare flesh. She arched back, resting on his hands, and drew the robe off, tossing it on the floor, her breasts swaying heavily as she moved.

"Molly—"

"Sshh." She put a finger to her lips, then pointed it up at the ceiling corners. She leaned down and whispered, "Big brother, remember?"

To his surprise, he felt himself grow harder, an unexpected erotic kink. He could hear their breathing, the faint ringing of the trams outside, and he imagined someone cupping headphones, straining, aroused. Then she bent down to kiss him and he lost the room again, moving his hands over her skin, wanting to touch her everywhere. Still on her knees, she lowered her pelvis to him and he felt the scratch of her hair along his prick. It brushed over him slowly, back and forth, wiry and delicate, until every part of him was waiting for it, sensitive, so that he thought he might come just from the touch of the hair. Then, a little lower, he felt the wetness start beneath the hairs, the moist skin moving over him, slippery as quicksilver, until his penis was slick with it, ready to explode before he'd even entered her. Too soon.

He rolled over, pinning her under him. Her eyes caught the faint light, shining, and when he looked into them they stopped for a minute, no longer playful, and grew wider, as if her whole body were opening up. "Just us," she whispered, grave and trembling, then took his head in her hands, drawing him down. He kissed her, then moved his lips down along her throat to her breasts, sucking them gently, making it last, feeling the nipples grow hard in his mouth before continuing down, wanting all of her, his feet sliding off the bed as his head went lower, along her belly. When he heard her gasp in anticipation, the sound itself was exciting. Make noise. Drown out the trams, the static in the headphones, everything.

He was there. He kissed her inner thighs gently, barely touching the skin, moving steadily toward the crease between her legs, then rubbed his face lightly across the hair, breathing her in. She shivered, a kind of physical noise, then moaned out loud when he started licking the edges of her crotch, long upward strokes, wetting the hair. His tongue moved toward the top of her slit, teasing it; then, using his hands to part the outer lips, he touched her clitoris with the tip, a series of light flicks, until he felt her move under him, drawing him closer. He lowered his head and placed his tongue between her lips, parting them with one long stroke, then back again, resting for a second at the top, then back, until they were both moving in a rhythm, her body rising to meet him, moving against him. Her cunt was wet now, as wet as his mouth, and he licked deeper, sucking, rolling her clitoris between his lips, then burying his face in her as she seemed to stretch wider, no longer secret, the wonderful pink skin all open to him.

When he stopped, then began the slow long strokes of a new cycle, she moaned again and grasped his head, trying to stop him and move with him at the same time. "Soft," she whispered, but when he licked more lightly, a wet kiss, she didn't want that either and pulled him harder into her until he was buried again and her body squirmed around him. Her breathing had become a kind of ragged pant and he felt she was close now and moved up again, covering the top of her slit and tonguing it from below, a constant stroke. "Come with me," she said out loud, gasping. "Come with me." But when he moved up onto the bed and slid into her, his mouth still wet with her, he could feel her walls clutching him, a tremor, and before he could move she was already there, coming around him with a cry, her body heaving.

He lay still for a second, feeling her, the moist inside now just part of his own body, permanently attached, then slowly began to move, drawing himself almost to the edge of her lips before sliding in again. Her vagina, already sensitive, continued to ripple against him, like aftershocks, urging him, and he began to go faster, adjusting his rhythm to her. She gasped out loud, a gift to the micro-phones, and he could hear the squeak of the bed-springs now, drowned out when his head had been down inside her, and their breathing, even louder, keeping pace, their strokes audible, a slapping of wet skin, the room alive with noise, as if the sounds themselves were racing, about to come. She clutched him and he felt her spasm again but now he couldn't stop, thrusting on top of her orgasm, trying to keep it alive so that when finally he spurted into her they were both shuddering.

Afterward they lay curled up, quiet, his prick soft against her bottom, his arm flung over her, protect-ing her from the night air that crept along their bod-ies, drying the sweat. Neither of them moved, and he lay surprised by the stillness, wondering what had happened. There was none of the odd embar-rassment he usually felt after sex, the impulse to cover himself, find his clothes and go. Now there was only an easy familiarity, as if they had finally run out of secrets and could lie here naked forever, everything known, an old couple. She turned and traced a finger along his face, reading it like Braille, wiping the wet from his mouth. "Look at you," she said softly.

He reached over and brushed the hair back from her face, smoothing it, taking her in. "I like your freckles," he said lazily.

"I used to have more."

"You did?"

"Uh-huh. You lose them as you get older. Like hair," she said, touching his bare temple.

"Careful."

She smiled, her eyes catching the dim light. "I was right, wasn't I?" She kissed him lightly, then snuggled closer. She reached down to pull up the covers, but he stopped her.

"No, I want to look at you."

"Then close the window. I'm getting goose-bumps."

"Where?" he said, running his hand along her hip. But he got up and went over to the window, closing the pane but keeping the curtains open to the streetlight.

"I love the way it jiggles," she said from the bed, looking at him. "How does it feel when it bobs around like that?"

"Little," he said. He stood by the bed for a moment, his eyes moving along her body.

"Oh," she said, turning away slightly from his gaze. "Don't. I feel so—exposed."

No secrets. He bent over and kissed her breasts, feeling her shiver when he opened his mouth on her.

She was already dressed, putting on lipstick at the mirror. He felt the air on his behind, jutting out of the tangled sheets, and covered himself.

"Well, it's alive," she said.

"What time is it?" He glanced at the bedside clock. "Christ."

"Sleep well?" she said. "It must have been

the—" She raised her eyes to the ceiling, then put two fingers to her mouth, pretending to draw in smoke. "You know what."

"Oh, that's what it was."

"What else?" She came over to the bed and sat on the edge, touching his chest. "Morning skin. Like a baby's."

He took her wrist, drawing her to him, but she shook her head. "You'll muss. Anyway, I'm off."

"Where?"

"See the sights. He wanted to meet you alone, didn't he? Národní Gallery. Better get cracking."

He got up, holding the sheet. "You always this cheerful? Where is it, anyway?"

"By the castle. Take a number 22 tram. You can't miss it. God, look at the bed. What will the maid think?"

He grinned.

She picked up her raincoat, then stopped. "Nick?"

He looked up, waiting, but she shook her head.

"Never mind." Then, hesitantly, "It's going to be all right, isn't it?"

He nodded, still smiling as she closed the door.

In the lobby, he wondered if everyone could tell, read his mood, like a permanent flush on his skin. His face felt loose, ready to break into a loopy grin, but he came down outside, deflated by another dreary Prague sky. The rain had left the city damp and grimy, as if nothing could wash away its essential grayness. For the first time, the thought of seeing his father depressed him.

On the tram, bottle blondes and grim faces; no one talked. Had this conductor been someone else once? They creaked through the old streets, the passengers' heads nodding with stolid patience, dazed with routine. No one had spent the night in someone else's body, alive with sex. When they crossed the river, even the Baroque stucco of the Malá Strana, pale yellow in the sun that first day, had turned dark, a dirty mustard.

The gallery seemed to be arranged chronologically, so that the rooms began in the Middle Ages, static allegories with pudgy Slavic babies and soldiers holding lances and spiked shields, Christ rising from his coffin, his feet still dripping blood from the crucifixion nails. Artists painted what they saw; here they'd seen atrocities, a culture of occupation.

He looked around for his father, but the rooms were empty. A guard, bored, stared at his feet. Nick thought he should wait near the entrance, but the room was oppressive and he moved along to the next—Italian, flesh pink with light, bowls of fruit. What would he say today? Another theory of history?

Nick found him in the room beyond, staring at a picture. He smiled when he saw Nick and lifted his hand to touch him, then withdrew it. They stood there awkwardly, a chance meeting in public. Nick glanced at the painting.

"The fatted calf," his father said, following his eyes. "A lot to expect, don't you think? After all that."

"The prodigal," Nick said automatically.

"You see how happy everyone is? Even the jealous brother." His father smiled shyly. "Maybe that's why we have stories. So things come out better." He paused. "It means wasteful, you know, not wandering. He wasted his inheritance, his gifts. Well." He turned to Nick. "So you got back all right? Anna was worried. We don't have much time," he said, looking at his watch. "I'm sorry. There's a service for František's brother. I have to go. It would be noticed."

"Do you want me to come?"

"A tourist? That wouldn't be appropriate," he said gently. "They'll all be there, watching. To write about Masaryk after all these years—everything about him is still political. Even a funeral."

"Then why go? Won't you be—"

"I have to go, for František. He and Anna were children together. If we don't go, it's political. It would mean that we knew what he was doing. Not just writing stories."

"I thought everyone knew. He said—"

His father nodded. "Now we pretend we didn't. Welcome to Oz. Walk with me to the Loreto. It's worth seeing—all the tourists go. The service isn't far from there. It'll give us a few minutes."

Nick followed him out of the room, then past the walls of impaled martyrs. "But we have to talk."

"We will. Later."

They were out on the cobblestoned square.

"Don't worry. I'll tell you exactly what to say."

334

He reached into his breast pocket and drew out an envelope.

"I can't carry anything out," Nick said, flustered, physically drawing away from it.

His father looked at him, then smiled, holding out the envelope. "No. These are tickets, for tonight."

"Oh."

"Benny Goodman. They're hard to get. Everyone wants to see Benny. Nothing changes, you see."

Nick said nothing, feeling teased. An evening out.

"I didn't know he was still alive," he said finally. They were crossing the square toward the Czernin Palace. There were no cars.

"Oh yes. He's very popular here—we're a little behind. His goodwill tour. You'll enjoy it. We can eat afterward."

Nick stopped, annoyed. "Look, I need to talk to you."

"I know," his father said, putting a hand on his arm. "You're worried. There's no need. You'll see." He continued walking. "This is where Masaryk was killed, by the way." He indicated the high palace walls. "In the interior courtyard."

"They found the lighter," Nick said suddenly.

"What lighter?" his father said, still walking.

"Yours. The one Mom gave you."

Now he stopped, his face bewildered. "What are you talking about?"

"They found it in the hotel room. That night. It's in the police report."

His father frowned, as if he'd misunderstood,

335

then looked away, thinking to himself. Nick watched him as he stared at the ground, apparently at a loss. Was he thinking of what to say?

"That's interesting," he said finally, but not to Nick, working instead on some interior puzzle.

"Is that all you can say?" Nick said, thrown by his response.

"But how is that possible?" his father said, again to himself.

"That's what I'm asking you."

"A police report? But it's a mistake. The FBI handled the case, not the police." He paused, still thinking. "Of course they would have been called first. At the hotel. But the FBI took it over. It was a Bureau case always. There's nothing like that in their file."

"How do you know?"

His father looked up at him. "Because I've seen it. Don't you think I would have remembered that? Why would they leave it out?" He shook his head. "It's a mistake."

"No," Nick said. But what made him so sure? "It's in the police report. Don't you understand what I'm saying? You can't go back. They know."

"Know what?" He looked at him again. "Oh, I see. I left it there. After I—" He paused, a new idea. "Is that what you think?"

"You tell me."

"Nick, how could I have left it? I already told you—"

"You don't tell me anything. Except what you want me to hear."

"I'll tell you again," his father said quietly. "I wasn't there."

"Then how do you explain this?"

"I can't." He looked down. "I don't know what it means. I have to think."

"Let me know what you come up with. But maybe you should think twice about traveling. *They* think you were there. The statute of limitations doesn't run out on this."

His father touched Nick's elbow. "You know who was there. We'll find him. Trust me." The cord again, pulled tighter.

"No questions asked," Nick said. "I'm not supposed to know what's going on. You said last night you had something valuable. What? Or am I not supposed to know that either?"

"It would be better."

"No. I need to know what you're doing. What I'm doing. You need to trust me. I'm not just a messenger."

"No," his father said. "You're the key to everything."

Nick stared at him.

"Listen to me, Nick. They're not going to accuse me of anything. Not some old crime." He glanced up. "Which I didn't commit. They're going to ask for me."

"They're what?"

"How else do you think this can work? A rescue mission to smuggle me out? I'm not worth an international incident. The Americans would never do that. It has to be a trade, a quiet trade. I can't escape—think what that would mean for Anna. I have to go legally. A plane from Ruzyné. With the comrades waving."

"What's the trade?"

"They can offer Pentiakowsky, a prize catch. For one broken-down defector. Do you think Moscow would resist such a deal?"

"Why would they do that?" Nick said, trying to follow the thread. "Why would they ask for you in the first place?"

"Because you asked. You and your mother. A humanitarian request. You came to see me—I know, all this secrecy, but that's only for now, until we're ready. Once the arrangements start, it's in their interest to protect me. They'll have to know you were here so the story makes sense. There's always the personal element, even in politics. You were shocked by what you saw. My health. I need an operation. That's true, by the way, I do. They know that. I can't get it here. So the trip would have a certain appeal, even to a dedicated old socialist. How we cling to life. So you appealed to your father, the other one. A man close to the president."

"What?"

"Yes, to Larry. No one else. He can make the deal, arrange things. I'll tell you what to say."

The surprise of it made Nick feel giddy, as if a missed step were pitching him farther down. "Larry," he said, trying to catch himself. "Why Larry?"

"Because he can do it. Arrange things. And he'll believe you. He'll know it's not a trick."

"No," Nick said quickly, not wanting to hear the rest. "You don't know what you're asking. He can't." Isn't it enough to involve me? He saw the mad plan spreading like a stain, touching everybody.

"I know what I'm asking. Do you think I would ask him if I didn't have to? He took my family." An edge, finally, in his calm voice, a bitterness not quite put away. "But now that's an advantage. He owes me this much. One favor. He'll do it." He paused. "He'll do it for you."

And I'll do it for you. A link snapping shut in a chain. Every link already assigned.

"It's the right story," his father continued, not seeing Nick's face fall. "Pentiakowsky for an old spy? Never. But I'm not just an old spy. I have friends in high places." He stopped. "A son in high places. Lucky for me, but even luckier for Moscow. To get Pentiakowsky back for a political favor? A stupid trade—but Americans can be stupid that way. Sentimental." He looked at Nick. "They'll believe you. Not just a messenger, you see. There is no story without you."

Nick looked at the ground, feeling his chest tighten, his breath grow short. "You have it all worked out," he said, thinking, all of us, he'll use all of us. "What makes you think Larry will do it?"

"He wouldn't. He's not sentimental. Or his boss. It's only the story, Nick. For Moscow. The truth is that I have to give them something."

"Something valuable."

His father nodded. "More valuable than Pentiakowsky. Then they'll do it. It's the only way."

"Then why would Moscow let you go?"

"They don't know I have it. They'll be suspicious—that's their nature—but they won't know. There's no trace—I've been careful. No one knows. Only you."

"Not yet."

"No, not yet."

Nick waited, his silence an unspoken demand. His father looked back toward the open square, then wet his lips, an old man's nervous gesture.

"I'm going to give them what they always wanted. Names. In America. I have a list. And documents." He saw the dismay in Nick's face. "I have to pay, Nick. You don't get a fatted calf, not in real life. What else do I have?"

"And what happens to them, the people on your list?"

His father shrugged. "They'll be replaced. Then it begins all over again. But meanwhile—"

"You get Silver," Nick finished.

His father shook his head. "Not yet. But they can lead me to him. One of them. There's a pattern, you see. People don't change. There's always a pattern if you can find it."

"And you did."

"I think so." His father looked at him carefully, then said, "You disapprove."

"They're your people."

"My people," he said, almost scornfully. "Yes. Agents expect it, you know, sooner or later. Somebody always gives it away. What do you want me to say, Nick? That it's not a dirty business?" He looked away. "It never seems so in the beginning. You just think you're doing the right thing, like a soldier. But in the end—"

His voice drifted and Nick followed it down the gray street, unable to look at him.

"So you do want me to take something," he said quietly. "The documents."

"No, of course not. I would never put you at risk. I told you that. Anyway, they're a passport for me. I take them."

"Then how will Larry know that all this is for real?"

His father looked at him curiously, as if Nick hadn't been listening. "Because it's you. He'll believe you."

Nick's chest, already tight, seemed to clench further. Not just a messenger.

"You see how important—that no one know. Just the fact of it, that such a list exists, is dangerous for me." His father paused. "Now you."

"Are you trying to frighten me?"

"No, protect you. I'll tell you what to say when you leave, not before. Just in case. Who Larry should contact. No one else, just the principals. He must understand this. Everyone talks. On both sides. But if we move quickly—"

"Before your names can run for cover, you mean," Nick said. "Your chips."

"No," he said, cut by the edge in Nick's voice.

"Before the leaks. There are always leaks. Before *he* knows. I wouldn't be safe here."

"You won't be safe there either. They'll know it was you."

"That depends. Sometimes it's better to let people stay in place for a while."

"To watch them."

His father nodded. "Or turn them. It's been known to happen."

"Come play on our side," Nick said evenly. "Your choice."

"Nick—"

"Do you know them, the people you're going to sell?"

"No."

"That must make it easier."

"Yes, it does." He looked at Nick steadily. "Your scruples are misplaced," he said, his voice cool, a kind of reprimand. Then, backing down, "Nick, it's the only way." He turned, wanting to bring it to an end. "Walk with me. I'll be late."

Nick stared at his back, the familiar hunch of his shoulders, then took a step, pulled along.

"And what if they don't leave them in place? Then what happens?"

"What you'd expect. The usual scurrying."

"I mean, what happens to you? Your life wouldn't be worth—"

"Like the old Comintern days? Send someone out to deal with me? Not anymore. I'll be all right, once I'm there."

"And if you're wrong?"

He smiled a little. "Never bet against yourself, Nick." Nick glanced up, recognizing it, his old rule of thumb, when they played cards at the cabin. "That sort of thing's a little old-fashioned, even for the comrades. I'll be all right, if we move quickly."

"How quickly? Larry's in Paris. You know, at the peace talks. He won't be able to just drop everything."

"To negotiate for me? Yes, he will. Nobody wants peace. But they'll want this."

I don't want it, Nick thought, so clearly that for a second it seemed he'd said it out loud. But his father's face, eager, full of plans, registered nothing, and Nick looked away before it could show on his own, the one betrayal his father did not expect. And was it true? Maybe it would be different later, when it was over. Maybe it was this he didn't want, the plotting and covered tracks, looking over his shoulder, the tired city, gray, expecting the worst.

"Then why wait?" he said suddenly, an escape hatch. "I could go this afternoon."

"This afternoon?" His father turned to him. "So soon."

"What's the difference? Nobody knows I'm here anyway."

"But they will later. They'll check. Visa dates. The hotel. It has to look right. It wouldn't make sense, your coming for a day. That's not a visit." He stopped. "Besides, I don't want you to leave."

"But the sooner we—"

"Just in case."

"In case what?"

"In case."

"Don't bet against yourself," Nick said.

"No. But sometimes—" He paused again. "In case it goes wrong," he finished. "At least we have this time." He put his hand on Nick's shoulder. "It's not so long for a visit. I'll show you things." A weekend parent, offering treats.

Nick nodded, embarrassed. How could he go?

But before he could say anything else, make an excuse that would play, he saw his father look past him. He withdrew his hand, alert.

"Valter, jak se máte?"

Nick turned.

"Anna," his father said, but it was another Anna, broader and short, slightly out of breath from climbing the hill. She said something in Czech, but his father answered in English, "No, we have ten minutes. I'll walk with you. An American," he said, nodding toward Nick, an explanation for the English. "I was showing him the way to the Loreto."

"Dobre odpoledne," Nick said, offering his hand. "Nick Warren."

"How do you do? Anna Masaryk."

"Masaryk?"

"My uncle," she said automatically, smiling a little at his surprise.

For a second he was jarred, as if she had stepped out of history, straight from the death scene in the Czernin courtyard over the wall. But she was no older than his father, someone you could meet in the street.

"You heard they took Miloš's book?" she said to

344

his father. "Now it begins all over again. How many years this time? All that work."

"Maybe he kept a copy."

"What difference? They'll never allow it now. They don't want us to know."

"You know," his father said, consoling.

"Me? I always knew. But to prove it—they'll never allow it. They're afraid of the truth." She caught Nick's glance and said, "Excuse me. You're visiting Prague?" Then Nick saw her look quickly at his father and back again, as if there were something she didn't understand. Had she noticed the resemblance?

"He's just been to the Národní Gallery," his father said before he could answer. "Now the Loreto." A tourist.

"Ah, yes. There's a very good Goya. I hope you saw it."

Nick nodded, hoping he wouldn't have to describe it. What Goya? Were they going to talk about art?

"Of course, the best are in the Prado. But this is very good. It's lucky that we have one."

"Perhaps one day you'll see the others," Nick said. "In Madrid."

The woman looked at him wryly. "I doubt it. It's not allowed, to go there."

"Oh," Nick said, stumbling. "Well, perhaps when things are looser again."

"It was never allowed. Not since '37."

"Czechoslovakia doesn't recognize Spain," his

father said, helping. "It's still considered a Fascist state."

"Oh," said Nick, feeling awkward. Another wrong turning in the maze. The old categories, still current, like Masaryk's death. Everything was yesterday here. No one had moved on. "I'm sorry."

"So am I," Anna said. "For the Goyas. You're staying in Prague long?"

"No, only a few days."

"Perhaps you would come to tea. If you have time."

A casual invitation, to a stranger in the street?

"Yes, if I can," Nick said vaguely, ducking it.

"Valter, you bring him. I never see you anymore. We'll have a salon." Was she trying to find out if they knew each other? "It's good to speak English," she said to Nick. "You can tell me about the new books. I like to keep up, but it's so difficult now. Well, we'll be late. Tomorrow then, if you can. Valentinská Street. It's in the book. But of course Valter knows." She took his father's arm.

"Goodbye," his father said, shaking Nick's hand, acquaintances. "I hope you enjoy the Loreto."

Nick looked at him, waiting for some sign, but his father avoided eye contact and moved off with her, an old couple on their way to a funeral. They reached the corner, and then his father stopped and walked back.

"I told her I forgot to ask your hotel," he said quickly. "There's something—the police report. How did you see it?"

Well, how? "A friend got it for me," Nick said.

His father nodded to himself, thinking. "Was it a copy? You know, a carbon?"

"I don't remember. Why?"

"They turned everything over to the Bureau. But if they kept a copy, that would explain it. Why they have it."

"Does it matter? It's there."

"But not in the Bureau file. It doesn't make sense." He shook his head. "If they found the lighter, what happened to it? It would have been evidence, something like that. So why didn't they use it?"

"You were gone." Nick looked at him. "Maybe they will."

"They still have it?"

Did they? "I don't know. All I know is they found it. Or said they did."

"In the hotel room," his father said to himself. "My lighter."

"Yes. The one with your initials."

"But how did it get there?" he said, frustrated, like someone searching for his glasses.

"Well, that's the question."

"Yes," his father said slowly, preoccupied again. "If I could remember—" His eyes narrowed in concentration, lost in his puzzle.

Over his shoulder, Nick saw Anna Masaryk still waiting on the corner. "I'm staying at the Alcron," he said.

His father glanced up, then nodded and turned without a word, the way old people hang up the phone without saying goodbye, their part of the conversation finished. Nick watched him go, his head bent in thought, until Anna called something to hurry him and he was back in his Czech life, offering her his arm, almost courtly. Then they turned the corner and Nick was alone.

Now what? Unexpectedly, he had the afternoon. But he didn't want to see anything. Not the Loreto and its famous chimes. He wanted it to be over. He stared down the empty street.

When he heard the footsteps behind him, he froze. Had someone been watching? The steps grew nearer, then passed—a man in a long winter coat, glancing at Nick out of the corner of his eye. He stopped a little farther along and turned, and Nick waited for him to speak, but instead he whistled, and then Nick felt the dog sniffing at his feet. The man said something, presumably apologizing for the dog, then called and began to walk again, looking back once over his shoulder, suspicious. Nick smiled to himself, relieved. What if everything were just as it seemed? A man with a dog. A friendly invitation to tea. Maybe she did like to talk about books, ordinary after all, just a dumpy woman with a magical name. Maybe they were all what they seemed here. Except his father.

He turned down the hill, toward the Malá Strana, replaying the conversation in his head. Easier not to know them. Was he any different? He remembered them shooting blindly into the jungle, everyone in his platoon, ten minutes of random fire. And then the odd stillness afterward, no sound at all, his ears still ringing. You couldn't trust yourself there either, all of your senses on alert. A twig snapping was enough to set them off. They were lucky that day, no snipers when they located the bodies. One had been shot in the face, his jaw blown open, hanging slack with blood and pieces of bone, and Nick had stared at him, wondering if he had done it. There was supposed to be a connection, the thud of your bullet hitting a body, maybe a scream, but he hadn't heard anything over the noise of the fire. Some actually claimed victims, like pilots after a dogfight, but they were lying. No one knew. It was easier. Later, in his safe job at the base, he walked around the airstrip with a clipboard, taking inventory on the shipments, and he would see the body bags lined up for the flight home, plastic, like garbage bags, held together with tape. He checked his list, then handed in the manifest and went for a beer. That easy, if you didn't know them.

He stopped for a minute on the street near some scaffolding where workmen were replastering an old melon-colored façade, and he realized he was sweating. When you started thinking about it, all of it came back, even the heat.

He followed the streets downhill, zigzagging as if he were shaking off a tail, a real spy game, so that when he reached the river he saw that he had overshot the Charles Bridge. It was warmer near the water, the trees in late bloom, and he stood for a few minutes looking at the city, couples huddled on benches, trams, everything ordinary. He started walking downstream toward the next bridge. Could a voice be the same if it lied? What did you trust, a muddled story full of loose ends, or an old man's hand, the same touch, unmistakable. He stopped to light a cigarette, leaning against a tree. It was when he looked up, blowing smoke, that he saw her on the bridge.

She was standing with a man, talking down at the water, and Nick, startled, moved further behind the tree. Who did she know here? His anger surprised him, a jealousy that went through him like a quick flash of light. Jiří, whom she wasn't going to see again. When had she arranged it? This morning while he was still asleep, drunk with sex? Nick leaned forward to see what he looked like. But he was ordinary too, his body hidden in a raincoat, his face down, a head full of brown hair. Anybody. But they'd been to bed, making private sounds, holding each other afterward. Until he'd moved on, feckless. Why see him again?

Now they seemed to be arguing, Molly shaking her head. He put his hand on her and she brushed it away. He took her by the arms, turning her toward him, saying something, but she broke away, stepping backward, and Nick realized suddenly that he had got it wrong. Not a meeting she'd wanted. She shook her head again, and Nick could imagine her refusal. No. There's someone else. He felt a flush, possessive. There *was* someone else now. Was she as surprised as he had been? Maybe she was tying up her own loose ends, sure now that it had happened. The one thing you could trust. Eyes deceived, not bodies. When he had been inside her, he had felt it, a different touch, just as unmistakable.

Jiří was talking again, and Nick saw her nodding, not looking at him. Then he leaned over and kissed her on the cheek, a goodbye, and this time she didn't resist it, letting his mouth stay next to her until he was finished and turned away. Nick saw him reach the end of the bridge and dodge across the street, not even a wave back, and felt in spite of himself a last prick of jealousy. Just an old boyfriend, but still a part of her he would never know.

He had moved away from the tree, but she continued staring at the river, absorbed, and even when she looked up her eyes went past him, not seeing what she didn't expect. Was she thinking about what to say to him later? I saw Jiří. He imagined her voice, breezy and matter-of-fact. I mean, I was *curious*. Wouldn't you be? But he's just the same. Her face, however, was somber, not jaunty at all, and in a minute she looked at her watch and walked away. Should he follow her? There was still the afternoon. But by the time he reached the bridge she was already gone, getting on a tram, her secret safe.

She was gone for hours. He lay on the bed waiting, listening to the maids pushing their carts in the hall, gossiping in Czech.

"You're back," she said when she opened the door, surprised. "What happened?"

"He had to go to a funeral."

"Oh. I wish I'd known," she said easily. "We could have spent the day together."

He looked at her. She wasn't going to say a word. Why not? "Where did you go?"

"The usual. Old Town Square, the clocktower." Not a word. She held up a Tuzex bag. "Shopping. I got something for your father. Rémy, no less. Not cheap, either, even with dollars."

"That's the last thing he needs."

"I know, but it's what he'll want."

"That was nice."

"We didn't take anything yesterday. You know, for a house present. So I figured—" She smiled at him. "I'm a well-brought-up girl."

"You could have fooled me."

She grinned. "Yeah. Well."

"So you've been busy."

"A little bee. What about you? Have you been here all day?"

"No. I took a walk. Down by the river."

He watched, expecting to see her hesitate, but she was fishing for something in her bag. Not a flicker. "Look what else I got." She held up tickets. "Laterna Magika. The hit of the Czech pavilion."

"The Czech what?"

"You know, at Expo, in Montreal. Don't be dense. Everybody's heard of them. We can't go without seeing Laterna Magika."

"Yes, we can."

"No, really, they're good. I promise you. Don't you like mimes?"

"I didn't mean that." He reached into his shirt pocket for the other tickets. "Benny Goodman. My father got them."

"You're kidding."

"He's very big here. So I'm told."

She sat next to him on the bed, taking the tickets. "What time? Maybe we can go after. Anna looks like the early-to-bed type." She slipped the tickets onto the bed. "Okay, no Magic Lantern. He's full of little surprises, isn't he?"

"All the time."

"What happened today?"

"Nothing. That was the surprise. We didn't even get to talk."

"So do you want to go out? Do something?"

"No."

"Nothing?" She leaned over him. "We have the afternoon."

"Let me think about it."

"I only do it once, you know."

"What?"

"Seduce you. After that you have to ask."

He looked at her. What had she really said on the bridge?

"So ask," she said, bending to him.

When he reached up to her he was sure again, the feel of her skin as familiar now as his own.

CHAPTER ELEVEN

It was late when they woke up, the bed tangled again from lovemaking, and they had to hurry to dress. The concert hall was nearby, in the New Town, and it seemed his father was right—the bright doorways were crammed with people, a mix of middle-aged suits and young people in jeans. Everybody loved Benny. Prague, usually so reserved, almost sullen, had turned noisy and eager. Inside, people shouted to each other over the crush, passing beers along from the lobby bar, and Nick wondered if the high spirits themselves were a kind of defiance, if simply listening to American jazz, even thirty-year-old jazz, had become a political act. But the mood, whatever its source, was contagious, and for the first time he began to look forward to the evening, ready for a good time.

His father and Anna were already in their seats, looking slightly frumpy in the younger crowd. Why such a public meeting, where everyone could see? Or was this part of the plan too, something that could be verified later? Anna was friendly, pleased to see them, but his father seemed preoccupied, as if he already regretted having come, bothered by the noise. When the lights blinked on and off, no one paid any attention, still talking in the aisles. Then the curtains opened on the band playing "Let's Dance" and there was a roar of recognition applause and a scrambling for seats. An emcee appeared at the mike, speaking Czech, then Benny in English saying how happy he was to be here, then the opening notes of "Don't Be That Way," more applause, and the evening, in this unlikely place, began to swing.

The music was wonderful. It was the standard program—next the "King Porter Stomp"—but the audience made it seem fresh, their enthusiasm flowing up to the band with such force that Nick saw some of the sidemen grin, bending into their instruments to send it back. "You Turned the Tables on Me," with its funny, innocent lyrics. How many of them knew what the words meant? But the music, just as they always said, was its own language, and the audience was answering it, some actually tapping their feet, squirming in their seats to the beat. Nick thought they might leap up to dance, and he saw that in the back of the hall, where the bar was, some of them had. Upstairs in the ring of boxes there were men in bulky suits, party bureaucrats, their wives fat and shining with costume jewelry, but the crowd on the floor ignored them. There were no uniforms anywhere. Just the music, an official time-out. "Elmer's Tune," where the gander meandered. American music, the happiness of it, as much a part of him as childhood stories. He smiled at Molly, who was drumming her fingers.

When Goodman started the clarinet lick of "When It's Sleepy Time Down South," the notes jetting out like liquid, he turned to his father. Nick expected to see his face soft with nostalgia, but it was cramped, white, and he realized that his father hadn't been preoccupied but worried. Even the music couldn't reach him, wherever he was. Nick looked at him for a second, wondering what was wrong, then made himself turn back. Don't ruin it. He'd find out later. Now they were here, not in some troubled past, not even anymore in Prague.

There was an intermission after "Avalon" and he went with Molly to the bar, his father staying behind, sitting it out. The lobby was filled with smoke and spilled beer, and the crowd was even more energetic than before, loud with drink. It took a while to get the beers, then a few more minutes to find Molly. She was standing near the door, her back to him, talking to someone. For a moment Nick hesitated. Jiří again? Then she moved slightly and he saw that it was Marty Bielak. Why not? It was his music too.

"Hello," Bielak said. "Enjoying it?"

I was, Nick wanted to say, but just nodded, handing Molly her glass.

"Of course, I remember the Meadowbrook," Bielak said. "Before your time. Helen Ward was the vocalist then. And the Long Island Casino. That was something."

Nick tried to imagine him young, skinny, with a date by the bandstand, raring to go.

"The good old days," Nick said.

Bielak glanced at him. "Well, the music was good. Maybe not the days." And then, wanting to be pleasant, "It was another time. Everybody danced. It was always dance music, you know. Not for sitting. To think I'd be here in a concert hall—"

"In Prague," Nick finished.

"Yes, in Prague. But the music doesn't change."

The lights flashed, the signal to return.

"Well, it's good you could come," Bielak said. "A taste of home, eh?"

Did he really think this is what they still danced to? An exile's memory, stopped in time. Nick saw his father suddenly, walking down streets he thought he knew, amazed at buildings that shouldn't be there.

"They seem to like it," Nick said, nodding to the crowd.

"What's not to like? Well, it's that time." He tossed back his drink.

He seemed to be waiting for them, but when Nick said, "We'll just finish these," he nodded and said, "Enjoy. I'd better get back upstairs. I don't want to miss anything."

"You're in a box?" Nick said involuntarily. With the party men. A bird's-eye view, to look over the crowd.

Bielak smiled weakly. "No, higher. The cheap seats." He moved toward the stairs.

"C'mon," Molly said, "they're starting."

"No. I don't want him to see us." A legman. "Wait a minute."

The crowd had started yelling and clapping, and

Nick heard the opening drums of "Sing, Sing, Sing."

"What's the matter?"

"Don't you think it's funny, his running into us like that?"

"Maybe. Anyway, he has seen us, so what's the difference? Come on."

But he held back. Were their seats visible from the balcony? "Not yet. Give it a minute."

"Okay. So what's our cover?" she said mischievously. "Want to dance? Can you?"

"Can you?"

"In this crowd?" She laughed, and Nick took in the couples around them, exuberant but awkward, as if they had picked up the steps from old movies.

"Chicken," she said, leaning into him. On the stage, the brass section stood up, horns blaring, infectious.

"Say that again."

"Chicken," she said, putting her hand in his to start the movement. And then suddenly he didn't care who was there and he swung her out and they were dancing, his arm reaching over to turn her around, then lead her back, laughing at the surprise in her face. How many years had it been? You'll never know when it will come in handy, his mother had said. Mrs. Pritchard's class, an agony on Tuesday nights. The girls tall, in flats to mitigate their growth spurts, the boys resentful, shirts never quite tucked in. When am I ever going to have to know the rumba? On boats, darling, she'd said. They dance on boats. And the lindy, another gen-

358

eration's dance, learned step by step but now, like riding a bicycle, all familiar and fluid, so that he could do it fast, Molly trying to follow, arm over, then back, finally come in handy, here of all places.

He felt the heat in his face when the drum solo began, but Molly was smiling at him, excited, and they kept up with each other now, the pleasure of the movement like a kind of foreplay that made everything else disappear. He noticed vaguely that people had made space around them, watching and stamping their feet, but he kept his eyes fixed on her. The song started its false diminuendo, everything running down and building at the same time, and they danced close, keeping pace, waiting for the break. Sweating. "Wow," she said, laughing, panting a little. "No, you," he said, meaning it, because he didn't dance, not like this. Then it came, the sudden loud blast of the finale, irresistible, and they were dancing wildly, grasping hands to hold on, their circle of movement spinning wider to fit the music, until the dramatic up-tempo crash, the real climax, and they hung on to each other, winded, while the entire hall shook with applause. Goodman's crowd-pleaser, the same frenzy.

The applause was for the band, not for them, but he heard it like an alarm clock, bringing him back. They were supposed to be inconspicuous, not drawing a crowd. He dragged Molly outside the circle of people and stood for a minute against the wall, catching his breath.

"Who would have thought?" she said, smiling,

hanging on to him. She reached up and wiped his temple, smoothing back the damp hair.

"We'd better get back," he said, but when he looked up he saw that his father had come to find them and was standing there watching. He felt embarrassed, as if they'd been caught necking. Molly followed his gaze and turned.

"Did you see?" she said to his father, still smiling.

"A killer-diller," his father said wryly. "We were wondering what had happened to you."

"My fault," Molly said lightly. "I couldn't resist."

His father looked around. "How about a cigarette?" he said. Then, to Molly, "Tell Anna we'll be right there."

Molly looked surprised at her dismissal, but he took Nick's arm before either of them could say anything and led him out the door. Nick felt the night air on his sweat and shivered.

"Outside?"

"Yes," his father said, still leading him.

"Sorry. We shouldn't have done that."

His father waved it aside, a matter of no importance. "Here," he said, lighting him a cigarette. "Listen to me, Nick. Carefully, please. We don't have much time."

Nick leaned against the building, still sweating, and took a gulp of air. Now what?

"We have to make a change."

"What's wrong?" he said, alert now.

His father shook his head. "Just listen. I need you to do something for me. Tomorrow morning go

360

to the train station and buy a ticket for Vienna—
you'll need your passport. The Berlin train at eight-
ten. You shouldn't have any trouble. An American.
Even at the last minute."

"What are you talking about?"

He put his hand up. "Just listen. If it comes up,
which it shouldn't, you had a quarrel with Molly—
these things happen. Take a bag with you, what
you'd take if you were leaving. After you buy the
ticket, go to the men's room, the one near the platform. First stall on the right as you enter. You leave
the ticket there—an accident, but you don't realize
it. You don't miss it until the train is about to leave,
so you retrace your steps, but you can't find it. Too
late. You don't report it. But missing the train—
maybe it's a sign you should make up. So you go
back to the hotel. You do make up—no need to
take the train after all. But leave that afternoon.
Drive to Vienna. Don't stay in Prague any longer."
He paused, as if he'd forgotten a detail in the rush.
"Don't talk to anybody at the station. That's important. You don't see me, not even if we're alone
there. Do you understand?"

Nick stared at him, trying to catch up. Was he
crazy? "You can't do this."

"Do you understand?" he repeated.

"You can't just get on a train."

"Yes. It's the ticket that's difficult. A Czech
would get it early, with the visa. No one goes to
Vienna at the last minute. But for you it's easy."

"No one goes to Vienna at all."

"Russian Jews," his father said. "They have exit

visas. This is the train that connects to Vienna. It's how they leave. Don't worry, I have papers."

"Yours?"

"Someone's. They won't bother me. Once I have the ticket I'm all right."

"No risk at all."

His father looked up at him but didn't answer. "When you get to Vienna, stay at the Imperial. I'll contact you. And don't tell anyone you're there— anyone."

Nick dropped his cigarette and took him by the arms. "What's going on? You can't do this," he said again. "What if it doesn't work?"

"It has to. It's not what I planned, Nick. But now we do it this way."

"But why? This morning—"

When his father didn't answer, it occurred to Nick, a chill like the night air, that it had always been the plan—not the elaborate exchange but an escape, clandestine like the rest of his life, drawing Nick in deeper, one story into another, until he was on a train platform buying a ticket, an accomplice. No risk at all, unless he was caught.

"What about your list?" he said. "Your documents?" Had he made that up too?

"There isn't time now. But they're also here," he said, tapping his head. "It should be enough."

If they exist at all, Nick thought. Now there were other papers, good enough to use on a train, insurance policies. How long had he had them?

But when he looked into his father's face, he saw that the smooth confidence of the morning was gone. Now there was the worry he'd noticed earlier, something hasty and makeshift. A new plan, while Nick had gone dancing.

"What's happened? Are you in some kind of danger?"

His father shook his head. "Not yet. I just have to do it differently."

"Not like this. Let me go to Paris and—"

"No," he said abruptly. "Go to Vienna. It's important, Nick, please. Do this one thing for me. There's no danger to you. A lost ticket—you can't be blamed for that."

"I wasn't thinking about me."

"No," his father said, his eyes softening, as if he'd received an unexpected compliment. "So you understand?"

"How long do I wait in Vienna? If you don't show up?"

"In that case you won't have to wait at all," he said, almost wry again. "But let's hope for the best. It's simple, Nick. Just keep your head. We'll be all right." He paused and looked around. "Well. We can't stay here. You don't want to be seen with me. Tell Anna to come out. Say I'm not feeling well."

Nick raised his head to speak, but his father's eyes were steady, pragmatic. There was nothing more to be said. Nick looked away. "I'll get them."

"Just Anna. You stay here." A little smile. "Have another dance."

When Nick moved from the wall, his father stopped him. "Nick?" he said, his voice anxious, then reached for him, a bear hug, no longer caring

363

if anyone could see. The platform goodbye they weren't supposed to have. He held Nick for a minute—the same clutch, unmistakable—then pulled away.

"What was that for?" Nick said, to cover his embarrassment.

"For luck. You always brought me luck, remember?"

Sitting at his side while his father played poker with the other men, watching the cards, happy to be up late. "Not always," he said.

"Yes, you did."

Inside, the band was still playing, the hall light and warm, as if nothing had happened. "Memories of You," a romantic low-register solo, calming the crowd down after the raucous opening number. Anna left even before he'd finished his message, snatching her coat, an attentive nurse. Molly raised her eyes.

"Tired," Nick whispered. "We're on our own."

She smiled, obviously pleased, and put her hand on his. He drifted with the music, relieved that they couldn't talk. What could have happened? Something at the funeral? This morning there had been a plan. This was more like flight, the bag ready at the door. What had spooked him? "Goody, Goody," a speakeasy song, fleshed out for the big band.

"You okay?" Molly said, looking at him.

He nodded, forcing himself to smile. Why was happiness so hard to fake? Everybody else was beaming, a kind of collective euphoria. This was the way his father had sat, not even hearing the music. He grinned. In case they could be seen from the balcony.

The band was brought back twice, and even when the curtain was down people kept clapping, reluctant to leave the party. They followed the crowd back to Wenceslas, where it spilled down the long street, clumping at tram stops and the few bars still open for a late drink. Molly wanted to go on to Laterna Magika—"We can still catch the end"—and because they wouldn't have to talk there either he went along, his arm around her shoulder, not giving anything away.

It was in a café at the bottom of the square, off Národní Street, and the minute he walked in he knew it was a mistake. The dark room, smoky, filled with shadows, was the part of him he'd been trying to push away. They couldn't take a table without interrupting the show, so they stood at the bar in the dark, and Nick found himself scanning the room, looking at faces to see if any of them were looking back.

The mimes worked in front of a bright spot, forming shadows against a screen, like children making rabbit ears on the wall with their fingers held up to a lamp. The play between the actors and their own larger shadows caused a trick of the eye, a clever chiaroscuro, but all Nick saw were the shadows, dancing, then elusive, sliding toward the edge until you could no longer see where they ended and the real dark began. The customers, sitting at cabaret tables, gave off the same effect, sometimes visible in the light, then vanishing into the recesses. No wonder the Czechs liked Goodman, the bright lights and the simple, bouncy music. This was the native product, all shadows, a city practiced at fading into doorways.

He went into the men's room, grateful for the light. A man, cigarette dangling, stood at the urinal, so he went into the stall. What if there was someone in the stall tomorrow? What did he do, keep going back until it was empty? He pulled the chain, looking up at the flush box mounted on the wall. He'd imagined a toilet with a back, a convenient shelf. Where did you leave the ticket, on the paper dispenser? Why had his father changed his mind? The man at the urinal said something in Czech over the plywood wall, hearty, maybe a joke about the effects of beer on the bladder, but it could have been anything. What if someone spoke to him? Nick just nodded to him blandly when he came out, not even stopping to wash his hands, afraid of being caught out by language. He pushed open the door to a round of applause.

"Aren't they wonderful?" Molly said brightly. "There's one more set. Want to sit?"

"No. Do you really want to stay?"

"You *don't* like mimes. Here, finish this." She handed him a brandy. "Ten minutes, okay?"

He took a long pull on the drink to burn away his mood. When he looked up over the glass, a shadow had come out of the wall.

"We meet again," Marty Bielak said. "You seem to be everywhere tonight."

"That makes two of us."

366

"Well, a nightcap." He held up his glass. Where else had he been? The Alcron. The Café Slavia. The legman making his rounds. Items for tomorrow's column. Just like the old days. The Stork. The Blue Angel. Another iron curtain joke. Café society was still alive here, lounge lizards and all.

"They're terrific, aren't they?" Bielak said, nodding toward the mime troupe. "I never get tired of them."

"You've seen them a lot?"

"Well, there aren't so many clubs here." He took a drink, standing closer. "I see you met one of our local celebrities." Prodding. "At the concert. He didn't introduce himself?" Insistent now, close.

Nick wasn't sure what to answer. How would it be reported? But Bielak was waiting, his lips wet with drink.

"Yes," Nick said finally. "I thought he was in Moscow."

Bielak nodded, his air confiding. "He married a Czech. A bourgeoise." The term threw Nick, some bizarre leftover from the old party meetings, those hours of dialectic and self-discipline. But Bielak didn't hear it as an anachronism, and when he saw Nick's look, he said, "Of course, not now."

"I didn't know," Nick said vaguely.

"What did he say? I'd be curious." He had leaned even closer, his whole body a kind of insinuation.

"Not much. How I liked the concert," Nick said. But this wasn't going to be enough. "I think he was a little disappointed that I didn't recognize him."

Too much? But Bielak seemed pleased. "Yes. He used to be famous, you see." He shook his head. "Nobody remembers, do they?" Delighted somehow, a press agent watching a falling star.

"We have to go," Nick said, signaling to Molly.

"So soon? They're not finished."

"No, but I am. We have to be up early."

Why had he said that? Bielak, however, was smiling, amused.

"Young people," he said. "In my day, we could dance all night." So he had watched. Was still watching. "One more drink?" Was it possible he just didn't want to go home? The empty apartment.

"Thanks, some other time. Molly?"

Bielak nodded and raised his fingers from the glass in a kind of wave. "I'll see you around," he said, his voice pleasant, not sinister at all.

Back in the street, Nick was rattled. A chance meeting? What if he was around tomorrow? In the lobby. At the station itself. As they walked along the street he found himself looking to the side, expecting shadows to move. It's simple, his father had said. But it wasn't. A quarrel with Molly? Who would believe it? Not Bielak, making his rounds. Nobody just got on a train, not here. Why risk it, all of a sudden? He started picking the story apart, uneasy.

Later it was worse. When Molly fell asleep curled next to him, he stared at the street light on the ceiling, looking for microphones that might not be there. You always brought me luck. Something was wrong. And what would Vienna be like? More cat and mouse. He wanted to turn his mind off, sleep, but instead he lay still with dread, awake with night fears, the ones that didn't even have names.

He shaved without running the water, careful not to wake her, and dressed quietly in the dim light. He put a few things in the small canvas bag, then crossed over to the desk and took her passport out of her purse. Both of them were leaving, a better story. No quarrel. She'd be late. When the floorboards creaked he stopped, but she didn't move, a mound under the covers. He turned the knob slowly, so that when he finally closed the door behind him there was only a soft click. In the hall a maid stared at him as if she'd caught him coming out of someone else's room, but he nodded and whispered *"Dobre ráno"* when he passed, just an early bird. He went down the stairs. The lobby was empty, but just in case he paused and took out his street map, a tourist plotting his walk, his head still down as he passed through the revolving door.

It was early, just a few people on their way to work, but he turned off Wenceslas at the first corner and took a series of side streets to circle back to the bottom of the square. Nobody was following. Near the Powder Tower he caught a tram, and watched out the window as it traveled back across Wenceslas, past the hotel, the doorman yawning. He walked to the university and headed left toward the station. The back streets, oddly, seemed less safe, without a crowd to hide in, but he kept going, one more deliberate wrong turn, then a glance at the map, another street, and he was there, the creamy art nouveau façade, vaulting shed behind, Wilsonova Street half filled now with sleepy commuters. Policemen stood near the doorways, looking bored, guns at their sides. No one looked at him.

The woman at the ticket booth said something in Czech and repeated it until Nick tried his little bit of German: *"Zwei nach Wien."* She took the passports and examined them, checking against sheets in a looseleaf binder, then leaned forward to look to his side, evidently expecting to see Molly. When she spoke Czech again, he gestured with his hands to indicate that she was following. The woman said something again, then, seeing his blank expression, gave it up, shrugging and stamping the tickets. Life was too short, even here. She took the money, grumbling at having to make change. *"Pĕt."* He stared and she repeated it, then grudgingly took a slip of paper and wrote "5," pointing toward the platforms. He nodded, thanking her in German, and moved away, putting the tickets in his pocket. That was it, as easy as he had said.

He walked across the hall toward the platforms, glancing around. Coffee stalls, newspapers. Any station. He found the men's room. Was there another one? A man stumbled out, obviously drunk, still zipping his fly. Inside was a row of stalls and sinks, urinals against the wall. He stood for a minute, too nervous to pee, then opened the door to the first stall. He couldn't leave the ticket yet, not for an hour, but there was a shelf, easy.

He made a half-circle through the hall to make sure it was the nearest toilet, then bought a coffee, wishing he hadn't come so early. Would the teller keep an eye on him? The newspapers were Czech. *Rudé Právo,* Red Truth. He walked out onto the empty platform, feeling conspicuous, then sat on one of the benches near the gate where he could see both platform and waiting hall. Where would his father be? There was nowhere to hide here. He'd walk straight to the men's room. Nick would follow. In an hour he'd be gone.

He had nothing to read, and in any case English might be noticed, so there was nothing to do but smoke and look at his watch, a pantomime of waiting. A soldier came up, machine gun pointing down, and spoke. Nick froze. Was he asking to see his papers? Then the soldier repeated it and made the sign for a match and Nick, grateful, handed him the disposable lighter. He looked at it curiously before he passed it back, an artifact from the West, then moved on to the next platform. But whom was he guarding? The hall was deserted except for the grim commuters, and Nick wondered what it had been like before, loudspeakers announcing the overnight expresses, wagons-lits connecting Europe. Now nobody went anywhere.

A man in a hat and a boxy suit, carrying a satchel, walked out on the platform. One passenger, at least. Nick followed his shoes. Not Western. Maybe a businessman heading back to Brno. Did the train stop before Vienna? There must be a border check, a customs search, rifling through the bags of the anxious Russian Jews. Too busy to bother his father. A cleaning man in a blue smock swept his way nearer, looking over at him, interested. Nick got up and went to the men's room again.

This time he could pee. He was alone, he could leave it now, but what if someone else found it? Why hadn't they set an exact time? He washed his hands and went back to the bench. A suburban train had pulled into the next platform, and people were moving off as if they were still asleep. Otherwise, it was the same as before, the soldier circling, the man in the suit waiting. Another man was on the platform now, pacing. Nick sat looking from one to the other. They all moved in silence, almost orchestrated, like the Laterna Magika. A train attendant checking a pocket watch walked out to the end of the platform. Any one of them could be someone else, waiting for his father. Two older women and a young man, one suitcase. Who was leaving? The boxy suit moved back toward Nick's bench, glancing over at him, then circled back. Would they know his father by sight? He used to be famous. Molly would be up now, wondering where he'd gone. But he couldn't leave a note. He'd get a taxi back.

When he saw the train coming in he began to panic. This was cutting it close. A ten-minute layover. But maybe that was right. A sleight of hand, quick. Where was he? There was a slow screech as the train stopped, doors banging open, a few people getting off, handing a suitcase down through the window. The people waiting on the platform began to move toward the train. He couldn't just stand there. Had he missed him somehow? He went back to the men's room. Maybe he was waiting.

The first stall was closed, feet visible underneath. He stood at the sink. It would have to be now. The whistle would go any minute. If he came now, Nick would have to hand it to him, tell him to run. He turned off the tap. Come on. And then it occurred to him that the feet were his father's, holding the stall. Of course. He'd been waiting all this time and now was late, Nick's fault. Nick darted over and pushed open the door, ready to hand him the ticket. A curse in Czech. A man, his pants down around his ankles, glared in surprise, then yelled. "Sorry," Nick said, yanking the door closed.

He ran out of the room and stood at the head of the platform. He'd have to pass this way, see Nick, not bother with the men's room. Just take the ticket and go. Nick looked around, frantic, then down at his watch. Not this close. It was stupid. They'd notice. The boxy suit and the pacer were gone, settled in the car. Only the attendant was now on the empty platform, looking at him. Nick turned to the waiting hall. He'd be running across the room now, late, accidentally bumping into

Nick, snatching the ticket before anyone could see. The soldier was coming back, smoking again. Then Nick heard the whistle and jumped, swiveling his head between the train and the hall. The soldier looked at him. The train was beginning to move. There was no one near, no one running. Nick looked at his watch—what else did you do when someone was late? When the soldier came up to him and said something, Nick turned his palms up and shrugged. She had missed it. Then he turned and saw the train sliding out, the attendant waving as it passed him, faster now, on its way to Vienna.

He stood for a minute, not sure what to do. The soldier was still looking at him. Play it out. The story was everything now. He'd wait for her. He arranged his face, concerned and annoyed, as if he still expected to see someone walk through the hall. He stood against the wall, giving it a few minutes, waiting for the soldier to move away. Then he picked up the canvas bag and headed toward the door, away from the ticket windows. His father would never be late. Something had happened again. For a second Nick was angry—why put him through this? Was he supposed to go back to the hotel, wait for the next plan? But all this was just pushing away the dread. He saw his father's face outside the concert hall, tense with worry.

Outside, he got into a taxi. If something was wrong, he should avoid him, wait for the right time. But he couldn't.

"Namesti sovetskych tankistu," he said, almost blurting it out. The driver looked at him—had he

374

mispronounced it, or was it too unlikely a destination?—but put the car in gear. Nick lit a cigarette, trying to calm his shakiness, and watched the streets as they started down the hill. Red street nameplates on building corners, indecipherable. Bouncing across the embedded tram rails, fast, as if the driver felt Nick's urgency. The river. Finally the tank at the foot of Holečkova, the empty traffic circle. He paid the driver and got out, unfolding his map and pretending to read it, part of the story. Then the taxi was gone and he was running up the long hill. No one ran in Prague. A workman coming down the hill scuttled to the side, avoiding him, flattening himself against the park wall. But Nick was running from his own demons now, not caring, the sound of ragged breathing in his ears.

The hill was steep and he stopped once, gulping, then started again, out of time. The apartment buildings appeared now, rising up against the park slope, set back from the sidewalk behind patches of banked lawns. White concrete balconies with their city views. He'd been lucky to get one. There was a black metal gate in the wall and Nick hung on it, jiggling the latch, then sprinted up the row of concrete steps leading to the building. Hell in the winter, slippery for old people. The entrance was in the back, at the end of the pavement. He raced up another series of steps, past some shrubs, the steep apron of lawn, a clump of pale blue shrub on the grass.

He stopped. Not a shrub. Pajamas. He walked across the lawn in slow motion, his chest heaving.

The legs were twisted, probably broken by the fall, the face lying on its side, blood underneath, a dried streak at the corner of his mouth. Nick sank to his knees, staring. He reached out to feel for a pulse in the neck, but the skin was already cold. Then, without thinking, he moved his hand up, brushing back the thin hair, stroking the side of his head, smoothing away the lines of his skin so that the face seemed to him again the one he'd always known, not old, the same high forehead and wavy hair. With his other hand he lifted the head into his lap, still stroking it, rocking back and forth a little in a silent wail. His eyes swam. How could it hurt this much?

He looked up. Everything quiet. Was there no one to help? The balcony above them. Had no one heard? Or had there only been a thud, a dull thump onto the grass cushion? He rocked harder, cradling the head, heavy in his lap, oblivious to the dampness of the blood. When he glanced at the pajamas and saw the dark stain on the pants where his father had soiled himself, a final embarrassment, he held the head closer, comforting a child, telling him it didn't matter. The quiet was unbearable, death itself, and he saw why people keened, made any sound to break the stillness so they weren't swallowed up in it too. But a part of you went anyway, seeping out like blood. He stared down again at the face, smooth, irretrievable, somewhere else. The only thing he had ever wanted.

He didn't know how long he knelt there, out of

the world, but when he came back all his senses were there at once—the sound of a car passing in the street, the stickiness on his pants, the tingling surge of adrenaline, fear. He should call somebody. Weren't there neighbors? Gently he moved his father's head, laying it back on the grass, and stood up. Maybe he shouldn't be seen at all. But now what did it matter? He walked over to the sidewalk and followed it around the building to the door.

A jumble of nameplates, two apartments to a floor, Kotlar on the top. He ignored the small elevator, afraid of being enclosed, and climbed the stairs, the landings bright through a wall of glass brick. Moderne. Instinctively he raised his hand to knock on the door, but who would be there? Then he saw that it was already ajar, as if someone hadn't closed it properly. Who? He pushed it quietly and stepped into the chilly apartment.

"Anna?" he called out, hearing nothing but the sound of a clock. He looked around the room—low Scandinavian furniture, bookcases, everything in order. The sliding door to the balcony was closed. He opened it, stepped out, and looked down. The body was still there, slightly to the right. He saw then that the balcony extended along to the next room and that the door there was open. He moved toward it, stopping when he saw the marks on the painted rail. Here? But his father had been barefoot, in pajamas, nothing to scrape against.

The bedroom was a mess, covers flung back, pillows scattered, as if he'd got up in a hurry. The night table was upright but at an angle, some pill vials and a book knocked to the floor, the lamp pushed near the edge. The desk chair was pulled back, out of place, where someone would bump into it in the dark. The desk wasn't ransacked, the drawers still in place, but somehow disheveled, at odds with the neat living room.

He stood for a minute, imagining how it might have been. The sudden impulse in bed, knocking against the night table as he got up, staggering (drunk?), bumping against the desk, yanking the chair out of the way, the rush to the balcony, and over. Soiling himself in the terror of the plunge. None of that happened. It would have been deliberate, planned out like everything else. A note. Nick looked on the desk, moving some of the papers aside, and then stopped. You weren't supposed to disturb the scene of the crime. The phrase struck him, another adrenaline surge. That's what it was, wasn't it? He looked at the room again. Another phrase: signs of struggle. Someone pulling him off the bed, dragging him, knocking against the furniture. Had he screamed? Nick leaned against the desk, lightheaded. Had he begged them to stop, fought back, one final swing, knowing his luck had run out? But no one had heard. The body was still lying there, unreported. Nick imagined instead a hand clamped over his mouth, muffling him, his arms thrashing as they forced him out, an old man, so terrified that he went in his pants.

No note. The papers were bills, scattered now from what must have been a neat pile, making sure everything was paid before he got on the train. Nick opened a drawer. Was there really a list? There seemed to have been no effort to find it, no search. The inside of the desk was untouched, folders of letters and bills and what seemed to be official documents with his name, the paper trail of socialist life.

Nick heard a noise in the hall, the whirring of the elevator. One of the neighbors would see the body now, glance across the lawn as he went out, curious, then cry out and run back for the telephone. Should he do it first? But the idea of calling the police in Czech defeated him. Let someone else do it. Maybe instead he should slip down the stairs, go back to the hotel and his own life. Call Anna later. What more could he do here? All this paper, receipts and letters, some in Russian, the desk of a foreigner. Only on the grass, strangely young again, had he been his father.

In the top drawer he brushed aside pens and paper clips. A passport, Russian, his father's. He drew out a manila envelope dark with age. Newspaper clippings, in English. His disappearance, his press conference, a loose scrapbook of disinformation. Why had he saved them? Then Nick saw that each of the clippings had family photographs—the three of them in front of the house on 2nd Street; the old wedding picture, blurred on newsprint; his parents shaking Truman's hand at a reception. Their tabloid life. At the bottom of the pile were two real photographs, worn at the edges. His mother, young, maybe during the war, shoulder pads and short skirt, a vivid lipstick smile, her mouth open with the beginning of a laugh. The other was a boy in hockey gear at Lasker Rink, a wintry Central Park in the background, the boy unaware that he was being photographed by a spy. Nick looked at himself. He wished now that he had been smiling, that every time his father had looked at it he'd seen what he wanted to see, his happy boy, not somebody caught from behind a tree. Too late. His eyes filled, and he wanted to make a noise again. The photographs were like the stillness of death. If you gave in to them, you drifted away to another place. Nothing ever came back.

He was still looking at the pictures when he heard the sound in the next room. He raised his head. Two policemen faced him, guns drawn, the small machine guns they held with two hands, more menacing than revolvers. One of them shouted in Czech, looking at the blood on his pants.

"I'm sorry. I didn't hear—"

Another shout. He pointed Nick toward the wall with the gun and said something in Czech, brisk. Now the gun was being jerked up, a signal to raise his hands. When he did, staring at the gun, the other frisked him, patting up and down his sides.

"I was going to call—"

Then a storm of Czech, perhaps to each other, their voices rising in frustration when he didn't answer.

"I don't understand." But then he did. When they snapped on the handcuffs and pushed him out of the room, the gun poking at his back, he understood, dazed, that he was being arrested.

CHAPTER TWELVE

There were people on the lawn now, huddled over the body, some in uniform, one old lady standing behind, clutching at her winter coat—the neighbor, finally?—but they wouldn't let him stop, pushing him with the guns down the path. He bumped his head against the car when they shoved him in, the sharp crack of pain the only thing real in what seemed to be a cartoon. His wrists, clamped behind him, were caught in the metal cuffs. One of the policemen in the front seat swiveled around, pointing the gun at him, and he watched the barrel bounce against the seat as the car took off down the rough road. A pothole could set it off. He closed his eyes. No siren, just the racing car, rumbling now over cobbles, taking a corner too fast, the speed itself official. He was pitched forward when they stopped, almost into the gun, then doors slammed and a hand pulled roughly at his arm.

The building was a blur, bulletin boards and clicking typewriters, heads looking up. They'd take him to a desk now, to someone who spoke English, so he could explain. Instead he was thrown into a chair and photographed, the flash blinding him, then yanked down the hall to a bare room. Not a cell. A plain table, two chairs, a picture of Husák on the wall. They pushed him down into one of the chairs, hands still behind his back, delivered another volley of incomprehensible Czech, then left. The door slammed.

No one came. What should he do—kick the door, demand to see someone, to have his one telephone call? But there were no rights here. He was a foreigner with blood on his clothes. Maybe they were watching him. He looked around. No mirror, just blank walls, Husák looking down. The bump on his head throbbed. They couldn't leave him here, throw away the key—a child's fear. An interior room, one small window facing a wall, the light always the same, no way to tell the time until it was dark. The story was the important thing now, what to say. The truth would start another web, catching him, sticking to him like his pants. He looked down. Would it never dry? He felt his eyes fill again. You always brought me luck. But he hadn't. Dancing, careless, while his father made a new plan, an emergency exit that hadn't opened. Why the change? He sat back, still dazed, and waited to see what would happen.

It was at least an hour before they came, or had waiting distorted his sense of time? His hands were numb. The two policemen again, with another, not in uniform, his fat neck spilling over his collar. He gave an order, the cuffs were taken off, and while Nick rubbed his wrists, the new man leaned over the table, glaring and talking into his face. When Nick didn't answer, signaling that he didn't understand, he said, "Ach," a sound of disgust, and sent one of the policemen out. Now they all waited, the big man in the suit pacing. Eventually there was a knock on the door and another man in a suit came in. This one was slight, with a mustache, and his eyes took Nick in like a jeweler. Then he listened to the big man grumble in Czech. He turned to Nick.

"This is Chief Novotný," he said, pointing to the big man. "Criminal Investigation Department."

"Am I under arrest?"

"He'd like to ask you a few questions," he said formally, sidestepping it. "I will translate. My name is Zimmerman." He caught Nick's glance. "Sudeten," he explained, "but Czech." An unexpected courtesy, almost social.

Novotný snapped at him, evidently telling him to get on with it. He nodded. Good cop, bad cop. Novotný handed him Nick's passport. What had happened to Molly's?

"You are Nicholas Warren."

"Yes."

"And how do you come to be in Holečkova this morning? In Pan Kotlar's flat. You were acquainted?"

"We met at a concert last night."

"Concert?"

"Yes, Benny Goodman." The sound of it absurd, even to him. Novotný grunted. "He invited me to come for coffee."

"A kaffeeklatsch," Zimmerman said. "Why?"

"He used to be an American," Nick said. Used to be. "I think he wanted—"

"News from home," Zimmerman finished.

"Something like that."

"So early. In the morning. Not the afternoon coffee."

"I'm leaving Prague today. It was the only time. So I went. But he was—I found him on the grass. He was dead. He'd been dead for a while."

Zimmerman looked at him sharply. "How do you know?"

"His skin was cold."

"I see. You examined him?"

"To see if he was alive. That's why the blood."

Novotný interrupted in Czech; the other answered him, annoyed but polite. Then he turned back to Nick.

"But you went into his flat?"

"To call the police."

"But you didn't."

Nick pointed to the policeman. "He got there before I had the chance. Someone else must have called."

"Yes. You were there long?"

"A few minutes. Look, what's this all about? He was dead. Do you think I killed him?"

"I don't know, Mr. Warren. I don't know that anyone killed him," he said carefully. "Do you have reason to believe someone did?"

"I didn't mean that."

"No. Last night, at the concert, how did he seem to you? Was he upset in any way?"

Desperate, Nick wanted to say. But had he been, or did it just seem that way now? "I don't know. I don't know what he was usually like. He seemed all right to me."

"So you were surprised, this morning."

"Of course. It was—horrible."

There was another exchange of Czech, then Novotný went to the door, said something, and came back with Nick's canvas bag. By the body. Why had he forgotten? Novotný handed Zimmerman Molly's passport and the tickets.

"You were going on from coffee? To the station?"

Caught. "Yes, later."

He opened Nick's passport. "Your visa includes an entry permit for a car. You are aware that it is illegal for you to sell a car to a Czech citizen?"

"I didn't sell it."

"A present, then, perhaps? You were not by any chance leaving it for Pan Kotlar?"

A hopeless tangle now. "No, why would I do that?"

"If you had just met. Yes, I agree. But you were traveling by train?"

Think. "It was acting up. I was going to have it fixed and come back for it."

"You're very trusting, Mr. Warren. To leave a car."

"The hotel would take care of it."

"But you couldn't wait."

"No, I had to be in Vienna."

"What is your business, Mr. Warren? You're a journalist?"

"No. I'm at the London School of Economics."

"A student?"

"A research assistant."

"With business in Vienna."

"I'm traveling with someone. She had to be there."

He fingered Molly's passport. "Miss Chisholm," he said, pronouncing it correctly. "Your friend?"

"Yes."

"She was not invited for coffee?"

"She had other things to do."

"It's a pity you did not join her, Mr. Warren."

He turned to Novotný and reported in Czech, a brief summary.

"You had better think of a better explanation for the car, Mr. Warren," he said, almost confiding. "He's interested in the car. By the way, the next Vienna train doesn't leave until late afternoon. I thought you should be aware of that." Nick stared at him. "Now, quickly please, what did you see in the flat? Had anyone been there?"

"I think so. Furniture was pushed around, as if there had been some kind of fight. Chair moved out of the way. I suppose he might have done it himself, but why?"

"Anything else?"

"Scrape marks on the railing. But there was nothing on him to make a scrape with, so I assume it was someone else."

Zimmerman nodded approvingly. "If it was

made then. How long did you say he'd been dead?"

"I don't know. I can't tell. He wasn't stiff, just cold."

"All right. Thank you." He stood up, talking again to Novotný. "Think about the car."

"Can I go now?"

"Go? Mr. Warren, I'm afraid you are in difficulties. Unless of course Pan Kotlar seemed— agitated to you last night. It might have been. Otherwise, the police will be interested in you."

"I don't understand. Aren't you the police?"

He smiled. "Actually, I was chief of police. Until last year. A year can make a great difference here, you see. Today, Chief Novotný. He's more comfortable with the regime, or perhaps they with him—it depends how you look at it. Now I help him." Another tram driver. "A research assistant," he said, his voice ironic. "But I'm glad of the work. It's hard, you know, to break the habit."

They brought Molly in sometime after noon.

"Nick. Thank god," she said, her face drawn and nervous. "What's going on? I've been frantic." She moved toward him, then looked at the police and stopped. Novotný watched them blankly, shut out by language, but Zimmerman followed her with interest.

"I don't know. There's some kind of mistake.

The man we met last night, at the concert—I found him this morning, dead. They didn't tell you?"

"Dead?" she said, stunned, not taking in the rest of it. Her face softened. "Oh, Nick."

"Mr. Warren was with you this morning?" Zimmerman said.

Molly nodded.

"What time did he leave?"

Molly looked to Nick for help. "I don't know. I was asleep."

"The maid said very early," Zimmerman said. "You don't know exactly when?"

"I didn't want to wake her," Nick interrupted. Then, to Molly, "I went to get the tickets. For the train this afternoon. You know. I didn't want to wait till the last minute."

"Evidently," Zimmerman said dryly, still watching Molly, who simply stared, following a game. "And yet you waited there," he said to Nick. So they'd already checked.

"I had a coffee. It was too early to go to his place."

"So much coffee," Zimmerman said. "You have business in Vienna?" he said to Molly. But she seemed not to have heard him.

"Dead?" she said to Nick. "He was dead? How?"

"That is what we're trying to determine, Miss Chisholm. A fall from the balcony. An accident, perhaps," Zimmerman said blandly. "But Mr. Warren's presence there naturally raises some questions for us. You understand. You have business in Vienna?" he said again.

Molly looked at him, unsure, then gave a nod, faint enough to be retrieved. He took up her passport, thumbing through it.

"You've been to Prague before. May I ask what brings you back?"

"I wanted to show Nick."

"Not on business then, this time? You did not apply for a journalist's visa, I see."

"No. It was a personal trip."

"To see Prague," Zimmerman said. "Again." He put down the passports. "So you cannot tell me when Mr. Warren left this morning."

"Sometime after six. He was still in bed then. I saw the clock." Had she?

"He left around six?"

"Later. I don't know when exactly. I fell back to sleep. Why?"

"It's useful to know these things. Chief Novotný will want it for his report." Novotný looked up at his name. "Or perhaps not. Perhaps he has his own idea. Don't be alarmed, Miss Chisholm. If you were under suspicion, we would have questioned you separately, before you could talk to Mr. Warren here. That's the usual procedure. Of course, Chief Novotný may not know that. He is new." Zimmerman sighed. "But it's useful, these details. For instance, you have not yet packed for your trip?" The disheveled room, noticed.

"Molly leaves everything to the last minute," Nick said.

Zimmerman looked at him. "Now she will have more time."

"But she has to leave today," Nick said evenly, facing her.

"I think Chief Novotný would prefer her to stay," Zimmerman said easily, "until we finish. Don't worry, the tickets will still be good. Unless, of course, your car is fixed in time."

Molly raised her eyebrows, finally thrown, but before Nick could say anything there was a knock and another policeman handed Novotný a folder. He pulled out a report sheet and grunted as he read, only handing it to Zimmerman when he had finished. Zimmerman went through it quickly, nodding and speaking to Novotný as he read. A small explosion of Czech back, then more talk, not quite an argument, Novotný bristling, clearly irritated by an inconvenience. Nick watched them, then looked over at Molly and saw that she was frightened. When he placed his hand on hers, it was cool to the touch.

"There was no blood in the flat," Zimmerman said, not a question. "Tell me again about the blood." He nodded to Nick's pants.

"When I was checking. To see if he was alive."

"Is that why you went back to the flat? To wash it off?"

Nick looked at him. "I didn't go back. I'd never been there. I found him and then I went in to call you."

"But not right away. First you went through his desk." He glanced down again at the report. "Pani

391

Havlíček—that's the neighbor—said she saw you holding his head." Molly took her hand away as if the blood were there, drawing her in. But her eyes were soft, upset now, the death real, not a story. "Is that usually the way you check a pulse?"

Someone watching, even then. "I don't know. I didn't know what I was doing. You know, I didn't expect—"

"What, Mr. Warren?"

"To see a body there."

"Pani Havlíček didn't expect to see you there either. She said you stayed for some time. Holding him." He glanced over at Novotný, who, bored, was now stretching his tight collar and looking out the window. "Of course, it might have seemed long to her. It's often the case. She also said she heard noises in the apartment. Just before dawn. Another light sleeper." He glanced at Molly. "A little commotion. Of course, it may have seemed louder to her than it was. It's possible, at that hour." He was walking around the table, talking to himself. "A noise when you don't expect it. Pan Kotlar himself, perhaps. There was alcohol in his blood. If he was unsteady—. It's difficult to be precise about these things."

Nick looked up at him. "What time is dawn?"

Zimmerman paused, a sliding look toward Novotný. "Before six," he said to Nick. "There were pills," he continued, walking again. "For illness. No marks on the balcony. Of course, these may have been missed, if no one was looking for them."

"They were there."

"So you said. What caused them, do you think?"

"I don't know. A belt buckle, buttons—something metal."

"And what could that mean?" Zimmerman said, almost playing.

"That someone scraped against it when he pushed him over," Nick said flatly.

For a minute no one said anything. Zimmerman looked down at the folder as if he were thinking it over, not just playing for effect. It was when Nick saw him glance at the window that he realized Zimmerman was just waiting to see if Novotný had understood.

"I see," he said finally. "That is your idea?"

"Yes."

"Oh, god," Molly said quietly.

"I don't know if Chief Novotný would agree with you. As I said, he has his own idea. And you know, sometimes the obvious solution is the right one. I've seen this many times."

"He didn't kill himself."

"You're sure? If I may say so, Mr. Warren, the obvious solution would be more convenient for you." Directly to Nick, almost an instruction. "An older man, sick, it's a common thing. Even the method. It's a disease with us Czechs, you know. I'm not sure why. All through our history. Defenestration. So many have chosen it."

A courtyard in the Czernin Palace. What had Masaryk said?

"The housemaid's way out," Nick said.

Zimmerman's eyes widened in appreciation. "I see you know our history."

"He wouldn't have taken it either."

"You know that, after so little acquaintance?"

Nick lowered his head, quiet.

"No, Mr. Warren, it would all be very simple. A sick man, a little drink. Our chief would sign the papers. Everybody goes home. Except, of course, for you. A foreigner. At the death scene. Now it's not so simple." He took one of the chairs and sat down, facing Nick. "What are you doing here, Mr. Warren? Why did you come to Prague?"

Nick looked away. "To see it."

"A tourist. Who drives in and takes the train out. Who meets a stranger, and the next morning he's dead. Mr. Warren, this is a charade. I'm not like our good chief. I like to know the truth. It's a habit. So."

Why not? Hadn't he been telling Nick all along that he knew it was someone else? The wrong time. The blood. Then why press at all? Simple curiosity? Or a final trick question before he'd have to let him go? There was no one to trust here. Nick said nothing.

Zimmerman looked down, opened the folder, and shuffled through papers. Newsclippings, yellow. Of course they'd gone through the apartment. Now he was fingering the hockey picture.

"A remarkable resemblance," Zimmerman said quietly, still shuffling, indifferent for Novotný's benefit. He didn't want him to know. "A relative?"

Nick said nothing.

"It's unusual, Mr. Warren, to hold the head of a dead man you didn't know." He paused. "Tell me, please."

"Why? You already know."

"I would rather you told me. It's better. For the report." He continued looking down, as if they were talking about something else.

"He was my father," Nick said.

"And yet you have different names." Zimmerman looked up. "A detail."

"My mother remarried. I took my stepfather's name."

"I see. Thank you. And now will you tell me why you didn't say this before? What are you doing here, Mr. Warren?"

"I came to see him. I didn't want anyone to know."

"Why?"

"It would hurt them, if they knew. My family."

"No, why did you come?"

"I wanted to see him."

"After so many years?"

"Before it was too late."

"You knew he was dying?"

"No. Old."

Zimmerman closed the folder. "You got here just in time. I'm sorry. This must be difficult for you. May I offer you a piece of advice? Do not create more difficulties."

"He didn't kill himself."

"How can we know that, Mr. Warren? From a few scrape marks?"

"Somebody killed him."

"Why?"

Nick looked down. "I don't know."

"Then let us confine ourselves to what we do know. For the moment. I understand that Pan Kotlar was much affected by the death of his friend Miloš Brokov. There was a discussion about suicide. You were there, I believe."

"That's not—" Nick stopped. "How do you know that?"

A flicker of embarrassment. "Pan Kotlar's wife returned this morning from visiting relatives." He looked up. "She was, by the way—visiting relatives." Had his father suggested it, knowing? Or had he just wanted to make it easier to get on the train? Had he said goodbye? "Chief Novotný was busy, so I took the opportunity to interview her. Separately. Our usual procedure."

"She told you about me."

Zimmerman nodded and touched the folder. "I confess I am not so clever, even with the resemblance." He paused. "Was there any reason for her not to mention this?"

"No." She hadn't known any of it.

"So you remember this discussion? She said Pan Kotlar was depressed. Is that so?" Building another case, away from the truth.

"No, he was drunk."

Zimmerman started, surprised by the bluntness.

"An emotional time," he said calmly. "A friend's death. And of course seeing you. Your presence—"

"Is that what she said?"

"She said he was not himself." The denunciations, already begun. The way his father said it would be, the standard procedure. "Was that your impression also?"

"I don't know what he's usually like."

"But he was upset by his friend's news?"

"Yes." A pinprick of disloyalty; so easy. "Anybody would be."

"Your visit, it was a pleasant one?"

"Yes."

"No quarrels? Sometimes, I know, these things don't always go smoothly. So many years. And of course the events of his life."

"That was a long time ago."

"Yes, but often there are feelings—you think it's over and then they come up."

"He was happy to see me."

"And you, were you happy to see him?"

Had he been? "Yes, very."

"Yet you were leaving today. A short visit."

"This time."

"A kind of trial run?" Zimmerman said, pleased with himself for knowing the idiom.

"Yes."

"Your father knew you were planning to return?"

"Yes."

"But would you say he was distraught? At your leaving? With his health—"

"No, I would not say that. You would. What are you trying to prove?"

"I'm trying to understand, Mr. Warren. How it was."

"No. You just want me to say he killed himself. I don't want any part of this. You don't need me—you already know. Can we go now?"

Zimmerman looked at him carefully. "I'm afraid you don't understand the situation. Miss Chisholm may go if she likes," he said, turning toward her. "Though I must ask you to cancel your business in Vienna. It would not be advisable for you to leave Prague just now. You, Mr. Warren, are another matter. It is not, of course, my decision—I'm only assisting Chief Novotný. But I suspect he would wish you to stay here."

"Am I under arrest? What for?"

"No, you are being detained for questioning."

"Whatever that means."

"It means you are being detained for questioning. You see, Mr. Warren, you are a spanner."

"What?"

"A spanner in the works. It's not correct?"

"A monkey wrench," Nick said.

"Ah, it's a Britishism, spanner?" Zimmerman nodded. "A wrench. It gets stuck in the machinery. A cause of industrial accidents. This is what has happened to Chief Novotný. Everything runs smoothly and then you fall in. Now he must decide what to do with you to fix it. How does he explain you? Just the fact of you raises questions. What if his idea is wrong?"

"It is."

"Then he must find another. I have been trying to

suggest to you—I hope you understand—that you should not make this difficult for him. He might—this can happen—he might find the wrong idea. He might find it in you."

Nick stared at him. "You don't think I did it."

"It doesn't matter what I think. I'm only an assistant now. You want him to believe this was a crime? Then it becomes a problem for him. Given the victim, perhaps a political problem. That would be serious. Me, I don't interest myself in politics. But I am interested in you. I'm a policeman. A man is dead and I want to know why, I can't help it." He paused. "I would like you to help me. But Chief Novotný has other concerns. Not why. What to do. You must understand that difference. For him, the wrong solution, any solution, might become the right one. Unless, of course, I can explain you."

"He can't prove anything."

"Proof can be a small thing, Mr. Warren, if you want to believe it. A telephone call that isn't made. A presence in someone's flat, stained with blood." He touched the folder again. "Perhaps a resentment that explodes—just like that, a kind of accident." He looked up. "A car that isn't broken. Many things. Which are important? Which do you believe? It's difficult to know, until they fit. Help me, Mr. Warren."

And not Novotný. Unless they were really one person, not separate at all, like the mimes' shadows at Laterna Magika.

"Nick, let me call your father," Molly said, anxious.

"No," he said quickly. The last thing he wanted, the wounded surprise on Larry's face, then the mess that would follow, with everyone in on the act. "We can work it out here." How? "This is ridiculous." He turned to Zimmerman. "Do I get a lawyer?"

"If you are officially charged. Let's hope that won't be necessary. We can inform your embassy, if you like, that you have been detained. Though I should warn you that that might take some time. I don't want you to think it's a lack of interest on their part, but there are procedures to follow." He lowered his voice. "And of course it makes difficulties for the chief. Questions asked. Paperwork. I speak from experience. I can recommend that you be allowed to return to your hotel tonight, if we need to continue tomorrow."

"But you can't guarantee it."

"No. Not if you are charged."

"Nick—" Molly said.

"It's all right. You go back to the hotel and wait." He turned to Zimmerman. "Can I call her later?"

"As you wish."

"I'll stay with you," Molly said.

"No." He looked at Zimmerman. "May I talk with her privately?"

Zimmerman shook his head. "It's not allowed."

"Can I go to the bathroom, then?"

Zimmerman held his eyes for a second, then nodded, a faint smile. "With an escort."

After an exchange with Novotný in Czech, one of

the policemen led them out. In the hallway Nick hugged her goodbye.

"Nick, stop arguing with him." Her voice was low, worried. "It doesn't do any good."

He stood still. Larry's advice to his father, years ago, in the study. You're not doing yourself any favors in there. Were they so alike?

"Somebody killed him, Molly."

"But he thinks you did. You've got to call your father."

"No."

"Nick, you've got to get out of here. You're only going to get in deeper. How are you going to explain—"

"Ssh. I'll think of something. Look, go to the embassy. They won't keep me here if someone makes a stink. Novotný doesn't want to charge me with anything—it would be a real pain. It's Zimmerman who can't get enough. By the way, I told him there was something wrong with the car—that's why we were taking the train. You heard the noise in the motor when we came back from the country, okay?"

"I don't understand any of this. I *hate* it. What train? What *happened*?"

"Later." The guard came over to nudge them apart. "Just go to the embassy."

"The embassy?" Nervous, her face dismayed.

"Yes, tell them to get me out of here. They can't keep me without a formal charge."

"And what if they do charge you?"

"Then they were going to do it anyway."

"What if he's right? That it takes them forever to—"

"Molly," he said, stopping her. But what if it did? An in box of tourist problems? He'd have to flash their attention. A flare, someone they'd know. "Tell them I'm working for Jack Kemper. In the London embassy. They'll move. I guarantee it."

"Who?"

"Just do it. Please. I'll explain it all later." He kissed her. "Do it."

"Nick, what are you doing?"

"Kemper," he said. "Don't forget. His wife's name is Doris."

"Doris?" she said, flailing, but before he could say anything else, the guard led him away.

"Later," he said over his shoulder, watching her fold her arms across her chest as if she were cold.

The guard stood at the door while he washed his hands. Flakes of dried blood, forgotten, came off in the water, turning it rust-colored. He stared at the drain, suddenly weak, then washed again, and again, until the water ran clear. On the way back, passing a long row of cubicles, he spotted Anna over a waist-high partition. She was bent over a desk, her arm moving, and for a moment he thought she was washing her hands too. Then he saw that she was writing, signing a paper. He imagined the statement—his father's depression, the upheaval of the weekend, his state of mind, all signed away now, more blood down the drain. When she looked up, her face blotchy from crying, she was startled to see him, as if Nick had died

402

too. Then she took in the guard leading him by the arm and looked away, refusing to meet his eyes.

"Anna," he said, forcing her to turn back. "I'm sorry."

"They said you found him," she said, her voice distant with grief.

"Yes."

"He wanted me to go to my sister's. After the concert. I thought he wanted to be with you. Was that it?" The troubling detail.

"No."

She nodded, piecing it together, then turned away again, cutting him out.

"I wish you had never come," she said.

Zimmerman was waiting with a pot of coffee, talking to Novotný, who sat on the windowsill eating a salami sandwich.

"Tell me about your trip to the country," Zimmerman began.

"It rained," Nick said dully.

"Yet you told the hotel you were going to Karlovy Vary. Why?"

Deeper. Zimmerman's voice droned on, elaborately polite, refusing to be discouraged by Nick's vague replies. There was always another question. He had all the time in the world, his patience as relentless as a light in the face. Wasn't that the way they were supposed to do it? The bright lamp hurting your eyes. No sleep. Shouts. Beatings. But nothing here was what he'd expected. He thought of the watchtowers at the border, his first sensation of fear, a movie iron curtain bristling with menace. But the countryside had been placid, the pokey guard interested only in his car. Now Zimmerman talked patiently, lulling him. But what did he really want? There was no way of knowing. The polite questions might be as deceptive as the placid landscape, still after all lined with barbed wire. So Nick stalled, repeating himself, giving away nothing that mattered. And after a while it was easier. The story became real to him. There *was* something wrong with the car. Molly did have business in Vienna. Why not? He saw that Zimmerman recognized it too, the tipping point after which nothing would be revealed, because the lies were now true. His eyes, shrewd, witnesses to a hundred interrogations, began to anticipate Nick's answers—the cards fell where he expected them. Why go on? Unless this was part of the weakening process.

They took a break. Zimmerman sighed and lit another cigarette, his manner easy and intimate. He reminded Nick, in fact—an odd thought—of his father, the resigned irony, the personal reaching out. Trust me. He'd watched his father the same way, trying to guess how much was true behind the words, sorting through his conversations as if they were index cards. Except his father was dead. What if everything he'd said had been true, all of it? No hidden meanings or little deceptions, just what he'd said, the story he'd proved by dying. While Nick had wasted time wondering if he could trust him. He looked up at Zimmerman. But not him.

Only the dead could be trusted here. Had Anna really been with relatives? Wouldn't it have been easy to— Improbable. But then, everything was improbable. A list. They'll want this, he'd said. What did Zimmerman want?

"Can I ask you a question?" Nick said suddenly.

"Yes, certainly."

"Did they find anything? When they searched his desk?"

Zimmerman stared at him, trying to figure out what he meant. So they hadn't. "What did you expect them to find, Mr. Warren?"

"I don't know. A note."

"No," Zimmerman said quietly. "No note." A beat. "You don't think a note would have been left out where it could easily be found?"

Then where was it? If the list didn't exist, then none of it was true, and it had to be true, because he was dead. But Zimmerman was waiting.

"Is that your experience?"

Zimmerman shrugged. "Every case is different."

More questions. The afternoon passing, only faint light now against the wall outside the window. They were alone, Novotný having left, giving up any pretense of following their talk. When he came back, it was with a burst of Czech, agitated. Zimmerman raised his eyebrows and followed him out. The quiet was worse. The interrogation at least was a distraction; his whole mind was forced to pay attention. Now it was released, skittering back to his father on the lawn, cradling him.

"Well, Mr. Warren," Zimmerman said as he

came back in. "You interest me more and more." He cocked his head toward the door. "Your rescue party is here."

"Molly?"

"No, your embassy. Remarkably efficient. They find it objectionable for us to detain you any longer. I didn't know you were so important."

"I'm not. We don't detain people in America."

"No doubt that explains why you have so much crime."

"So can I go?"

"For now. I have persuaded Chief Novotný that you're not such a dangerous character. It is as I predicted—an official protest would upset him. But I wish you had followed my advice. Now he will have to take an interest. So much work for everyone. Well." He opened his hand, a follow-me gesture. "I must ask, however, that you do not go far. We are not so accommodating as that. So you will stay in Prague."

"Until when?"

"Until we have no more questions." He stepped aside to let Nick pass. "Of course you have my personal sympathies. It is a difficult thing, a parent's death."

"Thank you." He was almost at the door.

"Oh, one last question. I forgot. Your father—the report does not say—did he by any chance lose control of his bowels?"

Nick stopped. "Yes. Why?"

"I was curious. For the details. Sometimes the reports—Thank you."

He opened the door. Chief Novotný, glowering. Next to him a man in a raincoat, extending his hand.

"Mr. Warren? Jeff Foster, American embassy."

Nick froze for a minute, his hand stuck in midair. Then he took Foster's, aware of Zimmerman watching him, not wanting him to catch the look on his face as he recognized the coat, the sandy hair, the man on the bridge with Molly.

CHAPTER THIRTEEN

"You want to tell me what the hell's going on?" Foster said outside. "We called Kemper. He never heard of you." Nick stared at him, his mind racing. Together on the bridge. "You okay?"

Say something. "I met him in London."

"Yeah? He never met you. Now he's got bells and whistles going off all over the place. Here," Foster said, indicating the car.

"Where are we going?"

"Back to the embassy. There's a little reception committee waiting to hear what you have to say. It better be good."

"Look, we did meet, at a party. I knew he was CIA. I wanted to get out of here and I figured that would get your attention."

"You got that part right." He nodded toward the police building. "You probably got their attention now too."

"How?"

"You think the Czechs don't monitor our calls? Christ, it's how half the country makes its living."

"Well, sorry. It was all I could think of."

"Sorry."

"Back off, okay? I came to see my father. He

killed himself and I got hauled into a Czech police station—what would you do? It worked, didn't it? I'm not going to tell anybody Kemper's CIA, I don't give a shit. I'm not trying to make trouble for anybody. I just want to get out of here."

Foster looked at him, surprised. "He killed himself?"

"He's dead. Maybe they think *I* did it, I don't know. Didn't Molly tell you?" Nick said, watching him closely.

"Nobody told me anything," Foster said smoothly. "I got a message sent up there's an American in jail says he works for Jack Kemper and would I go and get him. Now I've got this mess. He doesn't know you. You don't know him. How'd you know he was CIA, anyway?" Actually looking around as he spoke.

"I didn't," Nick said, not wanting to involve Larry. "I just figured it was a safe bet. All you embassy guys are, aren't you?"

Foster held up his hand. "I just work here."

"Yeah, stamping passports."

"Okay, let's just calm down. We'll go for a little ride and you tell the good folks what you told me."

"You tell them. Look, I've been answering questions all day. You're supposed to be on my side, remember? I'm just an American who pushed a button for help. The wrong button, I guess. Tell Kemper I'm sorry, his secret's safe with me. Tell him he has a nice wife. We sat together at dinner, that's why I remembered his name. That's all it is."

"That's all."

"I won't be hard to find if you want me tomorrow. The police are making me stay in Prague. Can they do that, by the way?"

Foster nodded. "It's their country."

"So can we skip the debriefing? I'm not a spook. I'm not anything—just tired. I just want to go back to the hotel." Did he? What would he say? Careful of her now. Quicksilver.

Foster was looking at him. "Some stunt." Then he smiled. "You don't know what you started. They've even got the ambassador jumping around."

"Well, make my apologies."

"You'll have to do that one yourself." He looked at him again, assessing. "Okay, tomorrow. He's got a dinner tonight anyway. You're out, that's the main thing. We don't want the Czechs thinking it's anything serious. That would really start something. Come on, I'll give you a lift."

"I'll walk."

"That makes it harder for them," Foster said, sliding his eyes toward a parked car. Two men. "They'll have to go slow, and it messes up traffic. Easier to follow a car."

"I'll never be alone again, huh?"

"Not in Prague."

"Nicholas?" He heard a voice at his side. Anna. How long had she been there? "Everything is all right?"

He nodded. She glanced at Foster, then handed Nick a piece of paper.

"It's the address. For the funeral."

"The funeral?" Already arranged.

"Yes, tomorrow. If you would come."

He looked down at the paper. A meaningless street name. "Tomorrow? Aren't they going to do an autopsy?"

She shook her head. "No one said. There's no need."

He grabbed her arms. "Anna, he didn't kill himself. They should—"

But she shrank from him, looking around to see if anyone was watching. "Please." She turned her back to Foster, who felt awkward enough to step toward the car. "You don't understand," she said to Nick, almost a whisper. "How it is here. It's better not to wait."

"Better? For whom, the police? I won't let them do this."

"*You* won't?"

"I'm his family."

"I'm his family here, Nicholas. Me." She glared at him, then lowered her head. "It's not for you to decide."

"But don't you want to know?"

"What? I know he's dead. It's enough." She moved back. "What I said before—I know you meant well. But now, leave Prague. There's nothing more for you to do here." She nodded at the paper in his hand. "Ten o'clock," she said, and walked away.

Nick got into the back seat with Foster, behind the driver, who had a Marine's shaved head.

"What was that all about? I thought you said he killed himself."

"She's his wife. What would you say?" He looked away, feeling in his pocket for a cigarette. "Let her think it was an accident."

"An accident. With an autopsy." Foster leaned forward to the driver. "The Alcron, over on Wenceslas." The car swung into the street. "You don't want to get involved in anything," he said to Nick. "Not here. There's only so much we can do, you know. We can make a little noise if they haul you in for no reason, but if there's anything wrong—"

"I'm on my own, I know." He lit the cigarette. "Don't worry. Nothing's wrong, not that way. They think he killed himself. Everybody does."

"But not you."

Nick looked at him. "He must have."

"I'm sorry. They said you found him. That's rough."

"Yes."

"After all these years."

"You know who he was?"

"Well, after I heard the name. He's the one that got away." Foster paused. "Must be a hell of a thing to live with."

The car was quiet with the tension of someone not rising to the bait.

"You guys keep tabs on him? Keep the files up to date?"

"We don't have the manpower for that," Foster said flatly. "By the way, before you get any other ideas, I don't work for the Agency."

"You just work at the embassy."

"That's right."

"Doing what?"

"Trade relations, mostly."

What had Kemper been in? Agricultural development.

"Really. What do we import?"

"Glass."

Nick took another pull on the cigarette. "I'd like to know. *Did* you keep tabs on him? Tail him, that kind of thing? Yesterday, for instance?"

"Why yesterday?"

Nick shrugged. "I just wondered. Something was bothering him. I thought maybe you—"

"I wouldn't know. I was in meetings all day." He turned to Nick. "Nobody was tailing him. I told you, we don't have the people for that. I don't think the intelligence guys—" He looked at Nick. "We have *some.* I never heard they were interested. Is there any reason why they should have been?"

"No good reason, no."

"Anyway, it would fit, wouldn't it? Something bothering him."

"Perfectly."

"Yeah, well." Foster turned away, embarrassed. "Hell of a thing, to live with that. I'm sorry. Here we go." The hotel doorman came to meet them. Foster put his hand on Nick's shoulder, a coach's gesture. "Do us a favor, okay? Keep your nose clean. We don't want to run interference with the police. The Czechs don't like it. They have to watch themselves too, since the Russians came in. You don't want to start anything."

Nick took in the friendly hand, the open face, an American kind of menace. What had he said on the bridge?

"No. I just want to get out of here."

"You and me both. I used to be in Paris. Now that's a place. Here you have to watch your back all the time."

Nick nodded. "I'll remember."

He got out and saw the Škoda two car lengths behind. In the hotel lobby he could feel the change immediately. The desk clerk's eyes followed him across the room, a disturbance, someone the police had asked about. When Molly opened the door and hugged him—the same smell, the same smooth skin—he felt they were onstage, with one part of him out front, watching. It was easy to do, being someone else. His father's son.

She sat on a chair a few feet away, curled into herself, while he told her about the morning at Holečkova, the body on the grass, feeding her only what he wanted her to hear, watching, measuring the distress in her face. They ate in the hotel dining room, old starched napkins and pork with sludgy gravy, sleepwalking through the meal. She took his distance for grief, picking at her food, waiting for him to speak. Then they sat drinking wine, almost alone in the faded room.

"You haven't told me about the train."

"Yes, I did."

"I mean why. I don't understand."

"Something happened yesterday."

"Yesterday? What?"

"I don't know. He was all right at noon. Then at the concert, all of a sudden he has to leave. Something happened." But how many possibilities were there? The gallery. The walk to the Loreto. The bridge. He looked at her.

"Did Anna know?" she said. "About the train?"

"I'm not sure. I don't think so."

"Is it possible that—" She stopped.

"What?"

"Please don't be angry. That he did kill himself?"

"No." She waited for more. "Why would he have gone to all the bother about the train? The whole plan, making me get tickets. Would he have done that to me?"

She shook her head.

"He was murdered."

She flinched. "But why?"

"Because someone didn't want him to leave. There can't be any other reason." He looked straight at her. "So who else knew he was planning to go?"

She didn't meet his eyes but looked down at her glass, somewhere else. Then she folded her arms across her chest, shivering, as if there were a draft in the stuffy room.

"What?" he said.

"I'm sorry. It's the wine."

"It's not the wine." Tell me.

415

"No, it's everything. It's my fault, isn't it? Starting this. We never should have come."

Not what he'd expected. "Stop."

"You blame me."

"I don't blame you." But why did you lie?

"It never would have happened."

"Stop it, Molly. Somebody killed him, not you. This isn't helping anything." He put his napkin on the table. "Come on, we're both tired. Let's go up." Play everything through.

"Sorry," she said, stung by his tone. "This is just making it worse, isn't it?"

And upstairs it was no better. They got into bed, an acting kiss, then turned away from each other, lying on their sides. He looked at the light on the ceiling, thinking of the other night, the tram bells outside, drowning in her. Now he was alert but absolutely still, as if he were afraid moving would wake her, even though he knew the reason he could not sleep was that she was awake too.

They took a taxi to the funeral address, a street out past the station, near the outskirts of town. The room, a kind of chapel with pews, was plain and functional, stripped down to a lectern, a Czech flag, one vase of flowers, and the wooden coffin on a platform in front. An undertaker in a black suit hovered near the door, an anxious maitre d' waiting for the room to fill, but after a few early arrivals no one came, and finally he had to start.

Anna sat in front, with Anna Masaryk behind her, like two squat matrioshka dolls. Zimmerman, in a suit, sat near the back, his curious eyes darting frankly around the room. There were four people Nick did not know, scattered off to the side, and František, sober now, who went to the lectern to speak. No one else. Where were the others? Would there have been more people in Moscow, old friends? Or was this the extent of his father's life, a pared-down circle and a son?

He and Molly sat across from Anna, and he kept his eyes fixed on the closed coffin. The eulogy was in Czech, so he had no idea what was being said. Probably the usual empty phrases, as comfortless as medals. In Moscow they would have mentioned the Order of Lenin, but not here. No socialist heroes, not since the invasion. His father had, somehow, become nobody at all.

The loneliness of the room was oppressive, and Nick shifted in his seat, causing a creak. Were they watching him? He had seen it in their faces, that he had a new role to play now, the cause of his father's despair, the unbearable reminder of everything he'd lost. His fault. And for a moment he gave in to it, became what they wanted. What if none of it was true, the whole story a pretense his father could no longer keep up? No Silver. No plan. Just a story whose plot had run out. Easier for everybody. What had he actually seen in the flat but the disorder of a final night? Then Molly squirmed beside him and he was alert again. He turned. People were nodding at the speech, their heads down.

417

Only Zimmerman was looking at him, his eyes bright, interested. Who knew it hadn't been suicide, only that people wanted it to be.

The Czech went on, František dropping to a guttural rumble, then chopping the air with his hand, making some point. Anna was crying quietly. A hurried funeral, her decision. Did she think it was Nick's fault too? Or had she discovered that his father was going to leave, even helped him? Out of the way, visiting relatives. But she must have been with him that afternoon, when something had happened. Nick looked at the wooden box, his mind freed by the droning language to sift through the last few days. Everything that had happened. Except for Molly, sitting next to him, pale, who couldn't be explained.

The words ended abruptly, and František sat down next to Anna and patted her hand. No one moved. Nick waited for music, some formal signal, but there was just the quiet. The undertaker and a helper came forward, said something in Czech, and pushed a button. Behind the platform, doors opened in the wall, and Nick saw that the coffin was on a kind of ramp, maneuvered now by the two men so that it began sliding toward what must be the crematorium, shuddering a little until the angle took it and it fell away, like a ship being launched into the water. Then the doors closed and his father was gone.

The room emptied quickly, a few polite condolences to Anna, then a shuffling toward the door. No one talked to Nick.

418

"I'm sorry, Anna," he said when the others had gone.

"Thank you for coming," she said formally. Then, softly, "He would have wanted that."

He felt his insides lurch. "I wish I had known him better."

"I think you knew him better than anyone," she said sadly. "You knew what he was like before."

"I'm sorry," he said again, at a loss. "Can we take you home?"

"No, no. I have to stay here. For the arrangements. Goodbye," she said to Molly, holding out her hand. "He liked you."

"Oh," Molly said, struck. She reached over and embraced Anna, surprising her. "Is there anything—"

"No," she said stiffly. "It's all arranged. Goodbye."

Nick looked at her, not knowing what else to do. His stepmother, a stranger. But she was already turning away from him, back to her life.

"Anna? Would you tell me something? What did he do that last day, before the concert?"

She looked up at him. "He took a nap."

"You were with him? I mean, did he see anybody?"

"No," she said, sterner now. "He took a nap. He was thinking. He would do that, lie on the sofa thinking and then fall asleep."

"He didn't go out?"

"No, I told you. Leave me alone now." She looked up, her eyes fierce. "Leave Prague." Then she turned her back to him and walked over to the undertaker.

Outside, the street was empty except for the Škoda, parked in front where he would see it.

"Maybe they'll give us a ride," Nick said.

"Don't," Molly said, nervous. "It's not funny. There's a tram stop down there at the next street."

They walked to the corner.

"Mr. Warren." A voice from a car window, rolled down.

"Miss Masaryk," he said, surprised.

"You remember. Good. Please, come to lunch." She handed him an address.

"That's very kind of you, but—"

"No, it's not kind. I want to talk to you. Alone." She glanced at Molly. "Excuse me."

"Why?"

"About your father. It's important. You'll come?"

"When?"

"An hour. Don't ring the bell, it's broken. The top floor. There's a good view," she said irrelevantly, then rolled up the window and started the car.

"Who was that?"

"A friend of his," he said, not wanting to give her a name. "She probably wants to talk old times."

"It didn't sound that way."

"I won't be long."

"Let me know if—"

"If what?"

"You're going to be late. I'll be worried."

■

A narrow street in the Old Town, near the river. The downstairs bell in fact was broken, the panel taped over, and the lobby itself, heavy stone cool as a monastery, was in disrepair. A pail sat in one corner to catch drips, and the broad stairs were worn down by the years, crumbling near the edges. When he began to climb, he could hear the echo of his steps in the stairwell.

She opened the door immediately, as if she had been listening for him, and motioned him in.

"Good, good, I was afraid you would miss it. The door, it's confusing. Come in. Some coffee? Maybe a brandy."

Nick shook his head, looking around. The room followed the curve of the eaves, vaulting near the windows, dipping lower toward the back. There were books everywhere, stacked to the ceiling on their sides, too many for shelves. Yellowing cream French spines, shinier English jackets. What wall space had escaped the stacks was crammed with picture frames, next to each other, a collage of old photographs and prints. The dining table near the window, already laid with open-faced sandwiches and pickles, was set for three. A pack of Marlboros had been placed in the center like an extra course.

He looked at the third plate, but she misinterpreted, following his eyes farther, to the window.

"Yes, come and see. It's why I stay. My little

nest. It's too small, but the view makes up for that."

A romantic view, the Charles Bridge and the hill rising behind it to Hradčany Castle, spires everywhere.

"I saw the tanks from here. A friend telephoned, so early. Who calls at such an hour? Go to your window, he said, the Russians are here. And there they were, coming over the bridge. I was standing right here all morning, watching them. The bridge was shaking. I thought, if one of the statues comes down. Bastards." She waved her hand dismissively.

"Is someone else coming?" Nick asked.

"Yes." He heard a kettle whistle. "Sit, sit. I'll make the coffee." Fluttering, not wanting to talk.

"How did you know my father?"

"Through Anna. We were at school. Of course, that's a long time ago. But she came back, so I met him. He used to come here to talk about books, many times." She stopped. "I'm so sorry for you." Then, obviously relieved, she heard the knock. "Ah, he's here."

Nick stood waiting as she opened the door. Zimmerman, still in his mourning suit. They exchanged greetings in Czech, a social kiss.

"Mr. Warren, you don't mind? Anna was so kind to arrange. It's easier to talk here."

"I've told you everything I know."

He held up his hand. "You misunderstand. It's not the interrogation. I want to talk to you in a different way. No questions. Well, perhaps one."

"Sit, sit," Anna said, busying herself with the coffee, settling them in.

Nick sat down slowly, feeling ambushed. There was an awkward silence while Anna poured, neither of them saying anything. Zimmerman took one of the Marlboros.

"What question?" Nick said.

Zimmerman nodded to Anna, who went over to a stack of books and brought back an envelope.

"Your father asked Anna to hold this for him. He was going to collect it yesterday morning."

"I'm always up early," Anna said, as if that explained it.

"I took the liberty of opening it. Under the circumstances. Miss Masaryk, of course, had no idea what it was."

"Then why did she tell you about it?" Nick said, looking at her.

"She was concerned when she heard the news of his death. She thought it might be important. You understand, we are very old friends."

"It's Karl who started the investigation into Uncle Jan's death," she explained. "It's he who was helping František's brother with the manuscript. You can trust him."

Nick opened the envelope and drew out a Russian passport: his father's picture, Cyrillic type.

"Your father was not Jewish." Zimmerman pointed to the Cyrillic letters. "Not called Pechorvsky, either. But that is his picture, yes? Can you think why he would need such a thing? A Russian Jew's passport?"

"No." But Nick's heart was racing. All of it was true. His father's papers for the train—not at the flat, but ready. Everything was just as he had said.

"That page is an exit visa," Zimmerman said.

"But it's not his."

"No. Pechorvsky's. Who died of kidney failure." He picked up the passport, running his finger along the edge of the picture, the raised seal. "Not the best, but it would pass. The visa's good for two more weeks."

"I don't understand."

"I think you do."

"Well, I don't. Was that your question?"

"No." He slipped the passport back into the envelope. "Mr. Warren, a man with someone else's exit visa can only mean one thing. He was planning to leave. Perhaps by train," he said, looking away, casual. "But not, I think, to Israel, like poor Comrade Pechorvsky. My question is, why?"

"Why? Everybody wants to leave."

"Not everybody. A man with the Order of Lenin, who betrayed his country—would such a man be welcome in the West? What made him think they would want him back?"

"I don't know," Nick said, hammering each word in.

"No? But it's a question, don't you agree?"

"He's dead. The question is who killed him. Why don't you ask that?"

"Because I know who killed him, Mr. Warren."

Nick stared at him, almost afraid to go on. "Who?" he said quietly.

"That is, I know who must have killed him. It's not difficult. What interests me is why."

"Who?" Nick said again.

"So direct, Mr. Warren. Sometimes an answer is indirect. Please listen. More coffee, Anna?"

Nick sat silently.

"Of course, every case is different," Zimmerman said. "It's the similarities that intrigue."

"What are you talking about?"

"Please. I said I had only one question. But I also have a story. That is why I wanted to see you. Will you listen to it? It will interest you, I promise. You are familiar with our history, I saw that at the station. 'The housemaid's solution.' How much do you know about the Masaryk case?"

"Hardly anything. Look—"

"Then listen carefully. I know a great deal about it, almost everything. It's as Anna says. Last year, under Dubček, there was an investigation, so we would know, once and for all. It's a national obsession, that case, our great mystery. Does it matter, after so many years? A little—you'll forgive me— like your President Kennedy. To know exactly what happened. So with Jan Masaryk."

"Everybody knows the Russians did it."

"But to *know*, Mr. Warren, to *prove* it. It's not easy. So many people have died—the night watchman, the doctor who signed the death certificate. Some natural, some not so natural. Just last year, a bodyguard who talked to me was shot on the highway. By thieves?"

"Karl himself was in danger," Anna said, touch-

425

ing Nick's arm, a conspirator. "He was threatened. They don't want the truth to come out, even now."

"But we learn things. So, the case. Nineteen forty-eight. The Communists are in. Masaryk is still in the cabinet, but not one of them. To the whole world he represents the old republic, his father's country. And every day in the cabinet, a new compromise. The death—how do you say it?—the death of a thousand bites. The Russians are taking over. So perhaps he feels despair. A way to end it all, the housemaid's solution. But there is also the possibility that he was planning to leave."

He looked at Nick. "An embarrassment for the Communists. Maybe even a government in exile, like during the war. His mistress had already gone—an American. So for them the jump was a convenient death. A public funeral. The end of the republic. But was he murdered? From the beginning there were inconsistencies. A more complicated case, let me say, than your own. The position of the body in the courtyard. A very wide jump. Violence in his room—even in the bathroom. Bottles broken, bedpillows on the floor. Even in the tub. Why, for sleeping? The window there had a high sill—not convenient. Scrapes. And his pajamas were soiled."

He looked again at Nick. "So many inconsistencies. A car was heard pulling away in the night. Was someone there? We'll never know. You see, Mr. Warren, the mistake I made was thinking that a criminal investigation would tell us everything. But this was a political crime. We can reconstruct the

426

evidence—what must have happened. But what I want to know is, was he planning to leave?"

Nick looked at him, quiet.

"You can't ignore the passport," Anna said.

"What must have happened?" Nick said.

Zimmerman rolled his cigarette against the ashtray, methodically tapping the ash. "Masaryk had had a full day. A meeting with Beneš, the president, his father's old friend. Very depressing, I've no doubt. Beneš may have told Masaryk he was going to resign. But that would work either way, as the last straw or an incentive to go. Either way. He had a meeting the next day with a Polish delegation, a speech to write. So he goes to bed early to work on the speech. He frequently did that, worked in bed. A bottle of beer and a sandwich. These details we know. The servants retired. Very heavy sleepers, unfortunately. Of course, the Czernin Palace is a large building and their quarters were not close. No one heard the lift being used. The guard at the front door reported no visitors. There is a side door for deliveries, unguarded. This much we know as fact."

"Go on," Nick said. Had they used the elevator at Holečkova? He thought of the milky light through the glass brick on the landing, enough to see by, even at dawn.

"Masaryk was a big man. There must have been two, perhaps more, a team. The side door, the stairs. Quiet. Perhaps they were surprised to find him still up, working so late. There must have been fighting. The room is knocked about, papers all over. In the bathroom, more smashes. They must have been angry at his resistance. But he's fighting for his life and he's strong. He must have knocked against the medicine chest, causing the bottles to fall on the floor. Then he is pushed, or falls, into the bathtub. And there someone must have held him down with a pillow over his face. He must have kicked, trying to get out, while they held him down. Until he stopped kicking." Zimmerman looked up from the ashtray, his voice dropping, almost husky now. "Of course, he was a vigorous man. Had he been older, it would have been easier. Not such a struggle."

Nick turned away, sick.

"Then they must have pulled him out—he would have been heavy—and dragged him over to the window, perhaps stepping on the bottles, kicking them out of the way. A high sill, the men grunting, propping him up. From the angle of the fall, they must have pushed him out back first. That was the first inconsistency. No one jumps backward. In its own way it's a brave thing, suicide. His fingers scrape the sill as they push him out. It's possible that the scraping happened earlier—that they tried to force him out the window and he resisted, holding on while he kicked them away. Then the same fight. No matter. He went out. That is the criminal evidence. That is what must have happened."

For a moment, no one spoke. "How do you know it was a pillow?" Nick said quietly.

"There were no signs of strangulation. Were

428

there marks on your father's neck?" Zimmerman said, no longer pretending to be in the past.

"No."

"But he soiled himself. That's very rare in someone who jumps."

"If he was frightened—" Nick began.

"So rare as to be almost nonexistent. It is, however, a common occurrence in cases of suffocation. It happens most frequently when people are hanged—that's why we have connected losing control of the bowels to fear. But jumpers don't do that. They are not afraid. But it would happen if he were smothered. During the struggle."

Clearly, as if in slow motion, Nick saw his father on the bed, gasping, his feet moving, then giving in. His papers ready. Nick touched the envelope. Nothing else, no list.

"Who?" Nick said finally.

"Who. Mr. Warren, do you blame the gun for going off? These men are tools. They are nobody. I'm not going to know who entered the Czernin Palace. I'm not going to know who went to your father's flat on Holečkova. I accept that."

"Then why are you telling me this?"

"So you will accept it too. So you are not tempted. To play the detective."

"My father wasn't Masaryk. He wasn't going to set up a government in exile."

"Then why was he killed? You see, I accept the limitations. How far we can take a criminal investigation—we've had to learn that. But it's still important to know, to protect ourselves. One day, you know, the Russians will leave—yes, I believe that. We can be policemen again, solve real cases. But meanwhile we have to know what they're doing. To hide, to play the fool if it's better. To survive them. This is what we do."

"Soldier Schweik."

"If you like. A man is killed. If I know why, then I know how far I can go. Contain the situation."

"By pretending it didn't happen."

"If that's necessary."

"Why do you want to protect them?"

"Mr. Warren, I want to protect you."

"Me?"

"Has it occurred to you how dangerous this might be for you? I came here to talk to you as a friend. I think you did not, at the station, understand how things are."

"And how are they?"

"They must protect the lie. They'll do anything to do that. Look at Masaryk—a crime twenty years old, yet still the lie. It's a curious thing, to care so much what people think when you have all the power anyway. Maybe they need to believe it themselves. So they stage a simple case of suicide. Who would doubt it? But you are there, something unexpected. Now there are questions, accusations, the Americans calling. If they feel the lie is threatened, they will have to protect it. So now a crime. But the most obvious person to have done it, Mr. Warren, is you."

"You know I didn't. The evidence—"

"Can be made to fit. It's not a criminal case, Mr.

Warren. That's what I'm trying to tell you. A political crime. All that matters is what they want people to believe. You were there, you had the motive." He paused. "And you cannot explain yourself."

"But you know—"

"If you are charged, there's nothing I can do. You must see that. Of course, it's a complication to arrest you. It becomes an incident. So many people involved. But they will do it, if they have to protect themselves. And you will be convicted. All proper and legal." He lowered his voice. "You will be your father's murderer."

Nick raised his head.

"Yes. They can do it. The question is, is it worth it to them? That's what I don't know yet. And I can't know that until I know why he was planning to leave. Why he was stopped. I can't help you if I don't know that. If you don't tell me."

Nick, shaken, said nothing.

"Will they accuse you? Is it that important to them?"

"I don't know."

Zimmerman sighed and reached for another cigarette, taking his time. "Of course, there is another possibility. The easiest way to avoid everything—no incident, no trial. What do you know, Mr. Warren? They were willing to kill him. Why stop? They killed people in the Masaryk case—oh yes, even years later. If they thought you knew the reason. It would be easy, to make a new lie. A family tragedy. You found the body. Who can say how people react to such a terrible thing? Sometimes they blame themselves. It would be easy. If they thought you knew."

Nick stared at the precise, glowing ash of Zimmerman's cigarette. "Maybe they sent you to find out."

Zimmerman looked at him for a second, then nodded slowly. "Yes, maybe. In that case, I seem to have failed. You decide." He stood up, scraping the chair. "But I see I have accomplished one thing—to make you suspicious. Even of me. Good. You need to be careful."

"Like you."

"Yes, like everyone here. But we're still alive."

Nick didn't move. All of it true. But did they know about him? Had his father told them? Before the pillows made him quiet?

"Do you really think they'd—"

"I have no way of knowing, Mr. Warren. Perhaps it's my imagination. Only you would know that. If what you know is dangerous. But I would be careful. In fact, I would leave Prague."

"You're the one who ordered me to stay."

He nodded. "Yes, it's a difficulty. You understand, that was an official request, not mine."

"Then what—"

"Under the circumstances? Go with the suicide. Make a statement. About his despair. Be innocent." Zimmerman stared at him, serious.

Nick looked away. An end to it. What everybody wanted. He thought of Anna's arm moving, on the other side of the cubicle wall.

"Then I can leave?" he asked finally.

432

"I'll see. I don't know how far this has gone. Incidentally, has anyone talked yet to Miss Chisholm?"

"No."

"Then perhaps you would advise her." He paused. "My concern for you—if you know what you say you don't—would extend to anyone. It's one thing to put yourself at risk—"

"She doesn't know anything."

Zimmerman smiled. "But then, neither do you. Be careful, Mr. Warren."

"Thank you. For the story."

"A reconstruction. What might have happened."

"You said 'must.'"

Zimmerman shrugged. "It suggests itself. It's not the first time." He looked down at Nick. "But you have to be satisfied with that, with what must have happened. You understand that. You can stop playing detective."

"And that's why you told me? So I'd stop? Go away?"

"So you would not live with a mystery. It can be a poison."

"Yes," Nick said quietly, his eyes fixed on the ashtray.

"You were thinking of another?"

Nick looked up at him. "How he got here."

Zimmerman opened his mouth to say some-thing, then gave it up, turning away. "You will not solve that in Prague."

"No." Nick stood. "Do I have to sign some-thing?"

"At your convenience. I will call you." He gave Nick a wry glance. "If your embassy permits."

"They don't care. They want me to go too."

Nick picked up the passport and held it out to him.

"No. That would only confuse Chief Novotný." He turned to Anna. "Sometimes things are not found. It's a pity."

Anna nodded and took the passport.

"Not even by good Czechs who might need them," he said to her. "You understand? Not this one."

She nodded again. "You haven't eaten anything," she said.

"Another time, Anička. Thank you. Mr. Warren?"

They said goodbye to her, shaking hands, leaving her to her full table and wonderful view. On the stairs, there were no sounds but their shoes against the worn stone.

"I'll leave first," Zimmerman said when they reached the ground floor. "Wait a few minutes here, please. Go left, to the corner, so they can see you."

"Aren't they your own men?"

He smiled weakly. "But I'm careful. Like you." He took Nick's hand, peering closely at him. "I wonder what you know, Mr. Warren."

"I don't know anything."

"Then that is what I'll say."

"Will they believe you?"

"Oh, I think so. I was a good interrogator, when we were just police."

Nick waited in the dark stairwell, listening to the drips in the pail. Then he went out, turning toward the Old Town Square, the streets, like everything else, a maze.

CHAPTER FOURTEEN

Molly was sitting by the window, waiting for him.

"What happened?"

"A condolence call," he said, crossing the room, avoiding her.

She waited, then looked down, disappointed. "Anna called. She wants to see you, at your father's."

"She say why?"

"No. Just that she has something for you."

He stopped, attentive now. Not in the desk. Anna had found it somewhere else.

"Okay. I'll be back as soon as I can."

"I'll come," she said, getting up.

"You don't have to."

"Yes, I do. I'm going crazy here. I keep thinking they're picking you up again."

"They won't. I called Zimmerman. I told him I'd sign a statement saying my father was depressed. I was worried about him. That's why I went to see him that morning."

"But I thought—"

"That's how you remember it too, isn't it?" he said, partly to the walls. "He left the concert early, after that little fight we had. If they ask."

436

She stopped in front of him. "Nick, what's going on?"

"Just say it."

"If that's what you want," she said, trying to read his face.

"That's what I want." He turned away. "I'll go see him after Anna and get it over with. I won't be long." He went over to the window and drew back the edge of the curtain. "Our friends are still here."

"Where?" She came over and looked out. "Not very subtle, are they?"

"Not the ones we know about."

She shivered. "Stop." She picked up her shoulder bag from the chair. "I'm not staying here. I'm just not."

They walked down Wenceslas, past the *párky* stalls and half-empty shops, heading inevitably toward the Národní Street bridge. Where had Anna found it? Did she know what it meant? Molly, wary, said nothing, glancing over her shoulder. One of the men followed on foot, the Škoda lagging behind. They passed the corner where she had caught the tram and started across the bridge. He waited until they were halfway across before he stopped, looking over at the tree where he'd stood.

"What's wrong?"

"I don't want them to lose us. I like having a bodyguard."

"Why? What's going on?"

"My father was killed, Molly. Not depressed, killed. I don't want to end up the same way."

"You?"

"The guy from the embassy said I should watch my back."

"Did he?" she said, her face blank. "Why would he say that?"

"Maybe he's paranoid. They get like that over here. Maybe he knows."

"Knows what?"

But instead of answering, he said, "Molly, I want you to do something. Get out of Prague, today. The ticket's still good. Take the car if you want."

"Why?"

"Maybe I'm paranoid too. But do it. There's nothing you can do here. At least you'll be safe."

She shook her head. "Knows what?" she said again. *"Tell* me."

He turned to her, angry now. "You tell me."

"What?"

He grabbed her arm. "Who's Foster, Molly? Tell me."

"Why are you acting like this?" she said, pulling away.

"I'm watching my back. He didn't have to tell me, we learned that in the war. You get like that when people shoot at you. You start seeing things. You, for instance. Standing right here, having a little talk. Not shopping. Definitely not alone. I was over there." He indicated the tree. "But maybe I was seeing things. Was I? Tell me."

She took her arm away, subdued. "What did he tell you?"

"Him? Nothing. Not a word. A real gentleman, if

438

you like the type. Which I guess you do. So why don't you tell me?"

She looked down. "He's a friend. Was."

"A bed friend?"

"What difference does it make?"

"A bed friend?"

"All right, yes. We had a thing. So what? In Paris. He used to work there."

"But not anymore."

"No."

"So you came here. A Czech filmmaker—Christ, was that his idea or yours?"

"Mine."

"What else did you make up? Why?"

"I didn't think you'd come if you knew."

"And it was important to get me here. That was the idea."

"It was important for him. He wanted it, not me."

"But you made it happen. You arranged every-thing. A little family reunion, with the CIA sitting right there beside me."

"He's not with the CIA."

"So he said. What about you? Who do you work for?"

"Nobody. I did it for him."

"Why, if it was over?"

"I thought it would get him back."

"Did it?"

"Things—changed." She looked up at him. "You know that."

"I don't know anything, Molly, remember? I'm not supposed to. Is that why we went to bed? Was that part of the plan too? So I wouldn't suspect anything?"

"No."

"No, you just couldn't help yourself. Christ, and I was worrying about the Czechs bugging us, not our side."

"Stop it. It wasn't like that."

"You tell him about it? Was that part of the report?"

She shook her head. "That wasn't supposed to happen. It just did."

"What was supposed to happen?"

"You don't want to hear this."

"Yes, I do. I'm dying to hear it. How stupid I was, fucking an agent."

She flinched and turned away from him, facing the water. "I'm not an agent. I told you, he's not CIA. He hates the CIA, as a matter of fact. It's like a sports thing. They're these big rivals."

"Who?"

She bit her lip. "The Bureau. There, so you know, okay? You got it out of me. Happy? He works for the FBI."

Nick stared at her. His father's voice. I know *where.*

"In Paris," he said sarcastically.

"At the embassy. They're not supposed to operate overseas. It's against the law. Like they care. Anyway, they get around it by putting people in the embassies. Legats—that's what they call them. Legal attachés. The CIA knows, but there's noth-

440

ing they can do about it, so they make each other crazy." She stopped. "He's not an agent."

"And that's supposed to make it all right."

"I didn't say that."

"Some difference. So you get together in Paris. I'm amazed. An old rock groupie like yourself. I didn't think he'd be your type. How was it?"

"Don't do this," she said quietly.

"How was it?"

She glared at him. "Fine, if you want to know. It was fine. Look, I'm not proud of this. What do you want me to say? What about you? Are you proud of everyone you've been to bed with?" She turned to face the river. "We had a thing, okay? I was attracted to him—I don't know why. Kind of like sleeping with the enemy. It's so wrong it's—interesting. You know, what's that like? I mean, god, the Bureau. The last thing I would have imagined. I thought they were like Nazis. But he wasn't. He was nice—at least, he was then. So I was wrong. I thought it would just be that one time, but it wasn't. It went on. And then, when he left I didn't know what to do. Maybe I wanted him to miss *me.* But I didn't want it to be over."

"So you followed him here."

She nodded. "But things were different. I thought it was the place—everything's different here. But what was really happening was that it wasn't important to him anymore. Just his stupid job. Who wants to admit that? So I didn't. Then I met your father and he got interested again. I had him back for a while."

"Why was he interested?"

"He knew the Bureau would be. Your father was the one who got away. They never closed the file. Because of Hoover. It's never over for him. Jeff says he lives in the past. I guess when he isn't spying on the Panthers and whatever else they do. But that period, your father's time—that was *it* for him. So he'd be interested if anything turned up. Jeff just wanted to do himself some good, get out of Prague and back home. Prague's a dead end. But if he could get the director's attention—" She paused. "I don't know, maybe he thought he could get something out of him. That your father might tell you things he could use. He's like that. Ambitious. So he used me and I used you. Is that what you wanted to hear?"

"Every detail."

"I already told you. I was at a party with Jiří. There was a Jiří, somebody I met here. I didn't make him up, just what happened. Your father was there and I was amazed. I thought he was in Moscow or dead or something. It was like meeting a ghost. So I told Jeff I'd met him, what he'd said, and he got interested. I don't think they even knew he was in Prague. So what was he up to?"

"And you told him my father wanted to see me."

"Why not? As far as I was concerned, he was—"

"I know, a murderer. So you decided to catch him."

"No. I never thought I'd see him again. I went back to Paris. Then Jeff came and said he'd been thinking about it and why did your father want to see you and maybe I should do it, do what he asked, and it might be important and wouldn't I do it for him?"

"But not tell me."

"Would you have come?"

"No."

"So I thought, why not? I didn't even know you. Jeff really wanted it. And it was interesting. I wanted to know—I figured I owed it to her. To find out once and for all. And then when it started, I thought, I can't do this. It's like working for the FBI, not Jeff. That's when I realized what he was, really one of them. And by that time I knew you. I was going to call it off in Vienna—I was supposed to check in with him there, before we crossed the border. But you changed the plan, remember? You didn't want to wait and I—I went with it. I couldn't tell you. I thought, what if nothing happens? Just a visit. Nobody had to know. Your father never suspected."

"No, he had you checked out," Nick said. "He believed you." A love affair, his father had said, young people always had love affairs. Some plausible young man at the embassy, not CIA, nobody to worry about. "Everybody believed you."

"Yes."

"So you wanted to call it off, but you saw Foster here anyway."

"I had to. I couldn't just leave. I had to put an end to it, tell him to stop. I was afraid if I didn't—"

"What?"

443

"That he'd talk to you. That you'd find out from him."

"Oh. Instead of from you. Just when were you planning to tell me?"

She turned to look at him. "Never."

"Never. Not even after we were home. Why not?"

"Because I knew you'd look at me the way you're looking now." Her eyes were moist, filling.

"So no one would be the wiser," he said, angry at the tears, not wanting to be disarmed. "Especially me. But it didn't work out that way."

"No."

"What did you tell Foster?"

"There was nothing to tell. We went to the country. No dark secrets from the past. Nothing that would interest anybody at home. Just a visit. End of story." She hesitated. "I told him I didn't want you to know about me. That it would ruin things. I made him promise."

"Don't worry, he kept it. Your secret's safe with him." He took out a handkerchief and held it out to her. "But that wasn't exactly the end. You told Foster he was planning to leave. Didn't you?"

She blew her nose, nodding at the same time.

"Why?"

"I never thought he was serious. It was just some crazy idea. And Jeff kept hounding me. What did they talk about? What did they talk about? He wanted to know who your father's contacts were, who he saw in Prague. As if I'd know. So I said it wasn't like that. He was out of it, retired. He even

444

had this idea about going back and he wanted you to help. That's how out of it he was—in some dream world." She looked up at him, her face still covered by the handkerchief. "I didn't want Jeff to think it was real, get all excited. Maybe try to contact him. *I* didn't think it was real. I didn't." A thin wail.

Nick turned away, not wanting to face her, waiting as she caught her breath. "Tell me something else you were never going to tell me," he said quietly. "He wasn't going to leave it alone, was he? Not after that. He wanted you to find out more. From me. Stay close to me. Let him know. He made you promise to keep going, didn't he? Then he'd keep his."

He waited, hoping he'd overshot, his stomach turning when he saw her nod again into the handkerchief.

"But I wasn't going to," she said. "I just said it to make him stop. I wasn't going to."

"God, Molly." He leaned back against the bridge, feeling hemmed in. His Czech watchdog down the road was staring at the river. The American was closer, stifling a sniffle. "Tell me something. What did that feel like? In bed. Spying on me."

"I wasn't spying on you."

"What do you call it?"

"I thought we were making love," she said quietly. "That's what it felt like to me."

"Spare me."

She raised her head, stung, then shrugged and

445

gave him the handkerchief. "It's true, for what it's worth. Anyway, how would you know? Did you even know I was there?"

"Not both of you."

"Maybe you can't," she said, ignoring him. "You don't care about anything unless it happened twenty years ago. I hate what he did to you. Making you think you could get it back. Who could compete with that? You don't have room for anybody else. Just him."

He stood, saying nothing, only vaguely aware of the traffic sounds, as if someone had sliced him with a knife and he had to hold his insides close so they wouldn't slip out. Then it worked, he'd held himself in and was able to breathe again.

"Well, now he's dead. Somebody else didn't want him around either."

"That's unfair. I didn't mean—"

"I know."

"Then why say it? To make me feel worse? You don't have to. I can do that myself." She shook her head. "Oh, what's the use? You're too hurt to see anything. But what happened with Jeff—it didn't matter to me, Nick. It didn't matter."

"But it did matter. My father's dead, because someone knew."

"Because I told Jeff? But how could it? Do you think I've thought about anything else for two days? What if I did it? Me. Killed him just by—But how? Jeff didn't kill him. He may be a shit, but he didn't do that."

446

"But who else knew? Me. You. Foster. Unless he told somebody. Did he?"

"I don't know."

He hesitated. "But you could find out."

"How?"

"Use your wiles. They worked on me."

"Don't."

"It's not much to ask, considering."

"Nick—"

"Not for me. Do it for my father. He's entitled to one favor."

She looked down. For a moment there was nothing, just the sound of a truck going by. "Do what?"

"Go see Foster. Tell him I still don't suspect anything. And you'd like to keep it that way. Just between you and old Jeff. Has he talked to anyone else? In the embassy. Or even back home. Find out if he signaled the Bureau about this, if anyone in Washington has any idea."

"Why Washington?"

"And when. If he said anything before."

"Nick, what's the point? What does this have to do with anything? The Bureau didn't kill him."

"Maybe my father wasn't as careful as he thought. Maybe his friends already knew. But maybe he *was* careful. Maybe he got tripped up because somebody wanted a new job and thought he was the ticket. I just want to find out who knew. It's important. Maybe it stops with Foster. At least we eliminate possibilities."

Molly stared up at him. "If it stops with him," she said slowly, "that leaves me. Do you think I did it?"

"No."

"Really. Why not me? Why not Anna? It's usually the wife, isn't it? Why not the Bureau, who didn't even know where he was. Except in some old file nobody cares about anymore. Who else? Do you see what this is doing to you? It's crazy."

Nick nodded. "But he's dead. And whoever killed him knew he was going to leave. It's the only way it makes sense."

"Well, it doesn't make sense to me. Why not just lock him up? They lock up everyone else. What made him so special?"

"I don't know."

She raised her head, scanning his face. "You do, though. That's it. That's why you're so sure he was killed. Why you're worried. Signing things. I thought it was just an idea he had, but you didn't. You knew he could do it. You even bought him a ticket. There's something else. That's why you want to know who Jeff told." She glanced up, her eyes narrowing. "In Washington. That's what you want to know. Who in Washington." Nick said nothing, still not looking at her. "Leaving was only part of it. There's always been something else. That you wouldn't tell me."

He turned back to her. "Well, that makes two of us."

He saw the flush rise in her face, a kind of blood wince. She lowered her eyes. "Not anymore. Now there's just you."

"I can't."

"You mean you don't trust me."

"I mean I can't. It's not safe."

She shook her head. "You think I'm going to tell Jeff. You still think that."

"They killed him, Molly. It doesn't matter whether I trust you or not. It's not safe."

"But why?"

He hesitated, then said, "Just ask him who knew."

"I'm surprised you trust me to do that. What is it, a kind of test?"

"It's important."

"Then ask him yourself. I'm tired of playing Mata Hari. First him, now you. If I don't know what you're doing, I don't want any part of it."

"You are a part of it. That's the other thing. Find out if he told them about you, if anyone in Washington knows about you."

"Me?"

"Let's hope he took all the credit. He looks the type. Old matchmaker Jeff."

"What would he tell them?"

"That you arranged it. That you've been sleeping with me."

"So what?"

"Somebody might get the idea that I confided in you. That you know why too." He stopped, letting it sink in. "Ask him. And tell him we both think it's suicide. Can you make him believe that?"

She nodded slowly, her eyes wide. Then she reached out and touched his arm lightly, tentative. "We have to talk about things."

"There isn't time now." An echo, somewhere in the back of his head. There isn't time.

"I never meant—" She looked up, a new thought. "Nick, whatever it is—what he told you. Do they know?"

"Not yet. Nobody does. Not even you. Do you understand?"

"But it's true? You're sure?"

"It has to be. He's dead."

He left Molly at the corner and turned left toward the tank square, his mind buzzing. What if Foster hadn't told anyone after all? What if Anna didn't have the list? He'd have to leave Prague with nothing but a history lesson from Zimmerman, a half-answer eating away at everything. Silver safe and sound, still sending his useful reports. The woman is the key, his father had said, but that trail had ended in the Mayflower Hotel, as cold now as the snow on the car where she'd fallen. Now there was only the list, with the name that could lead him to Silver.

When he got to Holečkova, he looked back to see if one of the shadows had split off to follow Molly, but they were both there. Only interested in him.

The same hill, steep. Then the gate, the concrete steps leading up to the apartment building. He stopped when he reached the lawn, his eyes drawn to the spot in helpless fascination, like a car accident. No bloodstains, everything cleared away. Just grass. Surprised at how much it had hurt. You don't have room for anybody else. But it wasn't true. That elation, opening out to her, and then the ice pick stabbing at him on the bridge, betrayed, the way he had felt that night, looking at footprints. He had thought no one could make him feel that again, and here it was, the same surprised bleeding. Now there were two who had done it, touched that part of him. And oddly, some twisted joke, they were the only two he still trusted. He knew it now, looking at the lawn, his anger gone. You could trust a touch, despite everything. It came back again and again, a heartbeat, making room.

He took the lift, avoiding the stairs where the killers had crept past the brick glass. Or had they clunked their way up, heedless, not caring if the neighbors heard? Just following orders. Anna opened the door at the first touch of the buzzer.

"Nicholas, come in. You got the message."

He nodded. "You have something for me?" He looked around at the bland Scandinavian furniture. Everything was clean, almost antiseptic, as if it had been scrubbed down.

"Come," she said, leading him to the bedroom.

"Where did you find it?"

She looked at him, confused, then continued into the room. He stopped at the door. Everything the same—bed, desk—but tidy now, no signs of disturbance. He looked at the neat pillows, feeling queasy. Did she sleep on them? She went over to the desk and brought back a small urn shaped like a squat loving cup.

"The ashes," she said simply. "Here, I want you to have them."

He took the urn, stupefied. It was cool to the touch. "Anna, I—"

"No, it's better." She looked down at the urn. "You have them."

The urn was surprisingly heavy. He stared at it, not knowing what to say. His eyes wandered over to the desk. Not the list. Nothing hidden here.

"I can't."

"Yes. Take him home. That's what he wanted."

"Did he say that? Did he tell you?"

She shook her head. "I knew. I was his wife. He was never happy here. Only a little. Take him home."

So small. The tall body reduced to a bowl of ash. He could hold it in his hands.

"Perhaps you would bury it somewhere he liked. At the country house."

"It was sold," Nick said numbly.

But no list. In a minute he would have to go, turn his back on the flat for good, leaving the list behind. But was it here? What had his father said? The echo again. There isn't time now. But why wouldn't there be time if it had been here in the flat with him? He was careful. The passport had been safe with Anna Masaryk. Not at the flat.

"Nicholas, do you hear me?"

"Yes, I'm sorry. I was thinking."

"If it's not possible in the country, then wherever

you think best." She handed him a slip of paper. "This is the document. You'll need it for customs, so they won't open it. It's sealed."

Why tell him that? Was she afraid they'd violate the remains, spilling ashes in a clumsy search through the luggage?

"I can't take this."

"You must." Her eyes on him, an order. She nodded. "For him."

Unless it wasn't just ashes. He stared at her. His father had sent her away that night. Visiting relatives, or a last errand? Now that she had it, she'd be careful too, speaking in code for the listening walls. He looked down at the urn again, his hands clammy on the cool metal. Sealed. Was it possible? His father would carry it out after all.

"Thank you," Nick said finally.

"Be careful with it. The seal is easy to break."

"I understand." Another glance. "So he told you."

She looked hard at him, her face as closed as it had been at the police station.

"Nothing," she said.

She led him out of the room. At the door, when he leaned to embrace her, she stepped back awkwardly, extending her hand instead. *"Na shleda-nou,"* she said, using Czech to move away, no longer connected to him.

He carried the urn all the way back to the hotel, covering it with his raincoat, not risking a tram. The room was empty, and he locked the door before he sat down at the writing desk. He looked at the urn for an edge of wax or plastic, but there was nothing but the lid. Maybe the seal was only a tightly fitted groove, like the top of a jam jar. He took the urn and tried to twist the cover, his hand slipping on the smooth metal. A handkerchief. He gripped it and tried to unscrew the top. What did you do with jars? Run the top under hot water. Tap it with a knife. He squeezed again, straining, putting his weight into it. Then a tiny jerk, a loosening, and the lid began to turn slowly. He followed it around, then turned again. Easier now, coming off. He lifted the cover and looked in. Not the black-and-white ash of a fireplace, different. An unexpected brown mixed with gray.

He stared at the urn, queasy again. Human ash. He touched it gently, as if it might still be warm, but it was cool, so fine that it left a smudge, like cigarette ash. He pulled back his hand. He took a pen from the writing pad, poked it in, and stirred. It wouldn't be paper. Film. His father had said you could copy things on film, even a whole manuscript, like František's brother's. He pushed the pen through the brown-gray ash, as light as powder but dense, as if the pen were moving through fine sand. Better to think of it as anything except what it was.

A clink, something hard. He worked the pen around and hit it again. Impossible to bring it up like this. He reached in with two fingers and pushed the ash aside, searching for the round cylinder. Then he felt it, smooth. He drew it out, careful of the ash, and looked at it. A piece of bone. He

454

dropped it back in the ash, his stomach jumping, then took the pen again and poked more frantically. Another piece of bone. Once more through the ash, knowing now that it wasn't there but unable to stop. No film. His father hadn't told her. It's here, he'd said, tapping his head.

Nick took the pen out, covered with ash, feeling sick. Then he looked at his fingers, covered the same way, dirty with it, and ran to the bathroom and held his hand under the running tap until the smudges washed away, coloring the water like faint gray blood. He stood against the basin for a moment, breathing hard, ashamed. His hands in it, digging, like a grave robber.

But the list had to be somewhere. His father hadn't intended to rely on memory. He knew they'd want more. There just hadn't been time to get it. Nick went to the desk again, staring at the urn as he screwed the top back on. Bury it somewhere he liked. The country house. A formal name for a simple cabin. Reproduced here, a private place away from the prying world. Of course. Not with another Anna Masaryk, around the corner. But there wouldn't have been time for a run to the country. He'd have to leave without it. So it must still be there, waiting to be found. Where? Nick felt the pricking at the back of his head. Simple, if you knew him. People don't change. And if he was wrong? A wild goose chase. But with no other options, it was worth, at least, a try.

He left Molly a note—"back later, don't worry"—and rushed out of the room. He'd have to hurry to get back before dark. He ran down the stairs, making a plan—could he lose the watchdogs in the back streets?—so that he missed the expression on the desk clerk's face when he asked him to call the garage.

"But the police have the keys, Pan Warren. There is some problem with repairs, I think. Were you planning to leave Prague?"

Nick imagined for a second the clerk's hand on the phone, ready to send out the alarm.

"No, no," he said quickly. "It's just the trams. I suppose I can take a taxi."

"Of course. Shall I call for you?"

"I'll find one," Nick said vaguely. Why had he thought they'd let him go? He stood in the middle of the lobby, knowing the desk clerk was watching him but unable to move. There had to be a way. In America there would be fleets of rental cars and drivers for hire, but movement was a luxury here, the great privilege in a country under house arrest. He thought of Jeff, tearing easily through Prague with his close-shaven Marine. Who else?

His eyes scanned the room and stopped at the entrance to the bar, where Marty Bielak was already perched on his stool. Who would want to stay closer? His legman, tempted with a scoop.

"I need to ask a favor."

"Shoot."

"It's just that I don't know anyone else to ask."

"What can I do for you?"

"I need to borrow a car. Just for a few hours. I'll pay for the gas. Mine's in for repairs."

Bielak looked at him, waiting for more.

"I need to get something. You know Walter Kotlar was my father."

Bielak said nothing, too interested to pretend he hadn't known.

"He wanted me to have something. You know, a memento. But it's in the country, and I don't have any way to get there. Would you mind? I'd really appreciate it."

"I'll take you," Bielak said, almost eagerly.

"You don't have to do that."

"No, I do. See, over here—you're a foreigner, and we can't lend—" He paused, apologetic.

"You wouldn't mind?"

"I'm just taking up space here. Let me get this." He put some money on the bar. "Sorry to hear about it, by the way. To go that way. Sad. Must be hard for you."

"Yes."

"Well, I'm sorry."

"At least I got to see him again. That's something, anyway."

"Why didn't you want anybody to know? If you don't mind my asking," he said, collecting the change.

"He didn't want it. He was afraid—you know, if the press got hold of it. He wanted it to be just family."

"I heard he was sick." Bielak hesitated. "Is that why he did it?" A trial balloon for the party line.

Nick nodded. "I suppose. I don't know."

457

"No. We never do, do we, when they go like that. Not really."

"No, not really."

Bielak got up from the stool. "What did he leave you, anyway? That we're going to pick up. If you don't mind my asking."

What? What would he have left? "The Order of Lenin," Nick said, leaving Bielak, for once, with no reply.

Outside, he saw the tails come to attention, their faces registering surprise at Bielak's appearance.

"Listen, I think you should know that the police have been following me since he died. I mean, I don't want to get you in any trouble."

"Don't worry about it," Bielak said easily. He looked at Nick seriously. "Your father was a hero. What do they know? Traffic cops." Nick caught the tone: rival agencies, then, not colleagues, like the squabbling offices in the embassy. Who did Bielak work for? It occurred to him, a grisly irony, that he had inadvertently picked the perfect chauffeur, the only way he could ever have left Prague without an escort.

"How far is it?" Bielak asked.

"Out past Theresienstadt."

"Oh, nice," Bielak said. "The country, I mean."

What Nick hadn't counted on was that Bielak would want to talk, using the long drive as a pretext for a fishing expedition, casting for information. Nick's life. His father's health. And after a while Nick began to welcome the distraction, so preoccupied with shaping his answers, the careful feints,

458

that he had no time to think about what really concerned him, what he would do if the list wasn't there. A wasted trip. But it had to be. All of it had to be true. Everything he'd said.

The questions told him something else—Bielak hadn't known about him before, which meant his superiors hadn't known either. The connection had come out with the death, surprising them as much as the police, the unexpected son. His father had been careful right up to the end. The order to kill had come from somewhere else.

They fell behind a convoy of trucks, back flaps open to reveal sitting rows of soldiers. When the road opened out to a long stretch, Bielak beeped his horn and passed, waving to them as he pulled in front.

"Russians?" Nick said.

"And Poles. Some Hungarians. They're here for the Warsaw Pact maneuvers." Did he really believe it?

"You never see them in town. I thought they'd be everywhere. You know, since—"

"The invasion?" Marty said, almost playful. "That's what they call it in the West. Some invasion. See for yourself. You notice they never say NATO troops have invaded Germany. They're guests. Only the Russians are occupiers. But the Americans stay and the Russians go home when the maneuvers are over. So where's the occupation, Germany or here? It's always the same. Don't believe everything you read in the papers."

"No. So when do they go home?"

"When the government asks them to. Right now it's useful. We could use a little order. Things go too far. These kids—they play right into the hands of the capitalists, and they don't even know it. Your father understood. That's why he came last year, to help out."

Nick froze. "Help out how?" he asked quietly.

"Well, the Czechs wouldn't look at a Russian cross-eyed. But a Czech-American with a Czech wife? He could talk to anybody."

And report back. Selling them, the way he had sold sailors who jumped ship in San Francisco. Still in the game, not retired, not everything true. What had he been buying this time? The flat with a view? A way to bring Anna home? Or the chance to get in the files again, get something worth a few dissidents?

"How do you know this? Did you work with him?" Nick said, remembering his father's easy dismissal.

Bielak squirmed in his seat. "No, no. But you hear things." He paused. "He wasn't wrong, you know. Things were going off the rails here. They see the flashy cars, but they forget what the West is really like." He paused. "But maybe you don't agree."

Nick glanced at him, the unlikely defender. Who still believed in the great dialectic, without his wife, thousands of miles from the old Glen Island Casino. A capacity for self-deception as limitless as faith.

"What are your own politics?" Bielak said. "If you don't mind my asking."

"I don't have any," Nick said. "My father had enough for one family."

Bielak was quiet. "You know," he said finally, "when you get to be my age, you don't point so many fingers. It takes a lot of guts to do something for what you believe in. I mean, the Order of Lenin, that has to count for something."

"If you're a Communist."

"It still has to mean something to you. Isn't that why you want it?"

"It meant something to him."

"It's a shame you didn't get to know him better, how he thought. Maybe you have more in common than you think."

The voice was no longer casual but insinuating. Nick looked at him, amazed. Was Bielak recruiting him? Was this the way it worked—the awkward fumbling, looking for the right spot, promising something else? Like teenage sex.

"I never cared about politics," Nick said, trying to be light. "I don't think I'd make a very good spy, either. I don't even know if the police are still following us."

"No, we lost them just outside the city," Bielak said, sure, not inept, a professional after all.

The driveway was still muddy.

"I'll only be a minute," Nick said, but Bielak got out too, looking curiously at the cottage. Now he'd have an audience.

He went toward the woodpile at the side of the

461

house, where his father always hid the key. But before he could reach down and scoop it out, Bielak said, "Here we go," taking a key from under the terra-cotta planter near the door. Nick stopped, disconcerted. People don't change. But maybe the planter was Anna's idea, better than fumbling under logs.

"I figured," Bielak said. "If it's not the mat, it's always the flowerpot, isn't it? You'd think people would know better. Where're you going?"

"I have to take a leak," Nick said, improvising. "I don't know if the water's turned on. Go on in."

"Well, me too," Bielak said, moving away from the house. "That last half-hour."

So they peed together at the side of the house, backs to each other, while Nick looked toward the woodpile, wondering. Where else?

Inside, he switched on the lamp. The same room, so familiar to him that he could have moved through it in the dark. The table by the window where they'd had lunch, gloomy now in the fading light. Everything spotless, still. But not his. He walked quietly to the desk, feeling like a burglar.

Bielak had stopped by the door, looking around. "Not much, is it?"

"No."

"I mean, a man in his position, you'd think they'd—" He seemed genuinely surprised, a little shaken. What had he imagined? A hero's dacha.

"He said they never really trusted Americans," Nick said, then, seeing the wounded expression on

462

Bielak's face, instantly regretted it. Why not leave him his faith, when it was all he had left?

The medal wasn't on the side table. Now there were two things out of place. Nick opened the desk drawer and pushed papers aside. The list wasn't at Holečkova; it had to be here somewhere. Bielak, subdued now, was looking at the bookshelves. Nick sorted through clipped articles from Russian magazines. Papers. It could be anywhere. Wedged behind a book. Think.

He went upstairs, leaving Bielak to the shelves, and turned into the bedroom. The nightstand drawer, nothing. Then Anna's, face creams and tissues. He found it on the bureau, a flat box next to their picture, out in plain sight. He opened it to find the medal and its piece of ribbon lying on a square of velvet. But what about the other? Somewhere personal, where she wouldn't have looked. He went to the bathroom and opened the medicine chest. Pill bottles, about the size of a roll of film. He started opening them, twisting off caps, his fingers clumsy.

"How we doing up there?" Bielak called.

"Got it," Nick shouted down. Two more bottles. Nothing. He took a last glance at the room where he'd helped his father to bed and went downstairs. He handed Bielak the box.

"A few more minutes, okay?" he said.

"Take your time." Bielak opened the box. "This is something, isn't it?" He fingered the medal, fascinated.

Nick went over to the shelves. English books.

Anna never would have bothered with them. He ran his hands over the titles, pulling a few out, squatting to reach the lowest shelf, half expecting to find one hollowed out, a jewel cache. But they were neat and dusted, part of Anna's house too.

"Looking for anything in particular?"

"No, not really." He stood and looked around the room. He'd have to come back alone, go through everything. But how? "I guess we'd better go," he said, feeling helpless. "It's getting late."

It was dark outside, and they had to follow the faint shine of metal to the car. Somewhere she wouldn't have looked. Bielak got in the car.

"I can't believe it," Nick said, dropping the medal on the car seat. "I have to go again. Be right back."

He went toward the end of the woodpile, pretending to fumble with his clothes. Bielak started the car. The headlights were facing away from Nick. Could he be seen from this angle? He stooped quickly, not caring, and felt along the bottom logs for an opening. Yes, where the key would have been, as always. He shoved his hand through, scratching the top, and felt around the dirt, rummaging again through ashes, remembering the moment when he had felt the bone. Nothing.

He reached farther, groping, his arm pressed now against the wood. It had to be. A place she'd never look. He heard Bielak call, "You all right over there?" and then he touched it. Something cool. His fingertips grazed plastic, and he pushed a little more until he covered it with his palm. The size of a pill container. He pulled his hand back, feeling slivers biting his skin, and put it in his pocket. Then he stood up and hurried back to the car, exhilarated. All of it true.

"You left your fly open," Bielak said. "I'm not in that much of a hurry."

Nick yanked his zipper up, then put his hand back in his pocket, afraid to let go, and got into the car.

"I'll put the heater on," Bielak said, thinking he was chilled. Nick drew his hand out and rubbed it against the other, playing along. But it wasn't the heater that made his face warm as they drove toward the main road. He could feel the film in his pocket, heavy as a gun, the excitement of finding it curdling into a new kind of dread. Now he wasn't innocent. If they caught him, they would never let him go.

He felt the warm lump against his leg all the way back to Prague, while Bielak's one-sided conversation drifted in and out like a weak radio signal. How would he get it out? Maybe like this, in his pocket, where not even a legman would think to look. Molly and her tampons. Why not? The embassy car on its weekly lettuce run, immune to prying. Then he remembered what it was. Not a joint. Something only he could carry. He was back in the snow, with no one to help.

When they reached Wenceslas, Nick offered to pay for the trip, but Bielak shook his head. "Buy me a drink sometime." Then, when Nick's hand was already on the door handle, Bielak held out the medal and said, "Tell me something. Your father, he knew he was sick."

"Yes."

"I mean, it was that. Knowing he was sick." Convincing himself. Then, unexpectedly, "Do you think he ever had any regrets?"

Nick looked at him, dismayed. All that was left. "No," he said firmly. "Never."

Bielak sat back. "Well, that's something to think about it, isn't it?"

He found Zimmerman waiting in the lobby, his usual calm betrayed by an impatiently jiggling foot. When he stood up, Nick panicked, sure that he was looking at the pocket.

"So you're back. A pleasant trip?" Zimmerman's voice was angry.

"No."

"Where were you?"

"At my father's house."

"You were told not to leave Prague."

"I went to get this." He opened the box, showing the medal.

"And this has a special significance for you? You surprise me." Zimmerman nodded toward the door. "Do you know who he is?"

Nick shrugged. "I met him in the bar. You have my car, remember?"

"Again with the charades. Is it possible you

don't know?" Zimmerman shook his head. "No, I don't think so."

"Who is he?"

"It's possible you don't take me seriously. That would be a mistake. Have I not made myself clear to you? Your position?"

"You mean he's one of yours?"

"Stop it. Listen to me carefully. Don't make yourself too interesting. A man is questioned; his embassy immediately protests. He is ordered to stay in Prague, so he goes for a ride with—with someone who is known to do odd jobs for the security police. Please, don't look surprised, there isn't time."

"Is that why your men didn't follow us?"

"Their jurisdiction ends with Prague, Mr. Warren. Naturally they thought I would alert the other department."

"But you didn't."

Zimmerman looked away. "Such a call would take things out of my hands entirely. The security police have much to do these days—so many dangers to the state. It's unwise to burden them with false alarms. Luckily, you returned." He paused. "Don't do it again. You did not, I trust, confide in Mr. Bielak?"

"No." Nick smiled. "In fact, I think he wanted to recruit me. Maybe he thinks it runs in the family."

Zimmerman looked at him. "Maybe it does, Mr. Warren. But that is not my concern. I brought your statement." He pulled some papers out of his breast pocket. "Sign it, please."

"It's in Czech," Nick said, a lawyer's son.

Zimmerman sighed. "The second sheet is the English. Sign the copy."

"But am I responsible for all of it, the Czech too?"

Zimmerman handed him the pen. "Sign it, Mr. Warren."

Nick read it through, a bureaucrat's account. His father's distress at his illness. In this version the depression had been deepened by Nick's visit, a new twist. He raised his eyes, then took the pen.

"Does this mean I can go?"

"That will depend on the STB. But it would be useful, I think, for them to have my police report before they begin their own speculation. That much I can do." He gestured toward the medal. "That's a nice touch. They'll like that. I hope Mr. Bielak mentions it."

"He will. Nothing else happened."

"Assuming they believe him. I wonder, Mr. Warren, has it occurred to you that you might have compromised *him?*" He nodded at Nick's surprised look. "Sometimes, you know, there's nothing so dangerous as an innocent man. Everyone has to explain him. Why you picked him, of all people." He took a breath. "Why your embassy was so eager to help. Why the police—well, the police are so often inept, losing people, not understanding the implications. For the STB there is nothing but implications. I hope they don't find you too interesting. I hope, for example, they don't find that you are involved with *your* intelligence group. Nothing

468

would interest them more than that, not even other Czechs."

Nick stared at him, chilled. Was Foster right? Had they monitored the call to Kemper? How long before they knew about it? He stood there, feeling the film in his pocket.

"You see," Zimmerman finished. "Nothing so dangerous."

"Well, at least you think I'm innocent," Nick said, trying to be light.

"Only of murder, Mr. Warren," Zimmerman said. "For the rest—" He took back the paper. "Thank you for the statement. Don't leave again. Don't do anything. Do you understand?" He turned. "Oh, by the way, your car is fine. What did you say was wrong?"

"A knock in the engine."

"Yes, that can happen. A knock for no reason. It's often the case with a new car."

Molly had double-locked the door.

"Thank god," she said. "Where have you been?"

"Getting this," he said, handing her the medal box.

She opened it. "So that's what Anna wanted."

He didn't correct her. "Did you see Jeff?"

She nodded.

"And?"

"Come for a walk," she said, raising her eyes

469

toward the ceiling. She picked up her jacket, then went over to put the box on the desk. "What's this?" she said, touching the urn.

"My father. His ashes."

She pulled her finger away, staring at it. "God. What are you going to do with it?"

"Take him home."

She kept staring. "It's so small."

Outside, it had begun to drizzle, so instead of walking they crossed the street to the broad island in the middle where the trams ran. Out of the corner of his eye he could see one of Zimmerman's men leave his car and follow them. The evening rush was over. Only a few people were waiting for the clanging bell of the approaching tram.

"What did he say?"

"What you thought. He couldn't wait to get back to Washington with the news. He called them right after I talked to him." Everything in place.

"Who did he tell?"

"His boss. Somebody called Ellis."

"Who else?"

"I couldn't exactly get a personnel chart, Nick," she said wearily. "He *hopes* it might have gone up to the director. In other words, it's around. People know." The agencies were like a sieve, his father had said, secrets dripping through a hundred holes. Anybody. "But I don't have to worry," Molly said, her voice a parody of Foster's. "You'll never suspect a thing. The Bureau keeps things to itself." The tram doors opened and they waited for people

470

to get off. She turned to him. "I can keep on going. Be your playmate." Nick said nothing.

They sat at the back of the nearly empty tram. Zimmerman's shadow was in front, pretending to read a newspaper.

"Did he tell them before?" Nick said, his voice low. He leaned into her, making them a couple out for an evening's ride, trying to find some privacy in the brightly lit car.

She shook her head. "Just that he had made contact."

The tail turned a page, looking in their direction. Nick put his arm over the back of the seat. When she felt it, she looked at him, surprised, as if he were making a pass.

"The man in front is watching us," he whispered.

But she kept her eyes on him, not bothering to turn her head.

"He didn't mention you?" he said.

"I don't think so," she said, throaty, so close now that he could feel the heat of her breath. "You were right about that too. He wanted it to be his show."

"Good."

"Not for him."

"What happened?"

"Ellis thought it was a joke—that Jeff was being taken for a ride, to embarrass the Bureau. Now it's not so funny. Especially since you called Kemper to rescue you. Everybody wants to know what's going on. How he died, whether he meant it about

471

coming back. All of it. So they're all over Jeff. He wants to call you in."

"When?" Nick said, aware again of the film in his pocket. How much time did he have?

The tram lurched to a sudden stop, throwing their heads together with a sharp bump. She raised her fingers to his forehead, touching it gently, as if she were soothing away a bruise. She left them there, a surprise of skin. "Nick—" she said. Then the tram started again and he saw an old woman coming toward them with string bags, glowering. She plopped down in front of them, as disapproving and unmovable as a duenna.

He lowered his head to Molly's neck. "When?" he said again, in her ear.

Molly was shaking her head, her face grazing his. "I said I could handle it."

"Handle what?"

She looked at him, her fingers now at the side of his head. "You," she said, in a murmur, intimate. "Isn't that what you want?"

He could smell her now, everything close, as if the film and her body were part of the same thing, the same unexpected excitement.

"I don't want you to do anything. It's not safe."

"I will, though. I'll do it." Her eyes on him. "Like a double agent," she said softly, the phrase itself suddenly erotic. "Ask me."

"No."

"Ask me," she said in his ear, her hair brushing his skin. So close he could not tell which of them moved, but her mouth was on his, the same touch, and then her hand was at the back of his neck, keeping him close, as if afraid he'd pull away. "I'll do it. I don't care," she said, her breath on his mouth. "You believe me, don't you?" She lifted her mouth to him again, a yielding. When he broke off and nodded, his head next to hers, he could feel her shake, a tremor of release, and she began kissing his face, moving over him. "I'm sorry," she whispered. "I'm sorry. I never meant—"

"Ssh." He kissed her again, almost involuntarily, caught by the smell of her, remembering her opening to him. She gave a faint moan, and the old woman turned, glaring, but her eyes were like the hotel microphones, making everything illicit, more exciting. Improbably, he felt himself growing hard, his prick rising to bump against the film.

"It's all right now, isn't it?" Molly was saying in a rush. "I don't want to lose you. I keep losing people."

"Ssh."

"I've been so worried."

"No, don't."

With a burst of Czech, the old woman made a show of gathering her bags and moving across the aisle. Molly, ignoring her, held him closer, her face next to his, necking.

"I'll help you," she said, kissing him again.

"You don't know what you're asking," he whispered, out of breath. He felt her moving against him, the rocking of the tram, in a kind of haze.

"Yes, I do," she said, nuzzling his ear. "I've got you back. I don't care about the rest."

He raised his head a little, catching sight of their tail in front, staring frankly at the unexpected blue movie. "We have to talk," he said, trying to bring himself back.

But Molly wouldn't listen, her hands on his face. "Not now." She put a finger to his lips. "Don't say anything."

"But—"

"Just keep doing that." She smiled, leaning her neck into his hand. "Keep doing that." Putting herself literally in his hands.

He looked down at her, so sure of him, and in that second he knew that what he did next would decide everything. Life could change without even thinking, a hair-trigger response, everything changed by a second, a phone call in Union Station, an accidental bump on the head. Make room.

"Let's go back," he whispered, his face on hers, giving in, letting the rest go.

She nodded absently, letting him kiss her, and then she looked up at him, a glint. "We'll make out." A backseat phrase. His skin jumped, like drops of water on a skillet, ready for her. The windows of the tram were shiny with condensation, catching the light of the bare bulbs that lined the warm car. Outside, the city slid by, drizzly, unseen.

"Do you have any idea where this goes?" he said, his face still close.

"It'll turn around," she said. "They always go back where they started."

When they got back to the hotel, he only left her

for a moment, taking the urn into the bathroom, shoving the film down into the ashes, then closing the door behind him, so that nothing else was with them in the room.

CHAPTER FIFTEEN

He watched the ceiling turn milky gray and realized it wasn't going to get any lighter. Another Prague morning. It was time. He'd been up half the night, dozing fitfully, then wide awake, listening to her breathe beside him, making plans. It had become a simple question of mathematics: how long? If Jeff's message had spread through the embassy, it was just a matter of time before the talk in the corridors leaked out into Prague itself. He wouldn't have to wait for Silver to act again. But how much time? Did they have people inside? And once the Czech security police knew, they would have to act. Real interrogations, the embassy powerless to help him. If they found the film, he would be guilty of espionage, kept, like his father, a prisoner here forever. All that protected him now was a little time and a discredited policeman. Unless, of course, Zimmerman wasn't discredited, the bad cop after all, one of them, quietly tightening a noose. Nick moved his body carefully toward the edge of the bed. If he waited, he would lose, his time finally run out. Except now there were two of them. He looked over at Molly, sleeping, hair tangled, her face smooth and unaware. In his hands.

476

He shaved and showered, knowing the sound of water would wake her. In the mirror his face seemed drawn and apprehensive and he took a breath, pushing his cheeks back to wipe away any trace of fear. It had to work.

She was lying on her elbow, the sheet drawn up modestly over her breasts, smiling drowsily.

"Where do you get the energy?" she said, her voice lazy, unconcerned. "I don't think I can move."

"I told Zimmerman I'd see him in the morning. To sign the statement," he said, dressing, not looking at her.

"Hmm. Wake me when you're back."

"It might take a while." He looked at the canvas bag. No, no things. Not even the Order of Lenin, still lying on the desk.

"Then I'll order room service. Have breakfast in bed like a capitalist. Maybe I'll spend the *day* in bed. What do you think?"

"No, you'd better get dressed."

"Where are we going?" she said, sitting up, pulling the sheet around her.

Nick walked over to the bed and sat next to her, lowering his voice. "Do you really want to help me?"

She nodded, no longer playing.

"Then listen. I want you to go see Foster, as soon as you're dressed."

She looked away, disappointed. "You don't waste any time."

"Listen to me, Molly, please. Tell him to get you

477

out of Prague in one of the embassy cars. They can make a lettuce run. Tell him you're scared. Whatever you think would work. But get him to do it right away, this morning. He owes you that much."

"But—"

"Stay at the embassy until you leave. You'll be safe there. Technically, you're on American soil. They probably won't even know you're there—they're not following you."

"What about you?"

"Just you. I'll come later."

"He won't want me to go."

"Tell him to talk to me himself. You've had it."

"I'll wait for you."

"No, this morning. As soon as you can." He reached up, putting his hand against her head. "Don't worry, I'll come. I think I can make this work with Zimmerman. They won't have any reason to hold me. Maybe even today. Tomorrow at the latest. Wait for me in Waldsassen, at the hotel. I'll find you."

"Don't leave me," she said softly.

"I'm not leaving you." He took her face in both hands. "Help me. I've got to settle this. I don't want to have to worry about you."

"They don't want me."

"They will. It's dangerous, if they find out about you and Foster." He stopped her lips with his finger. "It's dangerous for me." A beat. "You'd be a liability."

She stared at him, then turned away. "Are you telling me the truth?"

"Promise me," he said, bringing her eyes back.

"What if it doesn't work? With Zimmerman."

"Then I'll call Foster for help. I promise." He leaned over and kissed her. "I'll *be* there. It'll be all right. But you have to leave now. Do you understand?" She nodded slowly. "Good."

She leaned over and took a cigarette from the night table. "I don't want to be a liability," she said, an edge in her voice.

"You're not," he said, knowing he should say more. But there wasn't time. He got up and put on his jacket.

"But it was because of me," she said, brooding, "that he was—you know."

"No, not because of you. Don't think that."

"But Jeff called Washington. It's the same thing, isn't it? Your father knew."

Nick stopped. "No. I don't see how he could have."

"Then why did he change his plans?"

A wrinkle, something that didn't fit. "I don't know," Nick said slowly, standing still.

Molly looked up, watching him. "You'd better go if you're going." A small smile. "You've mussed your hair."

He picked up the raincoat and went into the bathroom, slipped the urn into the folds of the coat, and ran a comb through his hair. No time.

When he came back, she was still sitting there, looking at nothing. He leaned over and kissed her forehead, the coat awkward under his arm.

"Promise me?" he said, and when she nodded

again, he whispered, "Okay. I'll see you in Germany."

At the door he turned, and for a moment he wondered if this was how his father had felt leaving, the small lie, sure he could make things right later.

She looked back at him, smiling ironically. *"Auf wiedersehen,"* she said.

He went down the back stairs, passing a chambermaid on her way up. The lobby was impossible—Zimmerman's men would stick to him now—but there seemed to be no back door, just a long corridor leading to the kitchen, breakfast trolleys lined up outside, waiting to be delivered. A white-jacketed boy with a tray came out, looking at him curiously, so he went into the WC, locking the door behind him. The window was high, but large enough. If he climbed onto the sink he could reach it, then slither out to the back street. He stopped. He saw himself, feet dangling, dropping onto the pavement, amazing everyone in the street, a comic scene from a silent movie. Keep calm. The easiest way to be invisible was to be ordinary.

He went into the kitchen, all steam and banging pots, pretending to be lost. *"Vychod?"* he said to a girl folding napkins on a tray, a word he'd seen on exit signs, hoping he was pronouncing it properly. She giggled, either at his Czech or his hapless sense of direction, and cocked her head toward the end of the steam table. A fire door, half open to let in some air. Then he was on the street behind the hotel, just another morning walker, not even worth a glance.

He walked up the hill toward the university, not bothering to switch back on side streets, invisible because he had nothing to hide. At the station there was the same rush of commuters pouring out of the art nouveau arch, the same uniformed policemen standing guard, part of the scene, no more threatening than mailboxes. He bought a copy of *Rudé Právo* and went into the station café. When he handed over the Czech crowns for coffee, he wondered if there was a currency form for leaving the country, a mirror of the exchange document coming in, some small thing to trip him up. But crowns were worthless in the West; why would they care? Still, a detail he hadn't considered. How many others? Czechs walked literally through a minefield to the wire. Why did he think he could ride out with a ticket and a visa and a Western face, as if it were another stroll through the Alcron's kitchen? He took a table near the far end of the café window and tried to imagine everything that might happen, his face bent to the newspaper.

From his angle at the window he could see part of the big hall and the long row of platforms. The same ticket window and news kiosk, people hurrying across the floor. No one loitered. The same platform, marked BERLIN-PRAHA-WIEN, still empty. Next to it, a short train had pulled up, but the doors opened only on the right, to another platform, as if the boxy-suited commuters couldn't be trusted to mix with international passengers. Then Nick saw that they were handing in ticket stubs to a conductor at the gate. Not a plot; simple crowd control, to ease the morning rush. He sipped his coffee and looked at his watch. Molly would be at the embassy now, safe. A maid would be making up their room, maybe sneaking a look at the Lenin medal on the desk, everything still there, as if they were just out for the morning.

He was on his second cup of coffee when he saw the men. There were two of them, not in uniform but with the unmistakable swagger of policemen, ready to take charge. They spoke briefly to one of the attendants, then placed themselves at the entrance to the Vienna platform, waiting. For a moment Nick thought they were meeting someone. But when the first passengers arrived, a family with innumerable suitcases, he saw that they were acting as a checkpoint. They examined the father's papers, then waved him onto the empty platform. This was something new. The other morning no one had stood guard at the gate. Were they looking for him? He told himself not to panic. In a police state, everybody was guilty of something. There could be a hundred reasons for a passport check. They couldn't know yet that he was leaving.

He watched them pass another man through with a bored wave, then a third. Maybe it was a routine security check, a morning assignment no one wanted, their bad luck to come up on the duty roster. But it wasn't a routine morning. Nick was unaccounted for. Even if they were looking for someone else, they would notice him, remember him later, an unexpected risk. How long before the train got to the border? If they were looking for him, it wouldn't matter. He thought of the other train pulling out, leaving his father behind. His eyes darted around the platform, which was beginning to fill up. There had to be a way.

"Nick."

When he turned, startled, he saw only thighs, barely covered by a miniskirt, then the blouse and her worried face.

"Zimmerman came to the hotel to see you," she said, explaining herself. She sat down.

"What did you say?"

"I said you'd gone to see *him,* to sign the statement." She took a sip of coffee. "But you didn't." A reproach.

"No."

"Why didn't you tell me?"

"Does he know I'm here?"

She shook her head. "I said he'd probably just missed you. Or you went to see Anna first."

"Good." But how much time did that buy? Then he looked up at her. "How did you know?"

"You took the urn. So—" She let it go, shrugging her shoulders. " 'I'll meet you in Waldsassen,' " she said, sarcastic.

"I will. I told you."

"You tell me lots of things."

"Molly, there isn't time for this. I will meet you there. Go to the embassy."

"And bum a ride from Jeff? I've already got one," she said, tapping her shoulder bag. "The ticket's still good, isn't it?"

"You don't understand. It's serious. The security police may be looking for me."

"Then we'd better get started." A promise, well meant, unaware that it would complicate things. "I won't be a liability," she said, reading him.

"Take a look over there." He nodded toward the platform. "See those guys? They've been checking passports. They may be looking for me, I'm not sure. If you're with me, they'll arrest you too. They'd have to."

Molly looked at the men nervously and Nick thought he had finally frightened her, but when she turned back her eyes were calm, in control. "Then I'll go first. If they stop me, you'll know."

"I can't let—"

But she stood up, ignoring him, then bent down and kissed his forehead. "If they don't, meet me on the train." She hitched her bag onto her shoulder. "Wish me luck."

"Molly?" But there was nothing to say that she didn't already know. "It's not a game. If I don't make it, stay on the train. Don't come back."

She looked at him, a tiny flicker of alarm, then said, "I'll save you a seat." She put her hand to her hair. "How do I look? I left in kind of a hurry."

"Don't take any chances."

"Now you tell me," she said softly.

He watched her walk across the hall, bag swinging, and onto the platform area. If they did stop her, what would he do? The men looked at her carefully as she dug into the bag for her ticket and passport, exchanging glances. Nick sat up in his chair, ready to bolt. They were talking to her, not the indifferent wave they'd given the others. Could Foster really help if they took her? Then there was a nod, the papers were handed back, and she was through. It was when they turned to watch her walk down the platform that Nick realized, another comic moment, that what had interested them was not her passport but her wonderful legs.

But what did that prove? They were obviously looking for someone. Why not him? He looked at his watch. The Berlin train hadn't pulled in yet. How long would he have once it did? He tried to remember the other morning. Ten minutes? Maybe he should go now, not make a dramatic last-minute sprint. But if they stopped him, Molly would see and try to help. He sat paralyzed, trying to think of a way.

The café was busier now. A few workmen were ordering morning beers, talking sullenly, glancing over at him with curiosity. An American reading *Rudé Právo*? He couldn't stay here much longer without attracting suspicion. Where was the train? He lit a cigarette, an ordinary gesture, and when he looked up from the flame saw Zimmerman through the glass, walking across the waiting room.

He was alone, without his watchdogs, but his eyes were scanning the hall, on the lookout. Nick sat back, away from the window, and watched him head straight for the Berlin platform, his movements as lithe and full of purpose as a dancer's. He went up to the two men, who acknowledged him with a nod and huddled with him, familiar. The conversation seemed to go on forever, beyond a courtesy chat, as if they were comparing notes. Zimmerman turned and looked once more at the station floor, ticket office to newsstand. When his eyes stopped at the café, Nick wondered if he could see through the glare of the glass, a policeman's radar. But he turned back, touched one of the men on the arm, and walked out onto the platform.

He'd see Molly. There'd be no missing her. Maybe lead her back to the gate. It was the weak link he'd overlooked before. For an instant Nick thought of leaving, a quick dash for the station doors, a taxi to Foster. But if he went there now, there'd be no chance of getting out, no friendly hitch on the lettuce run. They'd want to know everything, and Nick's safety would pass through the sieve, the same leaks that had killed his father. And maybe Zimmerman wouldn't stop her after all. Hadn't he advised Nick to go? Nick put out the cigarette. He couldn't stay here, in the open.

He left the café and crossed to the right, out of the line of sight of the gate, and went into the men's room. One man, washing his hands. Nick went past him to the end, entered the last stall, and slipped the bolt on the door. He sat on the toilet and took a breath, finally hidden, like an animal gone to ground.

But now he couldn't see. The view of the platform, his eye on the checkpoint, waiting for the right moment, all gone. He was blind. The train would arrive without his knowing it. He wouldn't know when Zimmerman left, or whether he was alone. His hiding place had left him only sound, magnified, the sensitive noises of the blind. When someone entered the men's room the steps came out of an echo chamber, the zipper, the splash against porcelain, then steps again. It went on like this for a few minutes.

Then there was silence. He thought he could hear the hiss and clunk of a train pulling in, but it might be his imagination. He checked his watch. Now every minute would count. But what had happened outside? He imagined opening the door and facing a circle of guns, trapped, the way he'd been at Holečkova.

The slam of the door made him sit up. Steps, but no peeing, no water from the taps. The steps continued, not hurrying, perhaps searching. When they stopped outside his door, he could see the neat shiny shoes underneath.

"Mr. Warren."

Nick made no sound, drawing further into his hole.

"Mr. Warren, open. There isn't time."

But how could he know? Nick's American shoes, as obvious as a billboard. Nick unlatched the door, caught.

"Why did you leave the café?" Zimmerman said. "We don't have time for hide and seek."

"Molly told you I was there?" A silly betrayal. It would have been so easy to lie.

"Miss Chisholm trusts me. I thought you did too. Evidently not."

"What do you want?" Nick said, standing up.

"I came to warn you."

"Those men outside?"

Zimmerman nodded. "STB. Direct orders from the Interior Ministry. I found out this morning. That's why I went to your hotel. But you had flown the coop." He mispronounced the word, like the French *coup.*

"Are you arresting me?"

"*They* want to arrest you. I have come in here to relieve myself, that's all. I saw no one. Now listen to me for once. Wait a minute after I've gone, then leave here and go straight to the taxis. Don't even look back. Maybe you'll be lucky. Then go to your embassy and stay there."

"I can't do that."

Zimmerman looked at him curiously. "Maybe one day you will tell me why. It would be interesting. But now, just go. You cannot get on that train. They're looking for you everywhere. They smell blood. I don't want it to be yours."

"What about Molly?"

"Miss Chisholm is getting on a train. No one asked me to look for her."

"You're taking a risk with all this."

"No, I don't take risks. I'm a Czech. Like the Good Soldier Schweik, a worm. A worm wiggles, he can move the earth without getting stepped on. We can't do that. But we can move a little dirt." He looked into Nick's eyes. "I know who killed your father, Mr. Warren. We both know. There's nothing I can do about that. We live under that boot. So, a wiggle only. I won't give them an innocent man. What will they do? A show trial? Another Masaryk case, somebody else to blame? We have to live with them. Let them live with themselves." He stopped. "You must hurry."

"Help me."

"I can't do that," Zimmerman said, surprised. "I just came to relieve myself. My friends want me on the platform. You see, I know what you look like. I can't let you get on the train."

"I can do it. You just have to distract them. You said yourself they're looking everywhere. No one expects me to leave—how could I? You have my car. I don't even know they're looking for me. Do those men really expect to find me here?"

Zimmerman looked at him thoughtfully, intrigued. "No, not really. It's a point, the car. Even the STB could not imagine leaving a new car behind." He smiled. "Even one with a knock."

"I only need a few hours. Call in Marty Bielak. Maybe I've gone to the country again. Somehow."

"That would be enough time, yes," Zimmerman said, considering.

"They won't stop the train at the border if I never got on in the first place. Their own men will know I didn't."

Zimmerman sighed. "You have the adventurous spirit, Mr. Warren. But you can't do it, you know. They have orders to check everyone. If you get on that train, you'll endanger Miss Chisholm. Go to your embassy."

"What makes you think they're not watching

there? If I were the STB, it's the first place I'd stake out. I wouldn't even have time to pay the taxi before they'd nail me."

Zimmerman acknowledged this by not saying anything.

"Help me," Nick said, closing it. "A wiggle."

Zimmerman looked at the door, an evasive spot-check, then back at Nick. "What do you want me to do?"

"Just distract them." He glanced at his watch. "The train must be there. I only need a minute. Pretend you see me somewhere else in the station. Someone who looks like me," he added. "Just get them away from the gate."

"And if I can't?"

"Try."

"No. If I can't, I want you to go to the phone and call your embassy. Have someone pick you up outside. Is that understood? I don't want you on my hands, Mr. Warren. And I don't want you on my conscience either."

"I'll never forget this."

"I hope you will. For my sake." Zimmerman turned to go. "Oh, one more thing. Don't sit with Miss Chisholm. My friends are thorough. They may search the train."

Nick looked at him, distraught. He'd never escape a search.

"You have a fondness for lavatories," Zimmerman said. "Stay in the WC. I'll try to check those myself."

And then a courteous nod and he was out the

door. Nick looked at his watch. Could Zimmerman manage it in a minute? A sighting near the ticket window—something. The door opened and Nick recognized one of the café beer drinkers. He glanced at Nick, then turned to the porcelain trough, mumbling in Czech. Nick washed his hands and dried them slowly on the grimy towel roll. A minute. Now. If he waited, the man might want to talk. He picked up his coat, still covering the urn, and walked out.

He went out to the track area on the right, as if he were heading for another train. At the entrance, he bent to tie his shoe, hidden by one of the pillars. Zimmerman was leading one of the men away toward the newsstand. But only one. The other stood as before, unmovable. Of course. What could Zimmerman have said to make them both move away? The Berlin train was there, a long row of open doors waiting for straggling passengers. Everyone else was already on. No time.

Nick stood up, shielded by a group of passengers heading for the short commuter train. The policeman never turned, focusing only on the Berlin platform. Nick moved with the others onto the commuter ramp, passing a signboard of indecipherable Czech names. It was more crowded than he'd expected, but no one else was carrying luggage either, so no one seemed to find him unusual, except for one woman who stared at his shoes. He walked to the end of the train, about two thirds the length of the Berlin train, and got on the next-to-last car. Open seats, not compartments, a few people reading newspapers and eating rolls.

He didn't turn into the seating area but crossed to the opposite door, pulled down the window, and looked out, just getting some air. The Berlin train was a few yards away across the empty platform, its passengers visible through the windows. So simple, if they didn't see. He stuck his head carefully out the window. No Zimmerman, just the lone watchdog, looking toward the station hall. Now. There was a rustling behind him, someone getting on, a woman with a heavy shopping bag. He pulled his head back until she passed into the car, then looked again. Still clear. He turned the door handle slowly and pushed. Nothing. He looked down at the handle, amazed. He had only a minute. He jiggled the handle and pushed hard, trying not to feel frantic. He saw himself trapped, carried away to some unknown Czech town, his chance gone. He slammed the handle. Was it stuck? No, locked, sealed from the international platform. He felt around it, afraid to bend down and really look. If it needed a conductor's master key—but there it was, the oblong deadbolt. He turned it, his hand slippery with sweat, heard the loud click, and swung open the door, free.

He glanced toward the station as he closed the door behind him, alone on the platform, vulnerable. Three of them now, but only Zimmerman facing in his direction. He caught Zimmerman's quick look, then saw him draw the others into a small circle, holding one on the shoulder to keep their attention.

Seconds. Nick stepped across the platform. When he heard the shrill whistle, his heart stopped. Then, instead of shouts, the yells of pursuit, he heard the *thunk* of a closing door and saw one of the attendants walking down the platform, bored and poky, slamming shut the open doors, getting ready to leave.

Nick jumped into the car, out of breath, as if he'd been racing to make the train. The same open seating arrangement, like an American train, no class compartments. He turned left into the car and started down the aisle, looking for Molly. But what if she were in front—could he risk backtracking? Pretending to look for a seat when there were so many available? A small family, looking harried, with piles of suitcases. Russian Jews? Businessmen. No tourists. Everyone looked up as he walked by, frankly curious. Where was she? She'd never leave without him, despite the promises. If he didn't appear, she'd get off the train, then get stuck with the mess his leaving would cause. Why had she gone to the front?

But there she was, staring out the window, anxious. When she saw him she smiled and began to remove her jacket from the seat, but he lowered his eyes, shaking his head as he passed her. He went into the next car, to put distance between them, and found the WC at the end. Almost there. He turned the handle. Another lock, a woman's voice behind the door. He saw the *Besetzt* notice above the handle: occupied. Why now? But maybe it wouldn't matter. Maybe Zimmerman had taken them away for a beer. He peeked out the still-open door onto the platform. They were getting on the train, all three of them, as the conductor methodically shut the doors. He wanted to bang on the WC door, tell the woman to hurry up. He couldn't wait here. They'd spot him down the long connecting corridor. He knew because he could see them, far off, beginning to move through the cars, coming toward him.

He slipped across the car to the opposite door. The same kind of bolt. He turned it with a heavy click and swung the door open. On this side there was no platform. Just tracks, two sets of them, no train waiting at the next platform. He looked down. Too far. He could jump down, wait it out, but then he wouldn't be able to reach the handle to get back in. He looked at the side of the train. Smooth, only a narrow runner of metal trim. But maybe just wide enough, if you were desperate. He put on the raincoat, wedging the bulky urn into the deep inside pocket. What if the runner didn't hold his weight? But it was a German train, solid workmanship. He was about to risk his life on a national cliché.

He reached along the car to grab the windowsill, then swung one of his feet onto the trim and found a toehold. With his free hand he closed the door behind him then, crouching, moved his other foot onto the runner. His feet slipped a little, but he held the windowsill tightly, his whole weight supported now by his fingers. Then his shoe caught, and he flattened himself against the car like a barnacle, hanging on with fingers and toes. How long could he keep it up? Already his fingers felt the pressure. It occurred to him that everything he had done up until this moment could be explained away somehow. Now he'd run out of answers. Hanging on to the railway car where anyone outside might see him, he had become visibly, absurdly, a fugitive.

Only sounds again, like the men's room. The conductor slamming the platform side door. Another door closing—with any luck, the woman leaving the WC. But too late now. A loudspeaker in the station, scratchy. The engine humming. If the train started moving, he'd never make it; the jolt would throw him from the car. Then voices, indistinct. Finally Zimmerman's, loud, as if he were announcing their presence as they moved through the cars. Nick felt sweat running down the side of his face. Worse, his fingers were getting numb. Come on. Then the voices were nearer, a door opened. "No," he heard Zimmerman say—the check on the WC?—and they were moving into the next car.

Now. He couldn't wait any longer. His breathing was ragged, as if his fingers were gasping for help. Gripping even tighter with his right hand, he slid his left toward the handle, straining, terrified he'd slip. It turned smoothly, without a sound, and then he had the door open and was moving his foot inch by inch until finally it was there, and shifting his weight to the supporting handle, he dragged himself back inside. He was panting. How much farther along were they? He glanced toward the WC door. *Frei.* He had to risk it. He couldn't stand in the open

495

back of the car, waiting for conductors and attendants to look at him in surprise. Don't slouch, act normal. He took a breath, straightened, and quickly crossed over to the door. He jerked it open and went in, waiting for a cry of discovery. Instead there was another whistle on the platform, a louder throb of the impatient engine. He clicked the lock behind him. *Besetzt.*

Another few minutes and the train had still not moved. How much longer would they be? A cursory second check, just to make sure? He took a rough paper towel and wiped his face. His shirt, he saw, had begun to soak through; his fingertips were red. Then he heard them doubling back through the car, presumably on their way out. Zimmerman's voice was disgruntled, fed up, his time wasted. Steps in front of the WC, a burst of Czech. *"Ano, ano,"* Zimmerman said, bored. A knock on the door. He had to open it; a refusal would be the end. But what if they were all standing there, looking in? He turned the lock and opened the door a crack. Zimmerman stuck his head in, meeting Nick's eyes, his colleagues inches away. I don't take risks. A worm. Nick closed his eyes, waiting.

"Ne," Zimmerman shouted to them and then, to Nick, apologetically, *"Prominte, pani."* He bowed his head and closed the door.

When the train started with a jolt, Nick was pitched to the side of the narrow cabin. The window, painted over for privacy, had no view. He could hear the slow moving of the wheels, then the clicks as they passed over the points in the yard, switching left, gathering speed, until the car was rocking steadily, on its way. They would be passing through the dormitory towns now, drab concrete towers with washing hanging from the balconies. He opened the door and started toward Molly, balancing himself in the center of the swaying car.

"You all right?" she said when he took his seat next to her, still breathing heavily. "You're sweating."

Through the window, the country was racing by in a blur. He took her hand and held it, then, an uncontrollable nervous reaction, broke into a grin, almost laughing out loud.

"How did you get past them?"

But all he said was, "We made it," still grinning, in a private haze of well-being.

"We're not out yet," she said, but she smiled back, catching his mood. "I thought I was going to throw up."

"You?"

She nodded. "We just learn to put a good face on it. Girls. In case you haven't noticed."

He looked at her, then down at her legs. "They did."

"I told you I could help," she said, then looked at him seriously. "I did, didn't I? Telling Zimmerman. I didn't know what to do. I thought, what if I've given you away? But he seemed so worried."

"You were right."

"Then, on the train, he never said a word. Didn't even look at me. I didn't know what was happening, except that they hadn't got you yet."

"He didn't want them to know about you. They'd have taken you off." He touched her arm. "It doesn't matter now. We made it."

He leaned back and reached for a cigarette, looking out the window, content just to breathe. No more buildings, just trees.

"What happens now?" Molly said after a while.

"We stop at Brno, I think. Then the border."

"No, I meant after."

He lit the cigarette. "We finish it. We find out who killed her."

"Oh, Nick, I don't care about that."

"It's the same person who killed him."

"In Washington," she said slowly. "That's what this is all about." She turned to him. "Whatever it is." A question.

"When we're out of the country," he said, answering it.

"For my own protection. Don't you think it's a little late for that?"

"No. I don't want you sticking your neck out for me."

"You still don't get it, do you?" she said. "Stick my neck out. I'm in love with you."

He stopped. Out of nowhere, like the whistle on the platform, a rush of adrenaline. "Don't say that."

"Why not?"

He looked at her, helpless. "I don't know what to say back."

She smiled. "You don't have to say anything back. I just thought you'd like to know."

He leaned over and kissed her, just brushing her lips, tentative, as if he were looking for words.

"Stick my neck out," she said, her face close. "My god."

"But if something happens—"

She put her mouth on his. They were still kissing, oblivious, when the conductor came into the car, trailed by the customs inspector. Nick sat up, embarrassed, then saw instantly that she'd brought him luck again. The men were amused, raising eyebrows at each other, glad of a break in the routine. Up ahead, tickets were taken, bags hauled down from the overhead rack. The luggage. Still not over. In a panic, Nick tried to think of the right excuse. Our things were sent ahead. We're just going to Vienna for the day. None of it was logical. They'd notice someone without luggage. But in the end they didn't even ask.

"American?" the conductor said, smiling, as he flipped the passport. "I have brother in America. Detroit. You know Detroit?"

Nick shook his head. "New York."

"Ah, New York. You have good time in Prague?"

For a second Nick wanted to laugh, hysterical. A wonderful time. But the man was addressing Molly, flirting, his eyes on her legs.

"It's very beautiful," she said, the standard answer. How many times could they hear it?

"Like yourself," the conductor said, courtly, handing the passports back.

They had begun to move along when the customs officer noticed the urn on Nick's folded coat and said something in Czech.

"What is?" the conductor asked, evidently translating.

Nick felt his palms grow slick. "Ashes," he said, then pointed to the end of the cigarette. "Ashes. My father."

The conductor frowned. Something that didn't make sense. "Open, please."

Nick picked up the urn, unscrewed the top, and held it out. "Ashes," he said again.

"Ah, ashes," the conductor said, pretending to understand. He rested his finger on top, preparing to go through it. What did he expect to find? Drugs? Jewelry? There had to be a word.

"Krematorium," Molly said suddenly, giving it a German pronunciation, catching the man just as he was about to poke inside. He stopped and made a face, squeamish, looking at a corpse, and handed the urn back to Nick. He spoke a line of Czech to the other, threw an odd look at Nick, then gave it up—Americans were inexplicable—and moved down the car to harass traveling Czechs. Nick screwed back the top, relieved, and put the urn under his coat. His father had made it out.

"You're shaking," Molly said, watching him. "What was that all about? Have you got something in there?"

Nick nodded.

"I don't think I can go through this again. That was like the station. What are you doing? You've got to tell me."

Nick looked at her, the worried eyes. In his hands. Willing to walk through a gate, sick to her stomach. "Yes," he said. "Everything."

He sank back against the seat and began to talk, his voice low, almost a murmur, so that the other passengers thought they were simply a couple making plans. Molly said nothing, afraid he would stop if she interrupted, but her eyes talked back, wide and interested, then grave, finally intimate, part of it now. Outside they were passing through a Schweik landscape, passive, gentle hills wriggling across the countryside. Once they paralleled a road, passing a car, and Nick thought of Zimmerman driving his colleagues through the same rolling country to the empty cottage, giving Nick time, shrugging his shoulders when they got there, mistaken again. Another glance at his watch. How much time? It would only take a phone call to the border. But who would leave a car?

After Brno, even Molly became fidgety.

"Maybe we shouldn't sit together," Nick said. "In case."

"You leave and I'll scream."

"You don't have to go on with this. Now that you know. It's dangerous."

"Will you stop?" She glanced up, a hint of her old spirit. "At least you're not boring. God. Imagine spending the rest of your life with Jeff Foster."

"I'm serious."

"So am I. Can't you see I'm just nervous? How much longer, anyway?"

But the border, when they got there, was empty

501

and placid, as quiet as the crossing where they'd driven in. The train screeched to a halt, then idled while Czech guards in gray uniforms boarded and did another passport run, to make sure everyone was stamped for Vienna. The conductor, following, beamed at Nick and said, "American," as if it were a kind of secret handshake. Minutes passed. Nick watched the guards move through the cars, examining papers, everything in slow motion. One phone call. Maybe this is how the Russian Jews felt, waiting for the cage door to open.

Molly sat rigidly, not saying anything. He was sweating again. Out the window the conductor was talking to one of the border guards on the tracks, this one in blue. What did the uniforms mean? Nick looked toward the control shed at the crossing, its roof laced with wires, where the call would come in. More minutes. Then the clump of boots, the guards getting off the train, a whistle, and the barrier gate began to rise.

The engine grew louder, revving up, but the train stayed in place, as if it needed a push. Then the car began to slide forward, slowly, into the no-man's-land between the barriers. Another crossing gate going up, another group of uniforms waiting, and they were across, shuddering to a second stop as the Austrians got on. Nick looked behind. The Czech gate was going down. Were they technically in Austria, beyond recall? The new guards, speaking German, were perfunctory but correct, somehow more sinister than the shaggy Czechs, like movie Nazis. They stamped passports and moved on, efficient. Nick kept looking back toward the Czech sector, expecting to see someone running out of the signal house, waving his hands. But it had to be all right now.

And a few minutes later it was. The train picked up speed, leaving the border behind, streaming into the woods. Molly took his hand and squeezed it, but he was too drained to respond. He had been so focused on the crossing, a pinpoint of space, that everything beyond seemed a blank. Vienna. What if the embassy knew, had people waiting for them? He moved his hand, feeling the urn, just as deadly as before. But what did the film actually say? They were out, but the air wasn't free, full of questions.

"Everything's going to be different now," Molly said, squeezing his hand again. But it wasn't. The landscape was the same, unassuming hills and fields. It still wasn't finished. They'd want him, if they knew. But they didn't, not even Silver. They might watch, but they didn't know. If he was careful. Nothing was different. Even the fear was the same, not left behind barbed wires. It stayed with you, like a new sense. There was no geographical alchemy. You took Prague with you.

PART THREE

NAMING
NAMES

■

CHAPTER SIXTEEN

Larry was furious, and wounded. They had lunch in the quiet dining room of the Knickerbocker, overlooking Fifth Avenue, because he wanted to avoid the communal table at the Brook, but even here, so private that business papers were not allowed at table, people came over to say hello, a hand on the shoulder and an innocuous comment about Uncle Ho's keeping him busy and who was the fine young fellow with him. Larry put on his Van Johnson smile, but Nick could see his irritation, each interruption wasting precious time.

It was a typical Larry meeting, caught on the run, with a return plane to Paris waiting, a phone call expected, so that Nick became marginal, someone he'd managed to fit in. But Nick hadn't wanted it either. Molly had taken the film to a photographer friend downtown, and Nick had watched it drop into her purse with dismay, afraid to let it out of his hands for even a minute. Outside, with its swarms of bright yellow taxis, New York was rich and busy and filled with sunshine, everything Prague was not, but all he could think about was Molly being followed or the photographer—how good a friend?—amazed at the pictures appearing in the fixing tray. But Larry had insisted; he had only the afternoon. So they both sat there, prickly, like pieces of tinder ready to ignite. When Larry said, "Chicken salad and iced tea. Two," Nick wanted to jump on him. I can order myself. A kid again.

"Why didn't you say anything to me? That's what I want to know. What the hell did you think you were doing?"

"I told you, he didn't want anyone to know."

"Well, that's typical, isn't it? I suppose you know your mother's a wreck. For Christ's sake, traipsing around behind the iron curtain without telling anyone. Now, of all times. What do you think I'm doing in Paris, going to the Louvre? Did you ever think how this would look for me?"

"No, Larry, I never thought about that."

"Well, thanks very much."

"It had nothing to do with you."

"Of course it did. You're my son."

"I was his too."

"I'm surprised you wanted to see him. After everything. Why didn't you ask me to arrange it if it was so important to you? Do it the right way, not sneak around like this. Like some—" He hesitated. "Spy," he said, unable to resist.

Nick looked at the man his father had thought would help. Mistaken about everyone to the end, except Nick.

"What's the right way? What would you have said?"

Larry looked away. "I'd have tried to talk you out

508

of it, I suppose. What was the point, Nick? All these years."

"The point was he wanted to see *me*. Before he died. I couldn't say no to that."

"Before he died?"

"I think he knew."

Larry looked away, disconcerted. "What did he want, to tell you he was sorry?"

"More or less."

"Christ. So off you go. Not a word. And the next thing I hear you're in a Communist jail—"

"I was never in jail."

"And now I've got the FBI all over me. Did you know your son is in Czechoslovakia? Oh, really. Fucking *Hoover* on the phone. Now I'm supposed to owe him one. God knows what that favor will be. Your son's been arrested, but we got him out. Well, thanks, Edgar, I appreciate it. Do you have any idea what it's been like?"

"They didn't get me out. You don't owe him anything."

"Well, they still want to see you. Is there something else I should know before they start calling me again? What's all this business about him coming back? What did he tell you?"

"He said he wanted to come home, that's all. Maybe the FBI thought he meant it. I don't know why. They don't know what they're talking about."

"Well, it wouldn't be the first time." Larry paused. "He said that, about coming back? Christ. What did you say?"

"I didn't say anything. It wasn't real, Larry, just

some dream he had." And here, with the sun flashing on the yellow taxis, was it anything more?

"How could he think—? Come home. He must
have been out of his mind."

"Yes, he must have been," Nick said, an edge.
"He killed himself."

Larry stopped and looked down, embarrassed.
"I'm sorry. I didn't mean—"

Nick said nothing, letting the moment hang
there, everything awkward. The chicken salad arrived. Larry sipped his iced tea.

"They said you found the body. That must have
been—" He switched tack, avoiding it. "How did
he do it? They didn't say."

"He jumped off the balcony," Nick said, matter-
of-fact.

"Jumped?"

"It's an old Prague custom. Like Jan Masaryk."

"Yes," Larry said, surprised at the reference. "I
remember."

Another awkward pause, a sip of tea.

"That doesn't always work. Was he still alive
when you found him?" Larry asked, his tone almost delicate, talking around it, like asking a cancer patient the details of his medication because
you couldn't ask how it felt to die.

"No. No last words," Nick said.

"It must have been terrible. Finding him."

Stay away from it. "That's why they thought I
killed him, at first. It wasn't jail, you know, just a
few questions."

"Christ, what a mess," Larry said. "You'd think he'd have waited. Not while you were still there."

"I don't think he was thinking about that, Larry," Nick said.

"No." A quick step back.

"Maybe it's *because* I was there. His seeing me. That's what the police think."

Larry grabbed his arm across the table, almost violent. "Don't you think that. Ever. Don't you do that to yourself." Then he pulled his hand back and looked away. "Hell," he said, general, meaningless, like shaking his fist in the air. He picked at his salad, letting the polite room settle around them. "What was he like?" he said finally, as if they were just making conversation.

"The same. Different. He was sick. I met his wife."

"What's *she* like? A Russian?"

"No, Czech. They met in Moscow, though. She didn't talk much. He wanted to talk about old times."

"Old times?"

"When I was a boy," Nick said. "Not politics. Not what happened."

"No, I guess he wouldn't."

"Jokes we used to have. You know."

"No, I don't," Larry said, irritated, then caught himself. "Never mind. What else?"

"Nothing. We went to the country. We went to a Benny Goodman concert."

"God."

"He was just happy to see me. I thought so, anyway. I had no idea he was thinking about—"

"No, he was always good at that. The old Kotlar two-face."

"Come on, Larry."

He sighed and nodded, an apology.

What else? How Nick's heart had turned over that first night at the Wallenstein? Putting him to bed? His face at the gallery, gazing at the fatted calf? The bottomless regret? None of it. "He showed me his Order of Lenin," Nick said instead.

"Well, he earned it," Larry said sourly. "I'm sorry, Nick. A couple of jokes and old fishing stories? I remember other things. I remember *you*. The way you walked around looking like you'd been kicked in the face."

"I remember it too, Larry," Nick said quietly.

"He shouldn't have done it," Larry said, as if he hadn't heard. "Making you go there. All these years, and he just crooks his little finger like nothing happened. Jokes. I'll bet he was charming. He was always charming." He spoke the word as if it were a kind of smear. "He charmed me. Well, they're all good at that. All smiles. You ought to sit across a table from them. Day after day. Not an *inch*. They don't want us out, they want us to keep groveling. Showing you his medal—was that supposed to make you proud? What do you think he got it for?"

Nick stared at him, amazed at the outburst. Larry put down his fork and looked out the window, visibly trying to retrieve control. "He shouldn't have

512

done it," he said. "You might have got in real trouble. I didn't know you were there."

Nick waited a moment. "I'm sorry you were worried, but nothing happened. I'm back. He wasn't charming. He was a sick old man. Now he's dead. It's over." He paused. "What's this all about?"

"I don't know," Larry said, still looking out the window. Then he turned back to Nick, his eyes thoughtful. "Maybe I'm jealous. It's hard to share someone." He picked up his fork, then put it down again, as if a prop would distract him. "You were so stubborn. Like an animal. You wouldn't trust anyone. And I thought, I'm not going to let this happen to him. Okay, at first it was for your mother. I never thought about having a kid, not even my own. You were just part of the package. But there you were. You wouldn't give an inch either." He paused, a smile. "Just like old Ho. Maybe you were my special training. But then it changed a little. Then a little more. The funny thing was, I wasn't winning you over—it was the other way around. I loved being your father. All of it—all those things I didn't expect. Christ, those hockey games." He looked up. "I thought you were mine. You remember the way people would say we were like each other and you'd give me that look, our little secret? But I loved it when they said that. We are a little, you know. I see myself in you sometimes. I don't know how that happens. Of course, I don't see myself farting around London when you could be making something of yourself here. Well, I had to say it. But I know you will." He looked straight at

Nick. "You're the hardest thing I've ever done. So maybe I'm jealous when someone has you so easily. One call and you come."

"And if you called, I wouldn't?"

"Well, you like to be the only one. Maybe it's wrong. I never thought I'd have to share you, but I do. So I'll learn. Even with him. I thought Walter was a fool—I'm sorry, I did, I can't pretend. But I don't want you to think I am too."

"I don't think you're a fool."

"Well, you will if I go on like this. A little unexpected, isn't it? Maybe I'm getting old, a little fuzzy. But a stunt like this, Christ, Nick. Wait till Hoover tells you your kid is locked up somewhere." Larry paused and Nick saw the hint of a question in his eyes. "But it's all over now."

"Yes, it's all over."

Larry glanced at his watch. "I have to run, I'm sure you'll be relieved to hear. Go see your mother, she's expecting you. You might skip the body details—you know, after he fell. She's been— It brings everything back. So maybe just the old jokes. And how you weren't in jail." He paused, a glint. "And his wife."

He got up and started out, Nick following. "I shouldn't leave her, but I'll be back Friday. It's like the shuttle, back and forth to Paris every week. They love face-to-face in Washington these days, I don't know why. Maybe they don't trust the phones. Well, they're right. Remind me to tell you the latest about Nixon and old Edgar. The War of the Roses. To tell you the truth, I don't mind the planes. No calls. You get to read the papers." They were on the bright marble steps, traffic honking, the quiet formal rooms behind them like some misplaced dream of London. "By the way, what's with the hotel? You've got a perfectly good room at home sitting there."

"I'm with a girl."

"Really?" Larry said, interested. "Serious?"

But Nick ignored it. "We're only here for one night. To see you. We go to Washington tomorrow."

"What's in Washington?"

"Friends."

"What friends?"

Nick smiled at him, the suspicious parent. "Hers. This must be your car."

"How do you know?"

"It's black and important. Big aerial. Isn't it?"

"Wise guy," Larry said fondly.

"By the way, did you get a call from Jack Kemper?"

Larry looked at him, suddenly alert. "No, why?"

"He's with the CIA in London. I used his name. I told the embassy in Prague I was working for him. That's why they got me out. Not the Bureau. You don't owe Hoover anything."

Larry blinked, taking this in. "How do you know he's with the CIA?"

"You told me. At the Bruces' party."

Larry looked at him, then smiled, an insider's laugh. "Who said my kid couldn't think on his feet? They'd better watch you."

"Well, they may. And you. I heard Kemper was upset. That's why I thought you should know."

"Thanks for the tip," Larry said, taking his hand, but Nick leaned over and hugged him. Larry held him for a moment, surprised and pleased. "I'm glad you're home," he said, no longer joking, an apology for the lunch.

"Get us out of Vietnam," Nick said as Larry got into the car.

"I'm trying, believe me," he said, then rolled up the window and the car slid toward Fifth Avenue.

The photographer was in a rundown building on Delancey Street, near the bridge, two unlit flights up.

"You Nick, man?" he said, opening the door a crack. Long hair, a face corrugated with old acne scars. When Nick nodded, the door opened into a huge empty space with exposed pipes littered with tripods, light cables, and back screens. The living quarters seemed to be a camp bed and a trestle table overflowing with Chinese takeout cartons. A young girl in a flimsy short dress sat on a stool, smoking a joint. "Molly's in there," he said, nodding toward a bare red bulb hanging over an enclosed space. "Your prints are still drying. What the fuck are they, anyway? I mean, they're in fucking *Russian.*"

What had Molly told him? *"Samizdat,"* Nick said.

"Samitz who?"

516

"Underground manuscripts. They have to smuggle them out. You know, like Solzhenitsyn."

"Far out."

"Want a hit?" the girl said dreamily, holding out the joint.

Nick shook his head.

"I'm not going to get in any trouble or anything, right?" the photographer said.

"No, nothing like that. I appreciate your help."

"Hey, no problem. Old Molly. Samizyet," he said, shaking his head.

"What kind of photography do you do?" Nick said, to make conversation.

"Fashion," he said, grinning. The girl giggled.

Molly came out, stuffing an envelope into her bag. "Hey, thanks, Richie." She went over and gave him a peck on the cheek. "You do great work."

"Fucking A. You got them all? Don't leave nothing in there."

"All here," she said, patting the bag. "I'll see you, okay?"

"Yeah. Say hi to your mom."

As they were leaving, the girl with the joint began lifting the dress over her head, her body as thin as a child's.

"The people you know," Nick said when they hit the street, bright after the dark stairs.

"Richie? We went to high school together." She laughed to herself. "In the glee club."

They stopped at a bookstore on Fifth Avenue to buy a Russian-English dictionary.

"What's the point?" Nick said. "We can't translate this. It'd take months."

"No, but we might get some idea what it *is*. What were you going to do, get one of the girls at the UN? Would you mind taking a look at these? Just a few espionage documents I happened to pick up. By the way, do you have a safe-deposit box or something? For the negatives."

"No. I'll put them somewhere at home. I have to see my mother anyway."

"Alone?"

Nick nodded.

"A little too early to take me home to Mom, huh?"

"A little too early for Mom. She's got other things on her mind."

"Okay. Maybe I'll run up to Bronxville and see mine. Since we're being so good."

"But you'll be back tonight?"

"Hmm." She looked at him. "I'm not that good. Besides, I always wanted to stay at the Plaza. How rich are you, anyway?"

He smiled. "Rich."

"And Catholic. You are Catholic, aren't you?"

"Baptized, anyway."

"She'll die. She'll just die."

The photographs, in impenetrable Cyrillic, seemed to be a series of reports, not a simple list.

"See how they're dated up here? Like memos."

"This is impossible, Molly. Even if we figure out the letters, we still have to translate the Russian."

"Well, the numbers help. We can figure out the

dates," she said eagerly. "And see the words in block capitals? They all have them. It's a format, if we can figure it out. They sign off that way too."

But the dates, once deciphered, were all recent, none of them reaching back to his father's time.

"They're the active ones, that's why," Molly said. "These are the reports they're getting now. I'll bet the caps are names. Look, this one's Otto. So who's Otto?"

"A code name," Nick said, then sighed. "We have to know the context, Molly. Look at the dates—they're not consistent. It's a selection. Maybe they're the incriminating ones. Each one nails somebody, if you understand it."

"Hold on," she said, distracted, looking something up in the dictionary. Nick walked over to the window and looked across the street to where the hansom cabs were idling in the afternoon sun.

"Serebro," Molly said, running her finger down a page. "Yes. Come look." But Nick was still eyeing the street, watching the taxis pull up under the 59th Street awning. She brought the book over to him, pointing to the word.

"Silver," he said. "By him or about him?"

"By him. The signature."

He glanced at the photograph. A report, exactly like the others, same format, so not original, typed by someone in Moscow. From cables? By Nina, perhaps, his father's friend, Silver's admirer. "Yes, but we have to know what it says. Didn't any of your friends go into the translating business?"

"No, only dirty pictures." She hesitated. "You could ask your father. He'd know someone."

"You could ask Jeff," he answered back. "Want the phone?"

"Look, let's think about this. What would reports say? Not necessarily who they are, just what they're passing on. I mean, the reports still might not identify them. You'd have to know who the code names referred to."

"Great. No, we need the context. I mean, if it's a trade report, it's someone in Commerce. Like that."

"But how would we know exactly who in Commerce? Are you listening to me? What are you looking at?"

"It's a pickup zone," Nick said, still watching out the window. "So why is that car just sitting there? The doorman acts like he doesn't even see it."

"Maybe it's waiting."

"I don't think so. Two guys. Feels like old home week to me."

"Let me see," Molly said, getting up, accidentally knocking the photographs to the floor. "Shit." She bent down, collecting them.

"One of them's on the corner, so they've got both entrances covered."

"Don't get paranoid," Molly said, still crouched down, sorting the pictures. "I'll bet it's a divorce. This isn't Prague, remember?"

Nick said nothing. The man below lit a cigarette.

"Well, bless me for a fool," Molly said. "Nick, look."

"What?"

"I thought they were all alike, but look. At the end." Nick came over. "It's a list."

He took the photograph. "But of what?"

"Code names and addresses. Five of them. See. That's NW at the end."

"Washington."

"There's Otto. Come on, we can translate this. The street names'll be in English."

"What were the letters for Silver?"

She glanced down the list. "He's not here."

But someone can lead me to him. "Never mind. Let's do the others." He grinned at her. "How'd you get so smart anyway?"

"Bronxville High," she said. "Look at Richie."

The maid opened the door, someone new, a thin black woman wearing a housedress and comfortable bedroom slippers.

"She's in there, feeling sorry for herself. See if you can get her to eat something."

His mother was sitting on the long couch, staring out across the park. The room was almost dark.

"There you are," she said, holding out her arms. "I was getting worried."

He leaned down and kissed her, smelling the gin on her breath. "Want a light?" he said, reaching for the lamp.

"No, leave it. It's nice like this. Anyway, I look terrible." Her face in fact was blotchy, like a blur

521

sitting on top of the sharp edges of her perfect suit and its gleaming brass buttons. "I'm having a cocktail." She glanced up. "Just one. You?" He shook his head. "I don't know why. I don't really like them." She took a sip from the wide-mouthed glass. "Did you see Larry?"

He took a seat beside the couch, unnerved by her voice—dreamy, the way it had been the day after his father left.

"He said you were in jail."

"No," Nick said. "The police just asked me some questions. I'm all right."

She turned her eyes back to the window. "What did he look like?"

"The same. Thinner. Not as much hair."

"Waves," she said absently. "It's hard to imagine—"

Nick waited.

"Was he happy?" But she caught the absurdity of it herself. "Before the end, I mean." She reached for a cigarette.

"No. Not happy. I think he just made the best of it. While he could."

"Isn't it terrible? I don't think I could stand it if he'd been happy. Isn't it terrible. To feel that."

"He asked about you."

"Did he?" she said, her voice almost eager, and then she was crying, her face scrunched like a child's. "I'm sorry," she said, running a finger under her eyes. "I don't know why I mind so much. I didn't expect to. You'd think—" She took out a handkerchief and wiped her face. "I must look like

522

hell. I've been doing this all day. Silly, isn't it? It's just that I keep thinking—" Nick looked at her curiously. All these years without a word. She blew her nose. "What did he say?"

"He wondered if you'd ever want to see him again."

"If I'd ever want to see him again," she repeated dully, staring at the handkerchief. "I won't now, will I? He's really gone, not just away somewhere." She paused. "I've never been a widow before. All of a sudden, you're alone." She tried to smile, airy. "Nobody to go dancing with. Hear the songs. He was a good dancer, did you know?"

"No."

"We used to have fun. I'd get all dressed up, he liked that, and—" She stopped again, catching his look. "Don't worry. It's just that it all comes back. All the fun." Her eyes went back to the window, fixed somewhere in the fading light. A silence. "See him again," she said slowly. "I wanted to see him every day. Every single day."

I hope you die, she'd said.

"I never knew you felt that way. I mean, after—"

"Didn't you? No, nobody did. Maybe I didn't myself. I thought it would stop," she said to herself, still staring out the window. "How do you stop? I was in love with him," she said simply. "The rest of it doesn't matter, you know. Not any of it. I was in love with him." Her voice was dreamy again. "People don't say that anymore, do they? 'In love.'"

Nick looked at her, remembering his awkwardness on the train.

"But then, we were all like that. Drugged with it. That was our drug. All those songs. It's what everybody wanted, to fall in love. Maybe it was the war, I don't know. But I did. Just like in the songs. He would just walk into the room." She paused. "Just walk into the room. That's all. And I'd be—" She stopped and looked at him. "Am I embarrassing you? Children never think their parents feel anything." Her face softened. "But you're not a child anymore. You look so much like him. The same eyes."

"He never stopped loving you either." A kindness, but wasn't it true? He remembered the look on his father's face when he asked about her.

"Did he say that?" Her eyes moist again.

Nick nodded, not quite a lie.

"No, you never stop. I don't think I realized it until I heard." She turned back to the window. "I thought he—took it with him. Everything. The way he took the fun. And then I heard and it all came back. He was there all the time. Nobody else. I didn't know." She started crying again, shuddering, shaking her head. "Nobody told me I'd miss him. Nobody told me. Then you're alone." She turned her head, a thin wail, no louder than a sigh.

Nick looked at her, dismayed. "You're not alone."

She reached over and put her hand on his arm. "I know, honey, I didn't mean it that way." She sniffled, visibly pulling herself back. "What would I have done without you? It's different, that's all."

"I mean you have Larry."

524

"I never loved Larry," she said flatly, putting out her cigarette. "I never loved anyone but your father. Not for a day. Didn't you know that?"

No, I didn't, Nick wanted to say. "But you married him."

"Yes. I don't know why. I suppose to make him stop asking me. Maybe I thought it would be safer—better for you. Who knows why we do things? Maybe I thought it would be a way to forget." Her hand was still at the ashtray, rubbing the cigarette out. "I was wrong about that. In a way it made it worse, all the pretending. Anyway, I did. Not very fair to him, I suppose, but it's what he wanted."

"He's crazy about you."

"Larry?" She looked up at him. "Larry was never faithful to me in his life. Not that I cared. Well, at first. Then it was a relief, really. I never had to worry about him. Larry always took care of himself." She paused. "Now I *am* embarrassing you."

"How did you know?" Nick said, disbelieving. Where had he been while their lives were going on?

"Oh, darling, people are always helpful. Telling you things. For your own good. I suppose they thought I'd mind. Divorce him, which is always interesting. But, you see, I didn't care. I mean, he never flaunted it, there was no reason not to go on as we were. He was always very fond of you." She shrugged, ironic. "A model husband. It's just the way he is. So why should I mind?"

"You don't really mean that."

"No, not really," she said quietly. "But that's the

525

way it worked out. I don't know what he expected, marrying me. I often wondered. I think he wanted it because he wanted it. The idea of it. But after a while it didn't matter. You get used to everything, even the looks. 'Poor Livia.' That's the only part that used to bother me, the way they'd *look* at you. As if you didn't know. Tim was the worst. Those *eyes.* Like he was praying for you." She touched Nick's arm. "You ought to go see him, by the way. He's had a stroke now. They were giving him speech therapy. Funny, isn't it, to think of Tim tongue-tied. Funny how life works out. One day you're—" She broke off. "And the next day you're a widow. And it's all gone." She turned to Nick. "I'm glad you saw him. No matter what. You were everything to him. Was it all right, when you saw him? The way it was? I remember when you were little, that look he'd get on his face—" She reached for the handkerchief. "He couldn't get enough of you."

"It was the same," Nick said, suddenly claustrophobic in the dark room, the air itself swallowed up in her longing.

"He must have known. To want to see you before. It's terrible, knowing like that." As if his father had been lying in a hospital bed, waiting for the end, not being hurled over a balcony. The only way she would imagine it now, her dying lover.

Nick stood up and turned on the light. "It's getting dark."

She looked up, surprised, then nodded into the handkerchief. "And here I am *wallowing.* There's not much point, is there? Going on like this. There,'' she said, wiping her eyes again, ''all gone. Now. How about taking an old lady out to dinner? We'll go somewhere nice.'' She stood up and glanced at him. ''I suppose you're dressed. It doesn't seem to matter these days. I'll just go put on my face.'' She stopped. ''I'll be all right. Really. Somewhere nice. Lutèce.''

Nick checked his watch. ''Can we get in? I mean—''

''Darling. Use Larry's name.'' She started to move away, then turned. ''Nick, all this about Larry—I shouldn't have told you that. You mustn't mind. He cares about you. All this other—it doesn't matter, really. It's just life. My life, not yours.'' She tried a smile. ''Well, I won't be a minute. We'll have dinner. You can tell me everything that happened. How he lived. All that. Was he still funny?''

''Not as funny.''

''Oh,'' she said, a catch in her throat, then dismissed it. ''Well, everything. Even the bad parts.''

''Are you sure you want to know? Maybe it's better if—''

''Yes,'' she said, looking at him seriously. ''It's important. Everything about him. I have to know. All these years, nobody would talk about him. I was supposed to be—I don't know, ashamed, I guess. Larry wouldn't. I think it embarrassed him. Maybe he thought it would hurt me. But it can't now. I *want* to talk about him.'' She paused, looking down, her voice faltering. ''You see, I didn't know before. There isn't going to be anyone else. I'm not

527

ashamed. He was the love of my life." Then she turned and left.

Nick stood for a minute looking at the rich, soft room, the dull sheen of silver boxes and picture frames in the half-light, their old ormolu clock on the mantel, then went over to the window. Across the park, the familiar apartment towers had begun to light up: Majestic. Beresford. El Dorado. Movie castles, not the grim Hradčany, looming over a dark city. None of it had to happen. All their happiness. To protect somebody else.

"I won't be a minute," she called from her dressing room, her voice almost an echo.

She took ten. But when she appeared she was ready to go out, hair brushed back, lips red, fixed in a smile, the prettiest girl at Sacred Heart.

"How do I look?" she said.

"You look beautiful."

Her face softened, a real smile. "You always say that."

Molly was late.

"Remind me never to complain about Czech trains again," she said, flinging her bag on the hotel bed, full of energy. "At least they run. I had to wait an hour and *then* we got stuck. And of course she had to wait with me. Good old Kathleen. Made me realize why I left home in the first place. Still, it was worth it. Wait till you see what I've got." She looked over at him, noticing his distant expression. "How was your mother?"

"Sad," he said quietly, not wanting to discuss it. "What have you got?"

"What they call evidence." Molly sat, poking in her bag. "Take a look. Rosemary's last letter. My mother had it all these years—not a *word.* She said she never showed it to anyone because it was too shameful. Despairing. Anyway, I wheedled it out of her."

"A suicide note?" The letter was written on old correspondence paper, one sheet folded over to make four sides, the writing thick and hard, almost pressed through so that the ink had barely faded.

"*I* don't think so. Look." No margins, the girlish handwriting running from side to side in a solid block.

Dear Kathy,

Thanks so much for the $. I know things aren't easy for you either and I wouldn't have asked but I'm almost flat. I'll pay you back when I'm on my feet again. I wish I knew when that will be. I honestly don't know what I'm going to do and when all this business is going to end. I could tell from your letter, Kathy, that you think it's all my fault but honestly it's not, please don't think that. I don't know how it started, it's like a bad dream, and I just wish it would end. The newspapers don't bother me much now but I guess they'll start up again and then I don't know what. At least now I'll have some $ for a new dress.

You ask me if I'm sorry I got involved with the "Reds" in the first place. I suppose you want me to say yes, so yes. But I still think what they say makes a lot of sense. I guess all I can say is that it sounded like a good idea at the time. I am sorry that I got talked into doing what I did. You know I would never do anything against this country. I didn't think it was "treason" the way they say in the papers. I was just helping out, for a good cause. Well, I know better now but that doesn't help much. I thought one confession was enough. At least it wouldn't be on my conscience. But I guess Washington isn't like the church. They always want more—no absolution. I thought I was finished with it but I guess I wasn't. So I don't know what I'm going to do. Pray for me, if you think God is still listening. Thanks again for the $. Give my love to Molly and don't be angry with me.

Love,
Rosemary

P.S. You'll be happy to hear I haven't been seeing my "friend." I wish I was, in spite of everything. Since this business started, it's been hard. "Good," I can hear you say, but he's not what you think. He's not even married like the other one so don't worry about that. Just scared, like everybody else here. I'm sort of a famous character here (!). I guess I should leave Washington when all this is over but where would I go? Well, maybe God will forgive this too. Got to run. Thanks again. I'll pay you back. Promise.

Nick read it twice, trying to connect the simple schoolgirl scrawl to the twisted figure on the car roof. Everybody wanted to be in love then.

"What's the evidence?" he said finally.

"Well, it has to be some kind of evidence. It's the last thing she ever wrote. What was on her mind."

"A new dress," Nick said quietly.

"Which you don't buy if you're going to—Not if you have to borrow money for it."

"We knew that. You don't take your nightgown either. Who's the man? Did your mother say?"

"She didn't know. Just that Rosemary was seeing somebody. The married one was in New York, before she went to Washington. She and my mother had a big fight about him—you know, how *wrong* it was—so she was probably a little gun-shy after that about her love life. Especially if she was borrowing money from Mother Kathleen. Anyway, it sounds like he ditched her."

"No, I don't think so," Nick said thoughtfully. " 'Just scared.' Maybe just careful. Of a famous character. Well, that's one piece of evidence, anyway. It wasn't my father. He was married at the time."

"Unless he lied to her." She caught his look. "Well, people do. All right, I don't think he did it either."

She took the letter back and looked down at it. "Maybe I'll try confession too. Look what it did for Aunt Rosemary. You notice how nothing's her fault? *Her* conscience is clear. Pretty crazy, the whole thing, the more you look at it." She glanced

531

up. "I don't think she was sorry about anything. She just wanted my mother to think so. The guy's not so bad. Even the Communists still make a lot of sense. She was just helping out. I love the exclamation mark—little innocent me. Just a bad dream. 'I don't know how it started.' How hard would it be to figure that one out? 'I don't know how it started.'"

"But she didn't," Nick said. "My father told us. She never volunteered. They went after *her.*"

"Well, either way. What's the difference?"

"The difference is somebody else started it. Everything that happened."

But he was talking to himself, another conversation, and Molly wasn't listening. " 'Give my love to Molly,' " she said, pointing to the phrase. "If she saw me twice in her life, it was a lot. She was probably just getting ready to put the touch on old Kathleen again. You know, my mother thought she was wonderful. Wild, but—you know. That's why she kept it. I'll bet she never thought Rosemary was just fooling her too. God."

"She wasn't fooling anybody. She seems more sad than anything else."

"You keep saying that. You've got sad on the brain. You need cheering up." She reached up and put her hand on the back of his neck, tossing the letter on the bed. "Let's forget about them. Kathleen asked me if I was in New York with a man." She giggled. "So I told her I'd seen Richie. I thought she'd die."

"So would I, if I were your mother."

"But you're not, are you?"

"No."

"And you're not married."

"No."

"So there's nothing to worry about. Just my soul." She stretched her neck and kissed him. "Here's an idea. Let's smoke a joint and make love. All night." She nodded to the ceiling. "No microphones."

"I liked the microphones," he said, smiling. "Where'd you get the stuff?"

"Well, I did see Richie. There's no end to his talents."

He kissed her. "Was he a good kisser?"

"Are you kidding? I couldn't get past the Clearasil. Anyway, I don't kiss just anybody."

"No?"

"No. Consider yourself lucky."

"I do," he said into her ear, a murmur. "But let's skip the joint. We have to get up early."

"We do? Why?"

"Our friends down there left after I got in," he said, still whispering, as if they were back at the Alcron. "So they're probably on a shift, not working all night. I figure they won't get here before seven, so if we leave early, they won't even know we're gone."

She pulled back, surprised, as if someone had turned on the news. "You're good at this, aren't you?"

"I have help. You're the one who got the letter."

533

"Maybe you should take it up. What are you going to do when this is all over?"

"Go work for Jeff," he said.

"I work for Jeff," she said, kissing him.

CHAPTER SEVENTEEN

They took a taxi at dawn and waited, groggy, at the Eastern terminal for the first shuttle. New Jersey was a nap, and then they were circling Washington, Nick at the window feeling he'd entered a time machine, twenty years compressed into minutes. The monuments lined up as they always had along the Mall, changeless. His house somewhere to the left of the Capitol. But on the ground everything was different, whole streets of boxy new office buildings beyond the White House, bland and faceless, a discount Bauhaus, like a rebuilt city in Germany. They checked in at the Madison, its ornate ballroom still littered with last night's wedding, then went for a walk. A few of the trees were still in flower. Everyone carried briefcases.

"Where are we going?" Molly said.

"The Mayflower. I want to see it."

And of course it looked smaller, the awning he remembered near the car in the picture just an awning, the public spaces inside a little tired, no longer waiting for Truman's car. He stood in the lobby for a few minutes, creating lines of sight between the reception desk and the elevators and the big room where the United Charities ball must have been, then gave it up. He'd imagined it a hundred times, the forbidden place of his childhood, but it was just a hotel.

They rented a car, a plain Buick, and started going down the list, driving out toward the grand houses on Embassy Row, only to discover that the first address was the Russian embassy itself.

"Well, it would be, wouldn't it?" Molly said. "Maybe it's like the Americans in Prague. They have to live in the compound."

"No, there wouldn't be room. They have too many people. Besides, I'll bet they like to live out. It's probably one of the attachés. They'd be in residence. It would help if we had the real names." He put the car back in gear. "Anyway, I don't want the Russians."

"Somebody will." She looked down at the paper in her hand. "Valuable little list, isn't it?"

"Yes, they killed him for it."

"Did they know he had it?"

"I don't know," he said wearily. "I don't know, I don't know."

She looked up.

"This isn't going to be easy. I thought once we had it—" He remembered that feeling, a jolt of triumph, when his hand had felt it under the woodpile.

"Five names," Molly said calmly. "They can't all be Russian."

The next address was a quiet row house north of Dupont Circle, on a leafy block not far from the Phillips Collection.

"God, you'd never think," Molly said. "So what do we do, just sit here?"

"Let's see what happens. Maybe he'll come out."

When the door opened half an hour later, it wasn't a man but a white-haired woman, who bent over to water one of the potted plants on the stoop, then idly looked up and down the street—an old woman with all the time in the world.

"This can't be right," he said impatiently. There was no one in the street but a mailman making his way down the row. The woman put the watering can inside, then came back on the stoop to wait; evidently the mail was one of the events of her day. She talked to the mailman for a few minutes, her mouth moving rapidly with words inaudible across the street, even with the car window rolled down.

"Look," Molly said. "She's getting a lot of mail, I mean a *lot.* Maybe it's not just her in the house. You know, maybe she rents out."

"She acts like it's hers," Nick said, watching her flip through the envelopes, absorbed.

"She's just nosy."

"Okay, I'll find out," Nick said, opening the door.

"What are you going to say?"

"I'm not sure."

But it was remarkably easy, an unsuspicious world away from Prague. He had only to identify himself as someone from the government—the Washington password—checking on her boarders, and she leaped at the diversion.

"You mean the Russian girl. There isn't any trouble, is there? They told me there wouldn't be any trouble. I mean, I never had a *Russian,* but she seems all right. Quiet. Of course, she plays these *records,* but I don't mind that really. You have to expect things like that when you rent. Has she done something?''

"No, no, nothing like that," Nick said. "We just like to keep tabs, see if she's giving *you* any trouble. They're guests here, you know. Sometimes they forget that. We do get complaints.''

"Really?" she said, interested, settling in. "Well, no, she's good as gold. No men coming around. Of course, I don't know what she does on her own time, but she's been no trouble to me. I won't rent to men, just girls. That's what Mr. Baylor said before he passed away. When he was fixing up the apartments. They'll make a nice income, but you don't want men in the house, it's not worth it. Me being alone. Of course, these days girls are just the same as men, aren't they? But Irina's all right. It's just those language records. But I suppose she's learning. The other girl doesn't complain.''

"She doesn't live alone?''

"Oh yes, the flats are self-contained. They don't even have to share a bath. Mr. Baylor put another one in, said I could charge more if people had their own place. *And* they'll keep to themselves. But of course you can hear the records, the way she plays them. Still, Barbara never complains, so I just leave well enough alone. As long as they pay on time, that's what Mr. Baylor used to say.''

"Mr. Baylor.''

"My husband." She looked at him. "Where did you say you were from?"

"Immigration," Nick said, on firm ground now. "We just like to check. Thank you. I'm glad there's no trouble."

"No trouble at all. Shall I tell her you were here?"

"You can," Nick said carefully, "but sometimes it upsets them. You know what it's like where they come from."

Mrs. Baylor nodded. "I *do*."

"We don't want them to think it's like that here. Not with a routine check." He had taken out a notepad and was pretending to write. "These last names," he said, shaking his head.

"Aren't they something? I can never remember either. Oh, well, here," she said, flipping through the mail until she found a store catalogue. "*K* at the end. Kova."

He glanced at it. "Thanks."

"Any time. You couldn't do better, letting people like her in. Better than some we're already got."

Nick got in the car and waved to Mrs. Baylor as he drove off.

"Irina Herlikova," he said to Molly. "Quiet as a mouse."

"I wonder what she does."

"She's learning the language."

"No. For them."

The third address, surprisingly, was on D Street, in a black neighborhood southeast of Capitol Hill. Not a slum, but tattered, the respectable brick fronts frayed around the edges, needing paint.

"Well, at least this one's not a Russian," Nick said.

"We can't stay here. Two white people sitting in a car."

"No, let's just get a look at the house. We'll swing back."

"As if no one will notice."

But they were lucky. The house was in better repair than its neighbors, trim, a neat front yard, and on their third pass a man in uniform came out, moved a tricycle to the end of the porch, and, taking out his keys, walked toward a new car parked in front. Nick turned at the corner and waited.

"Let's see where he goes."

"Have you ever followed anybody?" she said, her voice eager, enjoying it.

"I'm learning on the job."

It turned out to be harder than he expected. He waited a few minutes after the car passed, then rounded the corner to find it idling at a red light.

"Don't slow down. He'll notice," Molly said.

Green. Their luck held. Another block and a car came out of a driveway and put itself between them. Nick relaxed. More blocks. The new car moved smoothly, never running lights, as orderly and correct as its owner.

"But where's he going?" Nick said. "There's nothing this way. Why doesn't he go into town?"

They followed for ten more minutes, unhurried, and then Nick saw the wires and gates, the sentry checking passes. The black man held out an ID badge and was waved through. The sentry looked up at Nick, who turned away, pretending to be lost.

"What is it?" Molly said.

"Anacostia. The naval base. I forgot it was down here. Well, that fits, doesn't it? A little Red dot on the sonar screen."

They drove up around the Jefferson Monument, then out through the park along the river and over the bridge. The fourth address was in Alexandria, not the Old Town of cobbled streets and ice cream shops but the maze of streets behind, lined with two-family houses. Anywhere.

"They're certainly not doing it for the money," Molly said, scanning the street.

"No. A better world."

"1017. Next to the one on the end."

They found a space two houses down and parked, then sat and had a cigarette. Another quiet street, a few children coming home from school.

Molly looked at her watch. "I'll bet there's no one home. Not at this hour. They must all do something, work somewhere. Otherwise, what good would they be?"

"I forgot to ask where the Russian girl worked."

"We'll find out. It's only the beginning, you know. It's not going to happen overnight."

"It's not going to happen here at all," Nick said, putting the key in. "You're right. We'll come back in the morning."

"Wait. Let's find out who he is, anyway. Be right back."

She got out, walked over to the house, and rang

the doorbell. What would she say if someone answered? She rang again, then looked around once and put her hand into the mailbox, pulling out a few pieces and shuffling through them. It took a second.

"Ruth Silberstein. Miss," she said in the car.

"Silverstein?"

"Ber."

He drove past the house. "We'll come back."

"She gets the *New Republic,* if that means anything. Where's the last one?"

He looked at the list. "Chevy Chase."

"God, they're all over the place. Creepy, isn't it? No one has the faintest idea. You can walk right up and look at their mail. They could be anywhere."

"Undermining our way of life," he said, using a newsreel voice.

"Well, they are, aren't they?"

"We don't know what they're doing, Molly. Maybe they're just passing on the wheat crop estimates so somebody can make a good deal. Do you think Rosemary was undermining our way of life?"

Molly looked out the window, quiet. "Just her own, I guess."

"Maybe they're just small fry."

"Your father didn't think so."

"No." Names he was willing to sell, worth a life.

"What are you going to do after? With the list."

"I don't know," he said, a curve, unexpected. "I'm only interested in one."

"I mean, they're agents."

542

"So was my father."

"But they might be—"

"I don't know, Molly. What do you want me to do, turn them in to the committee? I can't. It would be like turning my father in. Besides, there isn't any committee anymore. It's over. Just cops. Let Jeff catch them. I don't take sides."

"Yes, you do."

"Not anymore. Not with this."

"So Ruth Silberstein just keeps getting her *New Republic*s and doing whatever she's doing."

"I guess that depends on what she's doing."

"So you'll decide," she said quietly. "You'll be the committee."

A pinprick, sharp. "Yes, I'll be the committee," he said, the sound of the words strange, as if even his voice had turned upside down. "What's the address?"

The house in Chevy Chase was a snug Cape Cod with shutters and a fussy herbaceous border running along the front. In December there would be a wreath on the door and candles in the window, a Christmas card house. The wide glossy lawn was set off on either end by tall hedges to separate it from the neighbors, modern ranch houses, one with a *For Sale* shingle stuck in the grass. There was no car in the driveway or other sign of life.

"You going to read his mail too?" Nick said.

"No, it's a slot," Molly said, having already looked. "They're showing the house next door."

"How do you know?"

"See, they're huddling, and he keeps looking at the roof. The one in the suit's the real estate lady. You can always tell. She's wearing flats. With a suit. They all do that. I guess it's hard on the feet."

Nick grinned at her. "Are you kidding me, or do you really know all this?"

"Everybody knows that," she said, pleased with herself. "You just never notice things." She turned back to the window and watched the scene on the lawn, another pantomime of gestures and nodding heads. "How'd you like to live in the suburbs?"

"I wouldn't."

"Yeah," she said, still looking out, "but when you see the right house." She opened the door, then closed it behind her and stuck her head through the window. "Maybe you'd better stay here. You look like somebody from Immigration."

He watched her dart across the street and up to the group on the lawn, disengaging the woman wearing flats, a nod toward the hedge, heads together, the couple left to the side, unmoored. A shake of hands, the woman rummaging in her purse for a card, a smile and a wave, every step light and sure. When she crossed the street she seemed to move like liquid, and he thought of her coming toward him at the Bruces' party, walking into his life, like the songs. Now she was grinning.

"What did I tell you? They're the CIA of the suburbs. *Everything.* His name's Brown, John Brown. Like an alias, but then who'd use that? The house isn't for sale—she's tried. They won't list it. But there are a few others I might like to see, just like it.

He's not married, by the way—he lives with his mother. Which is odd, considering."

"Considering what?"

"Where he works."

He raised his eyes, waiting.

"How much do you love me?"

"Where?"

She grinned. "The Justice Department."

"Bingo."

They couldn't sit there and wait, however, under the watchful realtor's eye, so they drove into the next street, then the next, driving finally because they couldn't stop, just being in motion a substitute for something real to do. Brown wouldn't leave his office until five, later if he was the diligent type, so they had the rest of the afternoon to kill. Like a homing pigeon, Nick found himself drawn back to Washington, trying to make the streets familiar again.

"We still don't know who the Russian is," Molly said as they passed Embassy Row again.

"It doesn't matter. He'd never use a contact from the embassy. They're probably watched as a matter of routine. He'd never risk that."

"So then there were four."

"Unless Brown makes one."

It was when they were passing the bland new buildings on K Street, glass boxes of lawyers and lobbyists, that he saw the sign and pulled up.

"United Charities Building," Molly said.

"It's just an idea." He pointed to the NO PARKING

sign. "Move the car if someone comes. Five minutes."

He was directed to the Events Office and a pretty blond girl who looked too young to have been alive the night of the ball. A Southern voice and perfect teeth. The office seemed a mystery to her, and Nick wondered whether she was paid or just a nice girl taking a semester off from Sweet Briar, doing good works for credit. She treated him like a prospective date from VMI, all smiles and helplessness.

"A social *his*tory? Do they know about it?"

"Not of United Charities, of Washington. Washington society."

"Oh," she said, interested now. "You want to know about the *ball*."

"I thought you might keep the guest lists. To update them every year. Is there a file like that?"

"Well, I don't *know*. I tell you what, you wait right here. I'll ask Connie. She'll know." Another smile. "Nineteen-fifty? Just nineteen-fifty?" Unaware that anything had happened then; a date from the archives.

When she returned, holding a few pieces of paper, she seemed surprised that they existed at all. Nick glanced at the long row of typed names. "That's it," he said, nodding.

"Would you like a copy? I can use the machine," she said, walking over to the copier.

Nick looked at the names as the sheets came out of the machine. On page two, Mr. and Mrs.

Walter Kotlar. He saw his mother dressing, her off-the-shoulder gown.

"I don't suppose they keep a list of who actually attended. You know, who showed and who didn't show. One with check marks or something."

"Check marks? No, this is all there was. You know, most everybody does show. It's our big event. I was there this year—you know, to help out?"

"I hope they let you dance. They should."

"Well, aren't you nice?"

Back in the car, he flipped through the list again. "I wonder how many are dead," he said.

"I still don't see what you're going to do with it," Molly said.

"Did you see at the Mayflower how easy it would have been? You could go from the ballroom to the elevators without even passing the desk. Two exits, in fact. No one would know."

"You could also just walk through the front door. Who'd notice, unless you were a bum?"

He glanced down. "The Honorable Kenneth B. Welles," he said.

She looked at him. "Come on. John Brown's body lies amolderin'."

There was traffic, and Brown's car was already in the driveway by the time they got there. They sat for an hour, watching the house lights come on in the late spring dusk, occasional shadows moving back and forth behind the sheer curtains. The carriage lamp by the front door was on, as if they were expecting visitors. A dark corner, suddenly visible through the window, curtains open.

"The dining room," Molly said, watching. "Look, a cozy dinner with Mom." Brown sat at the table, his back to them.

Afterward the woman cleared, then passed out of sight. A light came on at the other side of the house; the dining room light was switched off. More waiting. Then they saw the blue-white light of a television in one of the upstairs windows.

"Let's go," Molly said. "They're here for the night."

"Give it an hour. Let's see if anyone comes. The front light's still on."

But it was Brown who stepped into it, a middle-aged man with glasses, disappointingly nondescript, more clerk than G-man. He crossed to the driveway quickly and got into the car. A few seconds later, the glowing red taillights backed out into the street.

"Look alive," Nick said, waiting until Brown's car had turned the corner before he started his own.

They drove through quiet suburban streets, then finally into the busy broad sweep of Wisconsin Avenue.

"He's going back to town," Molly said. "Meeting somebody?"

"Maybe he's just going back to work, now that Mom's tucked in."

They stayed several lengths behind, almost losing him once in the confusion of a traffic circle, but he swung onto Massachusetts and they found him again and followed, unhurried, all the way into town.

The left turn came out of nowhere, without a turn signal, and Nick missed it. He doubled back, making a U-turn in front of an annoyed taxi. Brown's taillights were at the end of the block, turning right. At the next corner he took a right again, heading back to the avenue.

"He knows," Molly said. "Why would he do that?"

"I don't think so. He's not trying to lose us."

"No, to catch us, see if we're here. Look, there he goes again."

Another diversion, then back into the light traffic.

"Maybe it's standard procedure. To make sure nobody's following."

"Before a meeting? I always thought they met on park benches."

They drove past the White House, where Nixon was plotting the peace, then down around the Willard and back up 13th Street. The old downtown was deserted now, abandoned to drunks. Brown stopped at an intersection just down from New York Avenue and pulled over.

"He's parking," Molly said. "Well, it's not a bench."

The storefront was outlined with a marquee of flashing light bulbs, its papered-over windows shouting XXX-RATED. MAGAZINES. NOVELTIES. PEEPS 25c. Brown walked over, looking around furtively, and went in. A few minutes passed.

"The one place nobody looks at you," Nick said.

549

"They don't?"

"Stay here. I want to see who he meets."

Nick crossed over to the store but turned to the window, startled, when the door opened again. Brown. He glanced toward Nick, then, unconcerned, walked back to his car, a bag under his arm.

Keeping his head down, Nick pushed into the store, dazzled by the harsh fluorescent glare. Racks and racks of magazines, a riot of breasts and pink skin, but no one looking at them. In the back, a dimly lit room of cubicles for the film loops. The place was deserted. At the cash register, enormous plastic dildoes hanging behind, a kid in a T-shirt with shoulder-length hair pulled into a ponytail looked bored, or stoned.

"That guy who was just in here," Nick said. "He talk to anybody?"

"Who the fuck are you?"

"Back there," Nick said, nodding at the cubicles. "He go back there?"

"Fuck you."

Nick glared at him, a cop's look. "You want me to close you down?"

"Hey, man, I just work here. You see anybody back there? It's *slow,* you know what I mean? He bought a magazine, that's all. You want to buy one?" The kid reached under the register and picked up a baseball bat. "Then get the fuck out. You're not fuzz. I know fuzz."

"You sure?" He saw the kid hesitate, but let it go

and turned to the door. His hand on the knob. "What'd he buy?"

"A lez mag. So he likes lez. What the fuck."

"Thanks," Nick said, leaving.

"Yeah, peace. Hey, close the fucking door."

Brown's car was still there as Nick crossed the street.

"He's just sitting there," Molly said. "What do you think he's doing?"

"I don't know," Nick said, disappointed. "Beating off. He likes lesbians."

"What's wrong with you?"

"We're wasting our time. He wasn't shaking a tail, he just wanted to be sure no one saw him buying dirty magazines."

"There he goes. Let's make sure."

But the trip back to Chevy Chase was uneventful, no diversions, and when he went back into his house the carriage lamp went off.

"Now they can both settle in for the night," Nick said. "I wonder if he locks his door." He turned to Molly. "This isn't working."

"Yes, it is. It just takes time. They're spies. We know that. Sooner or later—"

"But how much later?"

"Let's get another car. That way at least we can cover two of them at once." She glanced at him. "Unless you don't think I can do it."

He smiled. "I think you can do anything. All right, I'll start with Ruth. You take the Russian girl."

"I thought you said he wouldn't use a Russian."

"Not at the embassy. Let's see where she works."

He was in Alexandria at dawn, but not up before Ruth Silberstein. A small light on upstairs, presumably the bathroom. He sipped coffee from a Styrofoam cup, prepared this time for a stakeout.

Twenty minutes later she was out of the house. Nick leaned forward and looked closely. Probably in her forties, carefully made up, dark hair teased into a kind of beehive helmet, like the Johnson daughters', a belted raincoat even though the morning was already warm. High heels and a black purse, the car keys ready in her hand, everything in its place. Even her walk was efficient, like the professional secretary she probably was. She got into a Volkswagen and ran the motor a few minutes before she pulled away. Ruth Silberstein, who are you? What do you do?

She took the direct route to the parkway, driving fast, breaking lanes. The river, shiny with sun, flew past the window. Nick got into the lane for the bridge, anticipating her, but she turned over to the Virginia side and he was forced to dodge cars to get back. Toward the cemetery. He stared at the little car, keeping her in sight, ignoring signs.

When she pulled off into a side road he had no idea where he was until he saw the vast parking lot, acres of it ringing the five-sided building. Well, the Pentagon, yes. Early, to get a space near the building, to minimize the distance in high heels. Or maybe her boss liked to start early, whoever he was, who probably thought the world of Miss Silberstein, because she knew where everything was. Nick watched her walk into the building, ready for whatever paperwork came her way, running two copies, to be on the safe side.

It was still early, so he decided to make another pass at Chevy Chase. The black navy man seemed unlikely somehow—would Silver pass on sub designs?—and Brown, whatever his taste in magazines, was somebody at Justice. The street still seemed asleep, only a garbage truck clanking its way down the row of cans, but after two cigarettes Nick saw the door open and Brown come out, his mother on the stoop waving to him after a kiss goodbye. He was carrying a suitcase. He got in the car without even looking at the street.

This time he didn't leave Wisconsin but headed toward the river, past the Georgetown cliffs and then over the bridge Nick had expected Ruth Silberstein to take, so that Nick found himself back on the parkway, going in the opposite direction. Not toward the Justice Department.

The car turned off for National Airport and inched its way through the crowded, winding access roads to the terminal's long-term parking lot. Nick circled around, to see if Brown actually went into the terminal, then pulled into a space and sat, not sure what to do. The Eastern entrance. New York. Or maybe New York to somewhere else. For an instant Nick was tempted to go after him, hide behind a newspaper a few rows behind, follow his taxi. But what if it turned out to be as pointless as the adult store?

He drove back to Washington. Anacostia was down to his right, the Pentagon behind him, Chevy Chase beyond, a little necklace of spies—what did they actually do?—ringing the unsuspecting city. Or half of it, the only part he'd seen. He looked up at the Capitol in the distance. If he kept going straight on Constitution, he'd be there. The house on 2nd Street. He turned a sharp left. Never.

"I think he spotted us," he said to Molly when he got back to the hotel room, slumping on the bed. "Going away the next day."

"It might not be the next day to him. Maybe he's on vacation." She smiled slyly. "That's why he got a magazine for the plane."

She took out the telephone book and flipped some pages.

"What are you doing?"

"I'm finding out. If you want to know something, the easiest way is to ask." She started dialing.

"What about Irina?"

"She works at the embassy," she said over her shoulder. "So." Then, to the mouthpiece, "John Brown's office, please." A minute. "Yes, is he in, please? Oh, and he told me to call today. I see. Well, when do you expect him? Uh-huh. All right, I'll try back. No, no, it's just a friend of his mother's." She hung up and turned to Nick. "Was that hard? Not a vacation. He had to go out of town today, she doesn't know why, he just called from the airport. But I should try back. He's very good about checking in."

"Which tells us what?"

"That he wasn't planning to go. Something came up. I suppose we could try the New York field office, but that's probably stretching it. I mean, what if he is there?"

"We don't even know if he's actually with the Bureau," Nick said.

"Mm. Or just someone down the hall."

"So now what?"

"Well, I knew you'd be bored. While they were at work. So I had a little idea of my own. Remember the police report on Rosemary? I got the name of the signing officer. Retired, but still alive. So I called. He'll see us. I think he was amazed."

"I'll bet. Where does he live?"

"Actually, not too far from Ruth Silberstein. Al McHenry. He wheezes. Maybe he drinks. Still."

The house smelled of medicine and old age, an oxygen tank and face mask standing guard near the lounge chair. He made tea, shuffling around in a cardigan and slippers.

"It's the emphysema. There's not a damn thing you can do for it, either. It's all the smokes, I guess. Well. Just throw it over there," he said to Nick, who was fiddling with the bulky sofa pillow. "So what can I do for you? I wasn't on that case long, you know. The FBI took it over. Moved right in, the way they do. National security. Noses up in the air, all of them. Like we're just flatfeet. But I don't see they got anywhere either, did they? We did everything right, you know, at the scene—the dusting, the plastic bags, the whole works, the way it should be. They'll say we didn't, but it's a lie. We did it all.

The fact is, there was nothing left for them to do, that's the truth of it. If there's one thing I'm always careful about, it's the scene of the crime."

"So you didn't think it was suicide?"

He looked carefully at Nick. "Well, let me put it this way. If it was, someone drove her to it. Right there with her. She was entertaining, you know. That's a crime to me, never mind what the book says." He stopped and looked again at Nick. "No, I never thought it was suicide. They didn't either, the Bureau boys, that was just the official line. I could never see it. They have a lovers' quarrel and she gets hysterical and jumps out the window? Hell, by the time she got it open he could've stopped her. No."

"Unless he never turned up. Maybe she got depressed, waiting, knowing he wasn't coming," Nick said, playing devil's advocate.

"Oh, he was there all right. They had a drink. Now look, you don't have to be Sherlock Holmes to get the lay of the land here. Girl checks into a hotel. No clothes, just her nightgown—not the wool kind, the other kind. You know. And she brings her douche." He turned to Molly. "Pardon. Then she orders a setup from room service. For two, mind you. Ice, bottle, mixer, two glasses. I'd say she had company."

"But no one saw anybody going in."

"No. That was a bad break. You know hotel people. Notice everything. Can't wait to help you out, whether they've seen anything or not. Gets them off work. But that night—well, they had everyone

556

running around with that dance. People every-where. Nobody's got time to notice anything."

"Like somebody leaving the dance and taking the elevator to the sixteenth floor."

McHenry looked up from his tea. "I thought about that too. Couldn't prove it, though. Couldn't prove it. Might have been anybody. The only one I can prove went into that room was the waiter."

"And he didn't see anybody."

"No. Hadn't got there yet. But she was getting ready for company. Said she was putting her lip-stick on when he brought the setup."

"Then how do we know he was there?"

"There was liquor in both glasses. Why pour two?"

"Prints?"

"No," McHenry said slowly, looking at Nick, as if trying to assess where the question came from. "But he was there. He was there and he killed her. I'm sure of it."

"Because both glasses had liquor?"

"Because it makes sense. And there were the marks on the window." He waited for Nick's reac-tion. "You see, I thought to look. Even a flatfoot could figure that out. They had those sash win-dows, you know, you lift it up." He stood up to demonstrate. "Now you don't usually push some-one out face first. I mean, what would they be do-ing at the window in the first place, getting some air? Usually their back's to it and you surprise them, they don't know there's nothing behind. Then they start falling, and the natural reaction is to

557

grab on to something. Like this." He turned his hands around and lifted them as if he were holding on to the sash, then fell back in the chair. "The nails dig in, you see? Then they slip. Or someone loosens them for you. And down you go. But you'd leave the scratches."

"And she did."

"Yes, sir, she did. But I couldn't prove that either." He gasped, out of breath from the demonstration, and sucked some air from the mask. "These days, there'd be all sorts of ways. Just one little flake of something under those nails and the lab boys'd have it licked in a minute. But back then—" He took more air. "We just had eyes."

"The report says you found a lighter," Nick said, getting to it.

"Yes, I did."

"My father's."

"Yes."

"So you think he killed her."

"No, I don't," he said flatly, looking up at Nick. "Does that surprise you? You thought he did, is that it? Well, he didn't. I'm not trying to be nice. As far as I'm concerned, he was a traitor. I'd have put him away for that in a minute. But murder, that's something else, that's police work. I suppose it isn't easy having a traitor for a father. 'Course, mine thinks he has a fool for a father, so take your pick. But you don't have to have this hanging over your head too. No, I don't think he did."

He took a deep breath, wheezing slightly, then continued. "Everybody *else* thought so. Everybody

558

wanted it to be him. Nothing makes me more suspicious than everybody wanting it to be someone. I think, you know, they just wanted to nail him for something. They couldn't get him for what he did do, but if they got him for this, it sure as hell would look like he did the other—why else kill her? Of course, in the end they couldn't get him for anything. You can't try a man who isn't there, not even the Bureau." He smiled. "I have to say, I guess they were frustrated, the bastards. They keep the murder stuff out of the papers, thinking they're going to get him—you know, pull the rabbit out of the hat the way they liked to do. I kept my mouth shut. They want to say it's suicide, fine, I can't prove otherwise. I can see they're just waiting. Then by the time they find out where he is, it's too late. Who gives a rat's ass? You can't hang a man who isn't there. You can't even accuse him. No point."

"If you've already proved your point. That he's a traitor," Nick said, thinking.

"Well, he gave them that one himself. From what I saw, they weren't going to prove nothing. But I guess he was right to go. For him, I mean. They sure as hell would have got him for this. He had the motive, all right."

"And you had the lighter. Why didn't you think it was him?"

"Well, there was a funny thing about that lighter. Very funny, I thought. No prints. None. *Wiped.* We dusted right away, don't let them tell you different. I knew about prints. We got hers all over the place. But the lighter's all smooth and clean. You asked

559

before about the glass—no prints there either. Now that I can understand. You have a drink, you kill somebody, you wipe the glass, nobody knows you've been there. But who'd wipe their own lighter and then leave it behind so we'd find it anyway?"

"Somebody who wanted it found."

McHenry nodded. "Right. I mean, if you're worried enough to wipe it, why not take it with you? Somebody else planted that lighter."

"Who?"

"That I don't know. They were all out to get him, but who'd want to get him that bad? Like you said, he had the motive and we had the lighter. Case closed."

"Even if you didn't think he did it?"

"Well, it wasn't my case, was it?"

"No." Nick paused. "You know, the lighter never appeared in the Bureau report."

"It didn't? Well, they sure as hell had it. I gave it to them myself. In a bag, sealed, everything the way it should be."

"Why wouldn't they mention it?"

"That I don't know either. Who knows why they do anything there? It's all politics over there, not police work."

"Who did you give it to? Who specifically?"

"The guy running the case, the Canuck. French name. La something." He snapped his fingers. "Lapierre. That's right. One look, he'd freeze your blood. Snotty little bastard." Again to Molly, "Pardon. Anyway, that's who had it. After that, I don't know. Maybe they got it over there with Dillinger's prick, who knows?"

"Do you know where he is now?"

"No idea. Still there for all I know. Well, twenty years—" He did a mental calculation. "Maybe not. Not with their pension. I wish I had it. Not this chickenshit they give you on the force." He waved his hand around the room, living proof. "You want to see him too?"

"Maybe there's something else."

"Well, I doubt it. Like I said, we did everything right. What are you expecting to find, anyway? Who did it?"

"No, just who didn't. My father did a lot of things, but I never thought he did this. I just wanted to be sure. Anyway, thanks. I'm sorry to bother you."

"No bother, no bother. What else would I be doing but hacking my lungs up?"

He walked them to the door, reluctant to see the meeting end, his eyes lively with interest, back on the case. "One other thing that never came out. Not about your father," he said to Nick. "About the girl. It was really out of respect to the family." This to Molly, tentative. "We figured they had enough on their hands already. Terrible thing, suicide, for a Catholic."

Molly looked at him, waiting.

"Maybe she didn't know it herself," McHenry said. "She didn't need the douche. She was pregnant."

Molly was thoughtful in the car.

"Is that possible?" Nick said. "Not to know?"

"I suppose. For a while, anyway. Maybe she did, though. Maybe that's why she wanted the money. Not for a dress."

"A good Catholic girl?"

"It's been known to happen."

"I don't know. Remember in the letter how she made this big point about his not being married? I'll bet she thought it was going to be all right. Once they got past the hearing."

"I wonder if *he* knew." She moved her hand, brushing the thought aside. "Anyway, you don't kill somebody for that. You get it taken care of."

"He did."

Molly worked her phone magic again with the Justice Department's Personnel Office, pretending to be unaware that her old friend had retired, and got Lapierre's address out in Falls Church. They decided not to call first. "What if he says no?" Nick said. But when they got there, a condo development pretending to be colonial row houses, there was no question of his not opening the door—he was in the garden. A slight man, still wiry, digging on his hands and knees. When he got up, slowly, his whole body seemed wary, not standing but uncoiling. His face was blank when they explained themselves, then drew even further behind an official wall. But his eyes stayed on Nick, curious, as if he were looking at an old photograph.

"I can't discuss cases."

"It's not a case anymore," Nick said. "The statute of limitations was seven years."

"On espionage. Not murder." He wiped some dirt from his hands. "It's still an open case."

"My father's dead."

"Yes? I hadn't heard that." He looked at Nick again. "You were the kid. I remember you. At the house." A man holding his hat, his face unfamiliar, just a blur even then. "Said you were playing Monopoly, wasn't that it?"

"Scrabble."

"Scrabble." He nodded. "Right. Scrabble." Noncommittal.

A woman opened the back door. "Dad, you all right?"

"Fine. We're just talking here."

She looked at them suspiciously, wanting more information, then had to give it up. "Don't forget your pills," she said, reluctantly going back in.

"My daughter," he said. "She's worse than Hoover." But the interruption had the effect of drawing him to them, like a little boy not ready to be called inside. His body relaxed. "Tell me something, since you're here. I always wondered after. Did he tell you to say that, about the Scrabble? Did you know he'd skipped?"

Nick shook his head. "I thought he was hiding somewhere."

Lapierre took this in and nodded again. "He had us all going, didn't he?" he said, his voice reminiscent. "They must have had every man in the Bureau on it. Turning over rocks. And all the time we were just chasing our tails. But who knew? The director didn't want to hear it. Just find the sonofabitch. I remember *that* all right. Of course, we were too late. We started late. You get the locals in, trail's cold before you get to it." He glanced at Nick. "Kid says he's home all night. Why not? We never thought he skipped. We checked everything. How'd he do it anyway? Do you know?"

"He went to Philadelphia, then Detroit, Canada."

Lapierre's face was busy putting pieces in his own puzzle, but all he said was, "Philadelphia. Huh."

"Now can I ask you something?"

Lapierre looked at him, wary again.

"He wasn't being accused of murder," Nick said. "That would have been a police case anyway. Unless they asked you in. Which they didn't. You just came." Lapierre didn't respond. "He wasn't being accused of anything else either. So why the big hunt? Every man in the Bureau."

"Well, when you don't turn up at a congressional hearing, that's—"

"The excuse," Nick finished. "You put a dragnet out for a subpoena violation?"

Lapierre glanced at him shrewdly, intrigued. "I wouldn't know about that."

But Nick kept staring at him until finally Lapierre nodded, conceding the point, wanting to go on, playing one more hand to see what Nick knew. "Let's just say the Bureau likes to take care of its friends. Welles was a very good friend to the Bureau, close to the director. Nobody likes to lose a star witness. All of a sudden you're sitting there holding the bag. So I would guess he asked for a little help. That's just a guess," he added quickly.

"You did it as a favor?" Nick said skeptically.

"Maybe you don't understand how things work. Everybody thinks the Bureau's on its own, but it isn't. Hoover's got his boss too. Sometimes the AG's on your side, sometimes not. Depends on the man, whatever his agenda is. That was a funny time. Tom Clark had just left—never any problem with him. He never gave a damn one way or the other. But the new one—" He left it unfinished, still discreet. "And you never knew what *his* boss would do. The director hated Truman. Mutual, probably. So it was important to take care of your friends in Congress. Kind of an insurance policy." He stopped. "Well, that's the political side. The director wasn't going to let Welles hang out there. He made Welles. But the fact is, Kotlar *was* guilty— you don't need an excuse to go after a spy. You can't blame the director for that one. I don't say he does everything right—that case was no picnic for *us,* I can tell you. No let-up. But hell, you've got a Red spy and you don't go after him? That's like putting blood under a hound's nose and then sticking him in a cage. He's *got* to do it. I don't think you can blame him for this one."

"I don't blame him. I just want to know how he knew."

Lapierre looked puzzled. "Kotlar was guilty. There's no doubt about that."

"Not now. But what made you so sure then?"

"I don't think I understand you," he said cautiously.

"One woman's testimony. Not proven. What made you believe her? What made you go after her in the first place?"

Lapierre took a step backward, physically retreating. "That's all before I got into it. You want to know that, you're going to have to ask Hoover yourself."

"And he'll tell me," Nick said sarcastically.

"The director?" A cool smile. "Not even on a good day." He turned. "Anyway, what's the difference? Turns out he was right. He usually is." He looked at Nick, appraising again. "What do you really want to know? Is that why you came all the way out here? You know what happened. There's no mystery about it. You know where he was. We looked for him, we didn't find him. So what do you want to know?"

Nick waited. "What happened to the lighter," he said finally, watching Lapierre's reaction. "The police gave it to you. You didn't put it in your report. Why did you lose it?"

Lapierre's eyes narrowed, a new appraisal, and Nick saw that what interested him was not that Nick knew but how—a bureaucratic reflex, a fear the system had been violated. "The Bureau doesn't lose things," he said simply.

"But it's not in the report."

"That depends on which report you saw." Again

the narrow curiosity: *how* had Nick seen it? "Nothing was lost."

"There's more than one report?"

"The files are cross-indexed. It may be confusing to someone from outside."

"So's double bookkeeping."

He glanced up, annoyed. "We're an investigative agency. That means sensitive material. Sources, for instance. It's more prudent not to keep everything in one place."

"Where somebody might see it."

"We don't own the files. A request comes down from the AG's office—" He shifted, careful again. "It's not always appropriate. You don't want the files used for, say, political reasons."

"No, of course not." Almost a laugh.

Lapierre hesitated. "You say he's dead?"

Nick nodded.

"All right, you ask, I'll tell you. The official file wasn't the same as the internal one. Couldn't be. We were investigating Communists, not murder. There are some who would have preferred that, you know, for political reasons. To take people's minds off the real issue. But we didn't want it to be a murder case."

"Then it might have been sent back to the police. Right out of your hands."

Lapierre looked at him sharply, then nodded. "With predictable results. You keep forgetting, he wasn't there. There would have been no case. They'd be spinning wheels." He paused. "Besides, we didn't want to get him that way. Not for murder."

"Welles would lose his Red."

"You don't think much of the Bureau, do you? Think we're just like the feet. Fact is, I didn't run it as a murder case because I never thought it was. I always thought she killed herself." He looked up. "While he was playing Scrabble."

"Then how did the lighter get there?"

Lapierre looked at him with mild scorn, as if he had missed the obvious. "She put it there. There weren't any prints, you know," he said, watching Nick. "A little clumsy anyway, don't you think? Leaving it like that. It was her. She wiped it on her skirt, or something—and out. She was going to take him with her one way or the other. What you said before, about going after her? It was always my understanding that *she* went to Welles. Her idea. Of course, I don't know where your information comes from." Lapierre's eyebrows went up.

"Welles got everything from the Bureau."

"Well, maybe you know that. I don't."

Nick stood for a minute looking at the ground, thinking. "But you kept it. Even though—"

"You can't destroy evidence. That's illegal."

"So is hiding it."

"It's not hidden," Lapierre said blandly. "I don't know where you get this idea. To my knowledge, no one's ever asked for it."

"You kept it just in case you needed it," Nick said to himself. "A little insurance."

"Insurance?"

"If the statute of limitations ran out."

"Don't let your imagination run away with you. We didn't expect it to run out. We expected to catch him."

Nick looked up. "And tell him you had it, in case he wasn't feeling cooperative with the committee. Loosen his tongue."

"I don't know about that. I was just supposed to catch him. But I didn't." He shrugged. "So the statute did run out."

"But there's no statute on murder."

Lapierre looked at him, eyes cold again. "That's right. Not on murder."

"You would have hanged him with it."

"That would have been up to the jury."

"With your help."

"I would not have withheld evidence, no, if that's what you mean. The Bureau would never allow that."

Nick felt a band of heavy air tightening around his chest, a kind of noose.

"What the jury made of it—" Lapierre wiped his hands again, free of dirt.

"One way or the other," Nick said, again to himself. "He could never come back." Silver's insurance.

"Come back? Why the hell would he come back? He got away with it."

The woman came to the back door again. "Dad." Insistent this time.

"All right," he said, turning back to Nick. "I don't know what you're trying to prove. Everybody wants to get something on the Bureau these days. The Bureau didn't do anything to your father. We never got the chance. We were the ones looking like jerks, not him. He got away with it."

"Yes. He got away with it," Nick said, seeing his father's thin white legs as he put him to bed.

Lapierre began walking away.

"Tell me one more thing," Nick said, stopping him. "You must have seen the Cochrane file." A beat. "The internal one."

Lapierre waited, interested.

"Was there a description of it, how she approached Welles?"

Lapierre thought for a moment. "No," he said, "just the first interview."

"Then how do you know she did?"

Lapierre began backing away. "Well, I guess I don't know that either." He gave Nick a thin smile. "Maybe you should ask Welles. He was there, not me."

Molly, who'd been silent during the meeting, opened up in the car. "That was a mistake," she said. "He's going to report it. He thinks he's still working for them. Did you see his eyes? Just like Jeff. I know something you don't know. Even when they don't. I'll bet they're all like that—they don't know how to stop."

"Well, so what? What if he does?"

"They'll start watching again. How are we going to watch our friends if somebody's watching us? God, it's getting like Prague. Everybody watching everybody."

"Maybe they'll do the Navy guy for us," Nick said lightly. "You don't like the neighborhood anyway."

"I'm serious. If they start tailing us, it's like handing them the list. You know that."

Nick nodded. "They have to find us first. Anyway, they're not watching now. You want to take Mother Brown?"

Ruth Silberstein went to the movies. While Molly was parked in Chevy Chase, waiting for Brown, Nick trailed the Volkswagen to a suburban shopping mall. Her friend, a woman waiting at the box office, handed her a ticket and began a conversation that would last off and on through the show and into dinner afterward. They both chose the chef's salad. Ruth drank several cups of coffee, her friend shared an envelope of snapshots—relatives or an office party, Nick guessed, when he passed by the table to look—and Ruth picked up a pint of ice cream on her way home. Then he saw the blue glow of the television set upstairs, the bathroom light as she got ready for bed, a small reading lamp for twenty minutes, and darkness. Nothing. It occurred to Nick as he sat smoking in the car that the only exciting thing about being a spy was the end, the final adrenaline jolt of exposure.

John Brown hadn't returned.

"Just an evening with Mom," Molly said, weary.

"One of them's the connection," Nick said. "It'll happen."

"I hope so. Who's on tomorrow?"

"Try Irina again. I'll do the Navy. Then I think I'll take the Bureau's advice and go see Welles."

"Why?" Molly said, looking up.

"I want to know how it started, why she talked to him. It's important."

"Is it?" Molly said quietly, watching him.

"Silver didn't start this. He just did what he had to do. Once it did. I want to know who started it all."

"Who did it to you, you mean." Her voice still quiet.

"Not just to me," he said quickly, disconcerted. "To all of us."

Molly started to say something, then backed off. Instead she went over to the mirror and started brushing out her hair.

"What makes you think Welles will talk to you?" she said. "You're the last person he'd want to see."

"I'll use Larry's name," Nick said, thinking of Lutèce. "It's a real door-opener."

CHAPTER EIGHTEEN

The drive to Anacostia the next morning was as uneventful as before, a careful swing southeast through the back streets, toward the sun and the crisp sentries' uniforms. When the black officer's car slid through the gates, barely pausing for its badge check, it seemed to melt into the lot in the slow motion of a dream. Navy whites. A few official cars. What did he do here? Nick watched his dark face move toward the building, unhurried. He decided to take a chance on the guard.

"That guy who just came in? I think he put a dent on my car."

"Lieutenant Williams?" the guard said, amazed.

"I guess. How do I get in touch with him?"

"You can't. Not without a pass."

"You have an extension? I just want to call, for the insurance."

The guard checked a clipboard. "5207," he said. "Big dent?"

"No, just a scratch. Thanks."

Nick pulled away, the guard not even bothering to look at the car, turning his face to the sun. The whole base was dozing, far away from the war.

The Senate Office Building, on the other hand,

bristled like a command post, phones ringing, secretaries' heels clicking along the halls, busy with itself. Nick dialed the Anacostia number from a pay phone in the lobby. A girl's voice. "Naval intelligence." Nick put the receiver back, nodding to himself, and went to find Welles's office.

There were two secretaries, both with beehive hairdos, both wrapped in sweaters against the air conditioning. A leather couch, piled with unopened mail, the walls filled with photographs of Welles shaking hands with everybody in the world. A portrait of Nixon. A framed campaign poster. Peace With Honor. Nick heard voices coming from the inside office, laughter.

Now that he was here, he felt a quiet panic at the ordinariness of it all, that the demon swirling through years of his imaginative life would be reduced to a man making jokes in an office, harmless, like a funhouse ride after the doors open. Welles belonged in the newsreel, gavel banging, cowing them into silence, always oversize, his malevolence so large it needed an expanse of screen or it would become invisible, too large to be seen in a small room with posters and crank mail. His father had said that when you shook hands with Stalin, the act itself was a violation of scale, allowing you to believe he was just a man.

The inner door swung open. No longer screen-size but still large, grown fat, his bulk filling the door frame. Everything the same, the straight nose and square face softened by the years of extra flesh. He was wearing a bow tie and red-white-

574

and-blue suspenders, sweating a little in the cool room. His arms were draped around a middle-aged couple whose faces had the pleased look of pilgrims granted an audience. When he saw Nick, his smile froze for a second, then spread back across his face.

"Well, there he is. Looks like Betty's got them back-to-back this morning. I swear, they don't give me time to pee sometimes." Genial, for the benefit of the couple, who smiled. "Now, bless your heart, you tell the club I wouldn't miss it. Wouldn't miss it. You just make sure Betty here has that date." He turned to one of the secretaries. "Darlin', you circle this one now, hear?" Then, to Nick, "Well, come on in if you're coming." And then a flurry of goodbyes and Nick suddenly felt himself being led into the room by a hand on his shoulder, everything smaller after all.

"Well, I *was* surprised. Your call. But you know, your dad—Larry and I go back a ways, both sides of the aisle, so I guess I owe him a favor or two. Hell, I owe everybody favors. Now, what's so important he couldn't call himself? They got phones in Paris last time I heard." Before Nick could reply, he held up his hand. "Let me tell you up front, if it's this peace talk business he's got himself into, I can't do it. No help at all. The people don't want it—they'd have themselves a lynching party with me in the rope. And I don't blame them. Peace with *honor,*" he said, last year's slogan for war. "That's what we're looking for here. Now, Larry knows that. Hell, that was the whole campaign. Can't

575

have him giving everything away over there. We've been *there* before. All our fine boys getting shot up and we're just going to hand it to the Commies? Another Yalta? No, sir." His cheeks puffed now, like bellows. Everything the same.

"He didn't send me. I wanted to see you myself."

Welles stopped, surprised. "You did," he said, marking time, not sure what was happening. "Well, what can I do for you?"

"Larry's my stepfather. You know my real father was Walter Kotlar."

A tic of recognition, not alarm, a reflex to a surprise question. "That's right. Larry married the wife. I never did understand that. There was a kid." Just a detail, lost over the years. "That's you?"

Nick nodded.

"Walter Kotlar," Welles said, sitting against the edge of the desk. "A lot of water over that dam."

"He died last week."

"Died? Well, that's something," he said slowly. "Dead. I'm sorry to hear that." He caught Nick's expression. "Oh, he was no friend of mine. Matter of fact, he was anything but for a while there. No end of trouble. Whole thing just folded up on me. But dead—" He shook his head. "You know, it's not just your friends. Makes you feel old when the other ones go too. Maybe more. Nobody left who knows the war stories. Kids don't want to hear it."

"I do."

Welles lifted his head. "No, you don't. There's no percentage in that. Scratching sores, that's all that is—you're better off letting them alone. It don't pay, staying mad. Your dad, he almost put me out of business. Terrible, him and that woman. But what are you going to do? You pick yourself up and roll with it. You don't want to look back. That's what's great about this country—you just go on to the next thing."

Nick looked at him, amazed. Just something that had happened to him. Was it possible it had never really mattered, the whole thing no more important than a hitch in the campaign, patched over with a booster's platitude? Or was this just another way of telling Betty to circle the date, a hand on your shoulder on your way out the door.

"My parents never talked about it."

"Well, that's right. They wouldn't." He peered at Nick. "So you came to see me, is that it? It's all there, you know. Matter of record."

"Not all of it."

Welles gave him a serious look, on guard.

"Look," Nick said, "my father's dead. It can't hurt anybody anymore. It's history. I'd just like to know, to fill in the gaps."

Improbably, this made him smile. "History. Well, I guess it is now. We did make some history there, didn't we? He did, anyways. What do you want to know?"

"Did Rosemary Cochrane really have new testimony, the way you announced? Did she tell you anything?"

This was clearly unexpected. "She *would* have," he said, with a sly glance back.

577

"But she didn't."

Welles frowned. "Now look, I'm not raking this up again. They all said I drove her to it, but that's b.s. I didn't drive her to nothing. You had to know how to handle her—you needed a little pressure if you were going to get anything out of her. In the beginning, you know, when she told me about your father, I have to say I scared her into it—had to, wouldn't have got anywhere otherwise. She knew she had to give me something. Then she just clammed up again. My opinion? Her friends got to her. God knows with what—probably scared her worse. But she still knew plenty. Thing was, how do you get her to open up? You had to turn the heat on somehow. Hell, that's just politics. You're from a political family, you ought to know that. You tell the papers she's already confessed, she's not going to have her friends to fall back on. Can't trust her. They're running for cover. She's out there all alone. Maybe facing perjury, if you play it right. And she didn't want to go to prison in the worst way."

"She was pregnant."

Welles looked at him, stunned. "How do you—" A sputter, like a candle.

Nick didn't wait but slipped in under the confusion. "Look, I never said you drove her to it. I just want to know what she said. After Hoover told you to talk to her, did she mention my father right away?"

Welles missed it. "I told you, with her it was always pressure. She knew she had to give me a name."

"Or you'd go after her."

"Of course. What else?"

"By the way, how did Hoover know?" Nick said, trying to sound casual.

"How does he know anything? You don't ask."

"But she didn't mention anyone else," Nick said, moving away from it. Hoover.

"No, just Kotlar."

"And she thought that was the end of it."

"I don't know what she thought. How could it be the end?"

"But you offered immunity."

"From espionage charges," he said carefully.

"Which you couldn't prove anyway. Without bringing the Bureau into it."

Another sly look, nodding. "That was the tricky part. But she bit. She thought we could. You know, she *was* guilty. There's no doubt about that."

"No."

"And after she gave me a name, well, then I had her." He smiled, then looked down, troubled. "How do you know she was pregnant?"

"She told her family. It never came out."

"I didn't know that. It explains a lot. Why she'd be so upset. To take her own life." Welles shook his head.

"If she did."

He peered at Nick, alert. "What's all this about?"

"I always wondered," Nick said flatly. "If he killed her."

"Killed her?" Welles said, surprised. "Now, don't you start thinking that way." He raised a finger. "He was your father," he said, as sanctimonious as his peace platform.

Nick shrugged. "It's possible. You must have wondered. There were a lot of people in the hotel. Anybody could have gone up and—Well, couldn't they? I mean, you were there at the time."

"Yes, I was," he said slowly. "With Mrs. Welles." Only his name on the list.

"But you weren't married," Nick said involuntarily. Two glasses.

"We married later," Welles said evenly. "She was my date."

Nick tried an apologetic grin. "I'm sorry. I wasn't asking for an alibi."

"I don't care what you're asking for. Your time's up." Welles glanced at his watch, physical evidence, then stood up. "Let me give you a piece of advice. Don't be like your father, going off half cocked. That woman was probably crazy, I don't know. You have to work with what you've got. What I do know is, it's over and done with. You'd best put your mind at ease and get on. You don't want to go digging around the past—there's no percentage in it. I've lived a long time in this town and I learned. There's only the next thing. There isn't any past here. You let your father be."

Nick nodded, message received, then glanced up at his eyes, now the same hard eyes that had peered over the microphones.

"When you looked at him," he said, "at the hearing, what were you thinking?"

Welles stopped, framing an answer. "That he

was the smoothest goddamned liar I'd ever seen. That I'd never get him."

"Maybe it takes one to know one."

Instead of taking offense, Welles smiled. "Maybe it does, at that."

"Thanks," Nick said, taking his hand, wanting to see how it felt. Small. Welles raised his eyebrows. "For your time. For telling me what I wanted to know."

But Welles misinterpreted. "It's true. Never thought I'd get him. And I knew he was guilty."

"What about all the others?"

"The others?" All forgotten, like campaign workers.

"The ones who weren't guilty."

"Well, they must have been guilty of something," Welles said easily, "or they wouldn't have been there." Attending meetings. Running mimeograph machines. Flubbing loyalty checks. Thousands. Welles put his hand on Nick's shoulder and smiled. "You know, son, you don't know shit about politics. You should just get on to the next thing."

Welles walked him to the door, taking a deep breath and drawing up his shoulders, ready for a new meeting. As Nick watched, the buffoon suspenders seemed to expand, his body filling back up with air, almost newsreel size.

The break came the next day. Molly took the vigil in Chevy Chase again, and Nick decided, as if he were sticking a pin in a map, to follow Irina. He drove to Dupont Circle, and by seven A.M. he was waiting halfway down her sunny street, thinking that the whole random exercise was futile. They needed five watchers, not two. He imagined the contact being made—an exchange on a park bench? How was it done?—while they were both somewhere else, never in the right place at the right time. In this lottery, Silver's luck could hold forever while Nick drew empty mornings of delivery vans and dog-walkers. Anyway, where was she? She'd be late for work if she didn't leave the house soon. Nick stared at her door, so preoccupied he didn't hear the steps behind him, stopping at his open window.

"There you are." A woman's voice. "I suppose I have you to thank."

Mrs. Baylor, carrying a brown grocery bag. Nick looked up blankly.

"I thought she'd be someone you'd *want*. Why send her back, if you don't mind my asking? Was something wrong?"

"You mean she's gone?" First Brown, now Irina.

"Well, don't *you* know?"

Nick shook his head, confused.

"Oh. Of course, she did say it was temporary, but she seemed to like it here."

"When did she leave?"

"Yesterday. Said she found something better. I don't know what she means by *better.* There's nothing wrong with the apartment. It's self-contained. I thought you people sent her home."

"No, nothing like that. Did she leave an address? They're supposed to."

"No. Of course, they come and go, the girls. But one month? No more for me, I can tell you, no more foreigners. Not that she wasn't nice."

"She was only here a month?" Could the list have been that recent? But his father must have had it earlier, when he had first planned to leave.

"One month. Hardly worth the time it takes to clean the place. Flighty." Mrs. Baylor's arm shot up in the air, waving. "There's Barbara."

Nick looked toward the house, where a girl on the stoop was waving back. His eyes stopped, and he felt a tingling along his scalp. Not the Russian, the other girl. She started down the street.

"Thanks, Mrs. Baylor. Sorry for your trouble. She'll probably check in with us this week, when she's settled. If she does send an address, let us know, okay? Just in case." He turned on the ignition. "By the way, how did she find you? She give you references?"

"Well, I never thought to ask. Barbara told her about it. They met at work, I guess. Not that I blame Barbara. She was good as gold about those records."

By the time Nick was able to pull away, the girl had turned the corner into the next block, shoulder bag swinging. A miniskirt, short heels, blond like Molly. Reliable Barbara, who'd met Irina at work. But she was heading downtown, away from the embassy.

Nick followed slowly, but even at this pace the

car was bound to overtake her. She passed a bus stop, clearly intending to walk. He went through the light into the next block, keeping her in his rear-view mirror. A car pulling away from the curb. He slammed on the brakes and backed into the spot, adjusting the parking angle until she went by. When he started down the sidewalk he kept his eyes on her hair, a tracking beam, so that everything around her blurred out of focus.

She was walking quickly, not stopping to look at windows, heading toward Farragut Square. She took a diagonal path across the park, unaware of Nick in the crowd. Downtown. The Bureau wasn't far away. Then she went into a coffee shop, forcing Nick to stop at the corner, exposed. He fed some coins into a newspaper vending machine and took out a *Post.* A peace rally. District police requesting additional crowd-control units. People streamed by, carrying briefcases. What if she was just a boarder after all? But the address had been there, on the list.

When she came out, sipping from a Styrofoam cup, Nick turned away and almost lost her. Then, in front of a DON'T WALK sign, the blond hair came into view again. She crossed the street and disappeared through a door: EMPLOYEES ONLY. Nick looked around, then at the block-long row of plate-glass windows, trying to orient himself. It was only when he stepped back to the curb, taking the whole building in, that he finally recognized it, as familiar to him as an old dream. Garfinkel's. Still. His father had said the reports never changed, the same pattern. You could tell just by the prose. One of them will lead me to him.

Nick went through the door. Don't show yourself. But how else could he be sure? He walked past aisles of cosmetics and women's handbags. She could be anybody. But when he reached the men's department, there she was, just arrived behind the counter, talking to another clerk as she arranged the tie display, the shelves behind her lined with row after row of white shirts.

"We have to figure out a way to get in there," Nick said later, excited. "I can't spend all day trying on suits."

They were in the lobby bar at the Madison, the soft spring light still flooding into the windows from 16th Street, not yet evening. Molly, unexpectedly subdued, picked out a cashew from the bowl of nuts.

"You want me to be her," she said, not looking up.

"No, he probably knows her by sight. But if you were there. They're always looking for extra help. You could talk your way in. Anyway, it's worth a try."

"No, I meant *her.* Rosemary. You want me to be her."

Nick said nothing, surprised at her mood.

"Do I have to?"

"Molly, we're so close."

She nodded and looked out the window. In the corner, a man in black tie was playing the piano. Cocktail hour. "These Foolish Things," one of the songs his mother must have danced to.

"It's funny," she said. "All my life, my mother kept telling me I was like her. Political. That's what she said when I wanted to go to Kennedy's funeral. A whole bus went down from school. You don't want to get mixed up in anything, not like her. God. Every time I brought someone home. You'll turn out boy-crazy, just like—" She broke off. "But I never thought I was. I didn't even know her. That was just my mother. Half the time I didn't know what she was talking about. Now it turns out maybe she was right. I am like her. I know just how she felt."

"What do you mean?"

"Well, she did it for him, didn't she? Mr. Right. Anything, right up to the end. New dress. Order up a bottle—I'll bet it was the kind he liked. Everything was going to be all right."

"Everything *is* going to be all right."

A weak smile, ignoring him. "And now I'm going to be her, do everything she did. Even sell the shirts."

"Molly, if it bothers you, don't do it. We'll figure out something else."

"Oh, don't worry, I'll do it." She paused. "I am like her. I'll do it for you."

"No. Do it for her."

She sighed. "She's dead, Nick." She turned from the window. "I'll do it for you. So you'll be finished with it."

"We're so close," he said again. "What do you want to do, walk away from it? I need to do this for him."

Another wry smile, looking down at the nuts.

"What?" Nick said, annoyed.

"Not for him," she said. "Don't you know that?" She raised her hand, stopping his response. "It's okay. I want you to bury him. But how do you end it, Nick? What are you going to do if this works, if you do get Silver? Have you thought about it?"

Nick looked down, embarrassed because he hadn't. It had seemed enough to know, to see a face. "This one we turn in," he said finally.

"But not the others."

"He's a murderer."

"Maybe they are too."

"And maybe they just sell shirts. Would you have turned Rosemary in?"

She shrugged, shying away. "I guess not. I don't know."

"Molly, what's wrong?" he said, touching her arm. "What are you so worried about?"

"You're just so determined. 'We're going to get him.' Then what? Push him over a balcony? Nick, let's just give the whole thing to the FBI now. Let them do it."

Nick took a drink, calming himself, so that when he spoke his voice was steady and reasonable. "Molly, for all we know it *is* the FBI."

"You just want to do it yourself."

"Yes," he said, still calm. "I want to do it myself. I want to see his face." A beat. "Then it'll be over."

587

"Will it?"

He held her eyes, sure. "Yes."

She glanced out the window, avoiding him, then busied herself lighting a cigarette. She exhaled, then nodded. "When do I go to work?"

"Tomorrow."

"Selling seashells by the shore," she said. "Let's hope I don't end up the same way she did." Then, before he could answer, "And just when I was getting somewhere with Mr. Brown."

"What do you mean? I thought you said he wasn't there."

"He wasn't. But there's another thing, *if* you had let me finish. I took a drive over to the parking lot at National—that's where you said he left the car, right? Well, it wasn't there. So what is he up to?"

Nick thought for a minute, then frowned. "It doesn't matter. It isn't him."

"But funny, don't you think?"

"We don't have time. She's the only one who matters now."

"Well, you have to do something while I'm playing salesgirl. Why not find out? Unless you want to protect him from the FBI. One of your innocent spies."

"What are you talking about?"

"See the guy at the end of the driveway? He's been keeping an eye on us."

Nick looked out the window. "You're sure?"

"I've developed this instinct—in my new professional capacity," she said airily, then nodded. "Pretty sure."

"He follow you here?"

"No. At least, I don't think so. I just noticed him while we were talking. I told you Lapierre would have them put a tail on us."

"Then he's interested in me. Good. We can't have anyone walking you to work."

"Take the car out tomorrow and see."

"Damn. Why now?" Nick said, worried. "What do they want?"

"Like old times, isn't it?" Molly said, her eyes back at the window.

"We have to get rid of them."

"The FBI?"

"Hoover can."

She glanced back, amused. "That would do it." Then, seeing he meant it, "Right to the top. Larry's name again?"

"No." He smiled. "I thought I'd use Jeff's."

But he didn't have to use either name: Hoover sent for him.

He drove out to National in the morning, avoiding Chevy Chase, his eyes almost fixed on the rearview mirror, but the tail, if it was there, had been trained in a better school than Zimmerman's—he seemed to be alone. He went slowly through the parking lot. No car. Had someone taken it? A day ago he would have felt uneasy; now it was only a piece of a different puzzle.

He took the direct route home, then doubled

back across the Mall, where they were putting up a stage for the peace rally. Still no obvious tail. Then, at the hotel, he saw they hadn't bothered. The two men approached him in the lobby, said the boss wanted to see him, and led him to the car. When they hustled him into the back seat with a peremptory shove, he was at Holečkova again, the same helpless anxiety, his palms damp, as if he were back in handcuffs.

The office, a suite of rooms, was on the fifth floor of the Justice Department, past a secretarial pool and a corridor lined with autographed pictures and plaques and framed awards, the tokens of a grateful nation. The visitors' office made Welles's look like a closet: a huge room with an oversize desk between two flags, whose only purpose seemed to be for taking pictures. A vast blue rug with the Bureau seal. A ghoulish death mask, mounted—Dillinger, 1934. More photographs, all of them with Hoover. Burly, in a double-breasted suit and crisp fedora, leading a fugitive up the stairs. Bending over to shake hands with Shirley Temple.

Nick's escorts knocked on the inner office door, nodded to the prim woman in a high collar who opened it, and backed away, like courtiers. One more large room, with windows looking out over Pennsylvania Avenue, this one for working—a line of wooden memo trays, another football-field desk, with telephones and a single open file. Standing behind the desk was the director himself, bulldog jaw sticking out just like it did in his pictures, glowering up at Nick with a theatrical intensity. A silence.

"Am I under arrest?" Nick said.

"No. I want to talk to you," Hoover said, the words coming as fast as bullets. Nick wondered if he had worked on it, practicing in front of a mirror until speech too had become an intimidating prop. "I hear you want to talk to *me.* If you don't, you can leave right now. I'm a busy man. Thank you, Miss Gandy," he said to the secretary, so that, ironically, the next sound Nick heard was the door clicking shut behind him.

"Now we could start friendly, but I haven't got the time. Nobody bothers my agents, Mr. Warren. Nobody. *Interrogating* them. Who do you think you are? Of course I know *who* you are." He tapped the open file with his finger. "The only reason I'm talking to you at all is that your father's been a friend to the Bureau." Nick realized after a second of confusion that in Washington he was always Larry's son first. "Sometimes. Depending. But I don't hold grudges, and the Bureau takes care of its friends."

"I'll bet."

Hoover jerked his round head and stared at Nick. "Don't do that again," he said evenly. "Talk smart to your father. Maybe he's used to it. I don't like it. As far as I'm concerned, you're just some kid who thinks he's having fun with the Bureau, and that's not smart. Ask your father, he'll tell you."

"He's my stepfather."

"I know that too. I know everything about you."

591

He touched the file again. "War record. Not much, but at least you weren't one of the dodgers. I'm not surprised you changed your name. We can't help our parents—I don't hold that against you. Maybe I should. They usually don't fall far from the tree. But right now I just want to know what you think you're doing. Talking to Lapierre, playing cute with us in New York."

"I wasn't trying to play cute. I just left early. They weren't there around the clock."

"You're not worth twenty-four-hour surveillance," Hoover said. "You're not that important."

"I'm not that important now, either. So call off the guys you have watching me here. I haven't done anything. If there's something you want to know, ask and I'll tell you. I don't like being followed. I had enough of that in Prague. But you expect it there. I didn't think we were like that yet."

Hoover peered at him curiously, sizing him up, then moved out from behind the desk. Involuntarily Nick glanced down to see if his shoes had lifts. Hoover had always been described as short, but here, on his carefully constructed set, the sight lines seemed to exaggerate his bulk, and the broad shoulders and thick neck gave the impression of a large man barely contained by his suit. What caught Nick's eye, however, was the hair, short but still dark, at his age a color that could only have come from a bottle. Nick wondered if he did it himself, towel wrapped around his neck at the mirror, or if a barber had been sworn to secrecy.

"Not yet, Mr. Warren. And we're not going to be.

We've still got a free country here, no thanks to people like Walter Kotlar. Why did you go see him?"

"Because he asked me to. Look, you're busy— let me make this easy for you. He sent a message that he wanted to see me. I went. I spent a few days with him and his wife. He didn't tell me any state secrets and he didn't tell me about the old days. He did tell me that he was sick and he'd like to come home. One of your people there—a legat, isn't that what you call them?"

Hoover nodded almost imperceptibly.

"A legat found out about it and ran with it, all the way back to the Bureau, where they started ringing bells so loud even you heard them. Is that about right so far? But he didn't come back. He killed himself. I found him. The Czech police thought I did it, or caused it somehow, or whatever. Who knows what they think? I wasn't going to hang around to find out. I got out as fast as I could, only to come home and get the same treatment from you. Which I would like you to stop."

Hoover looked at him for a moment. "I know all that," he said finally. "That doesn't tell me any-thing."

"What do you want to know?"

"Why he thought he could come back."

"I don't know that he did think it. He just said he wanted to." Nick paused. "He didn't know you had the lighter."

Hoover said nothing, stone-faced.

"I'd like it back, by the way. It's mine now. It's not evidence anymore. He's dead."

"You're talking about Bureau property."

"No, I'm not. The Bureau doesn't officially have it. You do. You've always had it. In one of your special files. Just in case. But you can't get him anymore. He got away again."

"You think you know all about it."

"No. Just that it was you. All along. You fed Welles. You fed McCarthy. That was your little war. Years of it."

"You think it wasn't a war? You're too young to know, all of you. The only reason you're walking around free today is—" He stopped. "It was a war. And we won it."

"Well, you did anyway. You're still here." Hoover glared at him. "And so is the lighter. The one time you really had somebody and he slipped through your fingers. But at least you could always get him for something he didn't do—if he came back."

"He did do it."

"Your agents don't think so. Neither did the police."

Hoover looked at him steadily, his voice low. "But I did. Naturally you don't want to."

"It doesn't matter what we think anymore, does it?"

"Then why are you bothering Lapierre? Nosing around where you don't belong? What are you really doing in Washington?"

"Research. Not your kind. History, that's what it

594

is now. It's important to talk to who was there while they're still around."

Hoover's eyes widened as if he'd been personally insulted. "Research," he said sarcastically. "For who? That pink in London you've been working with?"

"Yes, that pink."

He snorted. "Not far from the tree. Well, not with my agents, you're not. Don't expect any help from this office. And keep the Bureau out of it." Hoover held up a finger. "I mean that. I'm not interested in history."

And Nick saw suddenly that it was true, that all the stagecraft was there not to trick the future but to keep things going now, attorney general after attorney general, Hoover still at the desk. The only idea he'd ever had was to hold on to his job.

"Then it won't matter," he said.

"You know," Hoover said, more slowly now, "a lot of people come into this office just set on showing me they're not afraid of me. It's a thing I've noticed. Smart talk. They don't leave that way."

"How do they leave?"

"With a little respect for this office and what we're doing. They find it's better to be a friend of the Bureau." The eyes so hard that Nick had to look away.

"Would you tell me something?" he said.

"For your research?" Almost spitting it.

"No, for me. Just one thing. It can't possibly matter to you anymore."

Hoover looked up, intrigued.

"Who told you about Rosemary Cochrane? You told Welles, but someone told you."

"What makes you think I told Welles?"

"Because he told me you did. He didn't intend to, but he told me."

Hoover twitched, annoyed. "Well, that's not what I would call a reliable source. Ken doesn't know enough to come in out of the rain. Never did. Did a lousy job with your father, too."

"Despite all the help."

Hoover said nothing.

"You knew about her. How? It can't matter anymore."

"It always matters. That's Bureau business. We never divulge sources—wouldn't have them, otherwise." He paused. "But in this case, since it matters to *you*." He glanced up. "It was an anonymous tip. A good one, for a change. We never knew who."

"Yes, you did," Nick said.

"You're sure about that," Hoover said, toying with him.

"Yes."

Hoover glanced away. "I don't remember."

Nick stood, waiting.

"I don't think you understand how things work here," Hoover said, looking back at Nick. "Information, that's like currency to us. We don't spend it. We don't trade for it."

"Yes, you do."

For the first time there was a trace of a smile. "But you see, you're not a friend of the Bureau's."

Nick stared at him, stymied.

"Now I'll ask you something," Hoover said. "Why you? All those years, and you're the one he sends for, says he wants to come home. Why not just go to our people in the embassy?"

"Would you trust them? Every embassy has informers. If the Russians had found out—"

"Well, they did, didn't they?" A shot in the dark.

"If they did, Mr. Hoover, then they got it from you. Only the Bureau knew. Is that what you think happened, a leak in the Bureau?"

"No, I do not," he said, steel again. "We don't have leaks."

"You must have had one once. My father had his file."

Hoover frowned. "Lapierre said you'd seen that," he said, diverted now to the office mystery. Another witch-hunt, irresistible.

"But he might have got it a while ago. Actually, I never thought the Russians did know. But if they did, that means—"

"I know what it means. And that never occurred to you."

"No. I thought he committed suicide."

"With you there? He makes you go to Czechoslovakia so he can kill himself while you're around."

"People who commit suicide don't always make a lot of sense."

Hoover looked at him, then turned to the window, pretending to be disappointed. "I don't think you do either," he said, looking down at Pennsylvania Avenue. "Don't have too much fun at our expense—it's not worth it. I've been here a long, long time. And I knew your father. I *studied* your father. You want me to think it was just a pipe dream. Our man didn't think so. Some pipe dream. Your father knew how things worked. If he wanted to come back, he knew he'd have to buy his way back. But what was he going to buy it *with?* You'd need a lot of currency to do that." He turned back and stared at Nick. "And somebody to make the deal. Close, like family."

"I don't know what you're talking about," Nick said, holding his gaze.

"I hate to see good information go to waste, get in the wrong hands. Hate it." He paused. "Most people find that it makes sense to be a friend to the Bureau."

"I can't afford it. It's too expensive."

Hoover nodded and moved toward the table behind the desk. "There's all kinds of information," he said, and pressed a button on a tape recorder. Nick heard a scratch, then his voice, Molly's.

"Here's an idea. Let's smoke a joint and make love. All night. No microphones."

"I liked the microphones. Where'd you get the stuff?"

"Well, I did see Richie."

Hoover clicked it off and looked at him for a reaction.

Not the Alcron, looking up at ceilings. The Plaza, where they were safe.

"Where was the bug?" Nick said, stalling.

598

"The phone."

"You can't use it."

"No? For two cents I'd set you up, you and your hippie girlfriend. I can do it. For two cents."

Nick stared at him, the bantam chest and dyed hair, his eyes shining, about to win. The way it worked. "But you won't," he said finally. "You can't afford it either. Larry Warren's a friend to the Bureau."

Nick saw the tic, the flesh of Hoover's cheek quivering as if he'd been slapped.

"Two cents," Hoover said, machine gun speed again, trying to recover. But the air had gone out of it, his skin now slack with age.

Nick turned away. "Keep it with the lighter, just in case. Can I go now?"

"Think about what I said. Hard. Maybe something will come back to you."

Nick walked toward the door.

"Don't push your luck," Hoover said, wanting the last word. "Not with me. I hear you had a rough time over there. You might learn something from that. How things are."

Nick turned from the knob and looked at Hoover. "I did learn something. You know, when I walked in here I was afraid of you. The Boss. You want some history? That was Stalin's nickname too. Just like you. But you're not that scary. You're just a guy who likes to go through people's wastebaskets." Hoover's face went blank, amazed. "You know what I learned? Nothing is forever. You think you are. You're going to be disappointed."

For a moment Hoover just stood there, seeming paralyzed by the impertinence, then his eyes narrowed. "You'll change your mind. They always do. It's better to be a friend." He walked back toward his desk, pulling himself together. "So I'll give you something free. As a friend. The Bureau isn't following you. Maybe we should be, but we're not. And maybe you're not as smart as you think you are. Just a little paranoid."

"Maybe."

"You see how it works. Now you give me one. I know he talked to you. How else would you know about the lighter?"

Nick smiled and opened the door. "An anonymous tip."

He walked over to the Mall and sat on a bench watching them build the scaffolding for the rally. Kids in T-shirts and Jesus hair with hammers. Portable toilets. In a few days the buses would pour in. Speeches and peace balloons. All of it happening somewhere else, in the present, while he waited to find someone in the past. Hoover hadn't dyed his hair then. He'd been a real monster, not a creaky vaudeville turn, hanging on. He'd made Welles, McCarthy, Nixon, all of them. Passing out his currency. Now some were dead and one was in the White House and everyone had moved on to the next thing. Except Nick.

He noticed some men in suits loitering by the

construction site. The Bureau, getting ready? He should get up and go home. Which was where? A hotel with a piano player in the lobby. A room in London he couldn't even remember. He looked up toward Capitol Hill. That wasn't home either. But he was still living there, on 2nd Street, trying to find his way out. The trouble with history, his father had said, is that you have to live through it. A crime story where everyone did it, without even thinking, as careless as an anonymous tip. And then went on. But what if it stopped, a freeze frame? What if you were the one caught in the picture? Stuck—unless you found the one with his finger on the shutter. Who had told Hoover?

Molly was already at the hotel when he got back.

"They said no?" Nick said.

"No. Half-day. Orientation. They jumped at it once I said temp—no health plan."

"Her department?"

"Well, they rotate. But I told them that's where I'd done it before, so it should be okay. I start with ties—no sizes, even I can do it. She was doing hats today. I mean, who wears hats anymore? Everybody switches around except for the men selling suits. I suppose you really have to know about suits."

"What was she like?"

"Nice, but not too nice. She probably thinks I'm going to be a pain. You know, who needs a trainee? But the point is, I can see her no matter where they put me. It's all open except for the fitting rooms. So."

"So now we wait."

"You do." She grinned. "I'll be on my feet. And they're already killing me." She took her shoes off and lay back on the bed, looking up at the ceiling. "I wonder if she's in love with him too."

"He'd be a little long in the tooth now, don't you think?"

"Oh, men just keep going." She smiled at him. "At least I hope they do."

He sat on the bed and began rubbing her feet.

"Mm. What every working girl needs. Brown's still not back, by the way."

"You went out there?" Nick said.

"Well, I had the time. Just a drive-by. I was curious. There's something going on—it doesn't make sense."

Nick shook his head. "We should leave the others alone. What if they spot us? We don't want to complicate things now."

"I don't think anyone followed me."

"No. Hoover said they're not tailing us."

"Really? What about the man outside the hotel? He wasn't just waiting for a cab. I know he wasn't."

"That's what he said. Of course, it wouldn't be the first time he lied."

The real waiting began in the morning. Nick stayed at the hotel, afraid he'd miss Molly's call if he left, unable to read or think about anything else. So close. He played a game with the United Charities list, checking it against the phone book to see who was still alive, still in Washington. The others he could run through the *Post* obituary files, finally winnowing it down. Some names he could deal with by sight—politicians gone after failed elections, senators old even then, his parents, still together on the list. But there were too many. He might as well be doing crossword puzzles, just passing time. His father had said the reports were irregular. How was it done? Was there a prearranged signal, a call, or did he just stroll into the store, a man shopping on his lunch hour? Nick's worst fear was that he might appear without their even knowing it, the waiting all for nothing.

The next day, too restless to stay inside, he walked over to 14th Street and circled the building to fix the likely exits in his mind. When he walked into the men's department, Molly looked up in surprise, then cocked her head toward the blond girl folding sweaters. There were only a few customers. Nick moved slowly past the counters, browsing, familiarizing himself with the floor layout. You could see everything from the fitting rooms. He made his way to the shirt counter, where Molly was waiting, glancing at him nervously.

"Fifteen and a half, thirty-three," he said, then stopped. Not even his size. When she reached behind her and handed him the shirt, he felt, eerily, that he had crossed some invisible line into his father's life. Exactly the way it must have been, no one noticing. He fingered the shirt wrapped in plastic. You could slip an envelope underneath. Rosemary could take it, hand you another, ring up the sale, and carry the shirt back to the stockroom.

A crime so easy no one would ever see. He realized then that Molly was staring at him, disconcerted.

"I'll come back," he said, embarrassed, and walked away.

After that he stayed with the list, not trusting himself to go out. He reread Rosemary's letter, trying to imagine what her voice had been like. Throaty, maybe, like Molly's. The hotel room was claustrophobic, so he sat for hours gazing out the window, going over everything that had happened in Prague, some clue he might have missed. He wondered what had happened to Zimmerman, what Anna Masaryk had done with the exit visas. He could see them both vividly and realized that this is what people in prison did—floated out of their cells into some imaginative other life. She had been putting lipstick on when the bellboy brought the setup. Two glasses. Happy to see him.

The phone rang twice before Nick came back to his own room.

"She asked to switch with me Friday. Tomorrow. To do the shirts," Molly said. "I don't know if it means anything or not. But why switch? Nick?"

"I'm here."

"So what do you think?"

He paused, not sure.

"Well, it might be, don't you think?" Molly said eagerly. "Why don't you buy yourself a suit tomorrow?"

He tried on several, lingering in front of the mirror with one eye fixed on the shirt counter. Finally, when the salesman became impatient, he picked a blue pinstripe and stood on a raised platform while the tailor measured for alterations. But how long could he string it out? A few men, all of them too young, bought shirts. The blond girl, Barbara, kept looking around as if she were expecting someone, but nothing happened.

When the floor manager told her to go to lunch, Nick followed. A sandwich in a coffee shop, eaten quickly. When she went back to Garfinkel's, Nick stopped himself at the door, his excuses to go inside exhausted. He went across the street and kept watch from a doorway. Smoking, waiting to meet a friend. Then another corner, a newspaper. The afternoon dragged on. How much longer?

He went back into the store and caught Molly's eye. A quick shake of her head. He crossed the floor, positioning himself next to ladies' scarves, then bought some perfume, all the while keeping the men's department in sight. Almost closing time. Barbara looked at her watch and then toward the door. A missed connection, or just a salesgirl eager to go home?

When the bell rang, Nick's heart sank. He'd made himself conspicuous and no one had showed. He watched her close the register with Molly, chatting, then had no choice but to follow the other customers out. He waited across the street again and then, on the chance that she was meeting him after work, moved toward the employee entrance. A group of women, talking. He picked out the blond hair easily and began to track it back toward Dupont Circle. Maybe a drink after work? But Barbara, the reliable tenant, went straight home, and when he saw her go through Mrs. Baylor's door he knew the day, with all its nervous expectations, was gone.

"But she asked to switch again," Molly said later. "Maybe he couldn't make it for some reason."

"And maybe she just likes shirts," Nick said depressed.

"No, she never asked before. It has to be. Anyway, you could use the clothes."

The next morning was like the first: sleepwalking past the sales tables, picking through the suits, the clerk puzzled at his being there again but still wanting to make a sale. Nick said he'd try a few on, hoping the salesman would go away, and went into one of the changing rooms. The door was louvered, so that if you bent a little you could see between the slats. Barbara at the shirt counter. But he couldn't stay here forever, peering out. The clerk had someone else now and was leading him toward the tailor, but he'd knock in a minute, wanting to know if everything was all right. Nick thought suddenly of the station men's room, the sick feeling as the footsteps came closer.

He was about to give up and open the door when he saw Barbara's head rise, relieved, recognizing someone. She turned and pulled two shirts off the shelf, ready, then glanced to either side of her to see if the coast was clear as the man's back came into view. For a second Nick didn't breathe. The man was picking up a shirt, handing the other

606

back to her, turning slightly as she went to the register. Nick grabbed the slats with his fingers, lightheaded, steadying himself as his stomach heaved. He'd seen the face. A shouting in his head. He opened the door.

"Ah, and how did we like the gray?" the salesman said, but Nick walked by him, one foot in front of the other, as if he were underwater. Moving toward the shirts, a hundred pictures flashing by him, rearranging themselves in place. The same face through the cubicle slats, in a slice, just like the crack at the study door. Molly watching him, her mouth open. And then he was there, behind the familiar shoulders.

"Hello, Larry," he said.

CHAPTER NINETEEN

"He told you."

They were on a bench in Lafayette Square, across from the Hay-Adams, everything around them drenched in sun, surreal, Larry's voice as calm as the quiet park. A man feeding birds, a young woman pushing a pram—no one had the slightest idea. Larry had led him here by the arm, guiding him out of the store as if he were a patient, one of those men in Nick's unit who'd been too near a bomb and had to be helped away.

"No. He never knew," Nick said, almost whispering, foggy. "Except at the end." His voice was coming back now. "That's why he changed his plan that day. He figured out the lighter—that you were the only one who could have taken it. From the study."

"That was an accident. I must have put it in my pocket. But then I had it—"

"He was going to use you to make the deal for him. Then he realized you were the one person he couldn't use. He'd have to do it himself."

"He must have been out of his mind."

"Yes."

"Come back. Really, Nick—"

"Are you going to kill me too?"

"Don't be ridiculous. You're my son."

"You killed the other one." Then, to Larry's blank expression, "She was pregnant. Rosemary Cochrane. It was yours, wasn't it?"

Larry was silent. "I didn't know," he said finally, past denial.

"Would it have made any difference?"

"No." He looked away. "It was too dangerous."

"She wouldn't have named you. She was in love with you."

"You can't trust that," he said dismissively. "She was just a girl. Then she got—emotional. And she slipped up somehow. They got on to her. It was dangerous. She knew about me."

"But he didn't."

"No. But he was going to crack. I saw it that night." He glanced over. "When you were spying on us."

"I didn't understand anything."

Larry sighed. "Well, neither did Walter. That was the problem. He didn't understand how serious it was. He thought—I don't know what the hell he thought. Buy them off with a name and live happily ever after? It doesn't work that way. Once you start, you go to the end. And what name? He only had Schulman."

"Who recruited him."

Larry looked back, surprised. "That's right. And me. At Penn. The one point of connection. I couldn't risk that. If he'd given them Schulman, it might have led them to me." He wrinkled his face.

"The way things work out. I was the one who suggested he try Walter. He was always looking for prospects. I told him Walter might be promising material. But he turned out to be the weak link. You see that, don't you? He might have brought the whole thing down."

Nick looked at him, incredulous. Was he being asked to agree?

"They had to protect me. I was in the White House. We'd never had a chance like that."

"Why didn't you just kill him too?"

Larry looked at him with an indulgent expression. "Is that what you think of us? Of course we didn't kill him. Anyway, you take care of your own, unless there's no other choice. That would have been a foolish risk to run. Two deaths? No one would have believed the other was suicide. There'd be no end to it."

"The police didn't believe it anyway. You made sure of that. With the lighter."

"No, I was making sure of *him*. I wasn't sure he'd go. Walter was unpredictable." He paused. "He had reasons to stay. He might have thought he could tough it out, not accept our invitation."

"But not if he thought he'd be accused of murder. Then he'd have to go."

"Well, it never came to that. It was just a precaution. He did go."

"Convenient for you."

"Convenient for everybody. Except old Ken Welles, I suppose, but that couldn't be helped. Oh, you think we wanted him stopped? No—he was useful. He was so busy looking for Commies in all the wrong places, nobody thought to look in the right ones. Loyalty oaths for schoolteachers— Christ. But even a fool gets lucky once.''

''You had Hoover looking too.''

''Well, I didn't want him looking at me. All I had to do was suggest that Walter must have been tipped off by someone in the Bureau and he was off. Catching his rats.'' He stopped. ''I never wanted to hurt Walter.''

''You killed him.''

''We got him out. It was the best we could do. He had a life there, you said so yourself. We had to do it.''

''Not then. Now. You killed him. Or had him killed.''

''You don't know that.''

''We're sitting here, aren't we? How do you think I got to you?''

Larry looked up at him, serious. ''How did you?''

''First tell me why.''

''Why. What else could we do? Coming back. That could only mean one thing. He found out. I don't know how—we were careful about that. All those years. I knew how he'd react. He'd make it personal.''

''It was personal.''

''No. I was just another agent.''

''Who took his wife. And set him up for a murder charge. And got rid of him to cover your own ass. You ruined his life, Larry. What do you call personal?'' Larry turned away. ''Why did you have to

611

kill him? He was never going to get out—you know that."

"He didn't have to get out. Once he knew, he could have told anybody. A journalist. The spooks at the embassy. He wasn't *safe* if he knew." He paused. "Given everything."

"But he didn't know, Larry. Not until the end. You had him killed for nothing."

"What do you want me to say, Nick? I'm sorry? It's a death wish, to want to defect. There's only one way to do it. If he didn't know about me, then he knew others. He was going to turn them in. This isn't school. What did you expect them to do?"

"Once you told them."

"Yes, once I told them," he said impatiently. "Of course I told them. You don't wait. We're all at risk when somebody defects. He had to be stopped before anything got out. It had to die with him."

"It didn't," Nick said quietly. "He told me. That's what led me to you. Names. Her, your new friend. You ought to change your pattern, Larry. You made it easy. It didn't die with him."

Larry crossed his legs and looked down at his trousers, picking at the fabric, seemingly at a loss. "Well, that creates a little situation, doesn't it?"

"Yes. You'll have to kill me too."

"Does anyone know?" Larry said.

"Just me. Once I'm gone, you're safe."

"I didn't mean that. I was thinking of you. Are you sure? What about that girl?"

"No," Nick lied. "Just me. You'd be safe."

"Don't talk crazy. Kill you." He turned to Nick,

his eyes suddenly old and unguarded. "You're all I care about. Don't you know that?"

Nick felt a tremor, another shock to the system. Not a lie. His boy, the unexpected thing in his life, a knot too tangled to untie. Nick looked away.

"You should have been more careful in Prague then," he said. "I almost didn't make it. Or were you going to get me out of that one too?"

"But I didn't know you were there," Larry said, reaching over and putting his hand on Nick's arm. "I didn't know. You have to believe that. I would never involve you. Nobody said you were there."

"Didn't Brown tell you?"

"Brown?"

"One of yours. Over in Justice—"

Larry held up his hand. "Don't. I'm not supposed to know. It's safer."

"Then who did?"

"Hoover. He called. He had a report from one of his legats saying that Walter was planning to come back. Did I know anything about it? I suppose he thought I might, because of your mother. He never said anything about you. Why would I even think it? It was a damn fool thing for Walter to do, involving you. What was in his head? You don't do that."

"He trusted me."

"He didn't even know you. I was there, not him. No matter what you think of me now, that part's still true. He wasn't there. I was. I gave you everything."

Nick looked at him, amazed. "No," he said. "You took everything."

A pause. Then Larry looked down at his watch. "Well, this isn't getting us anywhere. And I have a meeting." He looked up. "You're being sentimental. Walter was a damn fool. But you're all right, that's the main thing."

"You have a meeting?" Nick said. Was he just going to walk away?

"Yes, at the White House. Walk over with me." He stood up.

"Do you really think I'm going to let you do that?"

Larry raised his eyebrows, genuinely puzzled.

Nick got up, facing him. "I know everything you've done. Your code name. What happened at the hotel. How you report. All of it."

"You'll make an awful mess trying to prove it."

"I can do it. I have documents. He gave them to me."

"Ah," Larry said, looking away. "Then I guess I'm in your hands. You might say we're in each other's hands. Sort of a protection racket."

"I'm not in your hands."

"Well, a minute ago you said I was going to kill you. Which I'm not, of course. But you're not going to do anything either. What did you have in mind? Turning me in? Your own father? I don't think so. You know, Nick, you're more like me than you think. We're both pragmatists. We take the world as it comes. You just got thrown a curve, that's all. But don't do anything foolish. What's in it for you? Patriotism? Not very pragmatic."

"You bastard. Listen to me—"

614

"No, you listen to me. Calmly. We're going to walk out of the square, and in a few minutes I'm going to sit down at a table and listen to fools and crooks tell me how they want to run the world. I've been listening to them for thirty years, different crooks, same fools. But I'm at the end. This is my last job. After that I won't be a threat to anybody, least of all the country. That you think you care so much about. It's over. Walter told you things he had no right to tell. You're lucky, no one knows except me. So you come back playing detective, all fired up to change the world. Just like Walter used to be. But you're not going to change it. Nobody does. What you might do is cause a scandal that would embarrass the government—not a bad thing in itself, given who they are. But it'll be a lot worse for us. It would kill your mother."

"No, it wouldn't."

"And what about you? You know what it would mean. Do you want to go through all that again? I'm not doing anything more than what Walter did. You want to make him a saint, that's your business, but don't drag the rest of us down trying. Do you think anybody wants to know? That time is over. You think Nixon wants his old Red-baiting days brought up again? Mr. Statesman? Hell, the only one who still cares at all is Hoover, and he's been nuts for years. No one wants to know. Who would you be doing it for?"

"For me."

"For you. Why? Settling someone else's scores. And you'd still have to prove it. I don't know what you think you have—is it really enough? I'd have to fight you, and I'm good, I've been doing it for a long time. I don't want to fight you, Nick. You're my son. You are, you know. We'd be killing each other. Like scorpions. We'd both go down.''

"You killed someone, Larry. Doesn't that mean anything to you?''

"Listen, Nick, I'm going to a meeting now with men who are killing thousands, and people think they're heroes. I didn't make the world. At least I did it to protect myself—that's the oldest instinct in the book. What's their excuse? Come on, walk with me. I'll be late.''

Numbly Nick fell in step at his side. "I don't care about them, Larry. You killed him.''

"He killed himself, Nick. He killed himself the moment he decided to turn. Those are the rules. They'd do the same thing to me—or you. Be smart. Let's all just retire in peace. Think of your mother. You don't want to do this to her.''

"Look what you've done to her.''

"I hope I've made her happy.'' He turned. "She can't know about this.''

"What's the difference? A wife can't testify against her husband.'' Nick stopped. "Is that why you married her?''

"Of course not. I love your mother. I always have.''

"You're a liar, Larry. You don't even know her.''

"I'm not going to argue with you, Nick. I did my best, that's all I can say.''

"You even lie to yourself.''

"Well, we all do that." They stopped near the entrance to the White House, across the lawn behind the tall railings. Barriers along the street to keep protestors away. Larry waved to one of the guards and turned. "But I'm not lying to you. There's no advantage here. Be smart."

"Like you. Maybe I'm one of the fools. Are any of them smart, or are you the only one?" Nick cocked his head toward the gate, where a black limousine was pulling onto the driveway.

"Well, they're not very bright," Larry said. "Anyway, it won't be much longer. I'll be out this fall. Would you like me to resign sooner? Would that ease your conscience?"

Making a deal, the way he always did. Sure of himself. Nick looked at him, the familiar face suddenly inexplicable. "Tell me. Why did you do it?"

"I thought I explained—"

"No. It. Are you a Communist? I mean, do you believe in it?"

"I used to. I thought it would fix things."

"But not anymore."

"I'm too old to believe you can fix things."

"Then why did you keep going?"

"Well, you have to." An easy answer, but then he stopped, thinking. "I don't know if you'd understand. It was the stakes. It was—you'd sit at a table, in there." He jabbed his thumb toward the gate. "You'd sit there while they all talked, and none of them *knew.*"

"That you were betraying them."

"That you had the secret. This big secret. None

of them knew." He shrugged. "But that's all over now. My son's going to insist I retire." He smiled his old Van Johnson smile and turned to the gate. "Call me after lunch."

"But—" Nick reached out to stop him, but Larry had already moved out of reach, so that Nick's arm just hung in the air, as if he were holding a gun. Then slowly he dropped it, unable to pull the trigger.

Molly was still at the store, waiting.

"I didn't know what else to do," she said. "What happened?"

"Where's the girl?"

"She split. But I got this." She held up the envelope. "She was too freaked to argue. Just ran."

"Did you look?"

Molly nodded. "What we're going to say in Paris. Talk about a stacked deck. If this doesn't put him away, nothing will. What *happened?*"

No more than what your father did—another lie. He was prolonging the war.

"Let's get out of here."

"I can't," she said, indicating the unmanned register. "There's no one here."

"Now," Nick said sharply. Then, seeing her surprised face, "What if she comes back?"

Molly grabbed her purse from underneath the counter. They walked down 14th Street toward the Mall, hearing the sound of loudspeakers in the distance, a chant. Molly listened to him without interrupting, her face worried. They turned up Pennsylvania Avenue. Nick could see the Justice building, Hoover's balcony overlooking the street, where he watched the parades. A short elevator ride, a deal—that's all it would take.

"So what are you going to do?" Molly said finally.

"Why did it have to be him?" he said, almost to himself.

"Because it is."

"I don't know," he said, answering her question.

"Finish it. That's what you came here to do. End it."

"It won't end. It'll start all over again."

"Nick," she said softly, "if you don't do this, it'll never stop."

"Just name a few names."

"That's their politics. I'm tired of being them. He's selling us out *now.* Us. I can't be that neutral. Is this how we're going to live, like them? They made a mess of their lives."

"But we won't," he said ironically.

"Well, we can do it our own way. At least then we won't know how it comes out." She took out the envelope and handed it to him. "Here. It's yours. You decide."

Nick looked down at the envelope. "I can't be his executioner, Molly."

"Somebody'd better be. He'll do it to you too."

"He's not going to kill me."

"Yes, he is. Every time you look at him." She hesitated. "It's a lousy deal, Nick."

He watched her turn away.

"Where are you going?"

"Over to the rally. If you want to join the living, meet me by the monument." She stopped. "Then I'm going back to New York. I hate this place." She looked up at him. "Come with me?"

"I'm not finished here."

"I am," she said, and walked away.

He went toward the Justice Department and stared up at the balcony, the envelope like a weight in his pocket. A lousy deal. But would this one be any better? Could you really buy freedom in a pact with the devil?

The lobby was busy, full of men in suits and short-cropped hair, Bureau style. A bank of phones. Guards, armed. Where Hoover had started the phony war that had finally circled them on 2nd Street and now—beyond an irony, something grotesque—Nick would hand him, so many years later, the unexpected paper to win it. The pragmatic deal.

But as he walked toward the reception desk, surrounded by Hoover's foot soldiers, he knew he couldn't do it. Not here. The old enemy. He saw Hoover snatching the prize, vindicated, unassailable at last. Which was worse, Larry for a few months or Hoover tape-recording for the rest of his life? How did you measure the damage? Molly had to see that. He'd be one of them. He turned, pretending he'd forgotten something, and walked out past the indifferent guards.

The rally was noisy and crowded. He walked past the line of police and portable toilets and parked ambulances—were they expecting trouble?—and into the mass swarming over the Mall. He felt a million miles from the somber candle vigil for Jan Palach. Bubbles and painted faces and scraggly hair. Shirts off in the sun. The defiant smell of dope. In the distance was a concert stage with loud-speakers, a group at its base yelling "Out now!" the chant rippling back through the crowd in a wave. Homemade posters and peace buttons.

Where was she? Everyone looked young. Nick realized with a start that no one in the huge eager crowd had ever heard of the hearings, that the old war was not even a distant memory to them. Like Welles, the survivors had moved on to the next thing. An embarrassing moment in the republic, not even worth teaching in school, so the children, absorbed in their own war, would not even know it had happened. And Larry would survive this one too, betraying them all. A lousy deal. Molly was right. They needed to breathe their own air.

He'd never find her in this. He scanned the broad slope by the monument. A scuffle had broken out near the transverse road, and policemen were wading in to contain it. A kid next to him was watching it through binoculars.

"Pigs," he said. "There go the pigs again."

"Could I borrow these for a sec?"

"Look at the pigs, man," he said, handing the glasses to Nick.

It wasn't yet an incident. People stood watching without getting involved, like a highway accident. The police were leading two men away, but no one was protesting. Probably a fight someone had to break up, not a bust. People stepped back to clear a path, then started up the road again. Nick moved the binoculars across the young faces, then stopped, jarred by something out of place.

The woman was looking away, a little farther up the hill, annoyed she'd had to stop, anxious. In the carnival of the rally her determined face stood out like a warning. Not just any face. Ruth Silberstein. Nick followed her, hypnotized. What was she doing here? And when she turned to speak to the man with her, Nick felt the fear begin. Ponytail and acne: the guy from the adult store. Then Ruth pointed and Nick followed her finger to Molly, standing on the curb, looking around. Waiting for him.

"Hey, man," said the kid, reaching for the binoculars.

"Just a minute. Please."

It hadn't been Hoover's tail. He'd been telling the truth. Brown, or someone, had been following her. Or had Barbara called in an alarm? And now they were here, just a few feet from her. He wanted to shout out. Hopeless. But she'd know them, run for it. Except she'd never seen Ruth Silberstein, never been in the store. Nick watched through the binoculars as they approached her. What story would they have? At first she smiled. Then a moment of panic on her face, a quick glance around for help. She stepped away, but Ruth pulled her in and the ponytail moved behind her, close to her back, and then they were moving off together toward Constitution Avenue in a huddle. Run.

Nick dropped the binoculars and started racing through the crowd, bumping into people, dodging section leaders with bullhorns. The chant came back from the stage again, and those who had been sitting, picnic style, jumped up. "Out now!" Nick tried to push through a wall of people, not even able to see the road anymore. Flailing through vines in a jungle, shoving them aside. "Hey, where's the fire, man?" Someone said "Peace," as if the word itself had power. Had they known all along, been aware of their amateur shadows? Brown's elaborate route, a lure. Not just a dirty bookstore. Nick's mind raced through the crowd, faster than his blocked feet. But why here, in public? What would have drawn them out? The envelope. They knew she'd taken the envelope. And then, as he edged around a group of girls, stalled, the other thought occurred to him. Larry. Of course he'd lie. There had never been any deal. You don't wait. The oldest instinct in the book. She really had become Rosemary.

By the time he reached the road, calling out her name now, they had disappeared. He ran faster, trying to catch up. Police glared at him. Then he saw a car across the avenue, the ponytail bundling her in. He screamed her name. As she got into the car, she turned her head as if, impossibly, she'd heard him, and he thought, a final panic, that it could be the last time he'd ever see her. He ran across the avenue, halting traffic, but the car was pulling away, too far for him even to make out the license plate, and then sped around the corner.

He stopped and stood still, heaving. They'd question her first. But for how long? It was the lawn at Holečkova again, feeling utterly helpless. He glanced toward the line of police. But what would he say? And then, another jolt, what if they were following him too? Or was she just bait, Larry's new bargaining chip? Bastard, he thought, and began running toward Pennsylvania Avenue. Somewhere they wouldn't follow, if he could make it.

He tried to calm his breathing as he walked into the Justice Department. Don't look out of place. He went to the row of phone booths and pulled out some change. If it had been Larry, they might not even question her. He already knew. Nick tried the Hay-Adams—not there. But you couldn't call the White House. Unless your life depended on it. He dialed. The switchboard believed the emergency— the operator could hear it in his ragged breathing.

"Nick, are you crazy?" Larry said when he came on. "Pulling me out of a meeting. What—"

"Be quiet. I'm at the Justice Department. I'm going up to Hoover's office unless you let her go. Do you understand?"

"No. Nick, these phones." Hedging. "They're not secure."

"I don't give a fuck. Let her go."

"Calm down. I don't know what you're talking about."

"You kidnapped her. Molly. I fucking *saw* them. Ruth and the freak from the porno store. They probably had Brown in the car. Where'd they take her, Larry? Christ."

"Stop it. You're babbling. I don't know what you're talking about." Was it possible? "Look, come over here. I'll meet you outside. Not the phones."

"Forget it. I'm not leaving here. It's safe. Even you wouldn't try to get me here. I'll go upstairs, Larry, I mean it. I'll tell him everything."

"What do you mean, safe? Are you all right?"

"No, I'm not all right. They've got her. They'll kill her unless you stop it."

"Nick, I'll say it one more time. I don't know what you're talking about."

"She was following Brown. He must have spotted her. Or your girlfriend."

"Nick—"

"I don't give a fuck!" he yelled. "You have to get her. Fix this. That's what you do, isn't it? They're your people—talk to your boss. You must have one. He'll know. Tell him I'm already at the Bureau. If they touch one hair, one hair, I'll blow the whole fucking operation. I can do it. I have the names, Larry. You want to hear them? You're not supposed to know. Nobody's supposed to know. But they will. Tell him I have the envelope too."

"What envelope?"

"Your envelope. Your last fucking report."

"Nick—" A beat. "Stay where you are. I'll be right there. Where in Justice?"

"In the lobby. Right next to an armed guard."

He took ten minutes. Nick sat in the booth, sweating, the receiver cradled at his ear, the constant dial tone drowning out the buzzing in his head. All that mattered—not any of the rest of it, all the complicated loyalties. He saw her walking past the guards on the Prague station platform. In the room at the Alcron. His. The only thing he hadn't lost yet. By the time he saw Larry walking into the lobby, the fear had set into something harder, without margins. The oldest instinct in the book.

"It wasn't me, Nick," Larry said, his voice brisk, setting things straight.

"I don't care. Just get her. John Brown works upstairs somewhere. He's the one who'd know her. He's probably had her watched. What about Barbara—she take packages from anybody else?"

Larry nodded.

"Then she must have tipped one of them."

"Let me see what I can do," Larry said, getting into the booth. "I can't promise anything. I don't know the others. It may be out of my hands."

"But you're in mine. Do it."

Larry picked up the receiver and began closing the booth door. Nick put his hand on it. "Secrets, Larry? Still?"

"Theirs."

He closed the door and dialed. Nick stood outside the booth, watching the Bureau pass by, unaware. Larry was right, there was an excitement in knowing the only secret at the table. He heard him make another call, brusque, a man used to getting his way. Nick looked at his watch. They'd question her first.

"All right," Larry said as he came out. "They've got her somewhere. They want to know what's going on."

"They tell you where?"

"Yes."

"Let's go."

"One thing."

Nick stopped and turned.

"I'd like the envelope," Larry said, holding out a hand. Even now.

"And if I don't?"

Larry just looked at him.

Nick reached into his pocket. "Here." He tossed it at him. "You're a lousy deal anyway."

"Nick—"

"Let's go."

Outside, they walked to the waiting black car. Larry opened the driver's door.

"Personal errand," he said. "Take an hour and I'll meet you back at the White House."

The driver, surprised, handed him the keys. "They don't like that."

Larry winked. "Wouldn't want to do anything personal on government time, huh?"

"No, sir."

When they pulled away, Larry said, "In my brief-case. Left compartment."

Nick took the case from the back seat, opened it, and pulled out a gun, staring at it.

"Just put it in my pocket."

"Why?"

"The man holding her doesn't know me. If my person doesn't reach him, we may need a little help. Just in case."

"God, Larry."

"Still enjoying yourself?"

They drove up 13th Street toward New York Avenue and stopped—why hadn't he thought of it?—at the adult store.

"That's why you didn't want the driver."

"They talk," Larry said simply.

There was a CLOSED sign on the door, nothing visible inside. Larry knocked.

"We're fucking closed." The ponytail.

"Joseph sent me," Larry said.

"Who?"

"John Brown," Nick said. The one man he'd have to know.

The door opened a crack. "What the fuck do you want?"

"We came for the girl," Larry said. "Come on, open. Quick. Before someone sees." He pushed the door.

The man was holding the baseball bat, his eyes widening as he recognized Nick. "Who the fuck are you? Nobody said anything about the girl."

628

"Where is she?" Larry said. *"Now."*

The man nodded toward the film cubicles in the back. "Nobody said nothing about this."

"Nobody had to. Put the bat down. You look like an idiot."

"Yeah, well, who the fuck are you? I gotta make a call." He went toward the register counter.

"Just put it down," Larry said, holding the gun. "And the bat."

"Fuck," the ponytail said, amazed. He dropped the bat, which clattered on the floor.

"I thought you said just in case," Nick said.

"Just get her. Where?" he said to the man.

"In the back on the right."

Nick stared at Larry, suddenly frightened, then moved quickly into the back. Dim, after the garish front room. Doors with light bulbs over them.

"Molly?"

He heard a pounding inside one of the cubicles. His eyes adjusted to the dark. At the end, a chair was propped against a door.

"Molly." He threw the chair aside and pulled the door open. She was standing there cowering, holding her forearm. "You all right?"

She nodded, still stunned. Her face was blotchy, and she moaned when he took her in his arms, hugging her.

"It's my wrist. I think it's broken. He grabbed— Oh god, Nick. What's happening?"

"Come on."

He held her by the side and walked her out of the dark room.

629

"They're coming back," she said. "Who are they?"

"Later. Come on."

She blinked when the light hit her eyes, dazzled by the slick covers full of flesh. "Where are we?" Then she saw Larry holding the gun and drew closer to Nick, clutching him.

"Get her to the car," Larry said.

"Nobody told me about this," the ponytail said.

"Shut up."

"Fuck you." He moved toward Molly.

Larry raised the gun. "Don't. I mean it."

The man stopped, glowering.

"Get in the car," Larry said to her. "Quick."

She looked at Nick, who nodded and opened the door.

"You don't know what fucking trouble you're buying," the ponytail said.

"I always know what I'm buying," Larry said. "Now you can use the phone."

The man snorted and turned toward the counter. The blast caught Nick by surprise, making him jump, so loud it was still ringing in his ears as he watched the man fall onto the counter, then slump and slide off, with magazines slipping around him. When he hit the floor Nick heard his head crack. He stared at the blood. Like the war—blood coming out, quietly. He looked up at Larry, for a second expecting the other shot. But Larry was taking a handkerchief from his pocket, wiping the gun, then tossing it next to the man.

"He saw me," he said simply.

Nick said nothing, lost in the stillness that follows a violent death. It had been that easy. No witnesses. A girl falling out the window. Barbara next, whoever else might be a threat. His father jerking under the pillows. No end to it, ever.

"Now get out of here," Larry said. "You've got her. We're quits."

"I saw you too," Nick said quietly.

"Then I'm in your hands again," Larry said, matter-of-fact. "But we have a deal." He wiped his hands. "Come on, Nick, we have to get out of here. You'll see. It'll be fine." He moved toward the door.

"You're going to get away with it."

"Yes, I am. Come on."

He lifted his hand to the door, his back to Nick, the familiar shoulders. No end to it. I won't be his executioner. Not to Hoover, giving comfort to the enemy. But no end to it. He reached down and picked up the gun. Larry turned. Nick looked down at his hand, outstretched, the way it had been at the White House gate, unable to pull the trigger. Locked together in the tangle Larry had made.

"Nick. Leave it. They'll—"

Nick fired, the sound splitting the room again. He saw Larry's shocked face, his graceless stumble and fall to the floor.

"Nick." A gasp, like a plea.

Nick wiped the gun, just as Larry had, and threw it toward the clerk. Then he went over, leaned down, and took the envelope out of Larry's pocket. No scandal. Just a crime. Larry's eyes were still

631

open. "Don't worry," Nick said to the ground. "Your secret's safe with me. That was the deal."

A pounding on the door. "Nick!"

He slid out, not opening it wide enough for her to see, and he took her good arm, leading her away from the corner.

"Leave the car. If anyone asks—when they ask—just say he dropped us at the hotel. We didn't see him after that."

"The shots—"

"They're both dead."

"We can't just leave."

He turned to her. "We were never here, understand? Nobody will ever know."

She nodded, frightened.

"Come on, we'll pack and get you to a hospital."

"Pack?"

"For New York. But first we'll see about the wrist."

"I'm all right."

"No, you're not. Besides, I have one more thing to do. Stay at the hospital until I get back. Don't leave. You'll be safe there."

She looked at him. "One more thing," she said dully.

"I have to see Hoover."

She glanced at the envelope.

"No," he said. "Only the others. They still know about us. Now I have to."

"But not him."

"No." He tore the envelope into small pieces, then bent over and tossed them into a storm drain, where they would float, like a shirt, to the Potomac. "He's not a spy anymore."

"They'll find out. What would he be doing there?"

"What does any man do in a store like that? They'll cover that up. Out of respect," he said, an edge in his voice. "He's a crime victim, Molly. Mugged. It happens in Washington all the time."

"Are you sure you know what you're doing?"

He looked at her. "Yes, I'm sure. It's over."

"Except for one more thing."

"Yes."

They took a taxi to the hotel and he made the phone call while Molly packed. No one was outside, watching. He drove her to a hospital out in Georgetown, the late sun still glowing on the buildings.

"Why Georgetown?"

"It's on the way to Hoover's. He said he'd see me at home."

"God, his home," she said, sounding better, as if movement itself had begun to rub away the shock. "I never thought of him *living* anywhere."

"Remember, don't leave," he said as they pulled up to the hospital. "For any reason. They're still out there."

Thirtieth Place was a quiet cul-de-sac near Rock Creek Park, large brick houses with Georgian windows set back on narrow lawns. For a second Nick stopped, disbelieving. Hoover's grass, a hardy even green, was Astroturf.

A Negro houseman opened the door and led him into the living room. At first Nick thought he had walked into a gift shop—there were hundreds of antiques, vases and statues, silver teapots and curios, oriental carpets laid on top of each other so that every space was filled. An oil portrait of a young Hoover on the stair landing. Hoover himself, in an open-necked shirt and slacks, came into the room followed by two Cairn terriers, who sniffed at Nick's ankles, then padded away. The voice, still quick, had lost its machine gun effect, as if it too had been softened by domesticity.

"Drink?"

A drink with Hoover.

"No. I can't stay."

Hoover indicated the overstuffed couch. He took the chair next to it, sinking into the cushion so that his body became foreshortened, the round head bobbing on it like Humpty Dumpty's. He made the first move, extending his hand and opening it. The lighter.

Nick took it, staring at the initials. No longer shiny, a dull gold, from the days when they used to go dancing. "Thank you," he said.

"Now what have you got for me?"

"I want to make a deal."

"The Bureau doesn't make deals."

"That's no way to do business. You haven't heard what I've got."

A flash of irritation, then a slow smile. "The father's son. Larry never comes empty-handed. What have you got?"

"Names. I want to trade you some names."

Hoover looked surprised, then distracted as a thin, once good-looking man shuffled vaguely into the room.

"Speed?"

"I'll be with you in a minute, Clyde."

"Oh, I thought it was time for drinks." He was illness thin.

"Why don't you start? I'll be down as soon as I'm finished with my young friend here."

The man nodded, still vague, and headed for the basement stairs, the rec room, where Larry had told him Hoover had an obscene cartoon of Eleanor Roosevelt. A joke from the past.

"Clyde's staying here for a few days," Hoover said, as if he needed to explain him. The rumored companion. But it was impossible to think of Hoover being intimate with anybody. Nick wondered what they talked about over dinner. The Dillinger days, maybe, filled with public enemies.

"Speed?" Nick said.

"A nickname," Hoover said, annoyed. "What kind of trade?"

"Five for one. Five Russian spies. Here, in Washington." Hoover looked at him, impressed. "You were right about my father. He knew he'd have to buy his way out. This is what he had. It'll be a coup for the Bureau. Headlines. You can pick them up now."

"On your say-so."

"The names are good. He knew."

"Proof?"

"You'll find it once you've got them. The Bureau's good at that, isn't it?"

Hoover's face was wary and eager at the same time. "Why so helpful all of a sudden?"

"My father wanted you to have them. You were wrong about him. He wasn't disloyal, he was trapped." Hoover looked confused. "This was his way of giving something back."

"A friend of the Bureau," Hoover said, almost sneering. "Why didn't you tell me this at the office?"

"I've been checking them out. But I'm not as good as you are—they caught me doing it. They know about me. Now I want you to pick them up."

A slow smile. "That's more like it. So you want me to save your behind. For two cents I'd let them take care of you. 'Not disloyal'—your father was a traitor. You just want me to save your behind."

"And yours," Nick said easily. "You could use a little press. Nixon wants you out. You made him, but now you make him nervous. You could use this."

"You don't know what you're talking about."

"No? One of them's in Justice."

Hoover raised his head, as if he'd heard a bell.

"If you don't want them, maybe Nixon will. He could make you look awfully pathetic. Director's so past it he doesn't even know he has a spy in his own department. He'd do it. With a speech about your long record of service." A twitch in Hoover's

636

jowls; anxious now. "But I'd rather give them to you."

"Why?"

"Well, for one thing, I don't trust him to get them off the street in time. You could do it in an hour. Keep my behind safe for walking around." He paused. "And I want something from you."

Hoover peered at him, waiting.

"I want to know who told you about Rosemary Cochrane. One name."

"For five."

"Well, four, to be precise. One of them's at the Russian embassy. I only have the code name. But you probably know all the players there anyway. Maybe on tape. I'd like that destroyed too, by the way, the tape you played the other day. I always sound funny on tape."

"A real wise guy, aren't you?"

Nick shrugged. "I grew up in Washington. You get to know how a place works."

"No, you don't. A trade. What makes you think I wouldn't get them out of you anyway?"

"What, with a rubber hose? Like the Commies? You don't do business that way. You do business this way."

Hoover said nothing.

"One name."

"What do you want it for?"

"I just want to know. It's worth it to me. But not as much as my names are worth to you. It's a good deal."

Hoover watched him, thinking, then leaned over

and picked up a silver pen from an antique set on the coffee table. He scribbled on a notepad, then tore off the page and held it up.

"There's not much you can do now anyway," he said with a sly smile, making the better bargain.

Nick reached over, but Hoover raised his eyebrows. Nick nodded and took the sheet of names and addresses from his pocket. He handed it to Hoover with a formal gesture, like a diplomatic exchange, then looked at the small piece of paper.

It took a second to sink in—a name, just a squiggle on a piece of paper. Rosemary's letter. The overlooked clue. One confession is enough. The start of everything that had happened to them.

"You're surprised," Hoover said, enjoying it.

Nick stood up. "Thank you for the lighter."

"I knew you'd be a friend to the Bureau."

Nick looked at him. "That's one thing I'll never be." He pointed to the list in Hoover's hand. "If you start now, you can probably get them before you go down for drinks."

"You're a cold bastard," Hoover said, a kind of admiring salute.

"I didn't start that way," Nick said.

He found her in the emergency room, her wrist taped but not in a sling.

"It's just a sprain. They don't know why I'm still hanging around."

"Just sit tight for a few more minutes. I have to pay a visit."

"Your face," she said, studying him.

"I've just been with Hoover."

She nodded at the TV monitor in the waiting room. "There's been nothing on the news, by the way."

"There won't be. Store's closed, remember? I doubt if any of our friends are running to report it. I'll be right back."

"A visit here?"

"An errand of mercy. Five minutes."

The night-duty nurse was sympathetic. "It's after hours. Just a few minutes, okay? He gets tired. It's difficult for him to talk. He still slurs."

Nick went into the private room and closed the door. There was a small reading lamp, but no books. Father Tim's head was raised on an inclined pillow, his body motionless. Only the eyes moved in recognition.

"Nick," he said, the word muffled by the twisted face. A string of drool hung out of one side of his mouth. His hands still had some movement. He was clutching a rosary, a nurse's call button nearby. "Nick," he said again, that awful forced sound. "Livia—?"

"You hateful bastard," Nick said.

Tim's eyes blinked in astonishment.

"You told me to think of him as dead."

A gargled sound came from the bed.

"Shut up. He is dead now. Isn't that what you wanted?"

"No—"

"It was you. Hoover told me. One confession. That poor, stupid girl. She'd never imagine, would she? It's supposed to be sacred. Did you run right over from church to tell him? You interfering sonofabitch. One of Hoover's little helpers. Root out the Communists, protect the Church. Christ."

"Godless," Tim mumbled, struggling to explain.

"She didn't know you were just like the party. Means to an end. She *trusted* you. You were a fucking *priest.* But you're the real party. No doubts."

Tim's eyes darted about the room in frustration.

"Just one bad moment, when you thought you caused her death. But you forgave yourself, didn't you? God always forgives if you ask him in time, isn't that the way it goes? And for such a cause. But I don't forgive you. I want you to die knowing that. Never. You ruined our lives. For what? So you could have dinner with Clyde and Edgar? Do God a favor? Rosemary Cochrane was murdered. My father was murdered. Does God forgive that? Maybe yours does, but it's a chance, isn't it? What if you're wrong? Maybe they're just beads." He brushed the rosary in Tim's hand.

"Communists—"

"Yes, they were Communists. So what? Anyway, they died for it. I want you to see their faces when you go. Do you know how my father died? Somebody took a pillow, just like this one, and held him down till he couldn't breathe. Till his legs stopped kicking. Yours wouldn't even move."

Tim, his eyes wide with fright, moved his hand toward the call button, but Nick snatched it and put it on the table, out of reach.

"Don't worry. I'd like to, but I won't. You're not worth it. Let God do it." Nick leaned over. "I just wanted you to know what you did. So you can live with it too." And then suddenly, the fury broken, Nick felt his eyes fill with tears. "You started everything. You unholy bastard. Just so you could be somebody—with your lousy piece of gossip."

He looked down at the figure, the still, wasted frame, the twisted face, already punished. What was the point? Tim's eyes leaping.

"You thought I'd never know," Nick said calmly. "All that time, watching it happen. My mother. Nobody blaming you. Not even blaming yourself—not after putting yourself in God's hands. I'll bet you made a private confession. Only a fool would trust the box."

"Nick—" Another gurgle, his breathing ragged.

"But I do know. So die knowing that. I do know. No absolution."

Nick turned to go. A frantic sound. He looked back. The breathing was a gasp now, Tim's hands motioning toward the call button. Nick started toward the table to get it, then stopped.

"No," he said. "Let God do it. He owes you."

The old man's eyes wild now, afraid. A grunt.

"Pray, Tim," Nick said, backing away. "Maybe he'll hear you."

Molly, seeing his face, said nothing in the car, fiddling with her bandage instead.

"Who were you seeing?" she said finally.

"An old friend of my mother's. He's dying."

"What a good little boy you are."

"The best."

She looked at him. "You all right?"

He nodded. "It's over. We're going to New York."

"They'll call. About your father." For a moment she was quiet. "You killed him, didn't you? Not the other man."

He looked straight ahead. "Yes."

She bit her lower lip. "Was it—self-defense?" Wanting it to be true.

Nick saw Larry's surprised face, finally betrayed. "Yes," he said. She was about to speak again when he turned to her. "It's over."

She nodded, then placed her hand on his, just a touch, and looked out the window at the river. "I wonder if they'll find John Brown," she said finally.

"Count on it. I hope Hoover nails him personally. He'd be just right. They both lived with their mothers."

He turned the car toward the Mall.

"This isn't the way to the airport."

"No. I thought we'd take the train. For old times' sake."

She looked at him, the first hint of a smile. "Okay."

He drove past the Mall, where crews were cleaning up litter from the rally, then up the hill, turning into the street behind the Supreme Court, the lighted Capitol dome. A spring night in the South, the magnolias thick and glossy, lights on in the row of houses. The big forsythia bushes spilling over the wrought-iron fences. He stopped the car, idling.

"Was that your house?" Molly said.

"Yes."

Lights on upstairs. His bedroom window no longer scratched by the tall tree, which must have been taken down. When? Inside, a woman passed in front of the window. Everything was quiet in the street.

"Does it bother you?" she asked softly.

"I thought it would."

And for a second, just one, he was looking out the back window on that last day, the sidewalk covered with moving cartons.

"But it's just a house," he said, shifting into drive, the frozen picture moving again.

She looked at him. "Your house."

"No," he said. "Not anymore."

643